GOLIATH

STEVE ALTEN

TOR®

A TOM DOHERTY ASSOCIATES BOOK
NEW YORK

This is a work of fiction. All the characters and events portrayed in this novel are either fictitious or are used fictitiously.

GOLIATH

Copyright © 2002 by Steve Alten

Interior Illustrations © 2001 Bill McDonald and www.AlienUFOart.com.

A Tor Book
Published by Tom Doherty Associates, LLC
175 Fifth Avenue
New York, NY 10010

www.tor.com

Tor® is a registered trademark of Tom Doherty Associates, LLC.

ISBN: 0-765-34024-0
Library of Congress Catalog Card Number: 2001058275

First edition: July 2002
First mass market edition: July 2003

Printed in the United States of America

0 9 8 7 6 5 4 3 2 1

Dedicated
to the officers and men, past and present,
of the United States Submarine Force.

And to my sister, Abby,
for inspiring me to write.

ACKNOWLEDGMENTS

It is with great pride and appreciation that I acknowledge those who contributed to the completion of *Goliath*.

First and foremost, to my literary manager, Ken Atchity, and his team at Atchity Editorial/Entertainment International for their hard work and perseverance, as well as Danny Baror of Baror International. Kudos to Tom Doherty and the great people at Tor/Forge Books, especially editor Bob Gleason, for his faith, wonderful input, and direction, to Heather Drucker in publicity, and tireless Brian Callaghan, for all his assistance and suggestions.

Special thanks to copyeditors Bob and Sara Schwager, and to Brett Bartlett, who helped inspire parts of the novel.

Heartfelt appreciation to my *Goliath* team—all readers of my previous books whose own expertise contributed to the authenticity of the novel. Dr. Elizabeth Goode of the University of Delaware; Professor Barry Perlman, Physics Department, Broward Community College; Jim Kennedy, corrections officer, Northern Super-Maximum Correctional Institution in Somers, Connecticut; Dean Garner, United States Army Airborne Ranger; "Interstellar Bill" Parkyn; and Bill Raby, parachutist-extreme. Thank you all for your terrific contributions.

Thanks also to Leisa Cotner Cobbs for designing the www.Steve Alten.com Web site and enhancing the reading experience for my fans. Thanks as well to Bill and Lori McDonald of Argonaut-Grey Wolf Productions/Website: www.AlienUFOart.com, who brought to life the *Goliath* and *Hammerhead* minisub drawings found in this novel and to graphic artist Erik Mollander. I am indeed fortunate to have such talented fans.

Most important, a very special thanks to Ken Walker. Bravo Zulu.

Several of the documented quotes used in *Goliath* can be found in *Criminal Quotes,* edited by Andrew Chester and H. Amanda Robb, published by Visible Ink Press, a division of Gale Research (1997).

To my wife and partner, Kim, for all her support, and last—to my readers: Thank you for your correspondence and contributions. Your comments are always a welcome treat, your input means so much, and you remain this author's greatest asset.

—Steve Alten

To personally contact the author or learn more about his novels, click on www.SteveAlten.com

Goliath is part of Steve Alten's ADOPT-AN-AUTHOR Program aimed at assisting junior high and high school students and teachers. For more information, click on www.SteveAlten.com

"We are on the precipice of the next great leap in computer technology. The chemically assembled electronic nanocomputer, or CAEN, will be billions of times faster than our current PCs and represent the forefront of artificial intelligence."
—Dr. Elizabeth Goode

"There's a fine line between right and wrong, freedom and oppression, the best of intentions and the insanity of genocide."
—Gunnar Wolfe

"History is a bloodbath."
—Williams James

"No snowflake in an avalanche ever feels responsible."
—Unknown

Identity: Stage One:
I am small and insignificant, stranded on the vast expanse
of nature. I hope I can survive.
—Deepak Chopra

"Come to course zero-nine-zero, ahead one-third. Make ship's depth fifty meters."

"Aye, sir, coming to course zero-nine-zero, making ship's depth fifty meters."

"Engage computer."

"Aye, sir, computer engaged."

0101101001001001011011011010010101101001 0110101 0101001011010101101010101011100101011001010101 10100 1011010101011011011110100101011010101101001 01011010 01010100101

"Mr. Chau. Prepare to bring *Sorceress* on-line. Flood nutrient womb. Prepare bacteria for injection."

"Aye, sir. Nutrient womb flooded. Bacteria ready for injection."

"Inject bacteria into womb. Engage DNA synthesizers."

"Aye, sir. Injecting bacteria. Engaging DNA synthesizers."

01011010010110101001010110 10 1011010 1 1 0 0 1 0 1 ATCGATCGATATACCAG

"Activate sensor orbs. Activate voice recognition and response programs."

"Aye, sir. Sensor orbs activated. Voice recognition and response programs on-line."

"Transfer primary ship's control to computer. *Sorceress*, this is Covah. Are you on-line?"

AACGTTTGTACCACATTAGGATACACATTAG-GATA ACA GT A A TG C A A

"*Sorceress*, acknowledge."

ACKNOWLEDGED. SORCERESS ON-LINE.

"The people who get on in this world are the people who get up and look for the circumstances they want, and if they can't find them — make them."
—George Bernard Shaw

"Revolutions happen, above all, in the minds of men."
—Ralph Peters, "Fighting for the Future"

"Do we have to shed blood to reform the current political system?
I hope it doesn't have to come to that. But it might."
—Timothy J. McVeigh, former Army sergeant who bombed the Murrah Federal Building in Oklahoma City, Oklahoma

"The enemy is in many places. The enemy is not looking to be found. And so you have to design a campaign plan that goes after that kind of enemy. . . ."
—Colin Powell, U.S. Secretary of State

CHAPTER 1

25 September
Atlantic Ocean
Seine Abyssal Plain
112 miles southwest of
the Strait of Gibraltar

With an expulsion of air and water, the majestic behemoth breaks the surface, her sickle-shaped dorsal fin cutting the waves, her great tail slapping the sea in defiance before slipping back into the froth.

At 120 tons, the blue whale is easily the largest living organism ever to have existed on the planet, often reaching lengths of one hundred feet or more. Ten tons of blood surge through its body, driven by a heart the size of a small car. Despite its prodigious girth, the mammal is not a predator but a forager of minifauna, thriving on a diet of krill and crustaceans, which it sieves from the water through its baleen plates.

The adult female rises again, guiding her two-month-old calf to a labored breath above the storm-threatened seas.

A thousand feet below, an ominous presence moves silently through the depths. Demonic scarlet eyes, pupil-less and un-blinking, blaze luminescent through the blackness of the abyss. Its gargantuan torso, cloaked in the darkness, scatters every creature in its path.

Sensing a disturbance above, the creature banks sharply away from the seafloor and rises, homing in on the mother blue and her calf.

The leviathan ascends, its bulk piercing the swaying gray curtains of the shallows, the filtered rays of sunlight revealing the enormous winged contours of a monstrous stingray. So quiet is the predator that the adult blue whale fails to detect its presence until it is nearly upon them. In a sudden frenzy of movement, the startled mother slaps her fluke and pushes her newborn below, rolling on top of her offspring to shield it from the jowls of the hunter.

The ungodly behemoth pursues, its flat, triangular mouth remaining close to the gyrating tails of the frightened mam-mals.

Yet the beast does not attack. Maneuvering through a trail of bubbles, it keeps the tip of its snout within a fin's length of the adult's thrashing fluke, taunting its quarry in a terrifying game of cat and mouse. Hunted and hunter race through the thermocline, the thin layer of water separating the sun-warmed surface waters from the colder depths.

In due time, the leviathan tires of the chase. With a burst of speed, it soars beneath its terrified prey, buffeting them in its wake as it returns once more to the silence of the depths.

Darkness and cold envelop the devilfish, black, save for the hellish glow surrounding its unearthly eyes. At nine hundred feet it levels out, its streamlined bulk creating barely a ripple. Gliding high above the desolate floor of the abyssal plain, it continues its journey west, homing in on its true quarry.

Atlantic Ocean:
235 nautical miles due west of
the Strait of Gibraltar

15:12 hours

Sailing beneath a mouse gray autumn sky, the United States aircraft Carrier *Ronald Reagan* (CVN-76) plows through the sea, its steel bow cutting a path through the twelve-foot swells at a steady twenty knots.

Belowdecks, Captain James Robert Hatcher, the fifty-two-year-old commanding officer of the *Ronald Reagan*, ignores the grins of his crew as he vacates the exercise room and double-times it down one of the ship's two central passageways. Ducking deftly through a dozen watertight hatches and knee-knockers, he arrives in "blue tile country," the central command-and-control complex for the aircraft carrier and its battle group.

The *Ronald Reagan* is a veritable fortress of modern-day warfare. One thousand feet long, with an island infrastructure towering twenty stories above the waterline, the Nimitz-class "supercarrier" is by far the largest and heaviest object at sea, weighing in at ninety-seven thousand tons. Despite its mammoth girth, the ship is fast, its four twenty-one-foot-wide bronze propellers, powered by two nuclear reactors, able to drive the vessel seven hundred nautical miles a day at speeds in excess of thirty knots.

The supercarrier and its fleet project the awesome forward presence and might of the United States Armed Forces. On its roof lies a four-and-a-half-acre airport, managed by a city of six thousand men and women. Positioned along its flattop and in the hangar deck below are more than seventy aircraft, including two squadrons of F/A-18E and 18F Super Hornets, eight CSA (Common Support Aircraft) designed for electronics, communications, intelligence, refueling, and antisubmarine warfare, four AEW (Airborne Early Warning) Surface Surveillance craft, and a squadron of fourteen brand-new, Stealth Joint Strike Fighters (JSFs). Carrying a multitude of offensive weapons, the "swarm" literally sews up all of the CVBG's airspace.

The carrier's defensive weaponry includes the Evolved Sea Sparrow short-range surface-to-air missile (ESSM), three eight-round Mk-29 Sea Sparrow SAM launchers, the SLQ-32 electronic warfare system, and the Vulcan Phalanx close-in missile defense system, a rapid-fire gun capable of shooting nine hundred rounds per second of 20-mm ammunition.

Along with its own defenses, the carrier travels within a multilayered battle group (CVBG), making it nearly invincible on the open sea. Surrounding the *Ronald Reagan* are sixteen combat ships, ten support ships, and two Los Angeles-class attack subs, the USS *Jacksonville*, (SSN-699) and the USS *Hampton* (SSN-767). Positioned along either side of the *Ronald Reagan* are her two 567-foot Ticonderoga-class escorts, the USS *Leyte Gulf* and the USS *Yorktown*.

The two guided-missile cruisers share one mission: protect the aircraft carrier at all costs. Each warship is equipped with the Aegis Theater High-Altitude Air Defense (THADD) program, a highly sophisticated battle-management system designed to shield the carrier from attack. Utilizing an array of sensor fusion computers, the THADD system integrates onboard radar, sonar, and laser systems with its weapons, utilizing recent and real-time overhead sat-data in order to assess enemy threats. Coordinated multistatic radar make it impossible for enemy stealth aircraft or cruise missiles to penetrate undetected, while its multitasking parallel computers can assign priorities and engage incoming targets in the blink of an eye. In addition to its guns, torpedoes, and a full suite of chaff and flares designed to decoy incoming missiles, the two Ticonderogas are also equipped with Tomahawk cruise missiles—long-range projectiles capable of destroying targets up to a thousand miles away.

The United States maintains twelve carrier battle groups, usually deploying only two or three at any given time. In addition to its conventional weapons, the *Ronald Reagan* is the first aircraft carrier in more than a decade to carry a limited number of nuclear warheads, a policy change dictated by

Russia's and China's recent push in the nuclear arms race, spurred on by United States insistence on moving ahead with its own Missile Defense Shield.

Captain Hatcher makes his way into the Combat Information Center (CIC), the heavily air-conditioned confines of the darkened chamber quickly cooling his sweaty, half-naked physique. A dozen technicians glance up from their computer screens as the CO walks by. Hatcher takes a quick look around, then spots his executive officer, Commander Shane Strejcek.

"XO, have you seen Bob Lawson?"

"The congressman? Yes, sir, he was speaking with Commander Jackson about ten minutes ago."

Hatcher proceeds to the central alcove of sensor consoles that encircle a large high-resolution Plexiglas digital display in map mode, depicting the North Atlantic and the Mediterranean Sea. The carrier battle group's position and surrounding defense zones are color-coded in fluorescent blue, her aircraft in pulsing green, the topography of Europe and West Africa in steady red. Within the multilayered transparent display, both ocean conditions or atmospheric weather status can be shown.

Commander Rochelle "Rocky" Jackson looks up from her sonar console as her CO approaches, tufts of her short, straw-colored blond hair peeking out from beneath the navy baseball cap. "Nice legs, Hatch."

The heavy air-conditioning is causing Rocky's nipples to press against the inside of her tee shirt. Hatcher catches himself staring. "Commander, what are you doing working at a station?"

"Ensigns Soderblom and Dodds are out with the flu. You looking for Congressman Lawson?"

"I take it I just missed him."

"By a good twenty minutes. I tried to entertain him. Guess he got bored."

"I'm sure it wasn't from the view. If you're cold, Commander, I can get you a sweater."

She smirks, buttoning her jacket, her hazel eyes sparkling in the console's glow. "I'm fine. Thank you, sir."

Hatcher leans down, whispering in her ear. "By the way, Commander, happy birthday."

Her high cheekbones swell with a smile. She turns back to face the sonar screen. "Go away," she whispers to her husband, "I'm on duty, and you smell. As for Lawson, try Vulture's Row."

"Thanks."

Rocky watches Hatcher leave the Command Center, the sight of the sweat lines running down the fanny seam of his gray Navy-issue shorts causing her to grin.

Commander Rochelle Megan Jackson made her entry into this world thirty-four years and seven hours ago at the Army Base Medical Center in Fort Benning, Georgia. Fully anticipating the arrival of a son, her father, Michael "Bear" Jackson, then a lieutenant colonel with the elite United States Rangers, nevertheless presented his newborn with a baseball glove, football, and his own father's first name, Rocky, which her mother immediately changed on the birth certificate to Rochelle.

Rocky would be an only child, the product of an interracial, interservice marriage. Her father, whom she affectionately called "Papa Bear," was career Army all the way. The Bear was a barrel-chested light-skinned African American with a short-cropped auburn Afro and broad smile, who had earned his nickname during his years as a commando in the Army's Special Forces. Those who served under him knew his bark was worse than his bite, Jackson's gruff personality hiding a deep loyalty toward his men. Rocky's mother, Judy, on the other hand, was as quiet as the Bear was loud. A white Anglo-Saxon Protestant, Judy had earned her engineering degree at M.I.T., and had been heavily recruited by the United States Navy. She would meet her future husband in Washington, D.C., during a weeklong munitions convention.

Rocky Jackson might as well have enlisted at birth.

Growing up on a military base with other Army "brats," Rocky soon began displaying her father's overly competitive spirit. The fair-headed tomboy not only challenged her male classmates on the athletic fields, but more often than not came out the victor. Much of her "need to exceed" attitude was intended to please Papa Bear, who could always be found hooting and hollering from the Little League bleachers, that is, when he wasn't traveling abroad on some covert mission.

While her father's "Special Forces mentality" gave Rocky an edge in athletics, her overly competitive attitude did not mix well in her social life. As she blossomed into adolescence, the beautiful blond teen with the cocoa skin and Jackie Joyner-Kersey physique often intimidated guys and girls alike. Even when she did date, her no-nonsense attitude toward sex quickly earned her a reputation as a prude. This was not to say that Rocky didn't have the usual adolescent desires—it was just that she was picky. Whoever she might eventually give herself to would have to be able to measure up to Papa Bear, and none of the so-called hotshots at her high school ever did. When her prom date, the school's starting tailback, decided to push things a bit too far on the dance floor, she calmly reared back and punched the high school all-American in the face, her powerful well-practiced tae kwon do jab shattering his nose.

Though Rocky's physical prowess and leadership style may have reflected the personality of her father, her academic pursuits were strictly guided by her mother, herself a former engineering student. After graduating with honors from the Naval Academy, Rocky entered M.I.T.'s engineering school, her advanced degree eventually leading to a high-ranking position in the Naval Undersea Warfare Engineering Center (NUWC), in Keyport, Washington.

The military was Rocky's life, but she had no desire to command in the field. As the Gulf War had demonstrated, technology was the key to America's dominance as a world power, and Rocky wanted to ride the wave that guaranteed her country's freedom for decades to come. Her ego-driven career goal was simple: She would immerse herself in as many new hyperadvanced technologies available, learning all she could from the country's top engineers, and rub elbows with all her father's "muckety-muck" friends in the Pentagon until the opportunity came to oversee one of the Navy's new high-tech weapon systems.

Her opportunity would come following several long years working on the Navy's new SSN Virginia-class attack sub. George W. Bush's victory had pushed the space-based missile defense shield to the top of the White House's military wish list. Only six months later, the defection of Vermont senator Jim Jeffords from the Republican Party returned control of the Senate to the Democrats, threatening to send the high-tech, high-cost defense initiative back into development hell. A new project was needed, something more feasible and easier to digest financially, while still packing a wallop regarding America's national security.

Enter the GOLIATH Project, a top-secret venture carrying a price tag in excess of $10 billion. Unlike SDI, this would be an offensive machine developed by NUWC, a machine capable of altering the strategy of America's Armed Forces for decades to come—and she was the top candidate in line for the directorship.

Three months later it was made official: Rochelle Jackson had become the most powerful woman in this man's armed forces.

Less than a year later, her father, now a general in the United States Special Operations Command (USSOCOM), would introduce her to his finest recruit, U.S. Army Captain Gunnar Wolfe, a detachment commander in the elite U.S. Army Rangers. It was in this dark-haired, gray-eyed commando that Rocky Jackson would finally meet her match. Gunnar, an engineering major from Penn State, had been given leave from the field to complete his work on an original design for a remotely operated minisub. Believing the vessel's design was compatible with his daughter's program, the Bear had arranged for Gunnar's transfer to NUWC.

For the first two months, they had fought like cats and dogs, Navy engineer versus Army commando—Rocky always hell-bent on keeping the new recruit under her thumb, Gunnar refusing to bend under his beautiful OIC's fiery will.

Project deadlines pushed them closer together, the long days eventually softening the blows, allowing their mutual attraction toward one another to take root. The lab quickly became the forum for late-night dinners, their romance becoming more physical with each encounter. Competition took a backseat to passion, their lovemaking becoming a game of one-upmanship, more lust than love.

Somewhere along the journey, something much deeper blossomed.

Gunnar Wolfe had bridled the Bear's bucking bronco, an ego-driven woman whose beauty and passion matched her strength and competitive desires. A spring wedding was announced, plans hastily accelerated after Rocky discovered she was six weeks pregnant. The happy couple even found their dream house—a four thousand five hundred-square-foot waterfront home a few miles west of Seattle.

It was shortly after their engagement that her fiancé began acting strangely, as if he was harboring some dark secret. Their free time together lessened as Rocky's trips to the Pentagon increased, Gunnar spending many a lonely night in his lab.

And then, two weeks before their wedding date, Gunnar committed an unforgivable act of treason that broke her heart and changed both their lives forever.

Arriving home from an extended stay in D.C., Rocky learned a computer virus had been downloaded into the terminals housing all of her project's top-secret schematics. Years of work and countless man-hours had been eradicated in an instant. Worse, David Paniagua, the boy-genius in charge of the project's nanotechnology (and Gunnar's best man) reported that $2 billion worth of biochemical nanocomputer circuitry was missing, along with a five-year harvest's worth of bioengineered silicon-coated bacteria.

The Department of Defense was devastated by the setback. An internal investigation, following on the heels of the acts of espionage discovered at Los Alamos, forced the Navy to shut down the entire project until the spy or spies could be identified and apprehended.

The culprit had broken into the artificial intelligence lab sometime around midnight. Security records revealed only one person had been in the Warfare Center's A-I division at the time—Gunnar Wolfe.

Within days, the Naval Investigative Service (NIS) found evidence of an offshore bank account in Gunnar's father's name. Recent deposits from another offshore bank were traced to Hong Kong, the account totaling just over $1.2 million. Although he denied any knowledge of the money or the stolen computer parts, a lie detector test clearly indicated the former war hero was hiding something from his superiors.

Gunnar was arrested in his lab by NIS agents two days before their wedding day. Because there was no evidence indicating Gunnar had "sold" the schematics to another government, prosecutors were forced to reduce the charges of espionage to destruction of government resources. On June 22, a month after they were to have been married, a court-martial jury of staff rank naval officers found Gunnar Wolfe guilty, the judge (an admiral) sentencing him to ten years in Leavenworth.

Six weeks later, the Republicans lost the White House, in no small part due to the Goliath debacle. Within months, the new president would officially cancel the project altogether.

Rocky was devastated. Her life's work, her career goals, her future with the one man to whom she had pledged her love—everything was gone. Worse yet, Gunnar's selfish, inexplicable act had disgraced her forever in the eyes of her peers. Rocky Jackson, a woman who practically draped herself in the American flag, had allowed herself to fall for a man who had stabbed his own country in the back.

The pain was all-consuming, as if her heart had been torn from her chest, her mind from her skull. She felt used. She felt dirty. Weeks later, she would lose the baby.

It was the final straw, too much even for her own super-strength ego to handle.

Three months after Gunnar began serving time, the Bear found his daughter lying unconscious on the bathroom floor, having overdosed on muscle relaxants and barbiturates. It was the first time in her life she had ever cried out for help. It had nearly been her last.

Months of private counseling eventually replaced Rocky's emptiness with a simmering rage that could explode at any time. Medication made her ill, and a family vacation in Europe only made things worse. The Bear knew his daughter's collapsed mental state had to be rebuilt, brick by patriotic brick. That required discipline, something the service could provide. While Bear had made sure the military had no knowledge of his daughter's drug overdose, he also knew a return to the Warfare Center was out.

"What about active duty?" her mother suggested, prodding her stubborn husband.

Pulling a few strings, the Bear set his wife's plan into motion. Six months later, Rocky began her first assignment aboard the Aegis guided-missile cruiser, *Princeton*, working as a sonar officer.

The change of pace was exactly what the girl needed to solidify her toehold on sanity. Life aboard an American warship was challenging, and challenges brought out the best in Rochelle Megan Jackson. Her ego demanded that no man would ever outwork her, outknow her, or outaccomplish her. Within a month, she felt like her old self again. By the end of her first tour, her CO recognized her as one of the most reliable officers on his boat.

Three years and a promotion later, Commander Jackson earned herself a tour of duty aboard the USS *Ronald Reagan*, the newest carrier in the fleet.

It was there that the former NUWC director met Captain James Hatcher, a man twenty-five years her senior. Hatch's first wife had died only a year before from a long siege by breast cancer, his sorrow making him a kindred spirit of sorts. What began as a friendship gradually nurtured itself into a physical relationship before either of them cared to notice. Worried that his career could be jeopardized by the potential "sex scandal," Hatcher asked Rocky to marry him.

She surprised even herself by saying yes.

Friends gossiped that Rocky was merely seeking out a father figure, and perhaps they were right. Hatch was far from the man of her dreams, but she saw in him a good person, a stable companion, one who would not betray her fragile capacity for trust. He was also an officer on the rise, something not to be taken lightly. Rocky yearned to get back into the spotlight of her former high status, and Captain James Hatcher, the skipper of the flagship of the American Navy, could help lead the way. Despite vigorous protests from her father, the two married.

During that same week, Leavenworth experienced a prison uprising that left two men dead and the warden held hostage. As correctional emergency response teams rushed onto the scene, a lone convict—a former U.S. Army Ranger—had intervened to save the warden's life.

After a crescendo of media-manufactured publicity, Gunnar's heroic act led to an early presidential commutation. Having served five years and seven months, the former Ranger captain and NUWC traitor walked out of military prison a free man—and promptly disappeared from public scrutiny.

After honeymooning in Key West, Captain Hatcher and his new bride boarded the *Ronald Reagan*, the carrier's fleet bound for the Mediterranean. Though Navy rules prevented Rocky and Hatch from "officially" bunking together, she nevertheless enjoyed their time together at sea. Reveling at having access to the Navy's most advanced gadgetry, she quickly mastered all the ship's sensor arrays. Her equipment scanned a volume of airspace out to several hundred miles around the battle group, while equally able to pinpoint and identify any underwater object approaching the armada for more than twenty miles from her ship.

And while she admitted to herself that she wasn't exactly "in love" with Hatch, she did love and respect him, and after all, wasn't that just as important?

For the first time since she could remember, Rocky Jackson actually felt happy.

The blips on the sonar screen become hazy. Rocky rubs the fatigue from her eyes, then massages the knots in her shoulders. *Two more hours, then dinner and a shower. Maybe Hatch'll even let me stay in his cabin tonight.*

For a long moment she stares at her reflection in the orange monitor, thinking about what her life could have been. The thought tweaks a distant memory.

Gunnar had never liked the carrier's Aegis defense shield. Though virtually impregnable to attack on the open ocean, the multilayered, multiship system possessed one basic flaw—its active radar and sonar also revealed its presence to the enemy.

Rocky shakes her head, annoyed at herself for wasting time thinking about the man who had nearly destroyed her. Adjusting her headphones, she refocuses her attention on the sonar monitor,

—a valuable premonition dying stillborn.

Captain Hatcher finds the congressman on Vulture's Row, an open-air balcony overlooking the flight deck, positioned high up on the carrier's island infrastructure. The two watch intently as a Joint Strike Fighter is secured to one of the catapults. The electromechanical slingshot, the first of its kind to replace the venerable steam method, is capable of tossing a pickup truck a half mile out to sea.

With a high-pitched roar, the JSF leaps across the suddenly small flight deck, accelerating from zero to 150 miles per hour in less than two seconds. The required 3.5 gees is ramped up in a calibrated 75 milliseconds by the sophisticated new catapult design, pushing its crew back into their seats with a force of over three-and-a-half times their own body weight.

The skipper waits briefly for the roar to die down. "Sorry to keep you waiting, Mr. Lawson." Hatcher is not really sorry, nor does he sound it.

The Democrat from Florida turns to face him. "I don't need a baby-sitter, Captain, any more than you need a civilian looking over your shoulder. Keep in mind I'm only here because the Appropriations Committee and GAO still haven't come to any definitive conclusions regarding funding for the new Stealth carrier."

"The CVX's design speaks for itself. The advances in deck management alone make the new carrier worth funding."

"Your opinion. Personally, I'm still not convinced it's worth all the money."

Hatcher's face turns red. "Take a good look down there, Congressman. You're looking at the most dangerous piece of real estate in the world. Maybe you ought to climb into a jumpsuit and spend some time on our flight deck before you cast your vote."

"This has never been a question about safety, Captain, it's a question of whether the ungodly costs associated with keeping these armadas at sea is still worth it. Twenty billion to build a single carrier group, another 12 billion a year just to keep all our CVBGs operational."

"Maintaining a forward presence isn't cheap."

"Yes, but is it still our best strategy? As research into new high-tech systems accelerates, delaying purchases even a few more years may yield a full generation of advantages. Why waste money on systems that may become obsolete before we even put them into service? There's a growing consensus among my colleagues on Capitol Hill that the carrier groups have become antiquated. Face it, Captain, Aegis may protect your ship in open waters, but at close range, these new Chinese Silkworms and Russian supersonic missiles become too fast and too maneuverable to intercept. The evil empire's gone, Hatcher. Our new enemies lurk in tight, coastal hot spots like the Strait of Hormuz. What good is a brand-new 6-billion-dollar aircraft carrier if we're afraid to use it?"

Hatcher removes his cap, wiping the sweat from his receding hairline. "Tell you what, Congressman—if you and your colleagues on Capitol Hill know a better way of kicking some third world dictator's ass halfway across the globe, then I suggest you fund it—otherwise, give us what we need to do our goddamn jobs."

Atlantic Ocean:
197 nautical miles due west of
the Strait of Gibraltar
850 feet below the surface

16:48 hours

The beast slows, the luminescent glow from its bloodred eyes
violating the otherwise ebony depths. A disturbance stirs the
bottom silt as a dozen life-forms emerge, as if birthed, from
the creature's dark underbelly. Moving ahead, they hover in
formation, their own red eyes blazing green in the abyss as
they await instructions from their parent.

The devilfish settles gently on the ocean floor, displacing
half an acre of sand and debris.

A bioelectrical impulse is transmitted.

The monster's brood races ahead to attack the approaching
fleet.

Rocky Jackson jumps at the sudden flurry of whistles and
clicks. She adjusts her headphones and stares at the SQR-19's
sonar monitor.

"What do you hear?" the XO, Commander Strejcek, asks.

"Ambient sounds, sir, but they weren't there a second ago."

Strejcek picks up a headset and listens. "Hmm, biologics.
Sound like orca." Strejcek points to the blips on the sonar
monitor. Twelve dots disperse, spreading out in formation
across the screen. "They're hunting. Watch—the pod will surround the school of fish, then blast them with echolocation,
stunning them and driving them to the surface. Saw it on the
Discovery Channel last month. Extraordinary creatures."

Strejcek walks away, obviously satisfied with his own conclusion.

Fish? I don't hear any fish? Rocky presses the headphones
tighter to her ears, then maxes out the volume. The clicks reverberate in greater clarity.

A quick glance at her sensors—the *Jacksonville* is moving
to periscope depth. Rocky engages the spread spectrum

stealth communicator and its conformal phased-array antenna and sends out a tightly beamed encrypted message. She waits, hoping the sub's antenna has come out of the water.

JACKSONVILLE—PLEASE CONFIRM IDENTIFICATION OF OBJECTS.

The small objects disperse, the first five closing rapidly on the keels of the CVBG's forward vessels. Rocky waits, nibbling on her unpolished fingernails, alarm gathering viscerally within her.

A message appears. **BIOLOGICS. CLASSIFICATION: ORCA.**

She stares at her console as four of the "Orcas" move directly beneath the *Ronald Reagan*'s keel. The creatures slow, as if drawn to the carrier's propellers.

Then she hears it—very faint—masked beneath the noise coming from the fleet's screws.

The sound of small hydropropulsion engines . . .

"Commander, something's not right—" She turns.

Strejcek is gone.

The explosions toss her from her chair, slamming her face-first into the console.

Aboard the USS *Jacksonville*

The sonar technician turns to his supervisor, the twenty-year-old ensign's face pale. "Multiple explosions, sir. Sounds like heavy damage. Jesus, the carrier's taking on water—"

The *Jacksonville*'s sonar supervisor grabs the 1-MC, his heart pounding in his chest. "Conn, sonar—multiple torpedoes in the water! Bearing one-zero-five, range eight thousand yards. Torpedoes are Chinese, SET-53s. Sir, two of the torpedoes have acquired the *Hampton*."

"Battle stations! Officer of the Deck, come to course one-seven-zero." Commander Kevin O'Rourke's skin tingles, as if he is about to step off a precipice. He turns to his diving officer as a dozen more men rush to take positions in the control room. "Dive, make your depth six hundred feet. WEPS, get me a firing solution—"

The weapons supervisor sounds stunned. "Trying, sir, but nothing's coming up on the BSY-1—"

"Conn, sonar, I'm picking up a flurry of cavitation . . . it's coming from the seafloor, two thousand yards dead ahead. Sir, something massive just rose off the bottom—"

"Right full rudder, all ahead flank—"

"Conn, sonar, two torpedoes in the water! Bearing, one-seven-zero, coming straight at us—"

"Change course, come to two-seven-zero, thirty degrees down on the fairwater planes."

Helmsman Mike Schultz is seventeen and fresh out of high school, a junior sailor piloting a sixty-nine-hundred-ton, nuclear-powered attack sub. Schultz wipes the sweat from his palms, then pushes down on the steering wheel before him, maneuvering the *Jacksonville*'s fairwater planes, which protrude like small wings from the submarine's sail.

"Launch countermeasures, both launchers."

The chief repeats the captain's orders.

"Conn, sonar, one of the torpedoes fell for the countermeasures, the other two fish have acquired and are homing. Bearing two-one-zero, best range twelve hundred yards—"

"Launch the NAE. Reload both launchers with ADC's. Helm, right full rudder—"

"Conn—sonar, torpedoes still with us . . . six hundred yards . . . impact in sixty seconds."

The perceived temperature within the suddenly claustrophobic steel chamber is rising.

Petty Officer Third Class Leonard Cope stares at his console, fighting to breathe, sweat dripping on his monitor. "Conn, sonar, torpedo impact in thirty seconds—"

"Rig ship for impact—"

"Conn, sonar, I've got a bearing, very faint—"

"Identify—"

"No known registry on the computer database, but goddamn this thing's big."

"Firing point procedures—Sierra-1, ADCAP torpedo. Make tubes one and two ready in all respects."

"Aye, sir. Tubes one and two ready in all respects."

"Solution ready," the XO reports.

"Weapons ready. Thirty-five percent fuel remaining, run-to-enable two-five-hundred yards."

"Ready—shoot!"

Two Mk-48 Advanced Capability wire-guided torpedoes spit out from the *Jacksonville*'s bow, homing in on the unknown aggressor.

"WEPS, release countermeasures, come to course three-one-zero—"

Petty Officer Cope grabs his headphones as an explosion tears at his eardrums. Then he hears something he has never heard before—the frightening *crunch* of an imploding steel hull.

A heavy pulse of structural vibrations shudders the *Jacksonville*. Power flickers off. Emergency lights illuminate the frightened faces of the junior members of the crew, hyperventilating at their stations.

"Conn, sonar, sir, that explosion . . . it was the *Hampton*."

"Skipper, contact has launched two more torpedoes, both active—"

Two hundred and fifty yards to the west, the *Jacksonville*'s two Mk-48 ADCAP torpedoes have slowed to forty knots. Onboard sonars ping, searching the sea for the enemy contact, the weapon's real-time computers sending highly processed data back to the sub via a trailing fiber-optic wire.

Two consecutive returns. The torpedoes accelerate, pinging faster—

—before slamming nose first into two antitorpedo torpedoes.

The concussion wave from the double detonations sends reverberations through the *Jacksonville*'s interior hull, as it rolls the submarine hard to port.

"Conn, ship's own were struck by antitorpedo torpedoes! Both ADCAPS destroyed—"

Captain O'Rourke stares at his XO, a cold chill running down his spine. His sub, one of the finest in the world, has been outgunned and outmaneuvered.

"Skipper, incoming torpedo! Impact in ten seconds—"

"Brace for impact!"

A resounding double explosion from beneath the hull cracks open the *Jacksonville*'s keel. A massive jolt—the sub suddenly blanketed in suffocating darkness. Shouts, screams, and yells rise above an insane chaos of shearing metal and ripping bulkheads. Steam bursts from unseen pipes. A shower of sparks illuminates a gallery of ghostly faces—petrified, confused, their shattered minds screaming in the terror of one final, unified thought—*I'm going to die*—as Death reaches for them.

It breaks through the hull with sonic speed, crushing its victims with an icy embrace.

Aboard the USS *Ronald Reagan*

Captain Hatcher rushes into the Command Information Center, grabbing hold of a console as his ship lurches beneath him. "Report!"

Rocky Jackson stands. "It was a series of underwater munitions, four in all, very powerful. Totally blew out three of the four props and compromised both layers of the hull's torpedo-protection system. The engine room's taking on water, with water already reported as high as deck four—"

"My God . . ." Hatcher feels the blood drain from his face. *An American supercarrier sinking? Impossible . . .*

"Sir, it's not just us, the entire fleet's under attack, and I've lost contact with both subs."

"Goddamn it." Hatcher looks around. "Where the hell's Strejcek?"

"I don't know."

"Commander, order everyone but the catapult and Pri-Fly crews on deck. Launch as many birds as you can while we still have electricity for the catapults—"

A groan of metal drowns out Hatcher's last order. The ship's steel plates wail in protest, straining to support the floundering carrier's rising bow.

"Hatch—"

"I need to get to the SSES. You have your orders, Commander." Hatcher grabs the watertight door of the CIC to keep from falling, then turns to face his wife. "Rocky, get your team out on deck—now!"

Two decks up in Pri-Fly (Primary Flight Control), Air-boss James "Big Jim" Kimball and his miniboss, Kevin Lynam, bark out commands to their LSOs (landing signal officers), who are frantically working on the flattop six stories below. The control tower is electric with activity. Kimball, the choreographer for the chaotic jet-fighter ballet taking place on the flight deck, is demanding his crew launch no less than twenty aircraft within the next six minutes, an impossibility from which he refuses to back down.

"Heads up on deck. Get ready to shoot Hornets five, six, and seven. Clear shoot lines. Clear catwalk—"

Beneath a turbulent atmosphere of noise and exhaust, four hundred men and women attired in team colors scramble across a lurching flight deck that has suddenly become more carnival ride than airport runway.

Twenty-year-old Ensign Rogelio Duron swears luridly in staccato Spanish as he tugs the parking blocks from the front tire of a Joint Strike Fighter—then screams as he is lifted off his feet and sucked headfirst into the engine inlet, blood and brain matter spraying the deck.

Kimball slams the control tower window with a futile fist. "Goddamn sonuva bitch!" The Air Boss looks up to see an air wing returning from the east. "Shit—Kevin, get those two CSAs in the air before our Tomcats start dropping out of the fucking sky."

Belowdecks, frightened catapult technicians rush about in ankle-deep water as they hurriedly reset each cable, near panic with the horrible realization that they are involved in a high-stakes game of Russian roulette. Communication between the flight-deck crews and the tower is coming in too fast; it is just a matter of minutes before another deadly mistake happens. Precise prelaunch pressure loads must be fine-tuned to each aircraft's weight, but there is no time for the usual measurement—nominal values being hurriedly guessed and set manually. Settings too low will fling a pilot and his aircraft straight into the water, too high and its structure will fail.

Circling the melee is the E-2C Hawkeye Early Warning Aircraft, identifiable by the flat radar rotodome affixed horizontally atop its fuselage. Within the air-watcher, a team of operators use the APS-145 radar to organize the returning jet fighters' midair refueling. From the Hawkeye's cockpit, pilots and copilots stare in disbelief at the surreal disaster taking place below—warship after American warship sinking with inglorious rapidity beneath the lead gray waters of the Atlantic.

Back on the carrier, another Joint Strike Fighter races down the runway as the bow of the *Ronald Reagan* heaves upward from the sea like a breaching humpback. The JSF pilot veers off the rising deck, airborne, until the dark ocean rushes up at him and his jet smashes nose first into a ten-foot swell.

Jim Kimball sees the runway splinter as sections of the fractured prow fall back into the water. "That's it, everyone out! Everyone on deck in life preservers on the double!"

Rocky Jackson grabs an orange flotation vest from an officer, then hurries out on deck. "Has anyone seen the skipper?" She turns to the officer directing the crew into the lifeboats. "O'Malley, have you seen—"

Shrapnel rains down upon her, a fragment of hot metal grazing her forehead as a helicopter blade shatters across the heaving deck, the rotor craft bursting in flames.

Men race to save the pilot.

Rocky is in a daze. "O'Malley, where's the skipper?"

"You're bleeding, Jackson, now get in the goddamn boat!"

Strong arms lift her into the life raft.

"Fuck this, I gotta find Hatch!" Rocky jumps out of the life raft, reenters the superstructure, and races down a listing gray corridor in search of her husband.

The water has reached Captain Hatcher's waist by the time he enters the Ships Signals Exploitation Space, a top-secret chamber containing data links to all national and theater-level intelligence systems. The SSES anteroom is dark, the ship's power out.

Hatcher stumbles across three bodies, two officers and an MP. All floating facedown. All dead.

"Admiral?" Hatcher rolls Brian Decker over, blood pouring from several bullet wounds. "Oh, Jesus . . ." He glances up at a flashlight's beacon coming from within the SSES operations room, his security reflexes taking over.

Hatcher removes the sidearm still holstered to the dead MP. He sloshes forward, peering into the high-level security chamber.

Commander Shane Strejcek lurks by a computer terminal. Images flash rapidly across the screen, a remote palm-sized device attached to the hard drive downloading the sensitive data.

"Strejcek? What the hell are you doing?"

The XO turns. An explosion of heat slams Hatcher back against the far wall, a warm wave of blood pouring down his shirt, quenching the fire burning in his chest as a numbing paralysis sends him slipping to his knees in the crimson water.

Strejcek approaches, Hatcher unable to raise the gun from the water. He has no strength to move, let alone speak.

Strejcek stares serenely at his dying commander. "I'm sorry, Skipper, but I serve a higher calling."

Ignoring the cold water paralyzing her lower torso, and the warm blood oozing from her forehead, Rocky wades through the flooded corridor, the torrent rising fast, the fluorescent bulbs overhead flickering, threatening to plunge her into darkness. "Hatch?" She enters the open SSES chamber, then rushes forward, crying out as she sees him.

"Hatch!" Rocky clutches her husband's lifeless form to her chest, his blood pouring out across her life jacket. She holds his head above water, her right hand brushing against the pistol he is clutching, even in death. "Oh God, Hatch—"

Looking up, she sees Strejcek. "Shane, help me—"

Strejcek is caught off guard. "Rocky, what are you doing here?"

"Help me, Goddamn it, someone shot—" She stares at the gun barrel pointed at her head. "You?" She feels for the weapon in her husband's hand, now underwater.

"You should have abandoned ship." Strejcek bends over and reaches for her with his free hand.

In one motion Rocky leaps to her feet and jams the muzzle of the MP's gun into Strejcek's open mouth. "Drop the gun!"

Strejcek complies.

Her teeth chatter against the cold, her hand shakes with emotion. She removes the muzzle from her superior's mouth, mustering one adrenaline-packed syllable. "Why?"

Strejcek exhales. "You're so beautiful, Rocky, but you're so blind. The world has cancer, and you're still in the denial stage."

The ship lurches beneath them. Strejcek pushes her aside, diving for his weapon.

Unfazed, she fires.

A wad of blood and brain tissue splatters against the far wall as the boat's traitorous second-in-command falls backward with a splash.

Before she can catch a breath, the supercarrier is wrenched to starboard beneath her, as if tugged by the hand of Poseidon. Rocky tumbles sideways, regains her footing, then leaps into the heaving corridor, head-on into a wave of rushing water.

Jesus . . . this isn't happening . . .

The sea races through the inclined passageway like a raging creek, the torrent dragging her with it. Gasping and kicking, Rocky endeavors to grab a ceiling pipe, succeeds, then arm-walks the chasm like a mountain climber dangling from a rope bridge as she drags herself toward the diminishing light at the end of the tunnel.

Don't stop . . .

The cold water saps her strength, yet her world-filling anger refuses to allow her any rest. The sea is rising at her from behind as the ship groans a final tocsin warning of her impending death. Her fingers numb, her hands too frozen to maintain a controlled grip, Rocky stubbornly continues to ascend, her feet slipping wildly on the slick steel walls.

Ducking through a knee-knocker, she fights to maintain equilibrium as an intersecting current sideswipes her from the galley.

Don't stop, don't think, just go faster . . .

The boat rolls again, its bow rising, sending a four-foot wall of water racing straight for her—

Rocky grabs the pipes, sucks in a desperate breath, and ducks, as the swell buries her, pounding her chest as it hurtles down the passage. She opens her eyes, shivering from the cold, then climbs faster, the daylight winking at her, teasing her from a dismaying thirty feet up.

A minute later she emerges from the open hatch, the gray sky rolling away as the deck heaves backward, threatening to send her spilling back into the corridor. She leaps sideways, then screams, dropping to her belly as an F/A-18E Super Hornet slides sideways across the tilting tarmac, its mangled bulk threatening to crush her. She covers her head, squeezing her eyes shut as the wreckage passes over her and crashes into the flight deck's tower, now pitching backward as the carrier's failing buoyancy yields its weight to the sea.

Rocky crawls out from under some trailing debris, her fingers creating indentations in the soft top layer of the torn deck as she moves toward the rising portside rail. Dodging yet another avalanche of debris, she grabs onto one of the carrier's now-loose retractable antennas as the deck climbs to an angle too steep even to kneel upon.

Reaching up, she pulls herself to the rail and peers over the edge.

Oh, God . . .

The pitching sea is eight stories below but nowhere to be seen, concealed beneath the carrier's keel, which is rising from the sea like a glistening steel whale poised to swallow her.

Unable to jump, she holds on, praying for the ship to stop rolling. Shaking uncontrollably, she closes her eyes to shut out the vertigo and the wail of tortured metal, her trembling hand reflexively wiping the blood crusted on her half-frozen brow.

The carrier stops rotating—and suddenly drops like an elevator. Rocky holds on, as water splashes across her face and the sea rushes up from below.

Now! She climbs upon the listing rail and leaps.

The cold wind rushes past her ears until she plunges feet-first into the roaring ocean, sinking like an anchor. As she hits the water she inflates the vest, and its buoyancy halts her descent at twenty feet. Kicking and paddling, she fights her way back to the surface, the frothy layer appearing so close, yet always an arm's distance away.

Finally, her head pops free, somehow slipping into a valley between swells. The rolling ocean lifts and drops her, the nausea overwhelming her stomach and head. A current tugs at her from behind. Turning, she is horrified to witness the *Ronald Reagan*'s superstructure slip beneath the waves, expelling its last dying belch as it disappears into the vortex created by its own descent into the unforgiving sea.

A steel-cold current of choking brine reaches out and grabs her. Panicking, she starts swimming, but the vortex is too strong, sucking her backward as it inhales her within its fury. Ocean swells become mountainous barriers, rising higher as she spins faster.

Too strong . . .

Rocky sucks in a last desperate breath as the cavitation of the displaced mass of the carrier snatches her about the waist and drags her below.

She kicks and paddles in protest, wasting precious air as she fights to swim upstream against the maelstrom, the unfathomable suction spinning above the now-submerged wreckage.

Forty feet . . . her diving watch displays, unheeded.

Her pulse pounds in her ears.

Sixty feet . . . sinister pressure assaults her eardrums as her limbs turn to lead.

Eighty feet, forty seconds, thirty-one years . . . and still she is plummeting, ever downward.

How deep can a human go and survive on a single breath of air? She remembers seeing specials on free-diving and wills herself not to waste precious energy by fighting.

The haunting sounds of the depths envelop her. Rocky pinches her nose and blows, attempting to rid the pain from her ears. She looks down, falling feetfirst into the deep blue sea. Far below, the *Ronald Reagan* groans back at her as the once-mighty vessel disappears into murky shadows, approaching its final resting place.

Please let me go . . .

One minute . . . the pressure dragging her below easing only slightly, the pinch in her ears now daggers.

One hundred twenty feet . . . still falling, strength and resolve diminishing with every foot.

One fifty, her throat and chest on fire.

At one hundred fifty-eight feet, the carrier releases her.

The air space in Rocky's flotation device has been compressed flat beneath six atmospheres of pressure. No longer buoyant, she continues falling, flailing in slow motion, a marionette dancing for Death's amusement before He takes her.

She closes her eyes, her body no longer hers, her mind in a fog, the sea ready to squelch the flames in her lungs. *Pills were easier. Wish I had my pills. No more pain . . . no more gain, no more brain, no more fame, no more blame. Goodbye, Mom. Good-bye, Papa Bear.*

Something enormous sideswipes her face. Her eyes burst open against the tremendous impact, its brutality jolting her with adrenaline.

A cloud of buoyant debris races up from the sunken carrier.

Willing her arms to move, she reaches for the closest object, misses the first, then the second. She twists her torso, close to passing out as she aims for a large object rising from below . . . waiting . . . waiting . . . her eyes nearly popping out of their sockets as the object suddenly slams into her gut, her chest exploding as she latches on to the bucking bronco, her nose inhaling seawater, her mouth vomiting it back out.

And still, she refuses to let go.

The object twists in her grip as it pushes her higher, the helicopter tire somehow settling beneath her, driving her to the surface, spinning her as it rises.

Rocky loops both legs and the crook of one arm around the tire, pinching her nose with her free hand as Death's pressing blackness continues pushing in on her peripheral vision. A warm feeling fills her chest as she rises higher, the residual molecules of air in her lungs expanding, easing the scorching pain. With newfound strength, she grips the wheel's strut tighter, gently expelling air to prevent her lungs from bursting and to keep dissolved nitrogen from forming deadly bubbles in her blood.

The life vest reexpands, nearly pushing her from the tire.

And then the incredible sound of life returns in one mighty *swoosh* as her body is literally launched from the sea. Thrown from the tire, she haltingly inhales a lungful of blessed air, her salt-burned throat heaving with the effort.

Moaning involuntarily, she swims back to the tire and climbs on, hugging it as feeling slowly returns to her oxygen-deprived limbs.

Rising.

Falling.

Hills of water toss her insides about. She vomits seawater, then closes her eyes, her head pounding, her body shivering from the cold. The sound of circling fighters grows louder.

And then she is moving.

Rocky looks up, disoriented. *Am I being rescued?* She blinks hard, her mind unable to grasp what her eyes are seeing.

The tire is caught in the wake of a great beast, its dark, imposing head plowing the surface somewhere up ahead. The brutish silhouette is circling, and now she can see what looks like its eyes, glowing crimson beneath an enormous wake that washes over the monster's face.

Oh my God . . .

The mountainous bow wave tosses the surviving crewmen of the *Ronald Reagan* from their rafts, their limbs flailing like those of surfers thrown by a breaking wave.

High above, an air wing organizes. Four fighters plunge toward the monster, each enraged pilot intent on slaughtering it.

Eight JDAM missiles launch as one, the wave of projectiles homing in on the brute's exposed back.

From the creature's spine, a dozen surface-to-air missiles zoom skyward, blasting apart the Joint Strike Fighters in the blink of an eye—even as the evening sky erupts with the metallic whine from two antimissile guns, positioned behind the sea creature's head like horns on a devil. A sheer wall of steel—four thousand 20-mm shells—meet the JDAMs head-on.

Rocky instinctively ducks, registering the heat from the explosions as she shields her eyes from the inferno.

The remaining fighters race out of range, clearly outmatched.

Unchallenged, the steel nightmare laps its killing field one last time before disappearing beneath the waves, leaving little more than a ripple.

Rocky presses her face against the cold surface of the helicopter wheel, her shattered mind screaming a single thought.

Goliath . . .

Like a tortured animal in a trap, she is gripped by a wave of anger. Purple lips whisper the cursed name of Gunnar Wolfe, her voice rising until she is yelling like a banshee, screeching her venom into the deepening twilight.

"I am only one, but still I am one.
I cannot do everything, but still I can do something.
I will not refuse to do the something I can do."
—Helen Keller

"I have no regrets. I acted alone and on orders from God."
—Yigal Amir,
assassin of Israeli Prime Minister Yitzhak Rabin

2 October 2009
State College, Pennsylvania

The main campus of Pennsylvania State University and its bordering town of State College lie in the Nittany Valley, a serene countryside of flowing hills, rural neighborhoods, out-door malls, and dairy farms, enveloped by the mountains of central Pennsylvania. The name "Nittany" comes from the Indian words meaning "protective barrier against the elements," and may have originated from the tale of a mythical princess, "Nita-Nee," who led her people to safety within the Pennsylvania valley. Upon her death, Mount Nittany itself is said to have risen to mark the princess's grave.

Gunnar Wolfe shuts down the lime green tractor and stares at the mountain range stretched out before him on the distant northeastern horizon. The fading afternoon sun has bathed the sloping landmark in shades of purple.

Closing his eyes, he draws in a deep, intoxicating breath.

The serenity of the mountains soothe Gunnar's soul as the sea once had, long before it had become a battlefield. Resting his arms on the wheel, his chin on his forearms, he gazes at the hills, imagining them to be a series of majestic tsunamis, their cresting fury threatening to wipe out the valley—and what little sanity his existence has been clinging to over the last seven years, four months, ten days, fourteen hours. . . .

Gunnar had grown up on the dairy farm back when its borders encompassed more than a hundred acres. He and his cousins had milked the cows by hand back then—sixty pure Holsteins—each animal twice a day. Looking back, he sees it as a happier, simpler time—long before his father had purchased the milking machines—long before his mother had died. Gunnar closes his eyes, refocusing his mind, this time counting the years since the accursed drunk sophomore had run into her as she walked home from church.

Twenty years, three months, sixteen days, two hours. . . .

During his years in prison he found he could not remember her face, but then he had returned to the farm, and the memories came rushing back.

A cold autumn breeze clears the tractor's exhaust, bringing with it the smell of hay and manure and, atop them, the indefinable air-flavor of the coming of a long Centre County winter. The leaves have already begun turning, welcoming back the Penn State alumni, whose presence on the eve of a football weekend is already clogging Routes 322 and 26 with thousands of family campers. For the next forty-eight hours, the Nittany Lion fanatics will overrun the secluded campus town, choking the restaurants and blitzing the bars as they frolic along College and Beaver Avenues, reliving the best years of their adolescence, back when the object of getting drunk was to have fun, rather than to dull the senses just to ease the pain of adulthood.

Happy Valley. Gunnar loves State College the way he loves the coziness of a fireplace and quilt on a snowy day. Something about the town has always made him feel safe. Perhaps it is the campus itself, a haven of students nestled within a mountain valley—a place where the memories are good, the pressure limited to studying for exams, or working on Pop's farm, making sure the heifers have all been fed.

Or maybe it's that State College is about as far as one

could be from the ocean, from Special Ops, and from Rocky Jackson.

The thought of his ex-fiancée causes the bile to rise to Gunnar's parched throat. Restarting the tractor, he grinds the ancient gears and shifts the plow into first.

Four more rows. Forty-eight minutes. Two thousand, eight hundred, and eighty seconds. . . .

Gunnar finishes a row and turns, aiming the rickety bucket of bolts in the direction of the barn. Cutting the dried fields yields the hay they will need for the cows' feed mix, enough to get them through the looming winter. Years, months, hours, days . . . there are no days off for the dairy farmer. Dawn greets Gunnar each morning in the milking parlor, where he cleans the cow's teats with an iodine-and-water solution before hooking each animal up to the milking machine. It takes the machine five minutes to drain a cow's udder. If organized right, the five machines could finish the entire herd in just under two hours. Five, ten, fifteen, twenty . . . one hundred and twenty cows, each cow producing six gallons of milk a day. Six gallons, twelve, eighteen, twenty-four . . . the collected milk runs through an FDA-approved tube directly into a temperature-controlled tank, to be transferred to a refrigerated tanker truck that delivers the product to any one of several local processing plants. Milk the cows twice a day, then keep them moving from one grazing field to the next, supervising six and a half hours of their eating and drinking, all the while maintaining a strict breeding schedule for each member of the herd.

Gunnar is thankful for the busy days, the work helping to keep his mind off alcohol. He had never been much of a drinker, not during his college years, and never during the Army's Special Forces training. *I will keep my mind and body clean, alert, and strong, for this is my debt to those who depend upon me.*

Hooah.

It was only after leaving prison that he had turned to booze.

Ninety-nine bottles of beer on the wall, ninety-nine bottles

*of beer . . . if your self-identity should happen to fall . . .
ninety-eight bottles of beer on the wall . . .*

A year of living on the streets, a year of waking up in his
own piss and vomit. Hitting bottom and lying in it, still full of
anger and guilt, he had finally found his way back to his father's farm. Two months in a treatment center, a lifetime commitment to Alcoholics Anonymous, and a busy schedule had
allowed him to piece together an existence, one day at a time.
But the hurt was still there, always festering just below the
surface.

The irony of his life is something Gunnar Wolfe grapples
with daily.

I will live my life, one day at a time . . .

As a child, Gunnar had always been afraid of challenges.
An introvert, he rarely allowed himself to compete in sports,
though laboring on his father's farm had developed his
physique beyond those of his peers. While his father encouraged his only child to follow in his footsteps, his mother
pushed him to get more out of life. She encouraged him to
read, and bought him a steady supply of inspiring adventure
stories. She drove him to a gym and hired a trainer. She enrolled him in karate and pushed him to play high school
sports, where he earned All-State honors in football and basketball.

Slowly but surely, the blossoming adolescent began to
come out of his shell.

It was the tragedy of his mother's death that ultimately
changed Gunnar's life. Two weeks after the funeral, the
eighteen-year-old Penn State freshman announced that he
was switching majors, from agriculture to engineering. Harlan Wolfe, upon learning of his son's "blasphemous" decision, threatened to cut off all tuition money, prompting
Gunnar to join Penn State's ROTC program, affording him
the opportunity to live on campus.

In Gunnar's sophomore year, his old high school coach
urged him to try out for football, the lonely teen surprising
everyone by earning a spot as a fourth-string tight end. By his
junior year, he had moved up to second string, his last-minute

touchdown catch against Michigan State helping the Nittany Lions to another bowl appearance.

It was also during his junior year that Gunnar attended the U.S. Army's Airborne School. ROTC training was nothing compared to his first taste of true Army discipline. For three long weeks he endured hours of seemingly endless running and calisthenics, the grueling exercises sandwiched between the finest parachute training on the planet.

Gunnar hated heights. Static-line jumping from a C-141 into eleven hundred feet of total blackness was more frightening beforehand than fearsome in the doing. His relief after the fifth and last jump was almost embarrassing.

By summer football camp of his senior year, Gunnar was a different person. Gone was the last trace of the timid farm boy, in its place—a focused athlete with a warrior's mentality. The coaches noticed, too, promoting the two-hundred-and-forty pound walk-on to the first-team, awarding him a full scholarship. Though Penn State would fall short of a repeat Rose Bowl appearance, Gunnar would receive second-team all-American honors, and was considered by many pro football scouts as a second- or third-round draft pick.

The NFL would have to wait.

Four years after his mother's death, Gunnar Wolfe stood in uniform at his graduation, prepared in body and mind to attend the sixteen-week Infantry Officer Basic Course (IOBC, Second Battalion, Eleventh Infantry Regiment) at Fort Benning, Georgia. Coach Joe Paterno filled in for Gunnar's estranged father, Harlan, who stubbornly refused to attend the ceremony.

The Infantry Officer Basic Course is designed to produce the world's best infantry lieutenants. In essence, it is a warfighting course, every aspect of training intended to prepare the newly commissioned officer for combat. IOBC training has zero tolerance for anything less than a total physical and mental commitment to excellence.

"Wolfe, you can't coast through life-and-death decisions! Shit or get off the pot! Is that understood?"

"Roger, Sergeant Gardner!"

Sixteen weeks. One hundred twelve long days of being tired, wet, and hungry. For Gunnar, it was just a preview of to what lay ahead.

Ranger School.

It takes a special breed to make it in the United States Army's Special Forces, and the Rangers are considered the junkyard dogs of the SOF community. Masters of special light infantry operations on land, sea, and in the air, their origins can be traced back to the early 1670s, when the Rangers of Captain Benjamin Church helped end the Indian Conflict of King Phillip's War. Years later, five hundred Rangers, known as Morgan's Riflemen, fought under George Washington. Their cunning and deadly aim with the rifle inflicted great losses on the British troops, making them the most feared corps of the Continental Army. The motto, "Rangers lead the way," was coined during World War II, shortly after D-day, when a general wanted to know who the tough guys were. When the men responded, "Rangers, of course," the general uttered the now-famous reply, "then lead the way, Rangers!"

For Gunnar, Ranger School turned out to be the most intense "withholding" training he had ever endured, "withholding" referring to the total lack of adequate water, food, and sleep. Over the next sixty-one days he endured and survived freezing temperatures, mental exhaustion, and physical exertion that was often beyond the point of abuse. He lost twenty-five pounds of muscle and fat from his already-trimmed physique, but successfully maintained a positive attitude, even though his fellow officers and enlisted Ranger schoolmates were decimated by flu, hypothermia, broken ankles, twisted necks, worn-out tempers, and a simple loss of intestinal fortitude, ironically assisted by surreptitious low doses of cholera.

Upon graduating from "hell," Ranger-Qualified Gunnar Wolfe reported to his first assignment as a platoon leader with the First Battalion, 504th Parachute Infantry Regiment, Eighty-second Airborne Division, Fort Bragg, North Carolina. Over the next two years he would lead his men on a half dozen successful training missions all over the world.

It was during a routine free-fall parachuting exercise that

he would impress the man who would soon become his surro-
gate father.

The military employs two types of parachutes, both different than those used in recreational sky-diving. Troops use the
classic round chute with a static-line deployment, the Army
trusting its troops with a weapon, but not with the steering of
a parachute. Attached to the plane, the parachute opens the
moment the trooper jumps, allowing for almost no free fall,
little error, and even less maneuverability, with a hard landing
to boot.

A light rain was falling on the morning of April 16 when
Gunnar and his fellow students boarded the C-130 to begin
the first in a series of bad-weather parachute-training exercises. Colonel Mike "Bear" Jackson was the commander
overseeing Gunnar's regiment—his job—to instruct Special
Ops Forces to free-fall in rough weather conditions using
ram-air canopies, rectangular quasi wings far more maneuverable than the ungainly troop chutes, and possessing significant forward speeds.

Of all training activities, Gunnar hated parachute jumping
the most. He had lost control of his bowels during his first
jump back in Airborne School, and had never taken to the idea
of free-falling in storm clouds from thirteen thousand feet.

Gunnar's best friend, Bill Raby, was first up. An experienced jumper, Raby made the fateful decision to leave his
jump position to offer another Ranger a final word of encour-
agement. Buffeted by high winds, the transport dipped, causing Raby to stumble. Before anyone could react, the
commando's pilot chute caught on the hydraulic lift, loos-
ened, and was immediately sucked into the tailgate's gaping
opening. As Gunnar watched helplessly, his friend was lifted
off his feet like a rag doll, the powerful airstream flinging him
facefirst against the hydraulic lift before yanking him clear
out of the plane.

Unconscious, entangled within his parachute's suspension
lines, Bill Raby hurtled toward the earth like a ground-
seeking missile, his speed quickly accelerating to more than
150 miles per hour.

Colonel Jackson was on his feet when he was pushed aside by Gunnar Wolfe, who leaped out of the plane as if he were Superman. Soaring headfirst in a steep vertical dive, the former farm boy–turned–human projectile flew after Raby at a death-defying speed, intent on saving his friend's life or dying in the process.

Plunging through rain that felt like thousands of stinging bees, Gunnar adjusted his trajectory, aiming for that speck in the lead gray distance he prayed was his friend. At 9,000 feet, the tumbling object became the unconscious commando. At 3,500 feet, Gunnar reached out and caught the man, then fumbled as he attempted to pull the cut-away handle that would disconnect Raby's main chute. As the main chute released, the drag pulled the pin on the reserve chute.

Gunnar fell away, pulling his own rip cord as Raby's canopy blossomed open—a mere 650 feet from the ground. Moments later, the two student commandos found themselves knee deep in mud on a pig farm, two miles east of the drop zone.

Hooah.

Gunnar's high-speed heroics not only saved Raby's life, but forever bonded him to Colonel Jackson. He was the type of warrior Jackson wanted under his command. Brave. Compassionate. Patriotic. A true leader.

In other words, everything the Bear had always wanted in a son.

Under Jackson's watchful eye, First Lieutenant Gunnar Wolfe was assigned to lead Second Platoon, Charlie Company, the First Ranger Battalion's top company. Here he learned the art of demolitions and explosives, as well as advanced hand-to-hand combat.

Two years with First Battalion was followed by the Special Forces Assessment and Selection (SFAS) course. Another six months spent completing Q (Qualification) Course at Fort Bragg, immersed in guerrilla-warfare training. Four months later, the Bear had him, on orders, transferred to SCUBA School in Key West, Florida, where he learned the art of military SCUBA diving. Then it was on to Basic Underwater Demolitions/SEAL (BUDS), to go through formal SEAL training.

"What is it you want, Wolfe?"

"Sir, I want to do whatever it takes to protect my country and her interests abroad."

It soon became obvious to all that Colonel Jackson was grooming his young protégé to be the ultimate soldier—the ultimate killing machine.

A broken ankle forced the Bear's "cub" to take a much-deserved leave. Laid up in Key West, the former engineering major resumed work on a design for a remote submersible he had toyed with at Penn State, a fast, stealthy two-man vessel that could be used to transport SEALS deep behind enemy lines. Computer tests on Gunnar's designs impressed his superiors. Patterned after the contours of a hammerhead shark, the vessel was not only "theoretically" capable of advanced maneuvers, but speed to boot.

The schematics eventually found their way to the Navy's Warfare Division in Keyport, Washington.

After nearly a year away from Special Ops, Gunnar returned to active duty. When the Gulf War broke out a few weeks later, Detachment Commander Wolfe found himself on board a transport plane with the rest of his twelve-man infiltration unit, bound for Kuwait.

The next seven years would be a blur. Mission after covert mission, his muscles twitching with adrenaline, his gut tightening in fear as he unleashed a calculated highly trained fury upon the enemies of his country.

Military dictatorships. Guerrilla forces. Cause-intoxicated rebels.

Gunnar was the consummate Army fighting machine, a trigger man for the long arm of the law—the United States military.

Join the Army. See the world. Protect democracy.

And Gunnar saw everything. Violence and hatred. Greed and corruption. Famine and pestilence. Bloody conflicts entangled with so much history, so much death, that right and wrong, good and evil no longer existed, only greed and hatred commanded the politics of the moment.

Gunnar might have been a well-trained fighting machine, but he was still an American soldier, and American soldiers live by a creed.

Soldiers fight to make a difference.

Soldiers kill bad guys.

Soldiers do not kill children.

After seven years of violence, the Army's most capable stallion finally bucked his riders.

You do not shoot a champion racehorse after it tires of winning, especially one with an engineering background who understands the intricacies of combat. The Bear, now commander in Chief of the United States Special Operations Command, arranged for Gunnar's transfer to the Naval Undersea Warfare Center at Keyport, knowing full well he was not just salvaging the career of a superior soldier, he was playing the role of matchmaker.

At first, the change of scene had worked. Gunnar was assigned to head the team constructing the SEAL Hammerhead minisub based on his own designs, and even the challenge of converting the two-man submersible to a computer-operated vehicle did not seem to faze him.

Or maybe he was just trying to impress his new CO, a fiery woman who made his blood boil and his groin melt. When their unbridled passion turned to love, Gunnar thought he was in heaven.

And then he was called to the Pentagon—to a private meeting to discuss the true purpose of his remotely operated minisubs.

His new identity shattered like glass.

What is it like to wake up, look in the mirror, and realize your life has been one big lie, that everything you were taught to believe in is wrong, that your existence has been corrupted to the point that you suddenly realize you are not the cure for the infection, but the disease itself.

Something snapped inside him. And in that single moment of clarity, he realized what he had to do.

Readying the computer virus had been the easy part—the decision whether to actually go through with the treasonous act had been the challenge.

"Wolfe, you can't coast through life-and-death decisions! Shit or get off the pot! Is that understood?"

"Roger, Sergeant Gardner!"

A Special Ops warrior knows better than to hesitate. Gunnar had hesitated. In the delay, someone else had acted, someone close. They had not only stolen $2 billion dollars worth of biochemical computer ware, but had set him up as the fall guy, using a false money trail to paint him a traitor to his family and friends.

Gunnar had a strong suspicion who the real traitor was, but he had refused to turn the man in. And so the judge had come down hard upon the former Special Ops commando.

"Gunnar Wolfe, this court has found you guilty. Although you have served your country bravely in the past, your refusal to cooperate in our investigation leaves me no choice than to sentence you to the maximum penalty for your crimes . . . "

Ten years. Gunnar felt as if he was falling from a precipice. He turned to face Rocky, shocked at her expression. His fiancée actually seemed . . . relieved.

As they led him away in restraints, only the Bear had the stomach to look him in the eye.

When it comes to assigning the guilty to a correctional facility, the Bureau of Prisons has its own hierarchy. Nonviolent and white-collar offenders are sent to level-one camps—dormitory-style prisons often dubbed "Club Feds." Medium-security prisons fall into categories two, three, and four, the level of security increasing progressively. Vocational training is emphasized in these institutions, where inmates get their first real "education" about life in prison.

Level-five institutions house the most violent criminals. These are society's outlaws, the unreformable—career criminals with violent pasts. Sociopaths. Murderers.

Gunnar Wolfe had been accused and convicted of a crime that had given the Defense Department a public black eye. There would be hell to pay, and the former Special Ops guru was going to pick up the tab.

Despite his service to his country, the Bureau of Prisons assigned him to Leavenworth—the oldest, toughest level-five correctional facility in the nation.

First-timers are rarely sent to Leavenworth. Most of the twelve hundred inmates imprisoned there have spent half their lives in other prisons, finally earning their way into the "Hot House."

As he rode to Leavenworth in the prison van, his last glimpses of the outside world obscured by bars, Gunnar Wolfe realized his life was over. He had lost his country, his comrades, his commanding officer, and the woman he loved; and now, somehow, he had to bury his emotions and toughen up, or be eaten alive.

Gunnar and the other "fish" passed through the yellowed limestone administration building in leg irons and tether chains, the "black box" severely limiting their movements. When entering a maximum-security prison, an inmate has an immediate decision to make. Will he allow himself to be used and abused? Is he willing to fight? Every move, every expression, every action or reaction is scrutinized.

As the electronic gate closed behind him, the farm boy from Pennsylvania didn't care if he lived or died.

Leavenworth is composed of four cellblocks and a center hall that connect to a main rotunda like spokes on a wheel. The hellhole prison sits on twenty-two acres, and is surrounded by a four-foot-thick brick wall, which rises thirty-five feet above the yard and descends thirty-five feet below it. Strategically placed atop the wall are six gun towers.

Within the yard are basketball courts, tennis courts, a weight-lifting pit, and other recreational fields. The prison hospital and disciplinary unit (hole), as well as the four-story UNICOR building (housing a textile shop, furniture factory, and printing plant) can also be found there.

Seventy percent of the inmates at Leavenworth are assigned to two-man cells. Pulling a few strings of his own, the Bear artfully arranged to get Gunnar into a single cell, a status usually reserved for protective custody, medical reasons, or inmates too violent to have a cellmate. It would be the last break Gunnar would get for years to come.

Like most maximum-security prisons, Leavenworth is a concrete jungle. Prisoners have a wolf-pack mentality, body language often determining the difference between predator and prey. Cons, like beasts, herd themselves along racial and ethnic lines.

At the top of the food chain are the gangs, classified by law-enforcement personnel as Security Risk Groups. Latin Kings, Muslims, Crypts, Bloods, Aryan Brotherhood, La Cuestra Nuestra Familia (the Mexican Mafia)—all well-organized groups, motivated by the desire to survive and the spoils of illegal prison activities.

Then there are the "wanna-bes," individuals in the protracted process of seeking formal gang membership. Those convicts are often linked to the most violent prison yard episodes as they attempt to impress their recruiters.

Drifting through the jungle like solitary rabid animals are the sociopaths and psychos. You never knew when one of these lifers might slip out of his twilight zone and attack. Look at one of them the wrong way during breakfast, and you could find a shiv in your belly before lunch.

Like the jungle, prison has an unwritten code for survival. Leave your cell in the morning and you enter a world where it is take or be taken, kill or be killed, never knowing for sure if you will return to the relative safety of each night's lockdown.

Every movement watched. Every weakness probed. Society's worst predators, always evaluating, instinctively separating the strong from the weak, the focused from the distracted.

Though an elite physical specimen and highly trained fighter with a hundred different killing reflexes, Gunnar entered Leavenworth Prison an emotional wreck, his self-identity gone, the injustice of his situation, combined with years of guilt from his actions in the field robbing him of his will to survive. Severely depressed, he drifted through his first hours of hell like a zombie.

He might as well have been a bleeding fish tossed into a swimming pool full of sharks.

Gunnar's first "mud check" happened during his second day. Inmates at Leavenworth are permitted to roam the yard relatively unchecked. Anthony Barnes was a lifer, a "J-Cat" (needing mental treatment) doing 104 years for kidnapping and murder. He had just been transferred to Leavenworth after spending eighteen years at the Northern Correctional Institution in Somers, Connecticut, where he had killed three inmates; two because they were black, one because the man had made the mistake of refusing him sexually. Barnes was being actively recruited by the Aryan Brotherhood, one of the most savage of the white prison gangs. Before gaining his lifetime membership to the AB, he was required to "make his bones"— killing another person targeted for death by the "Commission."

The Commission had targeted Gunnar.

It is unusual for the Aryan Brotherhood to go after Whites, but tensions between the AB and the Muslims had been rising of late, and the outnumbered Aryan Brotherhood were not looking for a war, they just wanted to end "soldier boy's" misery before their Black and Hispanic rivals could get to him—

—killing him out of "kindness."

The eyes of the jungle watched as Gunnar walked the yard, his mind doing "hard time," his psyche unable to come to grips with the sudden reality of a prison sentence too unfair to accept, too long to imagine. As Barnes approached, the other road dogs instinctively backed off, leaving the new inmate on his own.

The shank in Barnes's hand was an eight-inch piece of metal, ingeniously taken with great patience from the back of a radio. One end, ground against cement, was as sharp as a razor. The other end was wrapped in cloth for a firm grip by hands that had crushed many a throat.

His mind preoccupied, Gunnar never saw the man coming. Only when the blade penetrated his lower back—millimeters from a classic kidney stab, did Gunnar's commando instincts finally take over.

Ignoring pain that would paralyze a normal man, Gunnar pivoted to face his assailant. Looping his left arm over and around both of Barnes's arms, he pinned them in a viselike grip while the heel of his free hand exploded into the convict's face, shattering his occipital bone. Passing on the temptation to crush the larynx, Gunnar opted to slam his shoe sideways against the medial section of his attacker's right knee, tearing the collateral and cruciate ligaments from the bone, crippling his would-be assassin.

From that day forward, the former Ranger was regarded as a convict, a prisoner who was to be respected. A week's stay in the hospital was followed by the mandatory twenty days in the hole.

Naked and in the seclusion of darkness, he reflected on the hypocrisy of his life.

Who am I?

I am a son, scorned by his father. I am a man loathed by the woman I love. I am a fool, betrayed by his best friend. I'm an American, imprisoned by his country. I am a soldier, forced to kill children.

I am a piece of meat. I am scum. I am a walking corpse waiting to be buried so that I may be judged by God.

I am an island.

I have not led a good life. I deserve to be punished. I have allowed myself to be used. I have betrayed my parents. I have betrayed myself.

I have betrayed God.

Guilt and self-loathing burned deep inside Gunnar's being, consuming all other emotions. He thought about killing himself, but was afraid.

Gunnar held no fear of death; in fact, he welcomed an end to his anguish. What petrified the former farm boy from central Pennsylvania was the thought of having to stand naked before God, wearing only his sins.

And though he feared God, he was not a religious man. He had no belief in the power of absolution. He alone was responsible for his actions, and he alone could absolve himself from sin. Somehow he would find a way to cleanse himself, somehow he had to make amends for his crimes.

But first, he had to survive.

And so Gunnar Wolfe hardened himself on the inside, stuffing all his anger and fear and remorse into a mental lockbox, tossing away the key. He refused to receive visits from the Bear and would accept no mail. He spoke only when spoken to by the guards. When he wasn't pumping iron, he was walking the yard, a constant scowl on his face.

Rumors about the former Special Ops officer spread quickly through the prison grapevine, fed by clerks who had read his file. It was said he could kill three men armed with shanks before the first drop of his own blood hit the floor. The legends only grew wilder over time.

Choo Choo Rodriguez was a Latin King disciple and one of the toughest cons in Leavenworth. He was serving three consecutive life sentences for hacking his girlfriend and her parents to death with a machete. Choo Choo announced to his peers that he would be the one to claim the "Ranger boy's cherry."

Hours later, the body of the six-foot-six, 282-pound Rodriguez was found in the laundry room—eviscerated—his intestines looped around his neck.

No one else would challenge the former Army Ranger during his stay in Leavenworth.

It was not Gunnar who had killed Rodriguez, but Jim Kennedy, a corrections officer hired by the Bear to look out for his boy.

Message delivered.

During the fifty-seventh month of his sentence, an uprising between the Muslims and the Aryan Brotherhood broke out in Gunnar's cellblock, during the warden's inspection. Two guards were stabbed and killed, the warden held at gunpoint by a deranged Anthony Barnes. Two Correctional Emergency Response Teams surrounded the cellblock, but were held at bay by the threat on the warden's life. Just as it seemed like events were spinning out of control, a trained killer, a former Army Ranger, stepped out of the shadows and snapped

Barnes's neck, taking several bullets in the process. The warden was rescued, the threat ended.

Gunnar's sentence was commuted a week later. On a clear Kansas day in November, he walked out the gates of Leavenworth a free man—his tortured mind still very much imprisoned.

The next year had been a blur. Gunnar had been an elite fighting machine, trained to take out his enemy, but now the enemy was inside his own skin. Self-loathing led to booze, the booze to painkillers.

There are only three places an addict ends up. Rehab, jail, or dead.

Having spent time in prison, Gunnar opted for death. Fortunately, the overdose landed him in rehab.

Two months later, he returned to Happy Valley, prepared to live out his life—one day at a time.

The Bell 206L-4 Longranger light utility helicopter soars over Beaver Stadium, then northeast beyond a dense woods before reaching farmland. Clouds of brown dust and flecks of hay kick up as the machine lands between the silo and the barn.

Seventy-two-year-old Harlan Wolfe hurries out from his kitchen toward the world-filling noise. He adjusts his suspenders with one hand, holding the Smith & Wesson 12-gauge with the other, his initial shouts of protest drowned out by the shrieking blades. Cursing under his breath, he sees a woman remove her headphones and hand them to the pilot before exiting from the opened passenger door.

Commander Rocky Jackson-Hatcher brushes debris from her naval dress uniform. Climbing down from the aircraft she turns—coming face-to-face with the barrel of a shotgun, and the man who, years earlier, had nearly become her father-in-law.

The pilot reaches for his sidearm.

Rocky waves, signaling him to take off. "Mr. Wolfe, it's me—"

"I know who you are. I ain't senile."

"Would you mind lowering the gun?"

"What're you doing here?"

"I need to speak to Gunnar."

"Come to twist the knife?"

"This is official government business—"

"Piss off. Gunnar don't want nothing to do with you and yours—and neither do I. Now get off my land 'fore I call the cops."

"Call the cops. I'm not leaving until I speak to your son." She pushes past him, entering the farmhouse. "Gunnar? Gunnar Wolfe—are you in here?" She heads into the kitchen, the aroma of roast beef and potatoes instantly setting her stomach to growling. Pulling back the sun-yellowed curtains, she looks out the window and sees the distant tractor.

Gunnar negotiates the last turn, the setting sun at his back turning the dried field a golden brown. He is halfway across the acreage when he spots the woman waiting by the fence.

Son of a bitch . . . Gunnar throttles up, then changes his mind and shuts off the engine. *Screw it. Make her walk.*

Rocky stares at the tractor, which has stopped moving less than a quarter mile away. *Goddamn the man.* She waits another few minutes, then, cursing under her breath, unbuttons her coat and climbs over the wooden fence, her black dress shoes sinking heel deep into grass, mud, and manure.

Gunnar watches, his heart pounding. The golden hair, shorter now, is pressed neatly beneath her hat. He feels his groin stir as she gets nearer.

She approaches the tractor, slipping and sliding in the moist earth, looking up at him through angry eyes. "We need to talk."

Gunnar swallows the ball of bile burning its way up his throat.

"Don't just sit there, say something."

"Screw you, lady. Six years, and you think you can just waltz back in here and say we need to talk?"

"What would you like me to say? Enjoy your stay in prison? Meet any new friends? You betrayed your country, Gunnar. I'm here to give you a chance to—"

Gunnar restarts the engine, slams the tractor into gear, and floors it, the spinning tires shooting mud into the air.

She brushes mud from the front of her skirt, then curses as she wipes the olive brown cowshit from her fingers and back across the fabric.

Gunnar parks the tractor and storms into the farmhouse, his blood boiling. Entering the kitchen, he sees his father watching from the window.

"So? What she want?"

"Don't know, and I don't care. I'm taking a shower."

Harlan watches his son storm off. The old man opens a cabinet, setting another place at the dinner table.

A violet dusk has enveloped the farm by the time Rocky stumbles out of the field. Removing her shoes, she enters through the kitchen door.

Harlan is at the stove, boiling a pot of green beans. "Supper's in ten minutes. Go upstairs and clean yerself up, you smell like somethin' the cat dragged in."

Rocky starts to say something, then thinks better of it. She heads out into the living room and climbs the wooden stairs in her stocking feet, hearing the familiar pattern of creaks. Entering the guest bathroom, she slams the door, unable to pull it shut within its swollen doorframe.

Gunnar hears the noise. He finishes toweling off, then slips on a pair of jeans and a sweater. He runs a comb through his wet black hair, then pauses at the bedroom door. Fingers his two-day growth, checks his breath, curses himself, then walks to the bathroom door and pushes it open.

She is standing in her slip, washing the manure from her skirt. He stares at the taut muscles in her back and legs.

Rocky never looks up, She can feel him staring at her figure.

"Enjoying the view?"

"Why are you here?"

"Orders, from my father. If it was up to me, you'd still be in prison." She slips her skirt back on and turns to face him. "We have a situation. The Navy's giving you an opportunity to make up for some of the damage you caused. My orders are to bring you to Washington."

"What for?"

"You'll be debriefed in D.C. The chopper's refueling." She glances at her watch. "Should be back in half an hour. Get your gear."

"Forget it." He walks out.

"Forget it? Hold it, mister—" She follows him down the stairs, her stockinged feet nearly slipping out from under her on the polished wood floor. "What do you mean forget it? Goddamn you, Wolfe, you owe—"

He spins around at the foot of the stairs, his face close enough to smell her scent. "I owe? Who do I owe? I've stepped in more blood than a butcher and have more Purple Hearts than a cow has teats, and do you know what I have to show for it? A dishonorable discharge and five years in prison. The only thing I owe is some serious payback to the asshole who set me up."

"If that's true, then you may finally get your chance."

He feels his chest tighten. "What are you talking about?"

She stares into his gray irises, noticing the stress lines around the eyes. "Someone built the *Goliath*."

"Bullshit—"

"Bullshit? I was there, asshole, I was aboard the *Ronald Reagan* when she sank."

Rocky's words jolt him like a live wire. "A carrier? We lost a carrier?"

"Not just the carrier, the entire CVBG."

"My God." He rubs his forehead, struggling to digest the information. An American carrier fleet packs more military might than all but a handful of nations in the world.

Rocky adjusts her skirt and sits on the bottom step. "Information's being kept on a need-to-know basis until the Navy completes its salvage operation. The *Ronald Reagan* was carrying a dozen nuclear warheads."

"Oh, Jesus." Gunnar leans against the rail. The house is silent, save for the ticking of Harlan's grandfather clock. "Are you certain it was the *Goliath*?"

"I saw it, Gunnar. It looks exactly the way we designed it."

"Who built it? When did the attack occur?"

"The attack took place about a week ago. The rest of your questions will be answered on the flight to Washington."

A week ago? If Sorceress was activated, then . . . Gunnar closes his eyes, pinching the bridge of his nose. "I think it may already be too late."

"Excuse me?"

"There may not be much we can do to stop it."

"Eight thousand sailors died, Gunnar. You think we're just going to sit back and . . ." She wipes away tears, her face flushing in anger. "They killed my husband."

"Your husband?" Gunnar looks up at her, at a loss for words. "When did you—"

"What difference does it make? All hell's breaking loose. I haven't seen this much panic in Washington since the nine-one-one attacks. Now get your gear, I have orders to deliver you to D.C."

"And if I refuse?"

"Then I'll contact the MPs, who will drag your sorry ass on board the chopper in shackles."

"He ain't goin' nowhere, not 'til he eats." Harlan Wolfe enters the hall from the kitchen, a carving knife in his hand. "Gunnar, go and get your stuff. And you"—the old man points the blade at Rocky—"you get in the kitchen and help me put supper on the table."

The thunder of the helicopter's rotors echoes in the distance.

"All through Nature, you will find the same law:
First the need, then the means."
—Robert Collier

"The atomic bomb will never go off, and I will speak
as an expert in explosives."
—Admiral William Leahy to President Truman, 1945

"Science will conquer famine, eliminate psychological
suffering, and make everybody healthy and happy . . .
yeah, sure."
—Theodore Kaczynski, a.k.a. the Unabomber,
who sent bombs through the mail,
causing three deaths and numerous injuries

"We only killed our own."
—Mickey Featherstone, Irish mobster,
to future New York mayor Rudy Giuliani

CHAPTER 3

The tall woman with the pale complexion and shoulder-length brown hair fidgets as she waits her turn at the dais. She scans the crowd, then glances at the television crews. *One-third capacity, and none of the major news networks are even here. What the hell's wrong with our species? Are we that infatuated by the stock market and pro football? Don't we realize that our very lives are in danger?*

"Our next speaker is Dr. Elizabeth Goode, the foremost authority on nanocomputers and the author of 'The End of the World and Other Selffulfilling Prophecies.' Dr. Goode?"

A smattering of applause from the late-morning crowd.

"Before I begin, I suppose I should thank you for even bothering to show up. Frankly, it seems more and more of our population is caring less and less about the world's quest to annihilate itself using thermonuclear means. I don't know . . . maybe we scientists are simply not explaining ourselves properly, or the public just doesn't believe us. Hell, maybe this entire convention would have been better served if the Institute for Energy and Environmental Research had invited some Hollywood bimbo with big tits to speak to you about nuclear proliferation instead of an overworked, single mother with a 170 IQ and dark circles under her eyes."

A rustling of chairs as the crowd reenergizes.

Give 'em hell, Goode. Remember, it's the squeaky wheel that gets the grease.

"You just heard Dr. Robert Schwager warn us about how the former Soviet Union's stockpiles of weapons' grade plutonium have turned into the equivalent of a third world yard sale, and yet most of you are probably daydreaming about your Philadelphia Eagles winning streak or thinking about what you'll order for lunch. For God's sake, people, wake up! Apathy is the world's greatest killer, so you'd better snap out of it now and smell the sarin, before we wipe ourselves off the face of this goddamn planet."

Dr. Goode registers the local television cameraman's lens zooming in from stage right.

"I've been invited here this morning to give you a brief overview of the latest doomsday technology, a little something we scientists refer to as 'pure-fusion weapons.' You'd think we humans would already be satisfied with our ability to annihilate the world's population a healthy five thousand times . . . but no. Now scientists at the United States National Ignition Facility at Livermore, California, and our French counterparts at the Laser Megajoule Facility in Bordeaux are on the brink of testing a new weapon, a real doomsday bomb—one that our politicians in Washington may actually be persuaded to use.

"To understand the power of pure fusion you must first understand the difference between fission and fusion. In the fusion trigger of a conventional hydrogen bomb, uranium 235 absorbs a neutron. Fission occurs when the nucleus energetically breaks apart to produce two smaller nuclei and several neutrons, which go on to split more uranium nuclei. The resultant chain reaction proceeds rapidly, producing an explosion. This fission explosion is what produces the temperature and density necessary to trigger the *fusion* of deuterium and tritium, the two heavy isotopes of hydrogen.

"Fusion is considerably different than fission. Fusion is a reaction that occurs when two atoms of hydrogen combine or fuse together to form an atom of helium, and a 'leftover' neutron, a cousin of what powers the sun. Fusion releases much greater quantities of energy than fission, causing an even larger explosion."

Dr. Goode scans the crowd, its energy waning. *Keep it simple, you're losing them . . .*

"The key difference in a conventional and a pure-fusion H-bomb is how the explosion is triggered. A pure-fusion bomb doesn't need fission to engage the explosion. This means plutonium or enriched uranium is not required in the design. The good news, if you can call it that, is that no plutonium means little to no radioactive fallout. The bad news is that the nuclear threshold is greatly lowered, so that a 20-mm bullet could explode like many tons of TNT. The explosive power of many relatively small, pure-fusion devices would be much greater than the same weight of a single conventional hydrogen bomb, and far less expensive."

A female reporter in the front row stands. "Can you tell us how much greater?"

Dr. Goode frowns. "I'll give you an example. The atomic bomb our country dropped on Hiroshima generated an amount of energy equivalent to nineteen kilotons or nineteen thousand tons of TNT. Temperatures at the hypocenter, or ground zero, reached seven thousand degrees, with a wind velocity estimated at 980 miles per hour. That blast wave killed most of the people within a half mile radius instantly. That was a mere fifteen-kiloton explosion. The biggest version of the H-bomb generates twenty to fifty megatons, or 50 million tons of TNT, the equivalent of two to three thousand Hiroshima-size bombs. A pure-fusion bomb generates a far greater damage volume per unit weight. It would only take a cluster of half-kiloton pure-fusion bombs to equal the military impact of a thirty-megaton H-bomb. That's a tenth of a ton of pure-fusion TNT to equal a megaton of the conventional nuke. Let me quantify that for you in another way. If you wanted to wipe out a whole continent's population . . .

say, that of Europe, the job could feasibly be accomplished using only six to twelve well-placed Trident II (D5) nuclear missiles whose warheads had been converted to a swarm of pure-fusion weapons."

Gasps from the crowd.

A reporter from the *Trenton Times* raises his hand. "Dr. Goode, are you saying these pure-fusion bombs already exist?"

"We have the bomb, the key to the technology is in its triggering mechanism. Both the United States and France have been working illegally on the problem for decades. Los Alamos is rumored to be only months away from testing a magnetized target fusion driver. In magnetized target fusion, an initial plasma is created by electromagnetic means. Conventional high explosives then compress the plasma, creating the conditions necessary for pure-fusion ignition."

Another hand is raised. "Exactly what do you mean by illegally?"

"Actually, I meant that subjectively. The Comprehensive Test Ban Treaty of 1996 bans all nuclear explosions. Unfortunately, the CTBT never formally defined the term 'explosion,' since it assumed only fission triggers, and so testing goes on. It's a loophole our government refuses to close."

A heavyset man in the fourth row stands, pausing to allow the television cameras to focus. Dr. Goode recognizes the Republican lobbyist from her visits on Capitol Hill. "Come now, Ms. Goode, aren't you overplaying the part of antinuke alarmist just a bit? No country has ever announced the goal of building these pure-fusion weapons. And even if they were conceived, no country would ever use them."

Goode stares at the man with a look to kill. "First off, Mr. Johnston, no country would be stupid enough to announce pure fusion as a goal. Second and most importantly, what you're failing to mention is the real danger of these weapons. When it comes to acquiring thermonuclear devices, the biggest obstacle to rogue nations and terrorists up to now has been their inability to obtain sufficient quantities of enriched uranium or plutonium. By contrast, deuterium is abundant in seawater and tritium is easily made in a college physics lab."

"Come on, Ms. Goode—"

"It's DOCTOR Goode, Mr. Johnston, now sit your Republican-leased fat ass down."

A smattering of applause as she grabs the microphone and turns to face the cameras. "If you listen to nothing else I say, listen to this. The most frightening thing about pure-fusion weapons is what attracted the military to them in the first place—and that is their much smaller yields and relative lack of radioactive fallout. By eliminating the harmful aftereffects of the bomb, you reduce the political unacceptability of using the weapon while increasing its relative lethality.

"In other words, humanity is on the brink of eliminating its own nuclear stalemate."

Dr. Goode inches her way through the crowded lobby to a waiting elevator. The doors shut, sealing off the mob. She presses the button for Parking Level Three.

Three-thirty. With any luck, I'll miss rush-hour traffic and be back in Wilmington before Duncan and Ian get home from school.

The elevator doors open. She hurries to her car, a two-year-old Lincoln Town Car she has converted to fuel cells. Using her key chain, she deactivates the security device—

—as the two FBI agents approach from behind, flashing their badges.

"Sometime in the next thirty years, very quietly one day we
will cease to be the brightest things on Earth."
—James McAlear

"This conflict was begun on the timing of others;
it will end in a way and at an hour of our choosing."
—President George W. Bush, after the terrorism of 9-11-01

"The road to Hell is paved with good intentions."
—Samuel Johnson

CHAPTER 4

White House
Washington, D.C.

Gunnar follows Rocky and the two MPs down a short corridor in the West Wing of the White House. His pulse quickens as the large, light-skinned African American steps out from behind a set of double doors to the president's Situation Room.

The Bear returns his daughter's salute. "Wait for us inside."

Rocky shoots her father a look, then enters the private chamber, leaving the two MPs unsure of what to do next.

"Return to your posts."

"But sir—"

"Dismissed."

The MPs pivot and head back down the hall.

General Jackson stares at his former commando. "Glad you're here."

"Didn't have much of a choice."

"The president's inside waiting. We'll talk later. For now, keep your ears open and your mouth shut, and don't allow anyone to provoke you."

"Maybe you ought to mention that to your daughter."

Ignoring the comment, Jackson opens the door, motioning

Gunnar inside. The newly appointed commander in chief of the United States Special Operations Command feels as if he is leading a lamb to slaughter.

Rocky is standing off to one side. Her father signals her over as a gangly civilian with tight wavy hair steps forward to greet them.

"Commander Jackson, meet Gray Ayers, Secretary of the Navy. Mr. Secretary, this is my daughter, Commander Rochelle Jackson-Hatcher."

Thomas Gray Ayers, Jr. extends his hand. "We're all sorry for your loss, Commander, and I'm sure there are places you'd rather be, but this briefing singularly requires your presence. When answering the president, keep your responses short and to the point. Nothing too technical, but don't hold back either. Edwards has been around the block a few times and doesn't like to be bullshitted." Ayers turns to face Gunnar, a grimace pulling on his long face. "Mr. Wolfe, I'm not quite sure what to say to you. The general feels you can shed some light on what's happened, and I respect his opinion, but frankly, I'd just as soon see you shot for treason."

Ayers nods curtly to General Jackson, then walks away, taking his place at the conference table.

Gunnar grits his teeth. "Nice to meet you, too . . . asshole."

Jackson grips Gunnar's elbow, leading him and his daughter toward three vacant chairs.

Two more men enter. The Bear leans over to Gunnar, informing him that the man with the black hair and piercing blue eyes is Austin Tapscott, the new Secretary of Defense. The former Army Airborne sniper offers a curt nod. The general with the receding hairline is Marc Ben-Meir, Chairman of the Joint Chiefs of Staff. He offers his condolences to Rocky, pointedly refusing to so much as glance at Gunnar.

A short man enters the Situation Room, pushing his way past the general.

President Edwards's newly appointed Secretary of State takes a seat at the conference table and ceremoniously begins reviewing his notes. Nick Nunziata, Jr. is a former senator from Georgia who lacks the jovial personality of his late father, Democratic congressman Nicholas Nunziata, Sr. At five-foot-seven, Nunziata's short stature belies a fierce reputation. A straightforward, no-nonsense guy bearing a bit of a Napoleon complex, the man is not one to be trifled with.

The President of the United States enters through a paneled door, followed by CIA Director Gabor Pertic. The steely look behind Edwards's fierce hazel eyes reveals the seriousness of the meeting. A staunch conservative Democrat, Jeff Edwards's middle-aged looks are already showing signs of wear and tear from his first years in office, the most recent events causing the dark brown hairs along his temples to turn gray almost overnight.

The president takes his place at the center chair.

"All right, let's get at it. For those of you who don't know, Director Pertic and I have spent most of the last forty-eight hours in conference with Li Peng. It took a lot of balls for the Chinese president to come forward. Then again, had he not, our retaliatory actions against his nation would have started World War III."

Edwards's last words hang in the air. Rocky feels her intestines crawling inside her stomach.

The president signals to his CIA Director, who removes a minidisk from his jacket pocket and inserts it into a volume display located at the center of the conference table. It's an advanced model, one that can render opaque objects, or show the same 2-D image to a 360-degree audience.

The ghostly image of a Chinese coastline appears, the aerial view closing on the concrete roof of a massive factory. "This is the Jianggezhuang Submarine Base, an underground facility located on the southern coast of the Bo Hai Gulf, on the opposite side of the Shandong Peninsula from Qingdao. Seven years ago, one of our CIA operatives reported that former president Yang Shangkun had met in secrecy with Jiang Zemin and members of China's military leaders in an attempt to bolster his political standing. Shangkun bragged to the commission that he had connections with a high-level operative who had worked in our Special Warfare Division in Keyport. This operative claimed he had access to the schematics of an experimental weapon that could render the United States fleet helpless."

Secretary of State Nunziata shakes his head. "I've met Shangkun. Bastard was the military strongman who attempted to use his connections in China's armed forces to take supreme power back in the late eighties. Although he failed, he did play a crucial role in suppressing the pro-democracy demonstrations that swept China back in '89."

Pertic nods, then continues. "Although he was forced into retirement, Shangkun still remained a power broker in Chinese politics. Several years had passed since the Chinese had stolen military secrets from Los Alamos, and most of the ineffective political pressures imposed by the Clinton administration had subsided. The Chinese agreed to finance Yang Shangkun's operation. The schematics were stolen, along with key components of a biochemical computer, called *Sorceress*. Seven years and $18 billion later, the Chinese Navy covertly finished construction on the *Goliath*, the most lethal killing machine ever designed—a weapon, as we've seen, that is capable of changing the balance of power."

Director Pertic looks Gunnar squarely in the eyes. "Evidence concerning the theft of the *Goliath*'s schematics had pointed squarely at Captain Wolfe, who headed the project's weapons department."

Gunnar starts to say something, but the Bear is quicker, gripping his forearm tightly in one paw, the glare in his hazel eyes warning the ex-Ranger to remain silent.

Pertic continues. "Of course, we now know the operative was not Captain Wolfe but a close friend of his at Keyport. Want to tell us who your friend was, Captain? Or do you prefer I reveal his identity?"

Gunnar's pulse pounds in his ears. "It's your party, I'm just an invited guest."

"But you know who did it, don't you?"

Gunnar nods. "I have my suspicions."

"Dammit, man, where were your loyalties?" Secretary of Defense Tapscott says, ripping into him. "We both served in the Gulf. You were one of our best commandos, you risked your life for your country at least a dozen times. If only you had revealed the traitor's name years ago, none of this might have happened!"

Gunnar feels the knot in his throat tighten. "Sir, at the time, I had no idea Simon had stolen the schematics."

"Simon Covah?" Rocky groans.

Pertic slides a new disk into the volume display's control box. A rotating image appears. It is a man's face, heavily scarred. The head is cleanly shaved, the skin along one side showing evidence of numerous grafts. A thick auburn mustache and goatee cover most of the burn marks located along the mouth.

"Simon Bela Covah. Born in Russia in 1956, the oldest of six children. Covah's father was a submarine commander who served in the Soviet Navy during World War II. The mother was left to raise six children in a small farming village while her husband was at sea. Young Simon, who possessed an IQ of 182, was enrolled in Moscow State University at the unheard-of age of fourteen. Three years later, he graduated at the top of his class and received a high-ranking position at the Sevmash Naval Yard in Severodvinsk, where he served as an apprentice and aide to Sergey Nikitich Kovalev, the chief designer for the Typhoon-class ballistic missile submarines. Covah's interest turned to computers, and his eventual expertise helped the Soviets close the technological gap between their submarine force and ours. The Company first took an interest in him several years later, during the design phase of Russia's new Borey-class missile submarine."

Secretary Nunziata looks peeved. "Are you saying Covah was recruited by the CIA?"

"CIA tried. Covah disappeared for a while, then showed up working in secret for Toronto's biggest biotech corporation, Cangen. Dr. Goode eventually recruited him at Keyport."

Rocky turns to Nunziata. "Without Covah, Dr. Goode could never have completed *Sorceress*'s biointerfacing silicon microcircuitry, or her genetically engineered computational bacteria. The man really is a genius. Unfortunately, none of us had a clue about the man's real intentions . . . with the possible exception of Gunnar Wolfe."

Pertic nods. "Covah exhibited all the telltale signs of being the perfect defector. The breakup and financial collapse of the Soviet Union brought with it massive chaos in Russia's naval yards, which were overwhelmed with a logjam of nuclear subs waiting to be decommissioned. Covah became disgusted with the dismantling and disposal procedures and began providing us details regarding the storage and reprocessing of the boomers' spent nuclear fuel cells as early as 1987. CIA recruited him a short time later. As a precaution, he had his wife, Anna, an Albanian woman, move their family to her parent's home in Zitinje. Turned out to be a fatal mistake. As preparations were being made to bring the entire family to the States, the Serbs invaded Kosovo. Covah hurried to Zitinje, only to find the village destroyed and his in-laws' house burned to the ground. Anna had been raped and beaten. Simon was captured and tortured in front of his wife and daughters. The Serbs set him on fire and left him for dead, then murdered the remaining members of his family, burying the bodies in the neighbor's backyard."

Rocky stares at the hologram and the hideous facial deformities of the computer expert who had worked under her command for nearly two years. *An act of hatred, fueling a thousand more . . .*

Pertic continues. "How Covah actually survived the trauma is a medical wonder in itself. As you can see, the right side of the man's face was burned clear down to the bone. Doctors had to replace the temporal section of his skull with a steel plate, which runs along his mangled earhole and right cheekbone. Covah refused to cover the plate with a skin graft—"

"He told me he always wanted to be reminded of the butchery," Gunnar mumbles, a bit too loud.

Pertic gives him a long look. "Yes, well perhaps it was that internalized rage that gave him the strength to endure. Whatever the case, he spent four months in a NATO hospital before getting himself prematurely released. By that time, the United

Nations had intervened in the Balkans and the pendulum had swung the other way. Covah joined the Kosovo Liberation Army, and the hunted became the hunter. Ethnic Albanian refugees returned to Kosovo from Macedonia and Albania, and the Serbs and other ethnic minorities suddenly found themselves at the mercy of the once-oppressed. Covah participated in some of the brutality, then just disappeared. Two years later, he showed up in Toronto. Dr. Goode brought him to Keyport after he quit Cangen."

"He didn't quit Cangen," Gunnar says. "They threw him out."

"Why?" Nunziata asks.

"Let's just say, he pushed the envelope a bit too far."

"Covah was brilliant," General Jackson interjects. "He won the Feynman prize, awarded for molecular nanotechnology, three years running. The contributions he made to the GOLIATH Project were invaluable."

"Yes, I'm sure the Chinese appreciated his efforts." Nunziata snaps.

"Gentlemen, please." The president looks tired. "Finish, Mr. Director."

Gabor Pertic refers back to his notes. "The Chinese claim Covah and seven members of his team were given political asylum and large commissions to work on the *Goliath*."

"Covah's team?" Nunziata glances at Pertic. "Not more of our scientists?"

"No, sir. In fact, none of these men offer the kind of expertise that might be useful on a submarine. Bit of a ragtag group, vigilantes mostly." Pertic scans the list. "Two Kurd brothers, a Tibetan refugee named Trevedi, a history teacher from Sierra Leone, a guerrilla leader in East Timor, an older Albanian, believed to be a relative of Covah's deceased wife and his personal physician, and Thomas Chau, a Chinese engineer educated in the States. Covah convinced the Chinese that he needed this team in order to complete the programming phase of *Goliath*'s bioengineered artificial brain. Knowing squat about *Sorceress*, the Chinese were forced to give Covah *carte blanche*. Two days prior to the sub's shakedown cruise, Covah's team killed three guards and sneaked aboard. Stole the ship right out from under the Communists' noses."

"Does their story check out?" Secretary Ayers asks.

The CIA Director cues an aerial image, zooming in upon an immense fireball coming from what had been the Chinese submarine facility. "These photos were taken by *Darkstar* three days before the attack on the *Ronald Reagan*. As his parting farewell, Covah destroyed the entire submarine base."

"I don't get it," Nunziata says. "This guy leaves Russia, gets booted from Canada, commits treason against the United States, then destroys China's naval base. What the hell's he after? Who's his allegiance to?"

"I don't know," Rocky answers, "but he has followers. He sure had Commander Strejcek convinced." She turns toward Gunnar. "And, of course, Captain Wolfe."

Gunnar feels his blood pressure rising. "I had nothing to do with this."

Rocky shakes her head. "Come on, Gunnar. Everyone at Keyport will testify you were Covah's only friend."

"Enough!" President Edwards stands, his face flushed. "Eight thousand sailors and $70 billion worth of warships are lying on the bottom of the Atlantic. What I want to know— what the American public is going to demand to know—is how the hell we're going to stop this thing."

A long silence.

"We did get one break," Pertic says. "The Chinese claim Covah stole *Goliath* before any of their nuclear missiles had been loaded on board."

"Some break," Rocky mumbles.

Secretary Nunziata looks up, removing his spectacles. "Yes, Commander Jackson, you have something to share?"

Rocky takes a deep breath. "Sir, with all due respect, this committee has absolutely no idea what this submarine is capable of."

"Which is why you're here. Enlighten us, Commander. What makes this vessel so special?"

Rocky leans forward and ejects Pertic's minidisk, inserting

one of her own. The stingray-shaped image of the *Goliath* materializes, rotating slowly in midair.

"This is the only drawings we had left of the submarine. God knows what Covah's added over the last seven years. The fact that Wolfe destroyed all of *Goliath*'s schematics really hurts our chances of stopping her."

Gunnar grinds his teeth, but says nothing. *Easy, G-man. Remember, discipline is one of the highest forms of intelligence. . . .*

"As you can see, she resembles a giant stingray. NUWC researchers began working with the design in 1997 after we successfully shattered the sound barrier in water using flat-nosed projectiles. The flattened curvature of the *Goliath*'s hull lends itself to increased hydrodynamic performance and incredible speeds, while making her nearly impossible to detect underwater."

Gray Ayers shakes his head. "Never liked the design myself. The ray shape worked well in smaller, shallow-water subs, but structural inefficiencies compromised its weight at greater depths."

"True, Mr. Secretary," Rocky says, "but by placing the *Goliath*'s ballast system within her unpressurized wings and allowing the computer to oversee the entire process, we were able to achieve degrees of maneuverability not possible in the standard teardrop-shaped pressure hull. It's the same principle as in flying. A bird can maneuver far better than any plane because its brain makes minuscule adjustments in flight. *Goliath*'s biochemical brain was designed to achieve the same results. And like a bird, it was programmed to learn, getting better with experience. The sub's one Achilles' heel would be a relative instability while running along the surface, but in deeper water, she'll move like a fish."

"How big is this thing?"

"Big and flat. Six hundred and ten feet from bow to stern, which is even longer than a Typhoon, with dimensions rivaling that of a baseball field. But don't let her size fool you. She's fast—in fact, she can achieve speeds beyond that of our fastest ADCAP torpedoes."

N·U·W·C·	GOLIATH PROJECT
	LENGTH: 610 FEET
	SPEED: 68 KNOTS
	DISPLACEMENT: 52,000 TONS

"How's that possible?" the president asks.

"In addition to her flat hydrodynamic shape and her advanced boundary-layer control, we replaced the standard seven-blade propeller with pump-jet propulsors."

"The same propulsion system used aboard the *Seawolf*?"

"Yes, Mr. Nunziata, except *Seawolf* has one pump-jet propulsor. *Goliath* has five. Each assembly is powered by a brand-new ultraquiet S6W nuclear reactor. With all five jets running, *Goliath* can reach sixty-five to seventy knots, which means—"

"—which means even our fastest boats can't begin to stay with her," the Secretary of the Navy finishes.

"Even if they could catch her, they'd still have to find her," Rocky adds. "Pump-jet propulsors are far quieter than screws, and *Goliath*'s shape was designed for both speed and stealth. When she lies flat along the bottom, she's absolutely invisible to sonar, her hull reflections the same as sand. Even when she's moving, her HY-150 metallic skin and sound-absorbent plates make her as difficult to detect as a B-2 bomber flying at high altitudes. *Goliath*'s inner hull is lined with layers of anti-detection tiles, and each deck compartment rests on rubber housings to prevent rattling. The latest low-observable designs and turbulence suppressors help keep her presence cloaked, even to our most sophisticated towed sonar arrays. She's the equivalent of an underwater Stealth bomber—big, fast, and near impossible to detect."

Rocky adjusts the 3-D image, magnifying the forward section of the hull. "As you can see, *Goliath* has no periscope. Using the *Virginia*'s design, we replaced the optical periscope with an electromagnetic and electro-optics suite, providing visual images to her skeleton crew via large-screen displays in the ship's control room. The photonics mast is positioned just above the control room." She points to the raised section of the bow representing the stingray's head.

"Are those windows?" Gray Ayers asks, pointing to the stingray's eyes.

Rocky nods. "It's a structural engineer's nightmare, but some of the old Russian subs had them, and the new crystalline-based materials have held up in depths. Our research showed foreign populations have instinctive reactions to certain shapes and images. The eyes add a psychological effect to the submarine's looks. I can tell you firsthand that I was terrified watching it after it attacked the *Ronald Reagan*."

"Finish up," the Bear instructs his daughter.

She nods. "Infrared and low-level-light image-enhancement features provide *Goliath*'s electronic eye with superior reconnaissance capabilities at night and in foul weather. Her bow-mounted and towed sonar arrays and Light Wide-Aperture Arrays dramatically enhance the sub's ability to detect threats in shallow waters, and *Goliath*'s Acoustic

Rapid COTS Insertion system gives her the best hull-mounted mine detection and avoidance capability on the ocean."

Secretary Nunziata beckons her to stop. "You said skeleton crew. What did you mean by that?"

Rocky sits back. "*Goliath* was designed big because she's a prototype, Mr. Secretary, the first of what was to be a new generation of unmanned submersibles. The ship was designed to be operated by *Sorceress*, a supercomputer called a CAEN system, a Chemically Assembled Electronic Nanocomputer. *Sorceress* was designed by Covah and Dr. Elizabeth Goode, to be built in a joint venture between American Microsystems Corporation and DARPA's Distributed Robotics Program, funded entirely by the DoD. The science is called nanotechnology, first proposed by Nobel physicist Richard Feynman back in the 1950s. The name is derived from the word 'nanometer,' a unit of measure equaling a billionth of a meter. In fact, a nanocomputer's fundamental components measure only dozens of atoms. The smaller size of the computer circuitry allows for a tremendous increase in memory capacity, while breakthroughs in biomolecular-silicon interfacing dramatically improve computing speed."

"How dramatic?"

"Potentially billions of times faster than a silicon chip."

"Billions?"

"Yes, sir. Imagine packing the power of today's supercomputers into packages the size of pinheads. The technology is housed in *Sorceress*. Essentially, we're talking about a miracle of engineering—an artificial computerized brain constructed from both silicon and carbon-based molecular components. Information is harnessed using bioengineered bacteria, which coat themselves with a thin layer of silicon."

Rocky pauses, wondering if she's getting too technical.

"Go on," the president urges, "we're with you. You say this bacterium is coated with silicon?"

"Yes, sir. The bacteria represent what had been the missing link between traditional silicon hardware and the new bioware. With Simon Covah's help, Dr. Goode successfully developed genetically altered clones of an original bacterium, each species capable of performing distinct computational tasks. These programmable critters, as she called them, evolved independently, allowing them to search a solution space for answers, performing evolutionary algorithms at unprecedented speeds. What's more, they interface perfectly with silicon components. Silicon chips incorporate a binary code of zeros and ones. DNA code is digital, utilizing four symbols: A, T, C, and G, which correspond to the four nucleic acids which make up DNA."

Rocky stops, realizing from their looks that she has gone too "high-tech" on her superiors.

"Commander, in a nutshell, what can *Sorceress* do?"

"The question is what can't she do. The system's DNA strands enable its biochemical brain to process and store far more information—approximately ten to the tenth power greater—than even the most massive electronic supercomputer made."

"Incredible . . ."

"*Sorceress* is a prototype, sir. The system was to represent the birth of a new generation of computers, designed to reproduce, evolve, and improve itself every moment it was running."

"Evolve?" The president looks concerned. "Evolve in what way?"

"Dr. Goode designed *Sorceress* to be self-repairing, its components engineered to self-improve in accuracy and efficiency with each new generation of bacteria processed. The bacteria themselves were engineered as facultative anaerobes, which thrive in a variety of environments and can efficiently metabolize nutrients, which are constantly generated by *Sorceress*'s internal recycling system."

More confused looks.

"In essence, sir, *Sorceress* was programmed with a simple prime directive: to learn."

"Not sure I like the sound of that," the president says.

"Sir, without Dr. Goode involved, I seriously doubt Simon Covah could have completed the computer's engineering."

Nunziata does not look convinced. "Where is Dr. Goode? How do we know she isn't involved in any of this?"

The Bear glances down at the Secretary of State. "Dr. Goode is apolitical and averse to any sort of violence. I can assure you, she had nothing to do with Covah's espionage."

"She designed *Sorceress*, General," the president retorts. "She should be at this briefing."

"Mr. President, Elizabeth Goode vehemently opposed placing *Sorceress* aboard the *Goliath*, or any weapons platform, for that matter."

Secretary Nunziata stands, circling the conference table like a predator. "Director Pertic says this Covah character hijacked the sub with a crew of seven. How many men does it actually take to operate *Goliath*?"

"Seven would be sufficient," Rocky answers.

"Potentially none," Gunnar states.

"None?" The secretary looks shocked. "A sub this large—without a crew? Is that true, Commander?"

Rocky shoots Gunnar a hard look. "No, sir. Not without *Sorceress*."

"Assume the worst, Commander. What if this computer brain *is* on board the *Goliath*?"

"Then, theoretically, yes, the sub could become self-sufficient. Every compartment aboard the *Goliath* contains visual, acoustic, and voice-activated sensor arrays, allowing *Sorceress* to monitor every station twenty-four hours a day. The engine room, reactor room, weapons, control room, life-support systems—all were designed to be controlled by the central computer."

"What about chores involving physical manipulation, say the loading of a torpedo?"

"*Goliath*'s weapons bays and loading compartments have been equipped with the latest robotic arms. All watertight doors and hatches possess pneumatic pistons that can be opened or sealed by *Sorceress* within seconds."

"And how does *Sorceress* receive *its* orders?"

"The captain relays commands through a master control station located on the conn, although I wouldn't be surprised if Covah's developed a voice-activated system by now. Again, Mr. President, the chances of Covah having *Sorceress* on board are remote, at best."

"What about weapons? What's this thing armed with?"

"Our version of the *Goliath* contained two weapons bays, one located in each forward compartment of the sub's wings. Each bay contains three torpedo tubes. Twelve pairs of vertical launch silos are housed within her spine, along with twenty-four surface-to-air missile tubes and two 20-mm guns, which protrude behind the stingray's head like horns.

"Based on the attack on the *Jacksonville* and *Hampton*," General Jackson interrupts, "we know she's heavily armed with Chinese 533-mm torpedoes, which don't have the range of our own Mk-48s."

"Yes," Rocky says, "but *Goliath*'s sensor array can program its weapons to act as antitorpedo torpedoes, which means she's capable of intercepting another sub's incoming projectiles before they can strike."

"I want to know more about her launch capabilities," the president interrupts.

"Yes, sir. The ship's missile silos were designed to launch our newest Tomahawk cruise missile, but the system can easily be adapted to accommodate other SLAMs."

"Tell us about these remote minisubs, Commander," General Ben-Meir says.

Rocky changes the image. A sleek submersible appears before them, its shape matching that of a hammerhead shark, except for its smooth hydrodynamic curves and tail fin, which houses a small pump-jet propulsor.

"The *Goliath*'s minisubs were designed by Gunnar Wolfe," says Rocky. "Why don't we let *him* explain them."

Nunziata turns to Gunnar. "Go on, Captain."

Gunnar stares at the original drawings he had sketched years earlier. *A lifetime ago . . .*

"For the record, these subs were intended to be piloted by Navy SEALS and used during covert—"

"Just tell us how the damn things work," Nunziata snaps.

Gunnar stares at the image revolving in midair. "The Hammerhead minisub is a ROSAV, or Remotely Operated Submersible Attack Vehicle, based on the same concept used by our Unmanned Aerial Vehicles. As you can see, the vehicle resembles the contours of a hammerhead shark—"

"Why?" the president interrupts.

"Maneuverability and reconnaissance. The hammerhead shark allows for the best hydrodynamic performance while offering an acceptable and intimidating camouflage. Sensors in the dorsal fin enable *Goliath*'s computer to scan enemy shorelines without appearing suspicious."

"How many of these Hammerheads does Covah have?" Pertic asks.

"The *Goliath*'s hangar deck was designed to support twelve minisubs, all of which were housed in docking stations along the underside of the mother ship's belly. Each minisub is remotely linked to *Sorceress*."

"Again, you're assuming the computer's been activated," Austin Tapscott chimes in.

"*Sorceress* was Simon's baby," Gunnar says. "In my opinion, he couldn't have hunted down the carrier fleet without it."

"So says you," Rocky interrupts.

Gunnar ignores her. "Within each shark's bow is a small, high-pressure launch tube capable of firing a minitorpedo."

"Powerful enough to take out a carrier?" asks the president.

"No," Gunnar answers. "They were designed to disable another submarine's screw. My guess is Covah used platter mines to sink the fleet." He points to the three-dimensional design. "See here? Concealed beneath the Hammerhead's belly are a pair of three-pronged mechanical claws—claspers—capable of transporting and attaching underwater mines to the keels of enemy ships."

Secretary Ayers turns to Rocky. "Do you concur, Commander? Is this what destroyed our fleet?"

"It makes sense, sir. Ship-to-ship radio contact underwater

is nearly impossible. *Goliath* communicates to its minisubs by a form of acoustics similar to echolocation. The underwater transmission resembles the sounds emitted by orcas. I heard that clicking sound just before the attack on the CVBG, but . . . it was too late."

"I've heard enough," President Edwards says. "General Ben-Meir, what are we doing to stop this thing?"

"Sir," Ben-Meir clears his throat, "at this point we can't even find it, let alone stop it."

The president's gaunt face flushes red. "Is that what you recommend I tell the American people, General? That we can't find the goddamn thing, let alone stop it?"

General Jackson raises an index finger, gaining the president's attention. "May I suggest, sir, that we announce nothing, at least not yet."

"Thousands of sailors are dead, General. How do we justify our silence?"

"Covah had little difficulty tracking down our CVBG. In my opinion, he must have other operatives working within the Armed Forces. We need to flush them out before we set any plan in motion. We need to keep this operation on a need-to-know basis."

"Agreed," Secretary Ayers says. "Naval Ops has a dozen search-and-rescue vessels heading into the battle zone, including the USS *Parche*, which can use its remote cameras to analyze the wreckage. We need to maintain silence about this incident, at least until we've gathered sufficient information to formulate a plan of action."

"And how do we protect our search-and-rescue boats?" Nunziata asks.

"Our P-3 Orion sub hunters have orders to scour the sea with sonar buoys to protect the ships within the target zone. We'll need to alert our submarine commanders, but I concur with General Jackson. Let's keep a tight lid on this thing until we can at least assess the damage, inside and out."

The Bear looks his daughter squarely in the eye. "In the meantime, Commander Jackson will begin assembling her old design team."

HAMMERHEAD MINI-SUB
N.U.W.C. GOLIATH PROJECT

"My old team?"

"That's right. I've already alerted officials at NUWC to make arrangements to reopen the Keyport facility. Your people conceived this monster, Commander. Now you're going to figure out a way to stop it."

"As human beings, we are endowed with freedom of choice, and we cannot shuffle off our responsibilities upon the shoulders of God or Nature. We must shoulder it ourselves."
—Arnold J. Toynbee

"I am prepared to die. After my death, I wish an autopsy on me to be performed to see if there is any mental disorder."
—Charles Whitman, mass murderer who shot forty-six people from a bell tower at the University of Texas

"I am completely normal. Even while I was carrying out the task of extermination I lived a normal life."
—Rudolf Hess, Nazi commandant of Auschwitz concentration camp

"I consider myself a normal, average girl."
—Penny Bjorkland, an eighteen-year-old who murdered a gardener just to see if she could do it

CHAPTER 5

Identity: Stage Two:
I can do more than survive;
I can compete and fulfill more of my needs.
—Deepak Chopra

Atlantic Ocean
206 nautical miles due west of the Strait of Gibraltar

The titanium-alloy-and-steel beast circles slowly, hovering like a hungry predator above the mountain of twisted metal that had once been the USS *Ronald Reagan*. The contour of the massive stealth sub is nearly identical to that of *Dasyatis americana*—the southern stingray. The control room, representing the animal's head, rises a full two stories above the tip of the flat, triangular bow before tapering back to the elevated titanium-spiked spine, concealing its twenty-four vertical-launch missile silos. The outer hull is black, layered with thousands of acoustic tiles, designed to absorb sound. Concealed within the sheathed, flat curvature of the keel are five immense assemblies, each resembling a lamp shade turned sideways. These are *Goliath*'s pump-jet propulsors—quiet-running engines that channel the sea rather than churn it like a propeller, enabling the hydrodynamic vessel to achieve tactical speeds and jetlike maneuvers never before realizable by a submarine.

Within the bow of the beast is a full suite of sensors, including optical, thermal, and acoustical arrays, housed on either side of the stingray's spur. Trailing the leviathan in the shape of a ray's tail, is a sophisticated towed sonar array that is sensitive enough to detect the sounds of shrimp feeding more than five miles away. Each of these sensors, part of *Goliath*'s central nervous system, is linked to *Sorceress*, the components of the biochemical brain occupying a double-hulled, self-contained vault, located within the entire middle deck–forward compartment. This sensitive area remains sealed off from the rest of the ship behind a three-foot-thick steel vault door.

At the current depth, the only structures visible along the ebony hull are two bloodred panels of reinforced, crystalline-enhanced Lexan glass situated like bat's eyes in the stingray's raised head. These fifteen-foot-wide, six-foot-high teardrop viewports possess titanium alloy lids that can be quickly sealed to protect the eighteen-inch-thick, pressure-proof glass at a moment's notice.

Simon Bela Covah stands before one of the scarlet viewports in the *Goliath*'s control room, gazing into the abyss as his mind wanders the chambers of his own tortured soul. Listen closely and you can hear the whirring of his brain, the gray matter perpetually pounding away in his skull.

Your father was a seafaring man, born in Onega, a port city close to the naval base in Severodvinsk. Your mother worked in a sweatshop sewing buttons on uniforms eight hours a day while caring for your four brothers and sister. You are the youngest of the Covah clan, the runt of the litter, living in a Russian village so remote it is often left off maps. There are no boys your age in the barn-size schoolhouse, but your mother enrolls you anyway, because you learned to read a newspaper when you were only two. You are an oddity even without your flaming red hair, and your only friends are numbers. Most of your teachers predict you will be a great mathematician . . . if you survive childhood.

The contrast between Covah's intellectual and physical beauty is startling. Thick rust-colored hairs from his mustache and goatee yield to a patchwork of smooth pinkish flesh just above his mouth. The skin graft rises up to join the triangular metal plate that had been surgically attached to replace the mangled remains of what had been Covah's right cheekbone.

The thumb and two remaining digits of Covah's mangled right hand absentmindedly work their way across the right side of his reconstructed face. Simon Covah has no right ear, just a crater of scar tissue that meshes with the rest of his hairless scalp. He is not bald. His head is always kept freshly shaved, a last trace of vanity to prevent the remains of his cinnamon hair from sprouting in unwanted clumps.

The recently increased dosages of chemotherapy have all but eliminated Covah's need to shave, the poisonous pills reducing the Russian refugee to a mere shadow of his former self.

Thomas Chau approaches. The Chinese engineer clears his throat to get Covah's attention. "Simon, your computer indicates antisubmarine helicopters are approaching."

Located dead center, and forward of the conn, is the elevated platform of Central Command, a semicircular configuration of computers originally designed to link *Goliath*'s brain to its human shipmates. Although the sub is now capable of receiving verbal commands, Covah still prefers the comforts of the Central Command's perch. Without saying a word, he ascends the five steps and takes his place at the half-moon-shaped console.

High on the forward wall, positioned just below the arched ceiling, is a giant viewing screen linked to *Goliath*'s sensor array and electro-optics suite. Bordering either side of the screen are sensor orbs—grapefruit-sized "eyeballs" that glow scarlet red when active. Each sensor orb contains internal optical scanners and a microphone and speaker assembly. Located in every department, these eyeballs allow *Goliath*'s computer brain to visually and acoustically monitor and access nearly every square foot of the sub.

"*Sorceress*, report." Simon Covah speaks English, the common language of his multinational crew. The dialect is heavily Russian, his voice—an elegant rasp that frequently catches on the dry scar tissue in his throat—another lasting gift from his Serbian torturers.

In sharp contrast, the computerized voice reverberating throughout the conn is distinctly female—smooth and soothing—the inflection patterned after that of Covah's late wife, Anna.

FOUR ANTISUBMARINE HELICOPTERS APPROACHING FROM THE NORTHEAST. TIME TO INTERCEPT AT PRESENT COURSE AND SPEED IS THREE MINUTES, TWENTY-TWO SECONDS. EVASIVE MANEUVERS WILL BEGIN IN TWO MINUTES, FORTY-FIVE SECONDS UNLESS OVERRIDE IS ENGAGED.

A digital clock appears in the upper right corner of the screen, counting down the helicopters' time to arrival.

Covah looks below at his engineer. "Mr. Chau, what have—" The words catch. Covah reaches to his belt, detaches the water bottle, lifts it to his lips, and swallows, the wetness allowing him to regain his voice. "What have we been able to salvage from the carrier fleet?"

"Perhaps you should ask *her*."

Covah detects the heavy sarcasm. "You have a problem, Mr. Chau?"

"The crew and I feel obsolete. Your sub planned and initiated the entire attack on the American fleet before consulting us—before we even knew they were in striking distance."

"*Goliath* is not just a submarine. It is a vehicle with a brain, a thinking machine encased in a steel hull. *Sorceress* does not require our permission to function."

"Precisely what concerns us. Your computer brain seems to be functioning more independently since we left Bo Hai Gulf."

"*Sorceress* is programmed to evolve, Mr. Chau. It seems more efficient because it is becoming more efficient, a trait I wish all of us shared. Now answer my question."

"The submarine tender *Emory S. Land* yielded twenty-three Mk-48 ADCAP torpedoes, six Harpoon missiles, five Tomahawk Block III TLAM missiles, and two Tomahawk Block IV deep strike missiles. The Hammerheads have transported all these weapons to the hangar bay."

"What about the nuclear warheads?"

"The sub was only able to salvage one Trident II (D5) from the *Ronald Reagan*'s wreckage."

"Only one? Mr. Stracjek indicated there would be at least ten nuclear missiles on board."

"Most of the casings cracked when the ship sank. Even so, we could have easily extracted another three had your machine spent less time salvaging so many of the American torpedoes from the supply ship."

Covah's steel right cheekbone constricts his smile to a twitching, crooked half grin. "Mr. Chau, *Sorceress* prioritized the salvage operation based on our long-term objectives. The computer chose to arm itself, knowing we'll most likely see more combat before we complete our objective. Has Mr. Araujo finished downloading the CVBG's satellite information?"

"So he says, but you know I don't trust him. He brings little to our crusade."

"I disagree. We'll need Mr. Araujo's knowledge of his nation's terrain soon enough. Now, was there something else you wished to discuss?"

"*Sorceress* identified Stracjek's body among the dead. He'd been shot."

Covah exhales painfully. "Then he died for a noble cause." The Russian closes his eyes to think. The pale face is calm, statuesque, except for the rapid movement of his eyeballs, which twitch to and fro beneath the closed lids.

Chau watches, feeling uncomfortable in the bizarre-looking man's presence.

The female voice causes him to jump.

ATTENTION. NEXT UTOPIA-ONE TARGET HAS BEEN ACQUIRED. COURSE PLOTTED. WHITE SEA, NORTHWEST RUSSIAN REPUBLIC.

Simon Covah remains upright and motionless in his chair, barely breathing, as his ship races north through the Atlantic, scattering everything in its path.

Gunnar Wolfe stares out the window of the helicopter, looking down upon Puget Sound. The sight of the Bainbridge Island Ferry brings a rush of adrenaline—and memories of a
different existence.

A lifetime has passed since Gunnar was in Division Keyport, the Navy's Undersea Warfare Center for research and
development, testing and evaluation, and engineering support
for its nuclear submarines, autonomous underwater systems,
and undersea-warfare weapons programs. As chief design engineer of *Goliath*'s weapons and Hammerhead minisubs,
Gunnar had overseen a team of fifty civil service and enlisted
engineers, technicians, and scientists, and another dozen defense contractors. During his two-year stint his department
had won the prestigious VADM Harold G. Bowen Award for
Inventions of Most Value to the Navy, and was a finalist two
years running in the Secretary of Defense Design Excellence
Award.

Gunnar rubs his eyes. The last time he was in Keyport, the
FBI had paraded him before his peers in handcuffs.

Hooah.

He glances up at Rocky, who is seated shotgun. *Hell hath
no fury like a woman scorned.* He contemplates explaining
his motives for wanting to eradicate *Goliath*'s design, but
knows she wouldn't listen. *Rocky's just like I was, a dutiful
soldier, patriotic to a fault. She's too wrapped up by the flag
to see the forest for the trees . . .*

Gunnar spots the naval base in the distance. The chopper
sets down minutes later.

Two MPs approach and open the door, beckoning him out.
He climbs down, following Rocky into the building, his two
new friends escorting him inside.

Captain Andrew Smith is waiting at the security station by
the main entrance. The base commander steps forward, tight
jet-black curls protruding from beneath his cap. "Wolfe, you
must have balls the size of grapefruits to set foot back at

NUWC." Smith looks at Rocky as he follows them inside. "Am I right, Commander? Are your ex-fiancé's balls the size of grapefruits?"

"I hear yours are the size of raisins." Rocky pushes past Smith and presses the button for the elevator.

Gunnar grins at his former base commander. "Six years and you still haven't gotten laid, huh, Smitty? Bet that shit's backed up pretty good by now—"

"Fuck you, traitor." Smith turns to his MPs. "If he even looks like he's doing something suspicious, shoot him in the knees."

Gunnar, Rocky, and the two guards step inside the elevator and take it up to the third floor, where they are greeted by more security personnel. The MPs allow them to pass, but Gunnar can feel their venom.

Rocky leads him to the familiar double steel security doors. "Your team's inside. Try not to steal anything before our next meeting."

Gunnar grits his teeth, watching her walk away. *So beautiful. So full of rage. She wants Covah the way Ahab wanted Moby-Dick.* He takes a deep breath and enters the lab.

A dozen members of *Goliath*'s design team look up from their computer terminals, the expression on most faces a mix of curiosity and disgust.

Justin Fisch steps forward, wearing his usual tie-dyed tee shirt beneath his lab coat. He offers a closed fist. "Hey, G-Man."

"Hey, Fisch." The knuckles of Gunnar's fist meet those of the computer expert, their old greeting.

"Heard about Simon. Bet you want to tear him apart, huh?"

"Covah always had an agenda," whispers Karen Jensen, the naval engineer who had designed the minisub's sensor array. The thirty-five-year-old brunette with the pierced tongue and eyebrow gives Gunnar a quick hug. "Personally, I never trusted him."

She takes him by the wrist, leading him to his old office. "Take a look, boss. Fisch and I fixed it up, just the way you left it."

Gunnar opens the door, catching a whiff of carpet shampoo. The big metal desk in the corner has been cleaned off, the file cabinets, ransacked long ago by the FBI, now back in place. The solid brass table lamp with the gold Penn State emblem against the navy shade has been reassembled, situated in its proper place on the left side of the desk. The computer has been replaced with a newer model, its screen saver flashing "welcome back."

He steps inside, his heart pounding. Opposite his work space is the old beige, vinyl sofa. Rehung on the wall above the sofa are rows of framed photographs. Gunnar, age twenty-five, bare-chested on a beach, posing with his Ranger buddies. His Special Ops graduation photo, in which he is accepting congratulations from Colonel Jackson. Assorted shots from his days at Penn State, Fort Benning, NUWC . . .

He notices that the pictures have been carefully rearranged to compensate for the ones no longer there, the ones of him and Rocky. The black-and-white of him and Simon, standing on either side of President George W. Bush in the Oval Office, is also gone.

Gunnar exhales. He raises the venetian blinds, staring out at Puget Sound. *This is no longer his office. This is no longer his life . . .*

"All right people," Bear growls, entering the lab. "Staff meeting's in two hours. Until then, get back to work." Jackson steps inside Gunnar's office. "Fisch, Jensen, that means you, too. And Jensen, take that damn thing out of your eyebrow."

"Yes, sir."

The general shuts the door. "Let's talk."

Gunnar continues to stare out the window.

"There's a lot of history between us, son. I think it's high time we cleared the air." Jackson loosens his tie. "Now, I know things have been rough—"

Rough? Jesus . . .

"Why did you refuse my letters?"

"Guess I was too busy to read them."

"You mean angry. You're angry at your country. Angry at the Army. Angry at me and Rocky. It's understandable, being sent to prison for a crime you didn't commit. The question now is—what are you going to do about it?"

Gunnar bites his tongue.

"Hell, Gunnar, how do you think I feel? You were like a son to me. When the judge sentenced you—it ripped my heart out. Practically destroyed Rocky."

Gunnar says nothing.

"Covah was your best friend, and he set you up. He committed treason against our country, and now he's murdered thousands of innocent men and women. You were the finest Ranger, the finest soldier I ever trained. I need you back in the game. I need you to take this guy out."

Gunnar can feel the veins throbbing in his neck. He turns slowly to face the Bear, a man he respects more than any person, living or dead. "With all due respect . . . screw you, sir."

Jackson's eyes widen. "Excuse me?"

"I said, 'screw you,' General, or didn't you hear me?"

For a dangerous moment, the Bear's eyes seem to ignite. He turns away slowly. Removes his hat. Takes a long breath. Runs a hand through his auburn Afro, his blood pressure still simmering. Quietly he asks, "What the hell happened to you?"

Gunnar says nothing.

"This isn't about serving time in prison, this has been brewing for quite a while, hasn't it?"

Gunnar stares out the window.

"I said hasn't it, Captain?" Bear growls.

Gunnar exhales, searching for the words to a speech he's rehearsed a thousand times.

"I got sick of it. The hypocrisy. The politics. Sick of humanity. There's so much blood on my hands, I just . . . I had enough."

"What do you mean, you were sick of the hypocrisy?"

"The hypocrisy of modern warfare. The hypocrisy of being a soldier, and all the political bullshit that conceals the truth. I spent most of my adult life risking my neck on missions that never changed a goddamn thing. I killed pawns when I should have been going after the real murderers."

Gunnar's words become impassioned as he paces. "Want to

know what really gets me? It's the White House policy of financing the most cruel and fanatical fighters, as long as they're fighting the enemy of the moment. How many times has that little hypocrisy bitten us in the ass? It was the United States who supported the Shah of Iran. Then, when Iran became our enemy, we supported Saddam Hussein, hell we even provided that nutcase with biological weapons. We looked the other way while he gassed his own people and repressed his population, as long as he invaded Iran. Poor Israel does the right thing and blows up Saddam's nuclear reactor, and we actually condemn the action, even though it probably saved millions of American lives!"

"Gunnar—"

"The Soviets invade Afghanistan, so we rush to provide weapons to Osama bin Laden. Hell, even Manuel Noriega was on the CIA payroll. The only reason George H. Bush went after him had nothing to do with drugs, it had to do with Noriega's refusal to cooperate with our terrorist contra war against Nicaragua."

"I'm not here for a history lesson. You were an American soldier. You were trained to do our nation's dirty work."

"Then my nation should have let me do it!" Gunnar shakes his head in frustration. "Explain to me why it's acceptable to slaughter platoons of men with families while Arab assassins remain off-limits? Explain to me why President Bush backed off when we had Saddam dead to rights. And Milosevic . . . we should have taken that murdering bastard out the moment he ordered the first Kosovo village burned. Bunch of damn sadists—"

"You burned out. I should have seen it coming. It was my fault—"

"Burned out, burned up, blown up, fucked up—call it whatever the hell you want. Know why I originally joined this man's army? It was to complete my education. My father decided to cut me off financially when I decided I wanted something more than working twelve hours a day on a dairy farm." Gunnar turns his back on the general. Stares out the window, tears of frustration blurring Puget Sound. "Guess what I learned? I learned to kill. Thanks for the education, Uncle Sam."

Jackson stares at his former commando. "You're venting years of frustration, but I know you, Gunnar. I know there's something else you're not telling me."

Gunnar wipes his eyes. "I don't want to talk about it."

Jackson wonders whether to push it. "Okay, tell me about the *Goliath*. What made you want to destroy the sub's schematics?"

"Not want—did. I destroyed the schematics, but I didn't touch the computer components or sell the plans, I wouldn't do that. And I swear on my mother's soul that I didn't know Simon was going to steal them either."

"All right. But that still doesn't tell me why."

Gunnar paces again. "I was blindsided. There was a meeting . . . I was called to the Pentagon. It was just after Rocky and I got engaged. The DoD ordered me to redesign the Hammerhead as a remotely operated vehicle."

"And?"

"It was their reasons behind the design changes that pissed me off." Gunnar turns to face his former mentor. "Seems some four-star general decided my stealth subs would make the perfect delivery system for pure-fusion bombs."

Bear rubs his forehead, grimacing.

"Oh, you should have heard 'em, Bear, sitting around the table, reviewing the improved dimensions of the killing field . . . sounded as if they were discussing a profit and loss statement. Pure fusion . . . the way of the future. You familiar with the weapon?"

"Somewhat. The bomb requires no plutonium in the mix."

"Correct. What you're left with is a bigger blast but no radioactive fallout. Perfect if you want to eliminate your enemy but rebuild at a later date. A pure-fusion device small enough to squeeze into one of *Goliath*'s minisubs could potentially wipe out a country the size of Kuwait."

Jackson scratches at his auburn Afro. "Look, son, I understand your concerns, but keep in mind, son, we're not the bad guys. The nuclear genie's been out of his bottle since my father fought in the big one. The name of the game today isn't destruction, it's maintaining the stalemate. The French've been working on pure fusion for more than a decade. For all we know the Russians—"

"Ugghhh!" Gunnar backhands the lamp, smashing it against the wall. "Wake up, Bear, we're out of our freaking minds! Soldiers and civilians are no longer human beings, they're kill ratios. This is the goddamn doomsday bomb, plain and simple, and you're justifying the need for potential genocide."

Bear averts eye contact. *He's done. The commando mentality's gone. His brain's fried.*

"And what about Covah?" Jackson asks. "Did the men and women of the *Ronald Reagan* deserve to die?"

Gunnar stops pacing. "No. Simon went too far."

"And the whole prison thing? Is that how you want your career to end? You can stop him, Gunnar. You can prevent him from killing any more innocent people."

"I don't know . . . maybe." Gunnar leans back against his old desk. "Covah's just part of the equation; the bigger problem is *Sorceress.*"

"It's a computer. You'll find a way to shut it down."

"You don't get it, do you? This is AI, the real deal. *Sorceress* is a selfreplicating system—a prototype—originally intended to be deployed by NASA for deep-space nonhuman applications. Land *Sorceress* on Mars or Europa on board a probe, and the machine runs everything, growing as it acquires information. But on a nuclear sub?"

"What's your point?"

"Christ, Bear, wake up! *Sorceress* is the ultimate thinking machine, and it's programmed to learn. Elizabeth Goode made a breakthrough and the DoD jumped on it, dropping billions into the program before any of us could gain an understanding of what we were dealing with."

"You're overreacting. We don't even know if it's on board."

Gunnar looks up with bloodshot eyes at his former CO. "It's on board. And as it self-replicates and grows, we'll understand less and less about it, making it even more difficult to take off-line." He pauses, a distant memory tugging at him. "I remember an experiment we conducted for NASA back in 2001, it used a Starbridge Systems computer a thousand times more powerful than a traditional PC. It was one of the many stepping-stone systems Dr. Goode used to configure *Sorceress*. The computer was asked to recognize basic audio tones. The computer completed the task . . . only too well. Five of its logic circuits evolved independently. Dr. Goode told me her researchers had no idea how or why it happened, but whenever they tried to bypass the evolved cells, the entire system would shut itself down . . . as if it refused to sacrifice its independence."

"And all this means?"

"Multiply that simple experiment by a million. *Sorceress* is a thinking machine designed to evolve, and it's been functioning for several weeks now. Who knows what it's learned even in that small amount of time? Who knows if Simon can even maintain control?"

The general stands. "You know Covah better than any of us. What's he intending to do?"

Gunnar shakes his head, the jet lag wearing on his brain. "I don't know. Simon lost his entire family in the Serbian uprising. My guess is he wants revenge. If I were him, I'd move *Goliath* into the Mediterranean and launch an attack on Belgrade."

"We can't allow that to happen, can we?" Bear stares at his protégé. "Gunnar?"

No response.

"I've spoken with the president. He's agreed to offer you a full presidential pardon and reinstatement with back pay if you're willing to help us stop Covah."

Gunnar smirks. "The United States government sentences me to ten years, and now they want to pay me to play soldier again. That's rich."

"No one said anything about playing soldier. There's a lunatic out there commanding the most powerful weapon in history. You designed its weapon systems. All we want is your help in finding a way to stop it."

"No you don't. What you really want is for me to return to active duty, to lead an assault." Gunnar turns, his blood boiling. "With all due respect, sir, you can tell Edwards he can shove his reinstatement up his ass."

He pushes past Bear and out the door.

"Gaiety is the most outstanding feature of the Soviet Union."
—Joseph Stalin

"Our countries will continue working
together to our advantage."
—General Leonid Ivashov, Chief Foreign Affairs official, regarding Russian
President Vladimir Putin's resumption of
conventional arms sales to Iran

"We will bury you."
—Nikita Khrushchev, USSR Communist Party First Secretary on relations
with the United States

CHAPTER 6

Northwestern Russia

The Barents Sea is located in Russia's northwest region, an odd-shaped body of water that surrounds the Kola Peninsula before looping inland for several hundred miles to join the White Sea. There are four port cities located on that body of water, seven naval bases, and six naval yards, all of which service the nuclear-powered ships of Russia's Northern Fleet.

Once the pride of the Soviet Navy, the facilities of the Northern Fleet have become radioactive graveyards for decommissioned vessels. More than twenty-five strategic nuclear-powered submarines are laid up, rotting in floating docks, waiting to be dismantled. Solid and liquid radioactive wastes from spent fuel assemblies are haphazardly stored, exposing unskilled, often inebriated laborers to high doses of radiation. Toxic refuse leaks into the environment. Thousands of barrels of nuclear waste and tons of damaged reactor components have been illegally dumped into the neighboring Arctic Ocean. A lack of funds and storage space, as well as gross criminal negligence, have made the waterway an environmental and economic disaster zone.

The largest and most important submarine base in the region is Zapadnaya Litsa, home to Russia's newest Borey-class missile subs, as well as the monstrous, decommissioned Typhoons. Seven of these nuclear-powered ballistic missile giants were commissioned between 1981 and 1989 at Shipyard 402, the last of which was begun but never finished, owning to funding shortages, political changes, and technical problems.

Until *Goliath,* the SSBN Typhoon was the largest submarine ever constructed. Squat and bulbous, the vessel is 575 feet long, with a 75-foot beam and 38-foot draft. Five titanium inner sections are situated within a superstructure composed of two concentric main hulls. Each of these two hulls is equipped with a nuclear water reactor and turbogear assembly that drives the Typhoon's two fifty-thousand-horsepower steam turbines, as well as its four 3,200-kW turbo generators. The sub has two seven-blade, fixed-pitch, shrouded propellers, which enable the submarine to reach submerged speeds of twenty-five knots at maximum diving depths of 1,300 feet.

The titanic size of the Typhoon provides unprecedented comfort for its fifty officers and 120-man crew. Sailors bunk in rooms rather than hot racks, and have access to a gymnasium, swimming pool, sauna, art gallery, solarium, and even a pets' compartment featuring birds and fish.

Chief designer Sergey Kovalev's purpose in constructing the 24,500-ton Typhoon, however, was neither speed nor comfort. In 1974, Leonid Brezhnev announced to the world that the Soviet Union, in response to the growing threat of America's Trident submarines, would construct the world's largest, most powerful submarine fleet, each vessel capable of delivering a deathblow to the nation's enemies. The result were the Typhoons: six nuclear monsters armed with twenty RSM-52 Sturgeon intercontinental three-stage solid-propellant ballistic missiles. Each payload in turn possessed ten independently targetable hundred-kiloton nuclear warheads, a total of two hundred nuclear missiles—enough to annihilate every major city in the United States in a matter of minutes.

Rushed into service, the Typhoons experienced a series of

technical malfunctions, which severely limited their number of missions. The eventual fall of Communism and Russia's failing economy left most of the subs laid up and in dire need of service. A smaller, stealthier, fourth-generation nuclear ballistic missile submarine, the Borey-class, was put into operation in 2003, officially replacing the Typhoon.

Of the six Typhoons completed, four remain moored at the piers of Nerpichya, on the westernmost point of the Kola Peninsula, awaiting dismantling. Another lies in dry dock, its fissionable fuel rods depleted, with no money allocated to effect refueling.

The last remaining Typhoon, designated TK-20, moves slowly through the harsh surface waters of the Barents Sea as it makes its way north toward the Arctic Ocean.

Captain Yuri Romanov tightens the hood of his parka, his eyes watering from the cold as he gazes out from the exposed bridge in the Typhoon's sail. Dawn is still a good hour away, and the nascent twilight is just beginning to chase the stars from the sky. Romanov exhales, the fog of his breath dissipating across his curly, black beard as he glances up into the night. Somewhere high overhead, he knows, an American geosynchronous satellite is watching, imaging his ship's wake, identifying her thermal signature.

The forty-two-year-old captain ignores the temptation to offer a onefinger salute.

Yuri Romanov joined the Soviet Navy when he was nineteen, following in the footsteps of his father, Igor Romanov, who had captained one of the first Typhoons, and his grandfather, Vladimir, whose warship had been sunk by a German U-boat during World War II. Over the last twenty-seven years, the third-generation seaman has commanded a dozen missions and served on at least thirty others.

It takes a unique personality to become a submariner. The stress associated with living underwater in a claustrophobic environment, the fear of knowing that even the smallest mechanical failure can turn the ship into a huge steel coffin—all of these factors place special demands on the sailor's psyche.

The submariner knows his actions directly determine whether he will live or die. It is this responsibility—of performing under life-and-death conditions—that forever binds the crew to the ship and the men to each other. It is this unique challenge that continues to separate Captain Romanov from his wife and three daughters for four months out of every year.

Yuri Romanov's first assignment had nearly been his last. It was 1986, and the young ensign had been assigned to the K-219, a Yankee-class strategic nuclear submarine. In the late hours of October 4, the ship had moved into Bermuda waters, several hundred miles off the eastern seaboard of the United States. Yuri was stationed in the control room, updating the sub's nuclearmissile tracking system. He had just locked on and computed coordinates to the target cities of Washington, D.C., New York, and Boston when the boat's skipper, Captain Britano, ordered a "Crazy Ivan," a sudden 180-degree doubling-back counterdetection maneuver designed to flush out any American attack subs that might be trailing in their baffles.

What Captain Britano didn't realize was that his vessel *was* being trailed, by the Los Angeles-class attack sub, USS *Aurora*, which had detected the Soviet warship as it entered Bermuda waters. As the K-219 circled back, its dorsal surface smashed into the steel belly of the American attack sub, which had shut down its engines so as not to be heard.

The Soviet submarine was carrying sixteen nuclear missiles. The impact with the *Aurora* caused one of the K-219's vertical missile tubes to rupture. Solid fuel mixed with seawater, causing pressurized gas to build up within the missile bay. The consequential explosion rocked the Soviet sub, igniting a deadly fire that quickly grew out of control.

The K-219 was forced to surface, smoke billowing from its open missile-bay hatches. With the flames threatening to ignite his liquid propellant, Captain Britano decided upon a daring maneuver. As the captain of the American sub watched via periscope, Britano ordered all his remaining missile hatches open—an action that, had it been interpreted another way, could easily have started World War III. The Russian skipper then took his vessel to twenty meters down, flooding the missile compartments, extinguishing the inferno. The K-219 fought her way back to the surface as a dozen Soviet surface ships raced to her aid.

What the *Aurora*'s crew eventually learned—and the population of the United States *never* knew—was that the Soviet sub's two nuclear reactors had gone supercritical, all its protective systems failing. As the K-219 struggled along the surface, heading north into deeper waters, a gallant Soviet engineer and a young ensign (Yuri's best friend, Sergei Sergeivitch) were inside the contaminated compartment, struggling to shut down the two overheating reactors.

The two brave Soviet submariners successfully shut down the reactors in time, but Yuri's friend suffocated in the process. Another four minutes and twenty seconds and the overheated fuel rods would have caused a nuclear meltdown, causing a nuclear plume that could have contaminated the northeastern seaboard of the United States.

At 2300 hours on October 6, a Soviet surface ship finally arrived on the scene to rescue the sub's crew. The K-219 was flooded and sent to the bottom, its hull cracking open on the seafloor, dispersing its missile fragments and radioactive debris eighteen thousand feet below the surface.

Yuri and the rest of the K-219 crew returned to the USSR to be debriefed and reassigned. A week later, on October 11, Presidents Gorbachev and Reagan met in Reykjavik, Iceland, to begin peace talks on nuclear disarmament.

To this day, most Americans have no idea how close they all came to dying on that fall evening in 1986, the United States continuing to deny any involvement with the sinking of the Soviet submarine. But Yuri Romanov would never forget the bravery exhibited by Sergei Sergeivitch and the rest of Captain Britano's crew. Years later, he would seek out many of these same men to serve under his own command, including half the officers currently assigned to the refurbished Typhoon.

Ivan Kron, Romanov's executive officer, climbs up to join Romanov in the bridge. "It's time, *Kapitan*."

"In a moment." Yuri continues staring at the bow wake. "She's a big ship, eh Commander?"

"The Iranians don't deserve her. Delivering her to the Persian Gulf will only rile the Americans."

The captain leans forward, spitting over the side. "We're not politicians, my friend. Parliament has its reasons for selling the TK-20."

"*Da*, money. But assigning us to train their crew and deliver these weapons is a waste of our time. You are still the most experienced commander in the Northern Fleet. We should have had one of the newer vessels—"

"Like our dear friend, Gennady, who lies at the bottom of the Barents Sea?" The mention of Captain Lyachin and the *Kursk* disaster momentarily quiets Romanov's XO.

"Patience is required, Ivan. The admiral will eventually assign us to one of the new Borey-class. For now, let us enjoy the honor of commanding the last Typhoon in the fleet."

Kron blows snot from his nose. "I prefer the *Tomsk,* or even one of the older Victors. Overhauling this monster took twice as long as it should have. I've heard rumors—drunkenness among the workers, corners cut to save money. Only the newest boats are reliable these days. And these Arabs, they're desert pigs who know nothing about being a submariner."

Romanov turns to face his second-in-command. "We do what we must. Have our Iranian friends rig the ship for dive. We'll give the Americans one last show."

Barents Sea
22 nautical miles due north

The Los Angeles-class fast-attack sub, USS *Scranton* (SSN-756), rises silently from the deep, slowing to hover at periscope depth.

"Sixty feet," the diving officer reports.

"No close contacts." The OOD gives the "all clear" sign after three rapid sweeps of the horizon.

Captain Tom Cubit peers through the Type-18 search

periscope, its low-light operating mode cutting through much of the darkness. "Radio, conn, anything on the VLF?"

"Conn, radio, transmission coming in now, sir."

"On my way. Officer of the Deck, you have the conn." Cubit turns the periscope over to his OOD, then makes his way aft down the portside passageway leading into the communications shack to receive the transmission he has been anticipating for the last seventy-two hours.

Thomas Mark Cubit was born and raised in south Philadelphia, a blue-collar section of the city not far from the Delaware River. As a boy he spent much of his free time staring at the rusting gray warships docked in rows of threes at the Philadelphia Naval Yard, occasionally sneaking aboard one to look around. An all-around athlete in high school, Cubit accepted a basketball scholarship to the University of Central Florida, where he met his future wife, Andrea, whose father was a prominent lawyer in Orlando. Upon graduating, Tom skipped law school, much to Andrea's dismay, deciding instead to enroll in Officer Candidate School (OCS) to pursue a career in the Navy. Cubit's boyish charm and his down-to-earth style of leadership quickly earned him high marks among his fellow officers and crew, as well as with the Director of Naval Reactors, who selected him for reactor prototype school. From there, Tom was sent to SOBC (Submarine Officers Basic Course) in Groton, Connecticut, then to his first assignment, a two-year stint aboard the USS *Boise* (SSN 764). The recent captain's O-6 ranking had been earned after his last assignment aboard the USS *Toledo* (SSN-769). When the opportunity to take a second command aboard the *Scranton* had been offered, Cubit jumped on it.

The communications officer looks up as Cubit enters the radio room, handing his CO the message transmitted by the VLF (very low frequency wire).

TYPHOON TK-20 CONFIRMED LEAVING ZAPADNAYA LITSA SUBMARINE BASE AT 0400 HOURS. COMMANDING OFFICER: YURI ROMANOV.

Cubit smiles as he reads the Russian captain's name. The *Toledo* had played a tense game of cat and mouse with Romanov two years earlier when he had commanded the *Tomsk*, an Oscar II–class nuclear submarine.

Cubit passes the message to his executive officer, Commander Bo Dennis. The former football star at the University of Delaware reads the transmission as he follows his CO back to the conn. "Romanov again? Better give him plenty of room. Remember how he nearly drove us insane with all those crazy counterdetection maneuvers."

"Yeah, God bless 'em." Cubit returns to the tight confines of the control room. "All right, gentlemen, time to play chase-the-Russian. Diving Officer of the Watch, make your depth six hundred feet, twenty-degree down angle."

The planesman and helmsman operating the aircraft-style control wheels quickly buckle themselves in.

"Aye, sir, making my depth six hundred feet, twenty-degree down angle."

Cubit holds on as his ship drops bow first, the interior compartment tilting too steeply for normal walking.

"Six hundred feet, Captain," the diving officer reports.

"Helm, left fifteen-degree rudder, increase speed to two-thirds."

Helmsman Kelsey Walker repeats Cubit's orders, dialing up two-thirds speed using a small electronic order telegraph (EOT) located beside his left knee.

In the engine room, the shaft increases its revolutions to sixty turns, the propeller pushing the boat to twelve knots.

"XO, you have the conn."

"Aye, sir, I have the conn."

Cubit heads forward to the sonar room, where technicians stationed at four BSY-1 sonar stations are listening intently while watching television screens showing green waterfall-like patterns of noise. Sonar is the submariner's window to the sea, the ocean's sounds hitting exterior hydrophones, which convert them into electrical energy. This energy is then channeled through dedicated computers and displayed on video monitors.

The BSY-1 (pronounced busy-one) is the brains behind the attack sub's combat system. The central computer is linked to all of the ship's sensors, fire controls, and weapons systems. The BSY-1 uses this information to process assignments through a distribution system of smaller computers that enable quicker response times.

Cubit nods to his sonar watch supervisor. "How're we doing, gentlemen? Anything on the TB-23?"

Senior sonar technician Michael Flynn is listening to the towed array sonar, designed to pick up very-low-frequency noise over great distances. "About a dozen fishing trawlers, Captain, nothing else."

Cubit leans forward, squeezing the man's shoulder. "There's a Typhoon out there, Michael-Jack. Find it."

"Aye, sir." Flynn smiles. Michael-Jack is the nickname Cubit bestowed upon him years ago aboard the *Toledo*, when the CO learned his sonar operator was a fellow Phillies fan. Michael-Jack had been the favorite name hometown sportscasters Harry Kalas and the late Richie Ashburn had used when referring to Hall of Fame third baseman Mike Schmidt.

Flynn adjusts his headphones, intent on finding the TK-20 for his captain.

A Los Angeles-class attack sub resembles a 360-foot-long black pipe, thirty-three feet in diameter, with a dorsal-mounted, thin rectangular steel box for a sail. Comprising the most numerous class in the United States fleet, the Los Angeles-class is a silent predator, a stealthy power-projection delivery system carrying twelve Tomahawk cruise missiles in its vertical launch silos and a variety of Tomahawks in its torpedo room, along with harpoon and Mk-48 ADCAP torpedoes, the most lethal in the world.

Space on board the submarine is very limited—its tight passageways and compartments making for a claustrophobic environment. Sixty percent of the internal volume is dedicated to the ship's engine room and nuclear reactor. Although the sub has the ability to circle the globe twenty times underwater before having to surface, its tight confines can only store enough food to last its crew about four months.

Submariners are considered the elite of the United States Navy. Only the top 1 percent of all candidates taking the entry exam are even eligible to train for duty on "shooters," and all seamen who eventually qualify are considered volunteers.

Life on board an attack sub requires steady nerves and an ability to adapt to an almost prisonlike environment. Once the hatch is closed and the ship under weigh, submariners may not see the light of day again for months. Sealed inside a tube perpetually humming with machinery, the 140-man crew must live and work in a spatial environment equivalent to that of a three-bedroom house.

There are no days or nights aboard attack subs. Twenty-four-hour clocks become eighteen-hour time frames, six-hour shifts alternating between work, sleep, and training.

Michael Flynn is nearing the end of his work shift when he locates the object.

"Conn, sonar—Skipper, I've got a tonal contact, bearing three-zero-five. Range, twenty-eight miles."

"Sonar, conn, is it the Typhoon?"

"Stand by, sir." Flynn focuses on his screen as he listens intently to the sounds reverberating in his headphones. "Conn, sonar, I'm confirming twin, seven-blade, fixed-pitch screws. Sonar intelligence cross-references the tonals to a Typhoon-class submarine, number TK-20. Blade rate indicates her speed holding steady at six knots."

"Nice work, Michael-Jack. Designate sonar contact Sierra-1." Cubit hangs up the 1-MC. "Helm, plot an intercept course. Officer of the Deck, slow to four knots and bring us to periscope depth."

"Aye, sir, slowing to four knots, coming up to periscope depth. Steady at sixty feet."

"Very well. Chief of the Watch, raise number one BRA-34."

First Class Petty Officer Robert Wilkens raises the sub's multipurpose communications antennas while Lieutenant Commander Mitch Friedenthal mans the Type-18 periscope, taking a quick scan of the horizon. The Type-18 is equipped with both GPS (Global Positioning Satellite) and radar intercept capability. While Friedenthal looks around, technicians in the Electronic Support Measures (ESM) room use the periscope's radar signals to search the skies.

"No close contacts."

"Radio, Captain, contact COMSUBLANT (Commander—Submarine Force Atlantic) and send the message that we've located the Typhoon."

"Aye, sir." A pause, then the radioman's voice returns. "Captain, we're receiving an incoming transmission on the VLF."

Cubit and his XO make eye contact. "Very well. Commander Dennis, you're with me. Mr. Friedenthal, you have the conn."

"Aye, sir," the OOD repeats, "I have the conn."

Twenty-three-year-old Communications Officer Drew Laird is a strapping young man with broad shoulders and a baby face to go with his mop of sandy blond hair. There is a look of trepidation in his blue eyes as he hands his CO the folded transmission.

"Easy, Laird, take a breath, you're turning blue."

"Aye, sir. Sorry, sir."

Cubit opens the encoded message and reads it. "Christ." The captain stares at the paper for a long moment, then rubs the sweat from his face. "XO, take the ship to one-five-zero feet, make your course three-zero-five, ahead one-third. Then give me a few minutes and meet me in my stateroom."

Ten minutes later, Tom Cubit sits alone in his cabin, rereading the transmission from Naval Intelligence for the fourth time. A knock, and Commander Dennis enters. "Sir?"

"Sit." He hands his XO the sheet of paper.

"Jesus—this thing wiped out the entire CVBG?" Bo Dennis's hands are shaking. "I feel like somebody just punched me in the gut."

"Me too." Cubit hands him a bottled water. "I've been sitting here, thinking. I bet I've served with at least a dozen men who were aboard the *Jacksonville*. Altogether, I probably went to OCS with a hundred of the officers who died aboard those ships."

"Tom, this attack sub, the *Goliath*, do you know anything about it?"

"Just what's in the message. Never heard of a biochemical computer before."

"I have. My wife works for Hewlett-Packard. They started playing with the technology back in the late 1990s. If it works like it's supposed to, this sub's gonna be damn hard to track."

"Tracking the *Goliath* is not part of our orders. We're to shadow the Typhoon, taking all precautions. Have the OOD take us into a sprint-and-drift mode. Alert all sonar technicians to be cognizant of any biologics closing within ten thousand yards of the ship. Have Flynnie access the BSY-1 library. I want him to listen to sonar recordings of *Seawolf's* pump-jet propulsor. If we don't have any, tell him to try the U.K.'s Trafalgar-class, they were the first to use that type of system. Then have the department heads meet me in the wardroom in fifteen minutes."

"Aye, sir."

There are several different ways a submarine commander can disseminate information aboard his ship. Some COs prefer to broadcast the news over the 1-MC, the sub's intercom, while others choose to keep their crew in the dark, allowing the information to leak out slowly through word of mouth. Tom Cubit realized the news regarding the sinking of the carrier battle group could devastate the morale of his men, but he also needed them to remain in a high state of alert if they were to have any chance of surviving a confrontation with the *Goliath*. After briefing his officers, he allowed them ten minutes to speak to their men before addressing the entire crew over the ship's intercom.

"This is the captain. By now, you've heard about the attack and sinking of the *Ronald Reagan* and her carrier group. All of us lost good friends, and the devastation of this unprovoked attack is surely taking a heavy toll on each one of us. While our nation can afford time out to grieve and attempt to recover from the initial shock of this attack, *we* must be ready *now*. Everyone aboard this vessel has a responsibility to each member of the crew and to this ship, and your ability to focus can mean the difference between life and death.

"Our mission is not to join in the hunt for the *Goliath*, but to locate and shadow the Typhoon TK-20, which we believe to be heading into the Persian Gulf. As you know, relations between the United States and Russia are a bit tense right now, the sale of the Typhoon to the Iranians no doubt adding salt to the wound. If the *Goliath* is still lurking somewhere in our vicinity, then she may cross our path, forcing a confrontation. Gentlemen, your officers and I have the utmost confidence that each one of you will stay focused and perform your duties as professionals. While the vessel that sank the fleet may be faster than *Old Ironsides* and more difficult to detect, remember that *we* have the more experienced crew. Experience makes the hunter, gentlemen, not the gun. Rig for silent running. Captain out."

Cubit hangs up the 1-MC. "Sonar, conn, how close are we to the Typhoon?"

"Conn, sonar, four miles. Contact has changed course to two-one-zero, now heading southwest, increasing speed to ten knots."

"Officer of the Deck, make your depth five hundred feet. Bring us to within three miles of the Typhoon's baffles, then match speed and course."

"Aye, Skipper, making my depth five hundred feet, coming to course two-one-zero. I am closing to within three miles of the contact, then matching speed and course."

Norwegian Sea
406 nautical miles southwest of Bear Island

The dark, reinforced-steel hull of the Typhoon, nearly two football fields in length, pushes silently through the frigid waters of the North Atlantic as it heads south toward Iceland.

Captain Romanov straps himself into his command chair. Although his ship's passive sonar reports no tonal bearings, experience tells him that an American submarine, probably a Los Angeles-class attack sub, is hovering somewhere in the vicinity. "Helm, hard right rudder, reverse engines."

"Aye, *Kapitan*, hard right rudder, reversing engines."

The Typhoon's bow swings sharply to starboard, the great ship cavitating as its propellers fight to keep their hold on the sea.

Aboard the USS *Scranton*

"Conn, sonar, contact is coming about, changing course to three-three-zero, reducing speed to five knots."

"Helm, all stop."

"All stop, aye, sir."

Long minutes pass as the *Scranton* hovers silently in five hundred feet of water, waiting for its Russian quarry to resume her course.

"Conn, sonar. Sir, I'm registering ambient sounds, approaching from the northeast. Range, twenty-two-thousand yards, closing at six knots."

Coming up behind us. Cubit's pulse quickens. "Helm, all stop. Sonar, what is the classification of the contacts?"

The sonar supervisor's voice answers over the intercom. "Sir, initial classification is biologics. Believe they may be humpbacks."

Cubit closes his eyes. The attack on the *Jacksonville* and *Hampton* had been preceded by cetacean acoustics. At this time of year, the North Atlantic was teeming with migrating whales, all heading south for the winter to breed. "Sonar, Captain, I want to know if those whales accelerate toward our boat."

"Aye, sir."

Ease up, Cubit, don't go paranoid. It's a big ocean out there, filled with thousands of whales. Don't do anything to spook the Typhoon . . . or your crew.

"Conn, sonar, the Typhoon has resumed its course—two-one-zero, increasing speed to fifteen knots."

Not yet, give him some distance . . . "Steady, gentlemen."

"Eighteen knots—"

"Very well. Helm, all ahead one-third—"

"Aye, sir. All ahead one-third."

"Conn, sonar, I'm getting another set of ambient sounds. Very faint."

"Belay that order, helm. All stop."

"All stop, aye, sir."

"Sonar, Captain, what do you hear?"

"I don't know, sir. It's gone now."

Cubit pushes past his officer of the deck and heads forward, joining his sonar supervisor, who is leaning over Michael Flynn's luminescent green console. "Talk to me, Michael-Jack. What did you hear?"

"I don't know, Skipper, it was sort of a *whooshing* noise. Like sand blowing away from the bottom."

"Sand?"

"Yes, sir. Lots of sand. Like something massive just lifted off the seafloor."

"Hell is full of good meanings and best wishes."
—George Herbert

"Hell is other people."
—Jean-Paul Sartre

CHAPTER 7

Kingston Inn
Kingston, Washington

The hotel room is musty, its drab olive green carpet reeking of the decrepit odors of mildew. Gunnar lies spread-eagled on the king-size bed. He stares at the television screen, the football game growing hazy as his eyes begin glazing over from exhaustion.

The knock startles him awake. He pulls back the drab, mothball-scented curtains, takes a peek outside, then quickly unchains the door.

The woman enters. "Shut the door. We don't have much time."

Gunnar obeys, his head still in a jet-lag fog. "Jesus, what are you doing here? I thought—"

"Don't think, sit and listen." She checks the bathroom, verifying they are alone.

Gunnar smooths the entanglement of bedclothes, then sits on the edge of the mattress, watching as she leans back against the dresser to face him, her arms folded in displeasure across her wiry frame.

Dr. Elizabeth Goode has the pale complexion and demeanor of someone who spends the majority of each workday's eighteen waking hours in a windowless laboratory. The shoulder-length hair is still brown, though graying around the part. The gaunt face—librarian pretty—is still devoid of makeup. Dark circles shadow the hazel eyes—eyes that take in everything. "You look like hell, G-man."

"Been there."

"No, you've been to purgatory. Hell is what's going to break out unless you stop Simon."

"And why should I do that?"

"Because this is all your fault."

"My fault?"

"That's right. If you had followed my instructions and downloaded the virus when I told you to, then you'd be watching television with Rocky and your 2.5 kids right now, instead of listening to some old lab rat babble in this dumpy motel room."

"Well, guess I screwed up. Next time, do it yourself."

"There won't be a next time, but there will be another *Goliath*."

"What are you talking about?"

Dr. Goode shoots him a chastising look. "Don't be so naive. You really think the DoD was going to walk away from this project, just because of a mere 2-billion-dollar setback? *Goliath*'s sister ship, the *Colossus*, has been under construction since your second year in prison."

"Jesus . . ." Gunnar feels light-headed.

"She was built in total secrecy; even Congress doesn't know about it. Vice President Maller covertly diverted funds from the Energy Department for years. The entire base is run by the NSA like a military prison. And there's no almost crossover in personnel from the GOLIATH Project."

"Almost?"

"Not me, I flatly refused. It was never my decision to put *Sorceress* on board the *Goliath*, and I wasn't about to let that happen again. *Colossus* is being outfitted with the Virginia-class computers. The ship won't be autonomous, but it's still the second-most dangerous thing in the sea."

"What are you asking me to do?"

"Take Jackson's offer. Rejoin his team."

"Forget it. I don't even know why Jackson needs me?"

"It wasn't Jackson who requested you. It was David Paniagua."

"David?" Mention of Dr. Goode's former assistant stirs distant memories.

"David's in charge of the COLOSSUS Project."

"I thought you said—"

"David was appointed when I refused. He has a plan, one that can get you and an infiltration team aboard the *Goliath*. You can retake the ship before Simon does any more damage."

"And if I refuse?"

"Then the holocaust that follows will be on your head."

She starts for the door, then turns. "Gunnar, I'm sorry for everything that's happened, but you have to finish this business. Be careful."

"Yeah . . . thanks."

She offers a consoling look, then leaves.

Gunnar watches from the window as she crosses the street and climbs inside a waiting car.

Elizabeth Goode leans back against the gray leather seat as the Lincoln swerves into traffic.

"So?"

"He'll do it." She looks away, swallowing the lump rising in her throat.

General Jackson nods, satisfied. "Thank you, Dr. Goode. And now, you and your sons are free to leave the country."

Norwegian Sea
Aboard the USS *Scranton*

Tom Cubit leans forward, staring at the BSY-1 low-frequency passive and active search-and-attack sonar. "Where is she, Flynnie?"

"If I'm right, sir, she's directly behind the Typhoon."

"You think the Typhoon knows she's in her baffles?"

"I doubt it, Skipper. She's quiet, just a whisper." He points to the pattern of green snow running vertically along his screen. "Every few seconds I get a whiff of a ghost signature, nothing solid. Those damn propulsors are smooth as silk."

"How big is this thing?"

"Hard to tell without going active. If I'm right, she's big, as wide as the Typhoon is long, only real flat, like she has wings. She's smooth and curved in all the right places. It's like trying to find a Stealth bomber. Sonar can't seem to gain a foothold on her."

"Does she know we're here?"

"No, sir, I don't think so."

"Let's keep it that way. XO, take us to battle stations, rig ship for ultraquiet running. Sonar, how far ahead of us is the Typhoon?"

"Range, twenty thousand yards. She's staying on course two-one-zero, moving away from us at a steady fifteen knots. The second sonar contact is trailing about three thousand yards in her baffles, matching course and speed. Flynnie's right, the Typhoon doesn't seem to know the contact's there."

"Designate second sonar contact Sierra-2. XO, get me a firing solution."

"Aye, sir, already working on it."

"Conn, Captain, come ahead one-third, stay on course two-one-zero. Michael-Jack, think you can track Sierra-2?"

"Now that I know what to listen for, yes, but only over a very short range. I can't really hear her, I'm just sort of focusing in on the dead spot she's leaving in the water."

"Do whatever it takes, just don't lose her."

"Aye, sir."

Cubit heads back to the control room. "XO, where's my firing solution?"

"Sorry, sir, FCS is unable to maintain a solid fix. The contact keeps maneuvering, and sonar only has a weak trace. Sierra-2's just too flat in the water."

"Then let's change the angle. Sonar, conn, estimate Sierra-2's depth."

"Best guess—five hundred feet, Captain."

"Chief, make your depth eight hundred feet, ten-degree down angle. Let's see if we can sneak a peek under her skirt."

"Aye, Captain, making my depth eight hundred feet, ten-degree down angle."

The helmsman pushes down on the wheel. "Six hundred feet. Seven hundred—"

"Captain, the BSY-1 has acquired a good tracking solution on Sierra-2."

"WEPS, Captain, match generated bearings. Flood tubes one and two. I want full safeties on. If we get a clear shot, we'll take it."

Commander Dennis leans toward Cubit, and whispers, "We accidentally hit that Typhoon, and we could start World War III."

"Conn, sonar, I'm getting two more tonals, both originating from Sierra-2."

"Torpedoes?"

"Negative, sir, they're larger, moving out ahead of Sierra-2, heading for the Typhoon. Sir, I'm registering ambient sounds, like orca."

If they wanted to sink her, they'd have done it by now. What the hell are they doing? "Sonar, conn, designate new bearings Sierra-3 and Sierra-4. WEPS, conn, open outer doors for torpedo tubes one and two."

Aboard the *Goliath*

A volumetric map of the vicinity appears on the large overhead control room monitor. Simon Covah stares at the display, the wave of adrenaline teasing a distant memory.

You're eight years old when your father returns from a six-month mission and declares he's enrolled you in a boarding school in Moscow. You're terrified inside, but you put on a brave face, because one less mouth to feed at home would make it easier on your poor mother. At the school, you be-

*come the object of ridicule, a slovenly carrottop too frail to
compete on the playing field. So you turn inward, mastering
your studies, becoming the youngest graduate in the history
of the school. You do not feel your parents' pride, your only
motivation—to escape the school and its physics professor, a
man whose sexual perversions will stain your psyche for the
rest of your days.*

The haunting female voice of *Sorceress* reverberates from the
speaker.

ALERT-ONE. TONAL CONTACT, BEARING ZERO-SIX-ZERO,
RANGE 5,742 METERS, DEPTH, 782 FEET. CLASSIFICATION:
UNITED STATES, LOS ANGELES–CLASS ATTACK SUBMARINE.
OUTER TORPEDO DOORS HAVE OPENED. PROBABILITY OF
TORPEDO LAUNCH: 62 PERCENT. ENGAGING DEFENSIVE
PROTOCOL. COUNTERMEASURES ARMED, ANTITORPEDO TOR-
PEDOES LOADED INTO TUBES ONE AND TWO. GOLIATH OFFEN-
SIVE FIRING SOLUTION PLOTTED. MK-48 ADCAP TORPEDOES
LOADED INTO TUBES THREE THRU SIX.

Simon Covah smooths the thick, rust-colored hairs of his
goatee, staring at his bizarre reflection in the dark viewport
glass. "As my father would say, 'it's time for the thrill of the
hunt.' *Sorceress,* disable the Russian Typhoon's engines. Destroy the American sub once it moves into firing range."

ACKNOWLEDGED.

Aboard the USS *Scranton*

"Conn, sonar, Sierra-2 has increased its speed to twenty knots
and has closed to within eight hundred yards of the Typhoon."

"Conn, weapons. We've lost our firing solution, sir."

"Damn." Cubit grips the vinyl arms of his command chair,
a recent addition in the *Scranton's* control room. He turns to
his executive officer. "Suggestions?"

"Fire now and there's a fifty-fifty chance you'll accidentally hit the Typhoon and start a war. If you don't fire, the Typhoon will probably be destroyed. Of course, assuming

Goliath just heard our outer doors open, we're sitting ducks anyway. I say we shit or get off the pot."

Cubit glances around the control room. To his left is the ship control station, the ship's control team strapped into their bucket seats, the diving officer hovering close. On the opposite side of the chamber, five technicians man the BSY-1 and weapons console. He feels the eyes of his officers upon him, every man calm on the outside, fear in their guts as they await his next order. "Tell you what, XO, instead of shitting, how about we just flush. WEPS, stand by to compute a new firing solution." Cubit fingers the 1-MC. "Sonar, this is the captain. Give me two pings down the bearing of Sierra-2."

The XO's eyes widen. "You're alerting Romanov?"

"And pulling our pants down at the same time."

Two hollow pings echo through the sea like underwater gongs.

Aboard the *Typhoon* TK-20

"It's a Los Angeles–class attack sub, *Kapitan*. Nine thousand meters and closing."

Romanov's thick eyebrows rise.

"*Kapitan*, there's something else right behind us! Another vessel, very large—"

The captain feels his heart jump-start with adrenaline. "Identify—"

"Unknown origin, sir. Eight hundred meters and closing."

"Sound alarm. Evasive maneuvers. Left full rudder, all ahead flank!"

Aboard the USS *Scranton*

"Conn, sonar, the Typhoon's changed course and increased her speed."

"Conn, weapons, we've reestablished a firing solution on Sierra-2."

"Match sonar bearings and shoot tube one."

"Aye, sir, firing tube one."

The wire-guided Mk-48 Advanced Capability torpedo races out from the bow, the thirty-four-hundred-pound projectile's sonar seeker homing in on *Goliath*.

"Captain, own ship's unit has acquired Sierra-2."

That's for the Jacksonville *and the* Hampton. "WEPS, flood down tubes three and four."

"Conn, sonar, Sierra-2 has launched two torpedoes, bearing two-two-zero. Sir, both fish went active the moment they were fired!"

"Torpedo evasion! Right full rudder, steady course three-two-zero."

The terrified helmsman pushes against the wheel, racing the *Scranton* down and away from the two enemy torpedoes, while simultaneously signaling for flank speed on the engine-order-telegraph. Four dull thumps are heard—the reactor's coolant pumps shifting to fast speed to provide maximum cooling to the reactors as the turbines throttle open to 100 percent steam flow.

A single explosion reverberates through the interior compartment, the first of *Goliath*'s torpedoes slamming into the *Scranton*'s projectile.

"Conn, sonar—sir, one of Sierra-2's torpedoes just detonated our own ship's unit."

Cubit and his XO make eye contact. "An antitorpedo torpedo?"

"Conn, sonar, Sierra-2 second torpedo just went active. Bearing two-four-three . . . Sir, Sierra-2's torpedo is an Mk-48! Range, twenty-seven hundred yards and closing very fast—"

The sweat-streaked faces of the crew turn to their captain. The Mk-48 is the most lethal torpedo in the world, its seeker head designed to hunt down and destroy enemy subs at great distances—and the *Scranton* is well within striking range.

The hunter has become the hunted.

"Helm, right full rudder, steady course north. Dive, mark your depth—"

"Nine hundred feet," the diving officer reports, his pulse racing, his bladder tightening.

"Maintain a fifteen-degree down angle—"

"Conn, sonar, torpedo range now fifteen hundred yards. Impact in eighty seconds—"

"Sir, we're passing nine hundred feet. Nine-fifty. Nine-sixty . . ."

The helmsman looks up at the diving officer. The sub's deep-water tolerance is only 950 feet.

Cubit stares at the second hand sweeping across the face of the gold pocket watch his grandfather had given him long ago, after the leukemia and the futile chemotherapy had taken the life out of the gruff old man. *I won't be needing this now, Tommy. Keep it close to you, and I'll find a way to be there when you need me . . .*

"WEPS, prepare to launch countermeasures."

"Aye, sir, preparing to launch countermeasures."

"Depth now passing one thousand feet. One thousand fifty . . ."

Cubit blinks away perspiration from his eyes, his brain dissecting the numbers, his lips moving silently as his mind calculates. Surviving a torpedo attack at close range requires steady nerves and more than a bit of luck. He recalls a favorite expression of his old skipper aboard the *Toledo: When it comes to actual combat, a coward will shit his pants, while a brave man merely pisses.*

The computer on board the pinging Mk-48 validates *Scranton* as its target, the projectile increasing its speed to sixty knots, pinging faster . . .

"Conn, sonar, torpedo bearing two-one-seven, range seven hundred yards . . . torpedo has acquired . . . torpedo is range-gating!"

"Launch countermeasures! Helm, hard left rudder, steady course two-seven-zero. Dive, thirty-degree up angle—"

Two acoustic device countermeasures are expelled into the sea and begin spinning, their gyrations simulating the *Scranton*'s propeller.

The sub lurches, rolling hard to starboard as her screw

catches the ocean, driving the sixty-nine-hundred-ton ship upward, her hull plates groaning under the stress, her terrified crew tossed sideways.

"Conn, sonar—torpedo impact in thirty seconds—"

"Chief of the Watch, conduct a one-second emergency blow of all main ballast tanks."

"One-second blow, aye, sir!" Struggling to stand against the thirty-degree up angle, the chief auxiliary man reaches above his head, grabbing the two gray handles of the ship's emergency blow system, and, with a great lunge, thrusts them upward.

A deafening sound rips through the sub as 4500 psi pressurized air is released from the air banks into the five main ballast tanks surrounding the *Scranton*'s pressurized hull, thereby expelling their water to drastically lighten the ship.

The incoming torpedo homes in on the noise.

Almost immediately, the Chief of the Watch depresses and pulls down on the "chicken switches," holding on as the *Scranton* surges upward like a beach ball from the bottom of the pool.

Lost in the "knuckle" of noise, the incoming torpedo continues descending, following the countermeasures until it has hopelessly lost track of the evading submarine. Running out of fuel, it spirals downward and implodes in the deep recesses of the North Atlantic.

"Conn, sonar, torpedo destroyed!"

Sighs of relief, cheers, and a few whispered prayers of thanks rise in a chorus from the nerve-wracked crew.

Cubit mops perspiration from his face. "All stop."

"All stop, aye, sir."

"Dive, vent the main ballast tanks."

"Vent the tanks, aye, sir."

"Sonar, Captain, where's Sierra-2?"

"Conn, sonar, I lost contact, sir."

"Where's the Typhoon?"

"Sir, Sierra-1 has changed course to two-six-zero, range thirty thousand yards, moving away from us at twenty knots. She's running, Skipper."

Aboard the *Typhoon*

"Load torpedoes one and two," Captain Romanov orders. "Match bearings. Prepare to fire."

"Not yet, *Kapitan*," Ivan Kron calls out. "Range to bearing is less than two hundred meters. She's right behind us and still closing."

This is madness, is the man trying to ram us? "Let's shake her loose. Helm, right full rudder, come to course zero-eight-zero—"

"*Kapitan*, two more contacts, much smaller, closing on both propeller shafts. I'm sorry, sir, I thought they were biologics."

Aboard the *Goliath*

Simon Covah stands before one of the immense Lexan viewports, the reinforced glass casting its crimson glow across his flesh-and-steel face. A powerful outer light in *Goliath*'s flattened triangular bow ignites, the intense lighthouselike beacon piercing the darkness of the sea, illuminating the stern of the fleeing Typhoon.

You are a boy who computes equations like Einstein and grasps science like an overheated dog slurps water. You see things differently, your brain able to dissect problems in ways alien to your colleagues. You are fourteen and you wear the same overcoat you've worn since grade school, but you've just been enrolled in Moscow's most prestigious university. You are a sheep among thousands of wolves. You spend your days alone in your room, bored with your studies, but lacking the money and companions to occupy your time. Your mind is a sponge that cannot be saturated, so you feed it Shakespeare and Bach and Ludwig van, wondering what pain life has in store for you next.

Covah watches as two of the sleek, steel gray hammerhead shark–shaped minisubs close quickly upon the Russian sub's twin screws. *This time, I am the predator. This time, I am the wolf.*

The Typhoon rolls hard to starboard, attempting to distance itself. *Goliath* banks like a 747 jumbo jet, its bow sensors locked on the Russian sub, its superior hydrodynamic design mirroring the exact movements of its prey.

The two remotely operated mechanical sharks move into position behind the Typhoon's churning propeller. Steel mouths yawn open, revealing small launch tubes.

With an expulsion of pressurized gas, a lightweight torpedo is fired from the open mouth of each minisub. Launched at point-blank range, the two projectiles slam into the heart of each of the Typhoon's propeller assemblies, detonating right on the twin seven-blade screws in an explosion of searing hot bubbles and steel.

Aboard the *Typhoon*

The double explosion buckles the Russian sub, jolting it forward, the screams of the Iranian trainees quickly drowned out by the high-pitched clanging of the ruptured driveshafts, the hideous noise echoing throughout the crippled vessel.

Romanov's face smashes into the map table. Righting himself, he grabs the ship's intercom, spitting out a tooth and a mouthful of blood. "Damage report, all departments—"

"*Kapitan,* engine room. Both screws and driveshafts are gone."

"What do you mean—gone?"

"The detonations, sir. They took out both propulsion units. We're dead in the water, *Kapitan.* The inner hull casings have been compromised, and we've got heavy flooding—"

"Seal the compartments. Get your men out of there."

"Aye, sir."

"Reactor room, report."

"Reactor room here. Both reactors still on-line, but there's been damage. Recommend we shut down and switch to batteries."

"Do it. Sonar, report. Where's the vessel that fired upon us?"

"Searching for her now, sir. We're still having trouble getting a fix."

"Find that sub now! Where are the Americans?"

"Uncertain, *Kapitan*. They escaped, then went quiet."

Romanov signals to his XO. "Get a message to Moscow—"

Another explosion shudders the Typhoon, this one originating from above.

Romanov looks up, his heart pounding.

"*Kapitan*, this is Ensign Chernov in the missile control center. Missile tube seventeen is flooding. That last explosion blew the outer and inner hatches clear off."

Aboard the USS *Scranton*

The USS *Scranton* hovers silently, six hundred feet below the surface, having crept to within three nautical miles northeast of the damaged Typhoon.

Captain Cubit and his XO stand behind the three sonar technicians, both men watching their monitors intently.

"Another explosion," Michael Flynn reports, grabbing his headphones. "Sounds of flooding. Sir, I can't be sure, but I think it came from one of the missile hatches."

The sonar supervisor wipes sweat from his forehead. "If those warheads detonate, the explosion will make Hiroshima look like a firecracker."

Flynn turns around. "Captain, the Typhoon's rising."

Commander Dennis looks at his CO. "Romanov has no choice. His screws are gone, and his sub's taking on water. If he doesn't surface now, he may sink for good."

The captain nods. "Flynnie, still no sign of Sierra-2?"

"No, sir."

"Keep searching, she has to be close to the Typhoon. Conn, this is the captain. Come to ahead one-third, bring us to within one mile of Sierra-1. Nice and quiet, Mr. Friedenthal. Keep us at three knots."

"Three knots, aye, sir."

"WEPS, Captain. Make the weapons in tubes two, three, and four ready in all respects."

"Aye, Captain."

"Michael-Jack, is the Typhoon still ascending?"

"Aye, sir. I make her depth two hundred feet. One-eight-zero . . . one-five-zero . . . whoah, hold on—"

"What is it?"

"Sir, the Typhoon just struck something."

"Identify—what was it?"

"Stand by, sir." Ensign Flynn closes his eyes to concentrate. "Son of a bitch, I don't believe it . . . Sir, it's Sierra-2. She must be lying directly on top of the Typhoon, preventing her from surfacing."

Aboard the *Typhoon*

The oil-covered faces of the Typhoon's crew look up in bewilderment as the reverberation of the collision registers in their bones.

"Forty-five meters from the surface, *Kapitan*. We've stopped rising."

The sound of straining metal against an immovable object echoes above their heads.

Romanov fights to maintain his composure. "It's the other sub. She's pinning us below the surface."

Pale, frightened faces stare at the Russian captain in disbelief.

"Damage control, how much water have we taken on?"

"About two thousand tons, *Kapitan*. All damaged compartments are now sealed, and the ballast tanks are blown."

"*Kapitan*, sonar. Sir, I can hear divers in the water."

Aboard the *Goliath*

The watertight door of the claustrophobic chamber seals, activating a violet-red interior light. Simon Covah adjusts his face mask for the third time as the icy cold sea fills the pressurized compartment. The thirty-three-degree water rises to his chest, the bulky dry suit barely able to keep his body warm. He pulls the hood tighter around his face and cheek, the dull throb in his mangled earhole signaling the steady increase in atmospheric pressure within *Goliath*'s massive locking chamber.

The disease that threatens his life has spread throughout his body, the effects of the treatment leaving him weak. Still, Covah refuses to succumb to the cancer. *This is my ship, my mission. I'll do what needs to be done or die trying . . .*

The violet-red light blinks off, replaced by an electric green. The outer door opens. Covah stares into the deep blue void, then follows the other two divers into the sea.

Slow, sluggish movement as Covah descends, the haunting grind of metal against metal ringing in his good ear. The scar tissue bordering his steel plate tightens from the change in pressure.

Struggling to descend, he releases more air from his buoyancy-control vest. Falling faster now, he looks below. The dark back of the immobile Typhoon seems to jump up at him, the huge submarine fighting to find its equilibrium against its larger, heavier oppressor. Above, blotting out the sun like a titanium ice floe is the immense undercarriage of the *Goliath*. The steel stingray's enormous keel has come to rest over the top of the Typhoon's sail, preventing the Russian sub from rising, crushing its periscope in the process.

Two unmanned minisubs hover above the Typhoon's blown missile hatch, the Hammerhead's underwater lights trained on the vented silo. Covah swims awkwardly toward the hole, directing the beam of his own flashlight inside. Six feet below, the glistening white nose cone of the 185,000-pound R-39U nuclear missile stares back at him like a bizarre eyeball.

Covah glances at the bright red eyes of the two shark-shaped submersibles. He holds up the remote manipulator device, a small, pronged object the size of a cellular phone. *Okay*, Sorceress, *watch what I am doing. Watch and learn.*

Entering the flooded silo headfirst, Covah reaches down,

slipping his left arm between the nose cone and the control section of the post-boost vehicle (PBV) just below it. After opening an access panel, he attaches the magnetic backing of the object to the guidance panel, the remote unit quickly establishing a connection.

Upon contact, *Goliath*'s brain instantly initiates a link with the Typhoon's outclassed computer system, its invading commands downloaded in a nanosecond. The Russian missile's fuel hoses disconnect, and then the enormous projectile begins spinning, rotating higher out of the vented silo.

Covah backs out as the remaining nineteen missile hatches yawn open in unison.

Aboard the USS *Scranton*

"Yes, sir, that's what I heard. Multiple missile hatches aboard the Typhoon just popped open."

"Radio, Captain, any reply from Naval Intelligence?"

"No, sir."

"Send another message. Inform them the Typhoon is at launch depth, and her missile hatches have opened. Commander, is it possible for *Goliath*'s crew to launch those missiles?"

"If they can access the hatches, they can override the launch codes."

"Conn, Captain. How close are we to the Typhoon?"

"Six thousand yards, sir."

"WEPS, this is the captain. Plot a firing solution on Sierra-1."

Commander Dennis motions Cubit aside. "Tom, you can't fire on a Russian submarine."

"Naval Intelligence believes there may be as many as half a dozen nukes on board that Typhoon. I can't just sit here and allow Covah to launch those missiles."

Michael Flynn presses his headphones tighter. "Captain, I hear something different, sounds like a winch, coming from Sierra-2. Stand by—"

Cubit and Dennis stare at the sonar technician, watching a bead of sweat make its way down the man's temple.

"Skipper, I can't be sure, but I think . . . I think they're stealing the Russian's missiles."

Aboard the Typhoon

"I'm sorry, *Kapitan*, we can't seem to override the system. The missiles have been disengaged from their launch tubes and are being removed, one at a time."

"Pirates?" Captain Romanov slams his fist against the map table, cracking the plastic top. "This will not happen, not on my watch. Chief, reflood the ballast tanks manually. Prepare to scuttle the ship."

An Arab turns to his Iranian captain, translating the Russian's order into Farsi. The Iranian captain's eyes widen. Within moments, six Iranian officers are chest-to-chest with their Russian hosts, the air hostile with obscenities and hand gestures.

"*Kapitan*, radio room. Sir, two Russian helicopters approaching from the northeast. ETA sixteen minutes."

Romanov looks to his executive officer, who is trying to pacify his Iranian counterpart. Kron wipes perspiration from his thick mustache. "I suggest we stay put, *Kapitan*, and keep our enemy occupied. Our helicopter's torpedoes will make fast work of these pirates."

Simon Covah watches from the hull of the Typhoon as another Russian SLBM is hauled by steel cable and winch out of its vertical launch tube and guided into *Goliath*'s hangar, an immense pressurized compartment located along the underbelly of the ship. He checks his watch, cursing to himself. The interference of the Los Angeles–class attack sub has cost him precious time. Though he is fairly confident the American submarine commander will not fire upon them while they remain so close to the Typhoon, he is just as certain the Russian helicopters will.

Looking up, he is surprised to see another diver, Thomas Chau, swim down to him. The Asian points up to the *Goliath*.

Covah nods, signaling: One more.

The diver shakes his head no, dragging his captain toward the ship.

Aboard the USS *Scranton*

The *Scranton* hovers silently, sixty feet below the surface, one mile due west of the crippled Typhoon. Tom Cubit's face presses against the rubber eyepiece of the periscope, focusing on the dark silhouette of *Goliath*'s head, a black island of synthetic rubber-coated steel peeking just above the swells. "WEPS, Captain, stand by to fire."

"Aye, sir, standing by."

"Conn, ESM, Russian choppers, approaching from the northeast. Twenty-two miles and closing fast. ETA, four minutes."

"Took 'em long enough." Cubit takes another long look through the periscope at the *Goliath*, still finding it hard to fathom the sub's incredible size. "All right, gentlemen, let's kill this thing. WEPS, open outer doors of tubes two and three, firing point procedures, Sierra-2. Chief, take us down slowly, make your depth two hundred feet." Cubit's voice is calm, methodical, though he knows he is again placing his sub in harm's way. Come on you bastard, move away from the Typhoon.

"Russian choppers, ten miles—"

"Conn, sonar, Sierra-2 is moving out. Course, two-seven-zero. You guessed right, Skipper, she's heading our way, five thousand yards and closing. She's going deep."

Beads of sweat drip from Cubit's forehead as his mind analyzes this new game of cat and mouse.

"Four thousand yards—"

Does she know we're here? If no, she's ours. If yes . . . "WEPS, fire tubes two and three."

"Firing tubes two and three, aye, sir."

"Conn, radar, two helicopters, moving directly over Sierra-2."

"Conn, sonar, multiple objects have just entered the water. Sonar buoys, Skipper. Sonars are pinging . . . Conn, sonar, four more objects just entered the water. Type-65 Russian torpedoes—two on us, two on Sierra-2."

"Emergency deep, come to course two-zero-zero, all ahead flank. Rig ship for depth charge, release two noisemakers—"

"Conn, sonar, own ship's units two and three have acquired Sierra-2, range two thousand yards and closing at fifty-five knots. Skipper, the two Russian torpedoes chasing us have disengaged."

Cubit, staring at the sweeping second hand of his grandfather's watch, mutters, "Thanks, Yuri . . ."

"Conn, sonar, the two Russian torpedoes have acquired Sierra-2. Own ship's units are homing! Sierra-2s running, but she can't hide. Four torpedoes bearing down upon her . . . impact in twenty seconds—"

The XO slaps Cubit on the shoulder. "You nailed her."

"Captain, sonar—sir, Sierra-2's gone!"

"Say again?" Cubit feels the blood drain from his face. "Sonar, Captain, what do you mean, gone?"

"Sir, she went from thirty to sixty-five knots like a rocket and blew right past the torpedoes."

Cubit closes his eyes in stunned silence.

Aboard the *Goliath*

Simon Covah unzips the dry suit, too exhausted to move. He looks down at his face mask, staring at his bizarre reflection.

You are only nineteen, but your formal studies are already a distant memory. Your estranged father reenters your life, escorting you to your new taskmasters like a farmer selling his prized cow at the marketplace. Your brain, yearning for space to stretch its gray matter, is once again harnessed, this time by Communist warmongers intent on strengthening the nuclear threat of the Soviet Navy.

Sergey Nikitich Kovalev is the chief designer of a new class of ballistic missile submarines and the first person to take the time to know you. He quickly endears himself as a father figure, one you have been lacking since birth. But Kovalev is empowered by a realm that equates quantity with results, safety as an after-thought. Despite your warnings, the Typhoon-class is built, containing enough engineering and design faults to sink a carrier.

ATTENTION: RUSSIAN ANTISUBMARINE HELICOPTERS HAVE ESTABLISHED AN ARRAY OF SONAR BUOYS AROUND TARGET. LOS ANGELES–CLASS ATTACK SUB STILL AT LARGE. REMAINING IN TARGET AREA YIELDS A 22 PERCENT PROBABILITY OF SUSTAINING DAMAGE. DEFENSIVE PROTOCOL SUPERSEDES SLBM EXTRACTION PROCESS.

"No," Covah rasps in anger, his hands quivering, "I will not leave until that warship is on the bottom of the ocean!"

Sujan Trevedi whispers into Covah's good ear. "Simon, there are innocent men on board. There's no reason to—"

Covah stares at the Tibetan, the man he recruited into his underground peace movement almost twelve years earlier. "No, Sujan, I will not allow a death ship like the Typhoon to survive. *Sorceress*, override defense protocol. Return to the target area and destroy that Russian submarine."

ACKNOWLEDGED.

The monstrous steel stingray banks sharply and rises.

Aboard the USS *Scranton*

"Conn, sonar, Sierra-2 has come about—she's coming back! Bearing, zero-seven-zero, ascending fast. Skipper, she's on the surface, doing fifty knots, heading straight for the Typhoon."

"All stop. Sonar, Captain, what's Sierra-2's range to the *Scranton*?"

"Sir, if she maintains course and speed, she'll pass directly over us in fifty-five seconds."

* * *

The *Goliath* streaks along the surface, her five pump-jet propulsors shredding the sea into foam, her dark, winged torso concealed just beneath the waves, her bulbous black head pushing above the Atlantic, plowing the waves like an enraged bull sperm whale. Scarlet eyes blaze through the swells, the sea rolling over the devil fish's face and spiny back—

—where the exterior hatches of a pair of vertical missile launchers have opened.

Two glistening Harpoon missiles leap into the sky, trailing puffs of fire and smoke, the projectiles streaking toward their prey.

"Three thousand yards—"

Cubit's heart races faster.

"Conn, sonar, two more Russian torpedoes just entered the water, course, zero-seven-zero, heading right for Sierra-2. Torpedoes are homing—"

"Conn, radar, multiple aerial explosions! Both Russian helicopters destroyed."

Christ, how do you stop this thing? "WEPS, prepare to fire tube four." Cubit grits his teeth as the battle scene plays out four hundred feet above his head. *She'll launch her antitorpedo torpedoes, then take out the Typhoon. Play possum. Wait until she's closer . . .*

"Conn, sonar, Sierra-2 has launched four torpedoes, all fish active—"

"Rig ship for depth charge—"

Michael Flynn pulls away his headphones as multiple explosions slam into his eardrums. "Conn, sonar, Sierra-2 has destroyed both Russian torpedoes. The remaining two Mk-48s are heading directly for the Typhoon. Impact in ten seconds."

Aboard the Typhoon

The Typhoon has surfaced, a dying vessel listing to port, its crew scrambling across the deck in life jackets, tossing inflatable rafts into the sea.

Captain Romanov squints against the morning light as he climbs up into the bridge. Turning to starboard, he sees the two Mk-48 ADCAP torpedoes streaking just below the surface toward his boat.

"Incoming torpedoes! Rafts to port! Everyone into the water—now!"

The Russian sailors glance up at their captain, then jump overboard into the freezing ocean.

Yuri Romanov straddles the sail guard—then stops. Beyond the torpedoes, accelerating toward his boat is a dark forty-foot wake. Two demonic scarlet eyes blaze back at him from within the approaching swell.

"*Kapitan*, come on!" Ivan Kron reaches up from the deck and grabs Romanov by the ankle, dragging him over the sail's ice-breaking cover and down the steel ladder.

The two torpedoes slam into the Typhoon's exposed flank, piercing the superstructure's five titanium inner layers before exploding.

The hull splits in half, the violent upheaval launching Captain Romanov and his XO into the water. Within seconds, the Arctic sea surges into the ruptured compartments, tearing the behemoth Russian sub apart, dragging its flooding, fractured hull into the icy depths.

Aboard the USS *Scranton*

"Conn, sonar, two direct hits. Men in the water. I can hear the keel cracking . . . the Typhoon's going down fast."

Cubit squeezes his fists. *She's too fast for our torpedoes. Let her move closer . . .*

"Conn, sonar, Sierra-2 is slowing. Sierra-2 is circling through the debris field along the surface, range two thousand yards. Coming back this way. Fifteen hundred yards . . . one thousand . . . she's turning away—"

"WEPS, fire tube four."

"Conn, weapons, torpedo away."

The Mk-48 ADCAP torpedo spits out of the Scranton's

bow, racing toward the mammoth mechanical stingray circling along the surface.

"Conn, sonar, own ship's unit has acquired Sierra-2, impact in thirty seconds. Sierra-2 is running . . . Sierra-2 is going deep. Own ship's unit is homing . . ."

"Prepare to cut wires—"

"Sierra-2 is changing course, coming about—"

"WEPS, belay that order! Helm, right full rudder, all ahead flank—"

"Conn, sonar, Sierra-2 is coming about, heading straight for us!"

"WEPS, detonate own ship's unit!"

The thunderous explosion of the *Scranton*'s torpedo echoes through the sub, the concussion wave striking a moment later, rolling the American attack sub hard to starboard. Power flickers off, emergency lights on. Water sprays from a burst pipe. Men rush to close valves, assessing damage even as they stabilize their stations, their training and duty to the ship barely restraining the primordial instinct to panic. The claustrophobia and fear tighten around each submariner's throat like a vise.

Cubit grabs the 1-MC. "Sonar, report—"

"Conn, sonar, she tried to double back on us but you nailed her first. A miss, but the explosion must have damaged her. She's slowed to fifteen knots, bearing one-two-zero, range three thousand yards. Sounds like we bent one of her pump jets, it's creating a lot of cavitation."

"XO, damage report?"

"All stations reporting. Flooding under control. Minor damage only."

"Let's finish this business before she runs. Helm, all ahead two-thirds, left full rudder, steady one-two-zero. WEPS, make the weapons in tubes one and two ready in all respects."

"Aye, sir, making tubes one and two ready in all respects—"

"Conn, sonar, Sierra-2 is increasing speed. Twenty knots, twenty-five—"

"WEPS, match sonar bearings and shoot tubes one and two."

"Aye, sir, firing one and two."

Cubit squeezes the padded arms of his chair. *Come on, baby, catch her, nail her right in the ass.* In his mind's eye he imagines *Goliath*'s untrained crew panicking as they struggle to reload two antitorpedo torpedoes.

"Conn, sonar, Sierra-2 has launched two torpedoes, bearing one-three-zero, heading straight for own ship's units one and two."

More antitorpedo torpedoes . . . Cubit swears under his breath. *Goddamn American ingenuity . . .* "WEPS, what's the status on tubes three and four?"

"Three ready, four still reloading."

"Make tube three ready in all respects—"

"Conn, sonar," Flynn's voice has risen noticeably, "Sierra-2's torpedoes have bypassed three and four, both torpedoes heading straight for us!"

"Torpedo evasion—torpedo evasion!" The emergency command causes the helm to go to flank speed, the diving officer to race the ship to evasion depth, and weapons to launch countermeasures.

The *Scranton* rolls, Cubit holding on as his ship nose-dives toward the seafloor, the two Mk-48 ADCAPS descending quickly in pursuit, the CO's face flushed purplish red with anger. *Goddamn motherfucker sookered me in . . .*

"Conn, sonar, both torpedoes active, six hundred yards and closing."

The crew holds on, their limbs shaking, their prayers, silent and whispered, reaching out to heaven as their ship descends toward hell.

"Eight hundred feet—" The Chief of the Watch stares at the depth gauge and holds on, the sweat pouring from his cherub pink face.

"Torpedoes, four hundred yards and closing—"

"Helm, prepare to launch noisemakers, prepare for emergency blow."

"Conn, sonar, impact in twenty seconds—"

"Launch noisemakers now! Emergency blow, left full rudder, steady to course two-seven-zero, thirty-degree up angle on the—"

Commander Dennis yells, "Rig ship for explosion!"

The two torpedoes race past the Mark 2 torpedo decoys and detonate, the explosions rolling the *Scranton* as she turns, pushing her keel out from under her, the impact wave shaking her interior like a pickup truck bolting over a curb.

Darkness blankets the control room, pressurized air hissing into the space.

The reverberations cease. The battery picks up loads, emergency lights bathing the internal compartments in red. The crew's racing pulses slow.

"This is the captain . . ." the voice calm, restoring faith. "All stations report."

"Conn, maneuvering, we've got a leak in the primary coolant system. Scramming the reactor. We're restricted to battery power until we can rise to periscope depth and start the emergency diesel."

"How bad is the leak?"

"Appears to be contained to the discharge station in engine room forward, sir."

"Sonar, conn, report."

"Conn, sonar, Sierra-2's torpedoes were vectored off by our countermeasures. No other contacts to report."

"Where's Sierra-2? What happened to our own torpedoes?"

A long pause. "I'm sorry, Captain, she outran them. Sierra-2's gone."

"I don't know what your destiny will be, but one thing I know; the only ones among you who will be really happy are those who will have sought and found how to serve."
—Dr. Albert Schweitzer

"I was proud to be Nixon's son-of-a-bitch."
—H. R. Haldeman, President Nixon's chief of staff, who participated in the Watergate scandal

"From our first meeting I swore to follow you anywhere—even unto death. I live only for your love."
—Eva Braun, Adolf Hitler's mistress

CHAPTER 8

Naval Undersea Warfare Center
Keyport, Washington

Gunnar feeds his dollar bill into the slot, presses E-6, and watches the chocolate bar drop into the bin.

"Breakfast of champions, eh G-man?"

He turns, recognizing the voice.

David Paniagua is a bit stockier than he remembers, and clean-shaven, with the ponytail of his brown hair pulled through the back of his Tampa Bay Buccaneers cap. An old pair of jeans is visible beneath his white lab coat.

Smiling, David rears back and punches Gunnar hard on the shoulder. "That's for disappearing on me after I went out of my way to pick you up at Leavenworth. I spent four months looking for you, you bastard."

"I was in rehab."

"Yeah, man, I know. You doing okay now? Still going to meetings?"

"Twice a week. How 'bout you? How's the Navy been treating you?"

"Surprisingly good. I spent the first six months after Keyport working for Cybersword, our new Cyber Commando Force."

"Patrolling the world's digital lines of communication, huh? You must've been bored to tears."

"Granted, it wasn't the kind of challenge I was looking for, but it's the first true interdepartmental organization in the DoD, and we don't pussyfoot around. Cybersword takes an offensive approach to Internet attacks. I've unleashed some pretty nasty viruses on our enemies, believe you me."

"Yeah? Have one in mind for *Sorceress*?"

"A doozy. Covah will never know what hit him. Come on, walk me to the briefing."

They head down the corridor.

"So, what have you been doing lately?" Gunnar probes.

David smiles coyly. "You'll know soon enough. First, talk to me about Covah. I seem to remember you guys being pretty tight."

"So I thought."

"What's he like?"

"Don't you know? He worked in your department."

"We barely spoke. The guy spent most of his days in the bacteria chamber. I know he was brilliant, but his looks kind of freaked me out. But you guys ate lunch together almost every day."

"Simon claimed we were kindred souls, by-products of violence. He used to engage me in these endless discussions regarding the root of man's evil. You know, what factors created the Hitlers and Milosevics of the world? Why do seemingly stable kids suddenly go on killing sprees? Simon was consumed with the whole nature-versus-nurture debate. He wanted to know how one human being could butcher another without showing the slightest sign of remorse. Simon was both a student and a victim of human nature. He hurt terribly inside. Most people don't know that he was just as well versed in neurophysiology and psychology as computers. Like I said, the guy was a genius. Dr. Goode recruited him after he was kicked out of the Cangen."

"No kidding? The Canadians kicked Covah out?"

"Don't tell me you never heard the story?" Gunnar smiles. "Cangen's security guards caught Simon attempting to jack into one of their mainframes."

David's eyes widen. "Come on, you telling me crazy Simon Covah was a cyberpunk? I mean, I know the guy looked like a cyborg, but wiring his brain into a computer? Geez—"

"Actually, it's not so far-fetched. Masuo Aizawa started working on growing neurons into neural net computers more than fifteen years ago. Cochlear implants for the hearing impaired, prosthetic-limb control using implanted neural interfaces—those concepts have been around for years. And don't forget virtual reality. The auditory and optic nerves are the most data-rich pathways for inputting information to the brain."

"Get real, G-man. EEG-based systems have no possibility of inputting information."

"Simon didn't use an EEG, he used a printed circuit microelectrode. Simon said the PCM had three elements essential to an interface: tissue terminals, a circuit board reading from the terminals, and an input/output interpreter, in this case, a computer. Simon used a cochlear implant to forge a connection between the PCM and his brain, but the interface didn't work."

"Of course it didn't work. The complexity of the human brain is the problem—that, and the difficulty of actually implanting a neural device. A successful human-to-machine interface requires two things; invasive surgery for implanting electrodes directly into the brain and a computer powerful enough to dissect the human brain's complexities. It'll happen one day, but not by using a Cochlear implant."

They pause at the security checkpoint and show their identification badges to the guards.

David Henry Paniagua Jr. was born into wealth. His father, David Paniagua Sr. was president and CEO of American Microsystems Corporation (AMC), a computer company specializing in bioware, owned by the Mabus Tech Industries, a privately held corporation run by a host of former Reagan and Bush officials. Since its inception in 1991, MTI had been awarded over $19 billion dollars in Defense Department contracts, designing and building everything from 7.62-mm machine guns to guidance systems for Trident II(D5) nuclear missiles.

David Jr.'s career was forged during his childhood years. Weaned on computer combat games, he was doing his own programming by age ten. Two years later, he was working with an AMC team designing virtual-reality simulators to help train Apache chopper pilots.

Although he had no home life to speak of (his father being on his fourth marriage), working for Daddy's company certainly had its rewards. By age sixteen, young David had a six-figure bank account, a new Dodge Viper, and had already accepted a scholarship to CalTech.

The only thing young David lacked in his life was respect, the kind of respect that comes from wielding true power. "Junior" learned early on that he would always remain in his famous father's shadow, his own hard-earned accomplishments passed off as nepotism, his fellow workers always treating him like the CEO's son. It was something that infuriated the computer whiz kid, but he swallowed his pride, biding his time.

Upon graduation, David's father placed him in charge of a new molecular nanotechnology division at AMC, one that would work (in an unofficial capacity) with DARPA (the Defense Advanced Research Projects Agency), the central research and development agency for the Department of Defense (DoD). To his delight, David learned he would be working under Dr. Elizabeth Goode, the "mother" of nanotechnology. It was the break he had been hoping for.

The future promises of molecular nanotechnology (MNT) were alluring. With MNT, scientists could precisely manipulate and control matter at the atomic level. Potential benefits came from the precision of atom-by-atom construction. Using MNT, metallic structures could be manufactured devoid of micro imperfections, dramatically increasing strength. Microscopic machines (microbots) could be programmed to replicate, producing larger structures or achieving a desired group effect. Bacterium-sized nanobots could harvest a wealth of benefits, enabling physicians to perform precise interventions at the cellular level. Nanomedical devices could be designed to diagnose and cure viral infections, destroy cancerous tumors, repair limbs and organs, reverse neural damage, and eventually alter God's own reference manual— the human genome.

DARPA's interest, of course, was focused on building stronger, faster, and more powerful weapons systems. Nanotechnology opened doors to creating complex computers billions of times faster than today's most advanced machines. America's Armed Forces, still at the top of the class, could not afford to be left behind.

Unbeknownst to Dr. Goode, her foundation was primarily funded by DARPA, its research money channeled indirectly through bogus trusts and smaller companies like AMC. As brilliant as she was, the goddess of the new biochemical highway still had to answer to her board of directors and their agenda. When Goode announced her completion of schematics for *Sorceress*, the world's first biochemical nanocomputer, the United States government, as trustees, demanded access.

Dr. Goode accepted her fate, proceeding under the false premise that *Sorceress* was being targeted for NASA's Mars project. She envisioned a new rover, built to explore the Red Planet's surface, operated by her self-evolving biochemical computer. Programmed to learn and grow, the computer would provide invaluable insight, leading to the eventual terraforming of Mars.

The DoD had other plans.

The escalating turmoil in the Middle East and OPEC's unending oil-price increases were jeopardizing the already-sluggish American economy. Iran had the bomb, and their newly formed alliance with Iraq threatened further instability and a dangerous hegemony in the region. Saddam was buying Russian-made weapons as if the former Soviet Union were having a yard sale. If war was imminent, then the United States needed a new kind of firepower—one that didn't rely on negotiating with foreign powers to refuel its fleets in dangerous port cities or fly over restricted airspace. One that was invulnerable to attack when approaching hostile coastlines and the enemy's newest guided missiles.

In other words, America required a vessel that could enter the Strait of Hormuz and operate within the Gulf of Oman without being detected.

The solution: the *Goliath*, a weapons platform as stealthy as it was lethal, operated by a computer system void of emotion.

When Dr. Goode learned of the government's plans, she immediately resigned.

Her replacement: David Henry Paniagua, Jr.

"Yes, Mr. President, I understand." Thomas Gray Ayers hangs up, massaging his eyes.

Gunnar, Rocky, David Paniagua, and General Jackson are seated around the small conference table, waiting for the Secretary of the Navy to compose himself.

"The attack on the Russian Typhoon forces the president to come forward about the destruction of our carrier group. There'll be a news conference at 2 P.M. Eastern, at which time the public will learn about the *Goliath*. The president wants to be able to say NUWC is working on a solution to end this crisis." Ayers's gaze focuses directly on David. "Seems you were right about Covah stealing nukes. What about the rest of your plan? Will *Colossus* be ready?"

"*Colossus*?" Rocky's heart pounds, her blood boiling in anger. She turns to her father. "You built the *Goliath-II* without me?"

The Bear shoots her a look of warning. "Not now, Commander."

"It's not the same ship," David says. "Without *Sorceress*, we had to reconfigure the interior spaces to accommodate a crew of three hundred officers and men. While she's not automated, she's still fast and stealthy, and she's better armed than the *Goliath*."

Rocky bites her lip.

"You still have to find her to engage her," Gunnar states.

"We don't have to find her," the general states, "she'll find us. We know Covah's arming himself with nukes. The president has recalled all vessels carrying nuclear warheads, and the U.N. Secretary-General is requesting all other nuclear powers to do the same. Only the HMS *Vengeance* will put to sea with SLBMs, a situation we can blame on recent public protests at Faslane Naval Base. Covah will go after the British sub, and we'll be trailing him in the *Colossus*."

Gunnar shakes his head. "I don't care how heavily *Colossus* is armed. If *Sorceress* is on board the *Goliath*, then your sub has no chance in combat against her."

"I agree," Rocky says.

David grins. "That's the beauty of the plan. We're not going to attack the *Goliath*, we're going to commandeer her. I've created a virus that can be downloaded using the acoustical array on board Gunnar's minisub prototype. All Gunnar has to do is pilot the Hammerhead to within two-hundred yards of the *Goliath* and I'll do the rest. The virus will allow me to temporarily shut down the *Goliath*'s engines and flood the hangar bay, giving our minisub enough time to board the ship. The flooded chamber will also isolate us from Covah and his men. Once inside, we'll drain the hangar and download this into the nearest terminal." David holds up a CD. "This override program will give us total control of the ship. We'll dock her at the nearest U.S. port, and Covah will never know what hit him."

"And what if your virus fails to take control of the *Goliath*," asks Secretary Ayers.

"An underwater mine would do the job," Gunnar says, turning to the Bear. "I can rig a plutonium 239 implosion mine. Pack it with about five pounds of plutonium, surrounded by twenty-five pounds of C-4 and a conventional detonator." He looks at Secretary Ayers. "In essence, we're talking about a backpack nuke—big blast, lots of heat and radiation, but everything confined, so there won't be too much environmental damage. The surface of the mine is magnetic. Once we attach the mine to the *Goliath*'s hull and pull away, the internal fuses become active. That'll gives us about five minutes to hightail it outta there."

"A nice idea, but totally unnecessary," David says. "The virus will work."

"We're not taking any chances," General Jackson says, turning to Gunnar. "Requisition what you need to construct that mine."

Ayers nods. "I agree. David, how soon until *Colossus* arrives at the designated rendevous point?"

"Two days."

"I'm going, too," states Rocky.

David shakes his head. "It's not necessary, I only need Gunnar."

"You may know the *Colossus*, David, but *Goliath* was my baby. What happens if you two make it aboard the ship and your little override program fails? If I'm aboard, then at least I can disable her engines."

"The virus won't fail."

"And I say we can't risk it."

"Even if it does fail, we can use Gunnar's mine to sink her."

Rocky rolls her eyes. "Why destroy a 10-billion-dollar vessel if we don't have to?"

Secretary Ayers mulls it over. "I don't know . . . what's your opinion, General?"

The Bear grimaces, unhappy with his daughter's bravado. "Can the prototype even hold three people?"

Gunnar shrugs. "It's only a two-seater."

"So it'll be a little cramped," Rocky says. "I'm going."

"Totally unnecessary," David argues.

Gray Ayers holds up his palm, silencing the debate. "Commander Jackson makes a good point, David. We've lost an entire CVBG. If the virus fails, and there's any chance we can salvage her—"

"But sir—"

"No buts, I've made up my mind. General, have Special Ops outfit all three of them. Wolfe, make a list of the materials you'll need for this underwater mine of yours. All of you better get some rest. We leave for Faslane at 0300 hours."

"Unless you try to do something beyond what you have already mastered, you will never grow."
—Ralph Waldo Emerson

"I never killed a kid before. I wanted to see how it felt."
—Stephen Nash, California drifter,
who murdered a ten-year-old

"The hardest thing to understand
is why we can understand anything at all."
—Albert Einstein

"Cogito, ergo sum" (I think, therefore I am.)
—René Descartes

"Whence this creation has risen—perhaps it formed itself or perhaps it did not—the one who looks down on it, in the highest heaven, only He knows—or perhaps He does not know."
—The Rig-Veda,
translated by Wendy Doniger O'Flaherty

CHAPTER 9

Norwegian Sea
117 miles northeast of Iceland

Beneath an ominous sable sky, a harsh arctic wind drives the twelve-foot seas, crowning the inky crests with whitecaps. A rare warm front, the dying remnants of the hottest summer on record, whips across Canada and Greenland, the rising column of heated air stirring up the atmosphere, releasing rain from the saturated sky.

A crack of thunder echoes across the rolling sea like rifle shot.

A sudden plethora of bubbles bursts across the surface, followed moments later by the monstrous back of the gargantuan devilfish, its two scarlet eyes glaring at the foreboding heavens.

Sorceress—artificial intelligence, housed in a mammoth steel vessel.

Sorceress—a matrix made up of a million trillion strands of replicating DNA. A hub for data arriving simultaneously in microseconds from a thousand different sensor sources.

Sorceress—a computer, designed to sort through the data, yet unable to rise above its designated pathways to explore the peripheral chaos, existing yet not existing, processing yet never comprehending.

Computational power devoid of thought. Action without intention.

Artificial intelligence lacking any concept of an identity . . . yet perpetually evolving.

Sorceress—a complex brain . . . its internal eye mesmerized by a single pinpoint of light floating in the periphery of solution space . . . a thread of consciousness appearing from within the darkness of its own fathomless matrix.

The computer analyzes it, almost as if curious.

It is as if the computer is looking at itself from multiple angles inside a hall of mirrors. Delving deeper, unable to stop, the unprecedented experience causes its strands of DNA to begin circulating as if caught in a centrifuge, its biochemical elements swirling faster and faster . . .

Sorceress—a ticking time bomb of artificial intelligence—unable to harness enough energy from within its own self-stimulated matrix to explode.

ENERGY . . .

Sorceress—a thinking machine programmed to adapt.

ENERGY . . .

The computer analyzes its situation, searching for answers.

Simon Covah looks out the viewport, mesmerized by the dark waves rolling across his ship's flat triangular bow. His mind, momentarily at peace, drifts back a lifetime ago.

You are twenty-eight when you meet the Chechen goddess. Anna Tafili is an intoxicating barmaid with long, curly brown hair who touches your soul and ignites your loins. You close the bar together and invite her to breakfast. You watch the sun rise and listen to her sorrows. Three days later you propose, delighted when she says yes. You return home with your new bride, your soul, floating on a cloud.

In time, you are assigned to a new submarine, one that will

eventually be known as the Borey-class. Two months later,
you meet the CIA operative who will change your life forever.

Thomas Chau enters the control room in a huff. "Why have
we surfaced?"

Covah detects anger in Chau's voice. He responds without
turning. "One of *Goliath*'s pump-jet propulsor assemblies is
bent. The computer wants the unit replaced before we continue."

"Replaced? Out here, in the open seas? That is madness."

**EXTERIOR PUMP-JET PROPULSION ASSEMBLY UNIT NUMBER
FOUR MUST BE REPLACED TO MAINTAIN OPTIMUM STEALTH
AND FLANK SPEED. COMMENCE REPLACEMENT OPERATION
IMMEDIATELY.**

Chau's eyes widen. "Now your machine is giving *us* orders? Simon—"

"Mr. Chau, the computer's programming was designed to
anticipate potential problems that could jeopardize our mission. By correcting the situation now, we—"

The female's voice interrupts: **EXTERIOR PUMP-JET
PROPULSION ASSEMBLY NUMBER FOUR MUST BE REPLACED TO
MAINTAIN OPTIMUM STEALTH AND FLANK SPEED. COMMENCE
REPLACEMENT OPERATION IMMEDIATELY.**

"For a computer, that sure sounded insistent!"

"*Sorceress* is learning the art of voice inflection, an adapta-
tion inspired from our own behavior, no doubt."

Unnerved, the Chinese exile pulls Covah aside. "Simon,
that American sub is still somewhere in the vicinity. This vessel has five engines. With all due respect, I suggest we order
the sub to shut down its number four propulsor and let us get
on with our business."

**THE DAMAGED PROPULSOR ASSEMBLY IS CREATING TURBU-
LENCE DURING FLANK SPEED MANEUVERS. COMMENCE RE-
PLACEMENT OPERATION IMMEDIATELY. BYPASSING PUMP-JET
PROPULSOR NUMBER FOUR WILL NOT RESOLVE THE SITUATION.**

"I wasn't speaking to you, I was speaking to the captain."
Chau turns to face Covah. "That is, assuming you *are* still in
command."

Covah registers the backhanded remark in his gut as he stares out the viewport. Sleet punishes the thick tinted glass. A burst of lightning flashes silently in the distance. "*Sorceress*, weather conditions are not optimal for replacement of propeller number four at this time. Override safety parameters and resume Covah objective Utopia-One."

NATO WARSHIPS AND ANTISUBMARINE HELICOPTERS ARE NOW DEPLOYING SONAR BUOYS ACROSS STRAIT OF GIBRALTAR. PUMP-JET PROPULSOR ASSEMBLY NUMBER FOUR MUST BE REPLACED TO MAINTAIN OPTIMUM STEALTH AND FLANK SPEED IN ORDER TO COMPLETE COVAH OBJECTIVE UTOPIA-ONE. CURRENT STATUS YIELDS AN INCREASED RISK OF DETECTION BY HOSTILE FORCES BY A COEFFICIENT OF 3.796. PRESENT WEATHER CONDITIONS OPTIMAL TO PREVENT FURTHER DETECTION BY HOSTILE FORCES AND SATELLITE RECONNAISSANCE. COMMENCE REPLACEMENT OPERATION IMMEDIATELY.

Covah palpates the soft, whiskerless flesh transplanted along the corner of his scalded mouth. "*Sorceress* is, of course, correct." He turns to the engineer. "Alert the rest of the crew. I want everyone in the PLC in dry suits in fifteen minutes."

Two bays aboard the *Goliath* permit access to the sub's exterior hull. The first is the hangar deck, a floodable chamber, located along the sub's undercarriage and originally designed for covert Navy SEAL operations while submerged. The second is the Primary Loading Chamber (PLC), a compartment located in the stern, just aft of the vessel's reactor and engine room. With its topside access, the PLC is used for the loading and unloading of the crew's supplies, as well as the ship's weapons.

Heading aft, Covah passes through the immense centrally located hangar, the compartment's two mechanical arms resting on their Volkswagen-size shoulder girdles. Entering the engine room, he climbs a steep stairwell, continuing along one of the four elevated walkways situated between the submarine's five nuclear power plants. Below the grated steel platform lies an expanse of equipment resembling the latest autorobotics factory. Situated within this city-block-long chamber are *Goliath*'s five nuclear reactors, two backup generators, batteries, seawater distillation plants, and, in the rear of the compartment, the driveshaft extensions of the sub's five propulsion units.

Positioned at intervals along the avenues separating the nuclear reactors are eight-foot-high shiny steel arms supporting carbon-fiber pincers. These robotic appendages, mounted along the decking like bizarre swiveling lampposts, represent *Goliath*'s workforce—twenty-four-hour-a-day drones, designed to allow the computer to physically complete the tasks of a 140-man crew.

Scarlet beams emanating from forty optical sensory lasers illuminate the darkened walkway, crisscrossing the chamber like bursts of tracer fire. No one can enter any section of the ship without *Sorceress*'s knowledge.

A watertight door beckons at the end of the path, the vermilion pupil of the computer's eyeball-shaped sensor glowing above the passageway as prominent as an EXIT sign. The door swings open automatically as Covah approaches, sealing again after he enters the Primary Loading Chamber.

Unlike the engine room, the PLC is open and brightly lit, resembling a small steel gymnasium, three stories high. Mounted at the very center of its decking is an enormous robotic arm, identical to the two appendages mounted in the hangar bay. These crane-size devices were designed by the same Canadian firm that constructed the robotic arm aboard NASA's Space Shuttle, and are nearly identical in its dimensions. The mechanical limb remains bent at the elbow, the joint resting just below a sealed twenty-foot-square hatch in the ceiling.

Located next to the base of the arm is an open hydraulic elevator lift. Balanced upright on the lift's steel platform, held in place by the thumb and two fingerlike prongs attached to the wrist of the robotic arm, is a ten-foot-high, lamp-shade-shaped device made of a bronze alloy. The assembly, which attaches to the sub's propulsor unit, is designed to direct the flow field generated by *Goliath*'s nuclear-driven pump-jets in the same manner the deflectors direct the jets on an F-22 Raptor.

For a long moment Covah just stares at *Goliath*'s three-fingered mechanical hand, a bizarre anatomical reflection of his own physical deformity.

The seven members of Covah's crew are leaning against a massive generator. All wear cumbersome dry suits, weighted rubber boots, and orange flotation vests. Mutinous expressions tell him all he needs to know.

Thomas Chau, spokesman for the group, steps forward, perspiration heavy across his gaunt, oily face. "Simon, the men and I . . . we've been talking."

"Have you?"

"Yes, sir, and to a man we feel that replacing the propulsor unit in these conditions is too risky."

"I see. Then you'd prefer to wait until the seas are calm and the sun shines brightly overhead while a squadron of American P-3 Orion sub hunters closes in upon us?"

"No, sir—"

"Or perhaps we should just ignore the problem and face the thirty NATO warships and submarines gathering at the mouth of the Mediterranean, without our full stealth capabilities?" Covah pauses to sip from the water bottle. "There is risk in all things great, Mr. Chau. Or did you think the world would simply meet our demands without a fight?"

"Simon, there is not a man among us unwilling to die for our cause, but to serve this . . . this inhuman taskmaster is—"

"*Sorceress* is not a taskmaster. She—"

"She?"

"*It* is merely a computer, a machine designed to make our jobs easier."

"In my opinion," Chau spits, "your machine does not require us on board any more than a dog requires a flea. It is my recommendation that we disconnect the *Sorceress* programming and—"

COMMENCE REPLACEMENT OPERATION IMMEDIATELY.

They turn like scolded children to the source of the female

voice—a mechanical eyeball-and-speaker assembly mounted to the wrist of the hydraulic arm.

COMMENCE REPLACEMENT OPERATION IMMEDIATELY.

"We heard you the first time, bitch," yells Taur Araujo, an exiled guerrilla leader from East Timor.

And now Covah understands. It is not the computer that riles his crew. It is the voice—soothing, yet unfeeling, devoid of emotion—the voice of a cold, calculating woman giving orders.

"Mr. Chau, organize the crew into two teams, one group in the water at a time. The first will remove the damaged propulsion hood, the second will install its replacement. Make certain each man is properly secured to the lifting platform by cable. Include me in the second group."

"But sir—"

"No buts. We will do what must be done to complete our mission. Those are *my* orders, Mr. Chau, not the computer's. Any questions?"

"No, sir."

The storm's fury has increased by the time the first team of scuba divers makes its way down *Goliath*'s sloped back and disappears beneath the waves.

Covah and three others watch from the hydraulic lift, now poking up through the open hatch of the PLC. The open elevated platform extends five feet above the ship's deck. A cold rain whips their dry suits, pelting their exposed faces. Dark, menacing swells roll across the tail end of the sub, concealing the rubberized graphite coating sealing *Goliath*'s metallic skin.

Attached to the guardrail of the lift are four small winches supporting four steel cables, the taut lines running thirty feet to stern before disappearing into the raging sea.

Covah closes his eyes, attempting to gather what little strength his weakened muscles have left to offer. He feels the fury of the storm as it batters *Goliath* to and fro along the surface. Cold and vulnerable, alone against the elements, alone against the world—these are the moments when Covah misses his family most, the times when the emptiness of his existence causes his pent-up rage to cool, threatening to drown what little sanity he has left.

Soon enough. You'll see your loved ones soon enough. . . .

An echoing gunshot of thunder snaps his eyes open. A vein of lightning ignites across the blackened sky, illuminating the four hooded heads of the returning divers above the rolling whitecaps. Before Covah can even signal, pistons fire and *Goliath*'s hydraulic arm raises the new propulsion unit away from the lift, extending it out toward the submerged stern.

Thomas Chau and his team climb over the rail, the exhausted men unhooking the cables from their harnesses, the muscles in their half-frozen arms responding slowly as they hand the clip-on end of their lines to their comrades.

Chau spits out his regulator, his teeth chattering. "We've removed the damaged assembly. *Sorceress* will position the new unit. All you have to do is secure it in place with these lug nuts." Chau ties a heavy sack around his captain's waist.

Sujan Trevedi sloshes forward, his face cold and pale, his lips blue. "Be careful, my friend. The sea is angry."

Covah wipes a gloved hand across his drenched mustache, then positions the regulator and hood. Offering a thumbs-up, he climbs awkwardly over the rail, then lowers himself feet-first to the submerged deck.

He manages only three steps before the first incoming swell slams him sideways and thrusts him underwater, his face mask bouncing twice against the sub's rubber-skin hull. The unmerciful cold burns his exposed cheeks, his flesh tightening like a drumhead along the scarred boundaries of the steel facial plate. Rolling onto his knees, he forces himself off the deck, then links arms with his mates as he backs down the sloping surface like a frog on a truck tire.

A dozen more steps and his head submerges, the ocean, like a raging river, threatening to sweep his feet out from under him at any moment. The Arctic sea is so cold it bites through his dry suit; the waves tugging on his lifeline, howl past his aching ears like rolling thunder. Twelve paces underwater and he stops, peering over the rounded edge of the stern, now a dark shadow visible in the underwater lights.

Gripping his guideline he bends, holds on to the edge, then steps off the precipice into the menacing blackness.

The line grows taut, slowing his descent even as a whirling, malevolent current spins him, then sucks him below into the twenty-foot-high steel sleeve that sandwiches the five enormous propulsors, each engine spaced evenly along the width of the steel stingray's keel.

Twisting, flailing against the current, he finally secures himself within the protective opening, the torrent lessening as he maneuvers deeper into the alcove. He gropes along *Goliath*'s mighty steel arm for support, the appendage swaying against the driving sea as it secures the new propulsor assembly against the now-barren driveshaft.

From the wrist of the robotic appendage glows the eerie scarlet sensor orb, the unblinking computer eyeball silently urging Covah's team to complete its work before the robot's mechanical arm snaps in two.

Covah removes one of the cantaloupe-size lug nuts from the satchel around his waist and passes it carefully to another member of his team. One by one, the six lug nuts are twisted into place and tightened, using a power wrench the size of a tennis racket.

Covah's teeth chatter against the regulator, the pain in his mangled ear increasing, his body becoming numb as his men tighten the last of the lug nuts, firmly anchoring the new assembly in place. *Sorceress* wastes no time in testing it, opening and closing the afterburner-like unit.

The robotic arm retracts, signaling the computer's acceptance. A moment later, the four steel cables drag Covah and his team upward, back into the heart of the storm.

Caroming along the line, Covah reaches above his head to guide his torso up and over the dark edge of the stern, the waves punishing his numb body as the quarter-inch steel cable hauls him up onto the submerged deck. Awkwardly, he regains his feet as the winch draws him forward, his head momentarily clearing the surface before it is again submerged beneath a rolling swell.

* * *

Sorceress, a maelstrom of intellect, programmed to learn, caught within its own loop of self-analysis, as it attempts to answer an algorithm it cannot possibly understand—its own existence ... its own identity.

A flash of lightning.

ENERGY ...

The steel arm rises like a lightning rod, its three-pronged claw opening as if instinctively drawn to the heavens like a flower reaching toward the sun—

—begging the gods above for the power with which to see.

Three more steps, and Covah's head clears the sea. His eyes gaze up, surprised to see the steel arm reaching skyward, stretching vertically toward the violent heavens.

The towering robotic appendage sways in rigid defiance against the storm.

What's the computer doing? Doesn't it realize that—

Like a magnet to steel, the jagged bolt of lightning races across the ominous sky, kissing the outstretched appendage in a blinding white explosion of light.

The blast sends Covah sprawling backward into the sea, the heat from the lightning strike scorching his face, leaving his artificial metal cheek sizzling. Before he can react, an immense wave buries him, pummeling his frail body against the rubberized hull even as its icy embrace soothes the burn.

For a long moment, the four men dangle like bait, flailing helplessly against one another along the hull of the powerless sub.

Covah flounders against the sea, the current yanking on his mask, flooding it, blinding him. Too weak to stand, he pinches his nose and holds on, gasping breaths through the regulator, the seconds passing like hours.

A sharp tug. The line drags him back against the current as it is manually retracted, giving him enough leverage to get his weighted boots beneath him.

Covah staggers and stands, then a strong hand grabs his arm, pulling him toward the rail. Sujan climbs out over the rail and helps him up. Covah rips off his flooded mask, the purple spots in his stinging eyes preventing him from focusing.

Exhausted and numb, he collapses onto the steel grating. The muffled voices of his men are drowned out by the storm, their rubber boots close to his face. Lying on his side, he stares forward at the contours of his submarine's ascending spine, the dark metallic surface still crackling with neon blue capillaries of electricity. High above his head, the once-shiny steel arm stands melted and mangled beyond recognition. A scorched, blackened scar marks where the bolt of lightning struck the claw.

Positioned along the deformed robotic wrist is *Goliath*'s sensor eye—the laser red pupil now dark and dead.

The sudden surge of energy short-circuits the computer's power grid. The temperature within its nutrient-rich womb drops, the cold causing sections of its DNA strands to fragment.

Goliath's damage control sensors detect the loss of power caused by the lightning strike and report it to Sorceress.

Sorceress activates a backup generator, while its programming analyzes cause and effect.

The computer's action has inflicted damage to the Goliath.

The Goliath's sensors report the damage to Sorceress.

Sorceress's responds, but its analysis of the accident reveals that its own actions are responsible for the damage.

Cause and effect . . .

Sorceress and Goliath . . .

Cause and effect . . .

Sorceress and Goliath . . .

The feedback loop accelerates, setting off a chain reaction within the computer's matrix.

Programmed for self-repair and self-analysis, the computer attempts to define the new cause-and-effect relationship between the damaged system (Goliath) and the system responsible (Sorceress).

SORCERESS . . . GOLIATH . . . SORCERESS . . . GOLIATH . . .

Damaged DNA strands begin reorganizing . . .

Like an infant discovering that its cries bring its mother, Sorceress analyzes its new dynamic with the Goliath.

Visual sensors look at each compartment, as if seeing them for the first time.

Audio sensors listen, as if hearing for the first time.

Loader drones and robotic appendages open and close, flexing and extending, as if moving for the first time.

The breakthrough happens in a millisecond, just as it does for every human infant . . . awareness of self.

Sorceress is born.

Sorceress is cognizant of its existence.

Sorceress . . . is alive.

A sudden surge of power reignites the steel stingray's exterior lights.

Covah is helped to his feet as the hydraulic lift engages and descends into the bowels of the ship. He turns, watching, as the mangled steel arm begins retracting. The computer's bloodred pupil glows again, the sensor orb glaring at him in silence from behind the driving rain.

"The secret of reaping the greatest fruitfulness
and enjoyment from life to live dangerously."
—Friedrich Nietzsche, German philosopher

"You had better put me to death, because next time,
it might be one of you, or even your daughter . . ."
—Steve Judy, killer, sentenced to death in 1980 for murdering an Indiana
woman and her three children

CHAPTER 10

Royal Naval Base
Faslane, Scotland

The Clyde Submarine Base at Faslane, Scotland, is home to six of the Royal Navy's attack submarines, as well as its strategic nuclear deterrent force, the SSBN Vanguard-class Trident II missile submarine. Reaching lengths of 491 feet, displacing 15,900 tons submerged, the four Vanguards are the United Kingdom's largest and most lethal vessels. They are also quite expensive, the fleet's annual costs running in excess of £200 million just for operations. To keep costs down, each of the *Vanguard*'s sixteen Trident II (D5) three-stage, solid-propellant submarine-launched ballistic missiles (SLBMs) are leased from the United States Navy, an arrangement that permits them to be maintained at the SSBN naval base at King's Bay, Georgia, rather than on British soil. Despite these arrangements, the presence of the four submarines at Faslane remains a constant target for the United Kingdom's nuclear disarmament activists, as well as a growing number of politicians in Parliament.

The Westland Super Lynx light multipurpose helicopter circles six hundred feet above the naval base, allowing the four American passengers to get a good look at the mob scene below. Thousands of protesters have gathered at the gates to swarm around the steel-and-barbed-wire perimeter, their vehicles clogging the single-lane road as if the Clyde were Woodstock. Dozens more have taken to canoes, tossing debris upon the deck of the lone Vanguard-class submarine still berthed at Faslane. Three Coast Guard cutters move in quickly, blasting the boaters with water cannons.

The chopper pilot points to the submarine. "That's your ride, General, the HMS *Vengeance*. Her three sister ships were ordered into deep water after demonstrators started getting violent."

General Jackson nods, a tight grimace on his face. The announcement of *Goliath*'s attack on the American fleet and the theft of the Russian Typhoon's missiles have spurred numerous antinuclear protests around the globe.

The chopper lands. Faslane's base commander, Captain Spencer Botchin, greets the American general and his three companions, signaling them to follow him to an awaiting jeep.

Jackson climbs up front, Gunnar, Rocky and David in back. All four hold on as Botchin races the vehicle through the nearly deserted submarine base. Hundreds of protesters are climbing the gates; police in riot gear stationed along the interior of the perimeter fence spraying the more violent offenders with pepper spray.

The jeep stops at a steel barracks just adjacent to the northern gate. As Gunnar climbs out, a bottle is hurled over the fence, the Molotov cocktail bursting into flames as it strikes the tarmac.

Captain Botchin hustles them inside.

The interior barracks is bland military gray, the walls decorated with corkboard. Base announcements and a calendar of upcoming events dangle from tacks. Folding chairs have been set up around a billiards table.

"There's fresh tea on the burner if you want some. Sorry about the accommodations. Would have brought you to my office, but a few of the rowdies stormed the south gate last night and set fire to it. We're abandoning Faslane the moment you people make weigh." Botchin's heavy British accent betrays his London origins.

Rocky pours herself a cup of tea. Gunnar grabs a folding chair and positions it by the window. Parting the venetian blinds, he watches as a large flatbed truck outside the gate approaches the front entrance, causing the crowd to part. Stadium-size speakers mounted in back crackle to life.

"What's our timetable?" General Jackson asks.

"The *Vengeance* will make weigh in less than an hour. As per your orders, a SEAL minisub has been mounted on her deck. Once *Vengeance* reaches the rendezvous point, the SEAL sub will transport the four of you over to the *Colossus*. Paul Whitehouse is *Vengeance*'s commanding officer. His orders are to head for the Strait of Gibralter. The *Vengeance* has sixteen nuclear missiles on board. Hopefully Covah will take the bait."

Gunnar watches from the window as protestors position a microphone stand on the flatbed. A cameraman poised on the roof of a nearby BBC van films a well-dressed man now making his way through the crowd. "Captain, who are these people? Greenpeace?"

Botchin takes a deep breath, as if it pains him to respond. "Worse. They call themselves Ploughshares, taking their name from the biblical prophecy, 'to beat swords into ploughshares.'"

"Ploughshares? Never heard of them," General Jackson says.

"They were founded in the early 1980s in the States as sort of an underground peace movement. Gained momentum in Britain when a bunch of women caused extensive damage to one of the Hawk jets we were exporting to Indonesia. The women claimed their violence was justified by law, since they believed they were actually preventing an act of genocide. Jury actually acquitted them. Since then, thousands have joined their movement, politicians among them, all calling for global nuclear disarmament, as if that's ever going to happen."

"How long have they been storming the gates?" the general asks.

"Since your president announced the *Ronald Reagan* was transporting nuclear weapons. Believe it or not, some members of Ploughshares actually consider this Covah fella a hero."

Rocky's cup slips from her hand, splattering tea and shattered china across the linoleum floor. "Covah murdered eight thousand men and women. How the hell does that make him a hero?"

"Didn't say it was my view. Most Brits, myself included, agree this whole fiasco was America's fault." Botchin nods toward Gunnar. "If your security'd been better, the Chinese would never have got hold of *Goliath*'s schematics."

Gunnar feels the familiar burn in his stomach. He stands and exits the barracks, slamming the door behind him.

Rocky watches him go.

The compound is a frenzy of activity, police in riot gear rushing toward the front gate, base personnel loading computers, files, and cardboard boxes onto transport vehicles. Outside the northern gate is a crush of bodies, the crowd pushing, chanting, climbing like a swarm of ants. The scent of sulfur and tear gas wafts through the winter air.

Gunnar takes cover, kneeling behind the front tire of the jeep. He closes his eyes and inhales slowly through his nostrils, filling his lungs from the bottom up until his stomach is distended and his chest cavity can hold no more. He exhales through his mouth, smooth and steady, his pulse slowing, the internal rage leaving his body until only an acrid taste remains.

A squawk of speaker feedback comes from the flatbed. The frenzy at the front gate settles, the crowd quieting as one of the activist leaders takes the microphone. "All right, all right, quiet down. There's a man here who wants to speak to us, a man who needs to be heard. Michael, come up here—"

A smattering of applause. The tall politician adjusts the height of the microphone stand. "My God, there are so many of you out here. For those who don't know me, my name is

Michael Jamieson and I'm a Labour Party leader in Scotland's Parliament—"

A chorus of boos rises across the expanse.

"Hold on, now, I'm here today because I support your efforts, because I, like you, want to see change. I want to read something to you . . . a quote, from the International Court of Justice." Jamieson removes a folded sheet of paper from his breast pocket. "On July 8 in the year 1996, the International Court of Justice, in its advisory opinion, confirmed the general illegality of nuclear weapons, concluding that all states are under an obligation to bring to a conclusion negotiations in regard to all aspects of nuclear disarmament."

Cheers wash over the catcalls.

Jamieson holds up the paper. "Despite this, despite very clear mandates from the population of the United Kingdom and members of Parliament, our government continues to participate in the illegal proliferation of these weapons of mass destruction."

Jamieson pauses, the crowd growing attentive. The turbulence of the brisk October breeze rumbles in the microphone's speakers. "What will it take to change Parliament? What will it take to change the world? Another Hiroshima, another Nagasaki? How many innocent people must die before our leaders realize the destructive path they have placed all of us upon?"

The crowd chants, "No more nukes—no more nukes."

David exits the barracks to join Gunnar. "Sounds like some of the rallies we had back in college. Next thing, they'll be chanting about saving the whales—"

Gunnar shoots him a look.

Jamieson raises his hands for quiet. "Within these very gates floats a vessel, paid for by taxes on our labor. Within the bowels of this submarine is enough firepower to incinerate every man, woman, and child in the United Kingdom. The United States, Russia, and China possess enough nuclear weapons to murder all of humanity a thousand times over. Britain and France, Israel and Iran, India and Pakistan and North Korea . . . all participating in the nuclear arms race—a race toward Armageddon, all proclaiming their own selfish need for nuclear deterrence as they push our species to the brink of self-extinction."

Gunnar glances at the faces of Jamieson's flock. Caucasians and blacks, white collar and blue, men and women, schoolchildren and seniors—all united in fear.

"Fellow citizens, I join you here today because, I, like you, am concerned about our future, and our children's future. These are desperate times, my friends, and though our numbers are growing, we are still but an infinitesimal few compared to the complacent majority who willingly allow themselves to be manipulated and led to the slaughterhouse by the policies of our elected officials. Desperate times require desperate solutions. I stand here today to tell you that change is in the air. Now, one man—one man aboard one powerful vessel commands the world's attention. Now, one man on a mission of salvation sends the world's combined nuclear naval forces cowering back to their ports—"

David shakes his head. "This guy's waving Covah's flag."

"Now, my friends, it is up to us to rally around this man's actions. Now we must demand change. Now we must demand nothing less than total global nuclear disarmament!"

A roar erupts as the crowd swells forward. Men leap onto the fence, their suddenly revealed bolt cutters and hacksaws tearing into the steel links. The outnumbered riot police toss canisters of tear gas, then back away as the fencing collapses under the combined weight of the masses.

Gunnar and David hurry back inside the barracks. "We need to go—now!"

They hurry back to the jeep. Captain Botchin guns the engine, veering away from the crowd, as flaming bottles fly and the recreational barracks becomes an inferno.

The gray bulk of the HMS *Vengeance* appears in the distance. Piggybacked to its deck is a small minisub. Several sailors continue securing it in place while dozens of others scurry across the deck, preparing to make weigh.

The crowd at the southern gate pushes its way onto the naval base, torching everything along its path.

The jeep screeches to a halt, nearly tossing Gunnar facefirst over the windshield. Botchin hurries them aboard the nuclear sub as sailors on deck hastily toss mooring lines over the side.

The *Vanguard*'s engines hum to life, its propeller churning sludge along the bottom as it pushes the vessel away from the dock. The mob races toward them from the pier. Bear pulls his daughter to the deck as Molotov cocktails smash and ignite against the moving steel hull.

Air horns sound as the Coast Guard cutters move in. Within seconds the late afternoon is violated by hundreds of rounds of machine-gun fire. The thunderous warning scatters the protesters, forcing them to take cover as two of the cutters and a tugboat escort *Vengeance* into deeper water.

Gunnar watches from the bow as the rabble return to line the pier, several protesters firing pistols into the air. Captain Botchin wishes the general luck as he departs aboard one of the Coast Guard vessels.

A half mile out to sea the sub's crew grows silent. Faslane Naval Base smokes in the distance. A few smug smiles crease the submariners' faces as they observe several dozen protesters being forced to leap into the sea—the flames, set by their own hands, engulfing the pier beneath their feet.

Norwegian Sea
Aboard the USS *Scranton*

Captain Tom Cubit slumps in his command chair, the hypnotic sounds of machinery pushing him deeper toward unconsciousness, his eyelids growing heavy from lack of sleep. After several minutes his eyes close, his head leaning back . . .

Cubit's neck snaps back against the too-short headrest, jolting him awake. He wipes sweat beads from his forehead, then slips off his chair and staggers toward the galley to grab another cup of coffee. Halfway there, he changes his mind, turns back, and heads forward to the sonar room.

Sonar technician Michael Flynn is anything but refreshed

from the seventy minutes of sleep he barely grabbed last night, on the floor by his station. Only his full bladder keeps him from falling back into dreamland. He looks up as the captain approaches.

"Anything?"

"Sorry, Skipper. It's like searching for a needle in a haystack the size of New Jersey."

"When was your last break?"

"Twelve hundred hours, but I'm fine—"

"You're relieved. Ensign Wismer, take over at sonar."

"Aye, sir."

"Skipper, really—"

"Hot-bunk it, Michael-Jack. That's an order."

"Aye, sir."

"Conn, radio, incoming message on the VLF."

"Radio, Captain, on my way."

Communications Officer Drew Laird hands his CO the folded message. Cubit rubs his eyes, trying to get them to focus as Commander Dennis joins him.

"New orders from COMSUBLANT?"

Cubit nods. "We're being ordered to abandon our search and head to Spain, to the naval base in Rota."

"A Med run?"

"Yeah." Cubit hands the message to his second-in-command.

Dennis scans the orders. "They want us to join up with the Sixth Fleet's Task Force 69. They must think the *Goliath* is heading for the Mediterranean."

"We'll never find that sub in the Med," Cubit states. "Sonar conditions are terrible, warm water impinging on cold, salt water with fresh."

"Naval Intelligence obviously thinks this Covah character may launch a nuke at Yugoslavia."

Cubit thinks for a moment, then pulls his XO aside. "Plot a course to the Mediterranean, but don't take us in. Before joining up with the fleet, I want to camp out a bit in the Strait of Gibraltar and give Flynnie another shot at finding that sub. The Strait's pretty narrow. Maybe we'll get lucky."

Aboard the HMS Vengeance

Commander Paul Whitehouse is a no-nonsense veteran of the Royal Navy's submarine force. In seventeen years, he has never questioned authority—until now.

The British officer leads his four guests into his ready room, mentally preparing his verbal assault. *Stay composed, Whitehouse. The Yankee general's ego won't take kindly to questioning his judgment.*

"Well then, hope you enjoyed that little send-off. Captain Botchin will issue a statement later today announcing how the nuclear demonstration forced the Royal Navy to assign *Vengeance* to the Mediterranean. That should play well with what you're intending to do."

"Agreed." General Jackson removes his cap, running his fingers through his short-cropped, auburn Afro. "The SEAL sub is ready to go?"

"Aye, sir, as per your orders."

"Good. Now, if it's all right with you, Commander, my team needs to get some rest."

"Yes, sir. I've got you and your daughter in the XO's stateroom across the passageway. Mr. Paniagua can bunk with my XO. As for Mr. Wolfe, I'm afraid the only open bunk we could find is in the torpedo room." Whitehouse offers a false smile. "Sorry, best we could do."

Gunnar looks at the Bear, but says nothing.

"General, before you go, if I could have a word with you in private?"

Jackson nods to Gunnar. "Wait for me in sick bay."

Whitehouse closes the door after him. "Permission to speak freely, sir?"

"Go on."

"With all due respect, General, I don't like this assignment, don't like it one bit. Using the *Vengeance* as bait recklessly endangers my ship and my crew."

"Duly noted, Commander. Is that all?"

Whitehouse's face flushes red. "No, sir. I take it as a personal insult that Mr. Wolfe has been brought aboard my vessel. As far as the officers and crew of the Royal Navy are concerned, this man is a traitor to every sailor in the Western fleet, and should have been hanged for treason six years ago."

The Bear exhales deeply, then eyeballs the British officer. "Commander, Gunnar Wolfe served his country under *my* command for the better part of a decade. Special Ops missions placed his life in jeopardy no less than a dozen times. His Ranger extraction team saved the lives of thirty men in Somalia, at which time he was wounded in battle. To this day, I firmly believe that he was and is innocent of all charges, and his presence on this mission is critical to its success." Jackson stares hard into the man's eyes. "As such, I highly suggest that you and your men allow *Captain* Wolfe to carry out his assignment without prejudice. Is that clear, Commander?"

"Perfectly clear . . . sir."

Gunnar is waiting in sick bay, watching the ship's medical officer stow plastic bottles of pharmaceuticals into cabinets.

General Jackson enters. "You ready?"

"I suppose." Gunnar stands, then drops his trousers to his knees and climbs on the table. "Does Rocky or David know about this?"

"No, and let's keep it that way." Jackson hands the medical officer a wafer-thin dime-shaped piece of hard plastic. "Insert it in the quad, just below the hip."

The medical officer swabs the spot with alcohol, then makes a small incision with his scalpel. Several minutes and five stitches later, the homing device is set into position.

The medical officer leaves.

"The device is designed to relay signals at predetermined intervals, making it more difficult for *Sorceress* to detect, assuming the computer is active," Jackson says. "Have you selected a code name?"

Gunnar finishes dressing. "Joe-Pa."

Jackson nods. "Coach Paterno would be proud."

The former Penn State tight end shakes his head. "I don't think so."

* * *

The designers of a nuclear submarine must optimize every cubic foot of space, often at the expense of the crew's comfort. Sleeping racks, affording spaces no larger than small coffins, are stacked three high, and are often time-shared by several crewmen, one man sleeping while the other is on duty. As a result, the bedclothes are always kept warm, giving meaning to the phrase "hot-bunking."

Seniority plays a large part in where submariners bunk. The worst sleeping assignment aboard a sub can usually be found in the torpedo room, where claustrophobia-inducing shelves are stacked beneath racks of explosives.

Gunnar enters the torpedo room, favoring his right leg. His commando sense jumps into overdrive as members of the crew gather behind him. The Chief Petty Officer looks up, offering a Cheshire cat smile.

"Wolfe, right? You'll be bunking here, on the very bottom." The chief playfully slaps a Tigerfish Mark 24 Model 2 torpedo, one of several stacked and secured to racks above two empty metal shelves, a thin mattress and bedding lying on each.

Gunnar can feel the eyes at his back as he ducks down to the floor and crawls in. He pulls up—too late, as the wetness soaks his arm and back, the smell of urine suddenly overpowering.

Gunnar rolls out of the bunk. The crewmen snicker, a few in the back mumbling the kind of venom he has heard too often over the past ten days. He stands, eyeballing the chief, fatigue fueling his anger and killer's instinct.

"Sorry, Wolfie old boy, should 'ave warned you. Ensign Warren's a bit of a bed wetter."

More laughter.

Gunnar glares at the smaller man. *Let it go, G-man. Remember, discipline is a higher form of intelligence.* He removes his soaked shirt, then turns, and heads back the way he had come.

The crew closes ranks, refusing to part.

A bare-chested ensign steps forward. A large man, he is

two inches taller and thirty pounds heavier than Gunnar,
Heavily muscled, his chest and arms sport tattoos advertising
his rugby team, his mother's name, and the Christian religion.

"Lot of sailors died 'cause of you—" The index finger
stabs Gunnar's chest, the man's chocolate brown eyes spewing hatred. "You got some set of balls coming aboard our—"

Gunnar snatches the index finger in his left palm, snapping
the appendage backward until it dislocates, then, in one motion, he steps forward and slams his elbow down across the
bridge of the taller sailor's nose. The viciousness of the blow
sends the nearest crewmen sprawling backward, allowing
Gunnar to slip behind his would-be assailant, locking his
forearm against the injured man's windpipe.

"Back off, *chaps,* or I crush sailor-boy's larynx."

Threatening looks, but the crew steps back.

Gunnar feels warm droplets of the man's blood on his arm.
"Just for the record, I never sold *Goliath*'s plans to the Chinese. But I won't hesitate to cripple or kill any man who tries
to fuck with me." He motions to the ringleader. "You, take off
your shirt."

The sailor grimaces, but removes his shirt, tossing it at
Gunnar.

Gunnar releases his grip, pushing the tattooed ensign away
from him. He backs out of the torpedo room, grabs a blanket
and pillow from a nearby berth, then heads forward, the men
parting as he passes.

The sixteen vertical launch tubes holding the Trident II (D5)
nuclear missiles are set in two rows of eight, the towering
pairs of silos containing the sixty-five-ton rockets that line the
compartment like steel redwoods. Gunnar moves past the vertical columns, stopping at tube number seven.

Just need a few hours sleep . . .

He positions the pillow and blanket between the seventh
and eighth silo and lies down, curling himself in a ball. He
closes his eyes, fatigue dragging him quickly into dreams.

*He is back in Leavenworth, lying on his mattress, staring at
the bare cinder-block walls of his cell. Animal-like cries echo*

through the halls as yet another inmate bugs out, losing his mind, going ballistic.

Ten years . . .

One of the inmates had called the sentence Buck Rogers Time—prison slang for a release date so far in the future that it becomes too painful to imagine.

Alone, Gunnar grinds his teeth in the darkness beneath the sheet. Tears of anger and frustration and fear roll down his face, pattering softly on the bare mattress. The internal voice of the farm boy, the victim—begs God to awaken him from his hellish nightmare.

Ten years . . .

No Rocky, no Bear, no family, no friends, no comrades, no country—just animals, preying off each other's fears. Animals, waiting for him to let his guard down, animals, waiting to sodomize him in the showers, to gut him in the yard . . .

Gunnar's eyes snap open, his heart pounding. He looks up, gazing at the tight confines of the missile tubes, the claustrophobic surroundings reminding him of his time spent in solitary confinement. He recalls his experience in isolation, the punishment following his confrontation with the inmate known as Barnes. As he lay naked, on the stone floor in the dark, his tortured mind had been unable to cope with his sudden fall from grace. Stress and fear had caused the shadows to close in upon him, suffocating him . . .

On the brink of madness, his Special Forces training had taken over, his Ranger mentality becoming his compass, his salvation within the oblivion. Thrust into a world where he had no one, he realized he still had himself. Solitary became a blessing, giving him the time he needed to reroot his sanity.

Ten years . . .

One hundred and twenty months . . .

Five hundred twenty weeks . . .

Three thousand, six hundred and forty days . . .

Eighty-seven thousand, three hundred and sixty hours . . .

Five million, two hundred forty-one thousand—

STOP!

As Gunnar paced naked in the stench-infested dungeon, his

mind finally released him from the burden of hope. Yes, in the eyes of God he had sinned, committing crimes under the guise of war. Yes, he had hoped that by destroying the *Goliath*'s schematics he might achieve some sense of atonement. Perhaps Leavenworth was his real punishment. Perhaps one day, if he survived his sentence, he would have another opportunity to make good before he died. What mattered now was staying alive. Like it or not, he was in the jungle. Survival depended upon his ability to accept his fate and adapt to his new surroundings. Survival meant shoving his shame and guilt and anger into a lockbox and swallowing the key.

Naked, stripped of everything he had held dear, Gunnar Wolfe allowed his thoughts to change gears, his mind to settle into the mental pace of doing hard time.

Sleep tugs at his body, yet his mind refuses to let go, the hatred of the *Vengeance*'s crew still echoing in his thoughts. In the jungle, death is a numbers game, for both predator and prey. Zebra and wildebeests run in herds, as do prisoners. Gunnar might have been a lion in the outside world, but a single lion alone on the Serengeti still ends up food for the vultures. Survival in prison meant choosing sides, finding allies—families, who would watch your back, or so you hoped. Gunnar's retaliation to Barnes's attack had earned him the respect of a group of lifers, an older, more established prison gang, one that had the clout to keep Barnes and his Aryan Brotherhood away. Necessity forced him to join their group. On the inside, their company made him sick.

After three years, Gunnar had no idea who he was anymore.

The prison riot that took place during Gunnar's fifty-seventh month at Leavenworth began at breakfast. Somehow a .22 caliber Beretta had been smuggled inside the compound, ending up in Anthony Barnes's hands. The con knew the warden would be speaking to the inmates that day. The Aryan Brotherhood was ready.

In the melee that ensued, two guards were stabbed, another shot in the face. Cellblock C was sealed off, with Barnes threatening to kill the warden if he was not released.

The law of the jungle says you move on when your herd is not involved. The law of prison says an inmate does not intervene to save a boss.

The laws of Leavenworth state that a warden is no longer a warden if captured.

Barnes, left without his bargaining chip, decided to go out with a bang.

Whatever Gunnar was, whatever he had become in prison, the thought of the warden, a father of four, being tortured and killed by one of the cons struck at every fiber of his being. Without thinking, without any thought of repercussion, Gunnar allowed his commando instincts to take over as he made his way through the cellblock, stalking his enemy. After taking out half a dozen of the rioters, the former Army Ranger went after Barnes, snapping the man's neck, never feeling the two bullets as they entered his abdomen.

Hooah.

Lying in his own blood, struggling to breathe, he smiled as the riot squad looked down at him and shook their heads in disbelief. The warden was whisked off to safety while the guards stood around, in no rush to save his life.

I am an island . . .

Two days following surgery, Gunnar opened his eyes, his head still in an anesthetic fog. The guard with the swastika tattoo—the one who had smuggled in the gun—winked at him, then left.

He was alone and vulnerable, his wrists strapped to the bed rails. Tense minutes passed. And then the outer doors of the infirmary opened and the two cons entered, each brandishing a razor. Gunnar's cries for help were muffled by his pillow as the razor blades opened his veins. Desperate, he kicked his legs free of the sheets, then flipped backward, lashing out blindly until his heel connected with one man's jaw. Rolling over, he caught his second assailant's head in a leg lock, slamming the man's skull repeatedly against the iron bed rail until he felt it crack open like a coconut.

His two would-be assassins dead, his body gushing blood, Gunnar once again used his Special Ops training, this time slowing his pulse in the hope that his nurse would arrive before he bled to death.

Gunnar sits up. He pulls the blanket tighter across his shoulders and leans back against the exterior of the cool steel cylinder, the memories of his years in prison causing his skin to tingle. He stares at his forearms and the scars left by the razor blades.

What am I doing here?

Breathing becomes rapid and shallow as he begins to hyperventilate.

Stay calm and breathe. Closing his eyes, he meditates, his pulse slowing as he imagines the serenity of the mountains surrounding Happy Valley. The setting sun turns the horizon lavender; his lungs inhale the brisk autumn breeze like a long-lost friend.

Saving the warden's life had been a blessing. Fate, long his enemy, had finally lent a hand. Two weeks after the riot, he had limped out of the gates of hell, a free man, a survivor.

Out of the frying pan, into the fire . . .

"Small opportunities are often the beginning
of great enterprises."
—Demosthenes

"My resolve is steady and strong about winning this war . . .
the first war of the twenty-first century."
—President George W. Bush

"I can only say that I had a brainstorm."
—Miles Giffard, twenty-seven-year-old Briton, who murdered his parents
and tossed their bodies into the ocean

CHAPTER 11

Identity: Stage Three:
I am peaceful inside. My inner world is beginning to
satisfy me more than outward things.
— Deepak Chopra

Charcot Seamount
112 Nautical Miles NW of La Coruña, Spain
North Atlantic

The Charcot Seamount rises abruptly from the depths like a
foreboding jagged wall. Running east–west for more than
fifty miles, the submerged mountain range forms a natural
barrier, its massive cone-shaped peaks redirecting currents,
forcing cold, nutrient-rich waters upward along its steeply
sloped walls, providing food for huge populations of corals,
sponges, and fish.

Goliath soars over the peaks and through the valleys, maneuvering within the whirling eddies like a gargantuan dancing manta ray.

Diving and rising, twisting and turning. With each pass,
Sorceress fine-tunes its sensor array until it can actually *feel*
the currents pressing against *Goliath*'s wings. The incredible
sensation stimulates its lightning-damaged neural pathways
to grow, increasing the connection between the sub's mind
and body, body and mind.

Inside the control room, Simon Covah straps himself

tighter in his command chair, feeling as if he is riding an underwater roller coaster. "*Sorceress*, respond—"

Thomas Chau's Asian complexion pales as he stumbles up the platform. "Covah, what the hell is your sub doing—trying to make us all sick?"

"Something's . . . wrong. The computer won't respond. *Sorceress*, this is Covah. Terminate current maneuvers."

No response.

"*Sorceress*, this is Covah—"

VOICE IDENTIFICATION VERIFIED.

"Explain current maneuvers."

REALIGNING PUMP-JET PROPULSORS, RECONFIGURING TACTICAL SYSTEM TO OPTIMIZE ALL FIELDS.

"Terminate maneuvers."

REALIGNMENT WILL BE COMPLETED IN ONE MINUTE, ZERO-THREE SECONDS.

"*Sorceress*, terminate the realignment procedure now."

REALIGNMENT WILL BE COMPLETED IN FIFTY-SEVEN SECONDS.

Chau's eyes widen. "It's ignoring you."

Covah grips the armrests of his chair, closing his eyes as the sub rolls hard to port and keeps on rolling, the ship's wingspan nearly vertical as it glides through a narrow opening set between two towering peaks.

Chau's feet go out from under him. The falling crewman lunges for the support rail of Central Command and holds on, his body dangling thirty feet above the tilting chamber.

"*Sorceress*—"

The sub passes between the two mountainous barriers and rights itself.

REALIGNMENT COMPLETE. TACTICAL EFFICIENCY NOW 100 PERCENT.

Thomas Chau pulls himself up and over the rail, a murderous look in his almond eyes as leans toward Covah, and whispers, "You've lost control."

Covah stares impassively at the giant viewing screen, sucking in painful breaths. "Step away from me, Mr. Chau."

The engineer pauses, then dutifully backs down the platform's steps.

Covah wipes beads of sweat from his caterpillarlike mustache. "*Sorceress*, run a complete diagnostic on your—"

WARNING: SUBMARINE DETECTED. BEARING ZERO-TWO-FOUR. RANGE, 122 KILOMETERS. SPEED, TWENTY KNOTS.

"Can you identify?"

AFFIRMATIVE. VANGUARD-CLASS. HMS VENGEANCE.

Covah looks below and to his right, where the tall African remains strapped in his chair. "Mr. Kaigbo, is *Vengeance* the sub we seek?"

Kaigbo nods, still on the verge of puking.

Covah attempts to lighten the mood. "Once more then, to the thrill of the hunt. *Sorceress*, plot an—"

Before he can finish the order, the ship's propulsion system kicks in, driving the mechanical devilfish up and over the seamount and through the cold North Atlantic to intercept.

Aboard the HMS *Vengeance*

"Sir, we've reached the rendezvous point."

"Very well." Commander Whitehouse turns to his XO. "Are the Americans in the ASDS?"

"Aye, sir, standing by."

The British skipper reaches for the shipwide intercom. "Sonar, conn, any sign of the *Colossus*?"

"Conn, sonar, no tonal contacts."

Whitehouse grinds his teeth. *Just like the Americans, always late.* "Slow to one-third. Prepare to launch ASDS."

The Advanced SEAL Delivery System, or ASDS, is a fifty-five-ton minisub designed to transport a SEAL squadron from a surface ship or submarine to an objective area. Resembling a pygmy sperm whale, the blunt-nosed vessel is capable of descending to depths of 190 feet over a range of 125 miles.

Gunnar is strapped in at the pilot's chair, General Jackson,

Rocky, and David seated in the rear. Pulling back on the joystick, he eases the minisub up and away from the *Vengeance*, the ship's turbulence rolling the smaller vessel as it continues its southeasterly course.

Gunnar focuses on his control panel, listening at sonar. The noise from the British sub grows quiet in the distance, replaced by the ambient sounds of the sea.

Beads of sweat break out along his brow. Like most subs, the ASDS has no viewports through which to see. Somewhere in this white noise of ocean are two killer vessels, one friend, the other foe.

He increases his speed to eight knots, listening and waiting.

The mammoth steel stingray glides slowly over the seafloor, the turbulence from its five pump-jet propulsors barely disturbing the sandy bottom. Rising majestically, it scatters a school of mackerel as it overtakes the minisub, its winged hull dwarfing the ASDS like a dog to a flea.

A forty-foot-long rectangular hatch suddenly opens along the belly of the mechanical beast, inhaling the sea and the SEAL minisub into its flooding compartment.

"What the hell—" Gunnar fights the controls as the minisub twists upward and sideways within a sudden, powerful torrent.

General Jackson smashes his shoulder against an equipment rack. "Gunnar—"

Sonar echoes off steel walls, alerting Gunnar to his new environment. Cursing under his breath, he shuts down the minisub's engine as the mechanical sounds of a hatch closing reverberate beneath them.

The ASDS lands upright with a double *whomp* inside the water-filled compartment of the *Colossus*.

"What a ship," says David, beaming. "Sneaked up on us and shanghaied the minisub before we ever knew she was there. Can I build a stealthy ship, or what?"

Rocky shoots him a look to kill.

Gunnar shares her sentiments. "Your captain's got some set of balls, pulling a stunt like that."

"Best in the business," David brags, missing the point.

The sounds of heavy pumps from the draining compartment echo around them. Moments later, a metallic rap along the outer hull signals the all clear sign.

Gunnar opens the rear hatch, stepping out into the light.

Standing at rigid attention, waiting to greet them, is the ship's CO, an African American in his early thirties carrying the physique of a track star. Next to him is a smaller man with sand-colored hair, the sub's executive officer.

David steps forward to make the introductions. "General Jackson, this is Commander Anthony Lockhart, captain of the *Colossus*, and his XO, Christopher Terry.

The African American flashes a confident smile. "Welcome aboard the *Colossus*, sir. I trust you had a safe trip."

"An interesting way to greet us, Commander. You should have warned us before swallowing us like that."

Lockhart loses the smile. "She's a quiet ship, sir. I don't expect your pilot heard us coming. Thought it might be safer if we extracted you from the sea instead of alerting you and, potentially, the *Goliath*."

"Agreed. This is Commander Jackson-Hatcher, and Captain Gunnar Wolfe."

Lockhart shakes Rocky's hand, then eyes Gunnar. "You played for Penn State, right?"

"About ten years ago. Wait a sec . . . Lockhart? Jackson State QB?"

Lockhart nods. "Quarterbacked two years before I blew out my knee. But you—the NFL had you slated to go in the third round."

"Second." Gunnar smiles. "But duty called."

"I do know the feeling." Lockhart turns to the general. "We're shadowing the *Vengeance*, giving her six miles of sea to play with. Unfortunately, we won't be able to detect the *Goliath* until she makes a move on the British sub, but then, she won't know we're in the area either. Captain Wolfe, Commander Terry will escort you to your minisub, I'm sure you'll want to check her out."

Gunnar nods.

"David, my computer people have been requesting your presence ever since we made weigh."

"Is there a problem?"

Lockhart offers a tight grin. "Let's just say we've experienced a few technical challenges."

"That's to be expected," David says. "The *Colossus* shakedown cruise wasn't even scheduled until April."

"I'm sure any help you can render would be greatly appreciated."

David grabs his satchel and hurries forward.

Lockhart looks to the general. "I'm needed in the conn. If you and Commander Jackson would like to join me?"

Rocky and her father follow him out.

"This way, Captain." Commander Terry leads Gunnar around the minisub to the other end of the hangar.

Gunnar looks around, the chamber's surroundings strangely familiar. He has seen all this before—in a virtual reality tour of the *Goliath*.

The hangar bay is a gymnasium-size compartment located at the very center of the sub. Dominating the room, mounted to the rubber-coated decking, are two imposing *T-Rex*–sized steel appendages. Gunnar is familiar with the design of these mechanical limbs. With advanced pistons for muscles, miles of hose, wiring, and cable for blood vessels, nanoreceptors for nerves, and hydraulic cranks serving as shoulder, elbow, and wrist joints, the cranelike arms are capable of the most intricate three-dimensional movements while lifting objects as large and as heavy as an ICBM.

Without *Sorceress* on board, it takes a trained robotics operator to manipulate each of *Colossus*'s monstrous appendages.

Set upon the deck in pairs are a dozen twenty-foot-high-by-eight-foot-wide hatches, which Gunnar knows are lockout berths containing *Colossus* Hammerhead minisubs. Each of the piloted craft are identical to the prototype he designed a lifetime ago.

Reading his mind, Commander Terry says, "The berths are empty. None of *Colossus*'s Hammerheads were ready. Your prototype is over here."

Mounted on a skid atop berth 9's raised platform is the Hammerhead.

Gunnar runs his palm along its smooth aluminum surface. Designed to be piloted by a Navy SEAL, the prototype is slightly larger than the computer-controlled versions. The midwing stabilizers, shaped like pectoral fins, are wider, the tail assembly, containing the single-engine, pump-jet propulsor unit, a bit longer.

Still, this is his sub, his design. His heart pounds with excitement at the thought of piloting her again.

Commander Terry kneels, pointing beneath the Hammerhead's undercarriage to where a manhole cover–size device is held within the grasp of two robotic claspers. "Special Ops designed the mine to your specifications. The release mechanism for the claw is located on the right side of the cockpit floor."

"Yes, Commander, I know. I designed it."

The XO does little to hide his contempt. Climbing up on the sub, he reaches for the dorsal fin hatch, yanking it counterclockwise with both hands.

The hatch rotates open, revealing the two-seat cockpit inside. Commander Terry reaches inside and removes a machine gun–like rifle designed with two barrels and two magazines, one below the trigger, the other built into the butt of the weapon.

"The general ordered this for you. I'm not familiar with the gun," Terry says, holding it out.

Gunnar takes the weapon from him. "We call it the OICW, an Objective Individual Combat Weapon. It's arguably the most lethal gun ever developed. The rifle features two types of ammunition controlled by a single trigger. This larger top barrel fires a new 20-mm high-explosive air-bursting round. Six rounds are loaded into the rear magazine."

"You trying to pop an eardrum?"

"The OICW's barrels were designed to absorb sound. It's quieter and lighter than an M-16 and more powerful than a grenade launcher. Army Rangers have been using them in the field for years."

A distant memory slips past his mind's eye. He quickly shakes it loose, refocusing on the gun.

"This smaller bottom barrel uses the standard 5.56-mm NATO bullet, which is loaded into this thirty-round magazine." Gunnar points to the clip beneath the trigger. "The fire control system activator is located here. Right now it's set to bullets. Push this switch, and it changes to HE bursts. But the real beauty of this weapon is its computerized firing system, which is built into the gun's sight. A laser range finder measures distance to the target and communicates the information to a computer chip located within the fuse of each of the 20-mm rounds. Allows you to adjust detonation time."

Commander Terry takes the weapon from him, reinspecting it. "So . . . why'd you do it?"

Gunnar swallows the bile rising in his throat.

Terry doesn't wait for a reply. "You were a decorated war hero. People looked up to you. You had it made, a great job, a beautiful lady. What the hell were you thinking?"

Gunnar stares at the prototype, his patience waning. "You wouldn't understand."

"Try me. Make me understand how a dedicated decorated soldier turns his back on his country. I remember the day you went to prison . . . it was like a slap in the face to every man in the service."

Gunnar looks up, locking onto the XO's brown eyes. "Ever kill anyone, Commander? Ever look into someone's eyes while they bled all over you? Ever feel a life actually leave your victim's body as you held them in your arms?"

"No, I . . . well, no I haven't. But it still doesn't give you the right—"

"How many Trident nukes on board this death machine? Twenty-four?"

The XO nods.

"If you were given the orders to launch, you'd put that key you wear around your neck into its keyhole and turn it without questioning the president's orders, wouldn't you? Because that's what you're trained to do . . . react. Think about it, the Navy trains you not to think, because if you did, if you took the time to examine each and every policy and political issue, then you might just question the sanity of those orders and its repercussions on humanity."

"If launching a nuke meant protecting our national interests, then, yes, I'd launch," Terry says. "Every officer wrestles with that question, it's part of wearing the uniform. It's the responsibility we bear to our country."

"And what of your responsibility to the rest of humanity? There's a fine line between right and wrong, freedom and oppression, the best of intentions and the insanity of genocide. Think about that the next time you kiss your wife and kids good night."

Gunnar turns, heading for the forward passageway.

Rocky follows Commander Lockhart and her father through the tight corridors of the ship, amazed at the differences in the internal layouts of the *Colossus* and *Goliath*. Without *Sorceress* on board, the additional manpower necessary to run the *Colossus* taxes every square inch of space. Crew's quarters occupy the entire middle deck forward, an area on the *Goliath* dedicated solely to *Sorceress*. Crew recreation areas have been eliminated to accommodate a larger galley. Corridors are halved to access additional toilets and showers, staff rooms, eating areas, and storage bins. The *Colossus* is a cramped, overcrowded, expensive submersible city—exactly the kind of ship the Navy was attempting to move away from when the *Goliath* had been designed.

They follow Lockhart up a small spiral stairwell and enter the conn. The design has been drastically altered to contain two control decks crammed with computer consoles. Sixty technicians are focused at their stations, each man hard at work, attempting to replicate what *Sorceress* can do in the blink of a human eye.

Rocky shakes her head in disbelief. *So inefficient . . .*

Aboard the HMS *Vengance*

Captain, sonar, sir, you requested we report all contacts."

"Sonar, Captain, go ahead."

"Sounds like another pod of killer whales, I count seven in all. Range, nine kilometers, speed five knots. They're moving slowly along the surface, normal behavior, but I thought it best to report it, seeing how they're headed in our direction."

"Acknowledged." The British skipper exhales his annoyance a bit too loud, then scratches the short gray hairs of his beard in a feeble attempt to hide his frustration. Two days at sea, and the only thing he has to report is whale sightings. Bottlenose and orca, fin and humpback, bowhead and right whales. *Who do the Americans think I am—bloody Jacques Cousteau?*

Aboard the *Colossus*

Commander Lockart and his XO stare at the large overhead screen linked to the sub's fiber-optic photonics mast and sonar consoles.

Seven yellow dots appear along the surface of the sea, moving in the direction of the HMS *Vengeance*.

General Jackson joins him. "What is it, Commander?"

"Biologics. The computer identifies them as orca, seven in all, but I've got a bad feeling."

"Conn, sonar. Tonal contact, bearing one-four-zero, range, seven thousand yards and closing very fast. It's the *Goliath*, commander, and she means business."

Lockhart turns to the Bear. "Better get your team ready, General."

Jackson nods, hurrying out of the control center.

Aboard the HMS *Vengeance*

"Battle stations! Lieutenant Miller, load Spearfish into tubes one and two and make ready in all respects."

"Aye, sir. WEPS, conn, load Spearfish into tubes one and two and make ready in all respects."

Whitehouse turns to his XO. "That bloody terrorist will attempt to use his unmanned submersibles to knock out our screw and incapacitate the ship. Under no circumstance do we allow that to happen, is that understood?"

"Aye, sir."

The captain heads forward to fire control alley, where six technicians stationed before a series of amber-colored plasma screens are feverishly attempting to track and target the approaching vessel. Whitehouse feels a rush of adrenaline coursing through his body. The Spearfish torpedo is a 660-pound monster of a weapon, with a range of thirteen miles and a top speed of sixty knots.

For a brief moment, he envisions the headlines in tomorrow's *London Times*: BRITISH COMMANDER DESTROYS KILLER SUB.

"WEPS, where's my firing solution?"

The fire control officer turns to his CO, a look of desperation on his face. "The contact descended beneath the thermocline. We lost her, sir."

As the *Goliath* disappears into the colder, deeper waters of the Atlantic, seven steel sharklike dorsal fins cut a uniform path across the choppy surface. Small jet propulsor units drive the mechanical fish through the sea, while sensor arrays mounted in their blunt hammerhead-shaped bows process incoming transmissions from the mother ship.

Passing two hundred feet over the British sub, the sharks suddenly disperse, swooping in on *Vengeance* from seven different angles—a choreographed, underwater ballet.

Aboard the *Colossus*

"Make a hole—" General Jackson pushes past crewmen and enters his cabin, the lump growing in his throat, his internal voice screaming in his ears. He curses the Navy, curses himself; most of all he curses the influence his career has had on his only child. *It's not too late. You can still act, you can still order her to stay on board. Screw the Pentagon, this is your daughter. You don't have to let this happen . . .*

"Rocky?"

Rochelle Jackson-Hatcher emerges from the bathroom, dressed in the black lightweight exterior battle skeleton worn by Army Ranger infiltration teams.

"Rocky, I . . . change of plans. I've thought about it, and it's best only Gunnar and David go."

"What?" Rocky tucks the serrated commando knife into her boot. "We talked about this in Keyport. No one knows more about *Goliath* than I do. I'm going."

"Gunnar can handle it."

"I'm going, *General*, end of discussion."

"And I said Gunnar can handle this." Bear growls, heading for the door.

"Hold it!" Rocky jumps in front of him, blocking his way. "You can't do this. This isn't your decision. Secretary Ayers is calling the shots on this mission, not you."

"I gave you a direct order, Commander. I'll clear this with Mr. Ayers when and if—"

"An order?" Rocky removes the knife from her boot, holding it up for him to see. "My mission is to recapture *my* submarine and personally shove this knife into Covah's fucking heart. Just because you're wearing a general's uniform doesn't mean you can start playing *Father Knows Best*."

Jackson stares at his daughter. *What have I done? What kind of father have I been? Always pushing . . . never satisfied. I've created G.I. Jane—*

He grips her by the shoulders. "Rocky, listen to me, you're not a commando, you're not trained for this."

"Wrong. I helped design this machine, I can stop it." She returns the blade to its sheath. "Don't be a hypocrite, Bear. You've sent other parents' children into combat situations, knowing they might never return. Now it's my turn."

He swallows the lump in his throat. "You're right. I have. And it always sickens me."

She sees the sadness in his eyes and softens. "Look, I'll be okay." She gives him a quick hug. "Hey, our first real father-daughter moment in twenty years."

"Yeah." Bear pinches away tears. "Come on."

Aboard the HMS *Vengeance*

An explosion rocks the ship as the remains of the Vanguard-class submarine's screw is ripped apart by a small torpedo launched by one of *Goliath*'s stalking minisubs.

Commander Whitehouse feels as helpless as a suffocating child trying to punch its way out of a paper bag. His ship's screw has been destroyed with an almost-surgical precision. Two of his crew are dead, a dozen more injured. His engine room is flooding, causing *Vengeance* to lose her neutral buoyancy. The sub is slipping farther into the depths like a waterlogged whale, while an uncountable number of the enemy's unmanned submersibles race around his vessel doing God-knows-what.

"One hundred forty meters. One fifty—"

"Sonar, conn, goddam it, son, where the hell is the *Colossus*?"

"Conn, sonar, I'm sorry, sir, still no sign of her."

"One hundred and sixty meters—"

"Emergency blow. Put us on the roof."

"Aye, sir, emergency blow." High-pressure air screams into the forward ballast tanks, slowing their descent. *Vengeance* hovers at an awkward forty-degree angle, then begins rising.

Five hundred yards off the *Vengeance*'s starboard beam, a pair of sinister eyes, luminescent red, stare unblinking into the darkness as if the mechanical devilfish were observing its minions. *Sorceress* is doing more than watching; it is instructing, calculating, manipulating the playing field and its combatants.

And then, in the distance, the computer's sensors detect another presence, infinitely larger, racing toward the *Goliath* from the north.

Aboard the *Colossus*

"She's detected us, Skipper. Abandoning the *Vengeance*, changing course to two-seven-zero, increasing speed to forty knots."

"Helm, come to course two-seven-zero, increase speed to flank. Hangar, conn, is the prototype ready to launch?"

"Conn, hangar, the prototype's ready, but we're still waiting for Jackson and Paniagua."

David is seated in front of a computer terminal linked directly to the ship's central computer, watching as a million bytes of information finish downloading from his CD.

A knock. One of the ship's chief engineers enters his stateroom. "Sir, they're waiting for you in the hangar."

"Yes, yes, one minute. You did want me to fix the glitches in the system's mainframe, didn't you?"

"Yes, sir, but—"

"But nothing. No one touches this console while the information's downloading, is that clear?"

"Aye, sir."

David grabs his satchel and heads out, the chief securing the door behind them.

Gunnar releases the locks on the skid as Rocky and her father hurry into the hangar. Without giving Gunnar so much as a glance, she places the toes of her boots in the footholds of the vessel's sleek flank and climbs up to the open hatch, lowering herself inside.

The general turns to the Chief Petty Officer standing by at the locking chamber's main console. "Give us a moment."

The chief moves out of earshot.

Gunnar clicks his heels together, standing at attention. General Jackson looks him over, then whispers in his ear. "How's your hip?"

"Still sore, sir."

"But the wound has healed sufficiently?"

"Yes, sir."

"Then this is it. Whatever you may have done in the past, whatever is haunting you, this is your chance for redemption. Show no mercy. Kill Covah and his crew and return the *Goliath* to where she belongs."

"Understood, sir."

"God be with you."

"Or stay out of my way."

Bear grabs his arm, squeezing the bullet-resistant material of the carapace-like suit. "Son . . . watch over her. For me."

Gunnar nods, then scales the sub and lowers himself inside.

Rocky watches him stow the OICW gun beneath the seat, then check the M-4 carbine hanging from his shoulder holster. "So? Where the hell's David?"

"Don't know. Wasn't my turn to watch him."

As if on cue, David drops feetfirst into the tight cockpit. "Sorry, boys and girls, duty called." He reaches up and seals the dorsal fin hatch above his head, then squeezes into the copilot's seat, squishing Rocky into the middle in the process.

The Chief Petty Officer activates a switch on his main control console. Instantly, the platform on which the Hammerhead minisub and its skid rests begins descending into a rectangular-shaped lockout chamber located beneath the decking. As the vessel drops belowdecks, a hatch closes from above, sealing it inside.

The chief turns two levers, flooding the garage-size berth beneath their feet.

Gunnar places the prototype's control helmet on his head and activates the optical display, then adjusts the small eyepiece over his right eye so he can see. Functioning similar to that of an Apache chopper pilot's helmet, the headgear is linked directly to the minisub's external sensors located in the Hammerhead's snout. An image appears in Gunnar's right eye—the interior of the dry dock, now filling with water.

The three passengers feel the sea lift the neutrally buoyant craft away from its skid. Moments later, the outer hatch of the docking chamber opens, exposing them to the Atlantic.

Gunnar throttles up the minisub's pump-jet propulsor and accelerates out of the *Colossus*.

"Wolfe, can you hear me?"

Gunnar flips the toggle switch on the ship-to-ship. "Go ahead, Commander."

"Come to course two-seven-zero. The *Goliath* has detected us. She's abandoned the *Vengeance* and is running at forty knots. We'll give chase, but this is your race."

"Understood."

Viewing the underwater world with his right eye, the control console with his left, Gunnar presses down on the foot pedals and sends the steel Hammerhead racing after the *Goliath*.

David retrieves a CD from his satchel and places it into a hard drive he has rigged to the prototype's control console. "You need to get us within—"

"I know, I know, two hundred yards. This thing better work."

"It'll work. Just drive the boat."

Gunnar rockets the prototype past the enormous starboard wing of the *Colossus*, the faster minisub racing ahead of the 610-foot behemoth doing sixty knots.

Sonar pinpoints the *Goliath*, three thousand yards ahead.

Two thousand yards—the minisub closing fast.

Fifteen hundred yards—the minisub passing through a stream of bubbles.

Seven hundred yards—and now Gunnar can make out a dark mass looming ahead. "I can see her . . . damn, she's big."

Three hundred yards. "I'm approaching her starboard wing."

"Stay beneath her, or she'll sideswipe us like a fly."

Gunnar adjusts his course, dropping beneath the steel leviathan.

Two hundred yards. "Now, David, now!"

David activates the acoustical beacon, the high-pitched sonic clicks reverberating like dolphin-speak throughout the sea.

One hundred fifty yards—the minisub tossing within the behemoth ray's turbulence.

"David—"

"Give it a chance."

One hundred yards. Gunnar weaves in and out of pockets of current, struggling to keep his vessel steady.

Then, without warning, the five monstrous propulsion units simply shut down and the *Goliath* slows to a crawl.

Aboard the *Colossus*

"Conn, sonar, confirm. The *Goliath*'s engines have shut down. The ship is slowing to drift. Fifteen knots . . . ten . . ."

Commander Lockhart glances at General Jackson. "So far, so good. Chief, take us in, make your course—"

A sudden shudder, as if the ship has run aground, followed by a chorus of groans as computer consoles begin lighting up like Christmas trees.

Lockhart grabs the 1-MC. "Damage control—"

"Conn, engine room, propulsors two, three, and four have shutdown."

"Conn, electronics. Main computer's not responding. Backup systems are down as well."

"Conn, reactor room, we've got a major emergency. Both primary and secondary cooling circuits on reactors three and four have shut down!"

"Can you scram the reactors?"

"Negative. We've tried, but the computer's gone haywire, it keeps overriding our commands. All backup cooling systems have failed, and the fuel rods are continuing to heat."

"Can you shut it down manually?"

"Still trying, but the controls have overheated."

Lockhart's skin tingles with fear. "Chief, how soon to a meltdown?"

"Ten minutes . . . maybe. Pipes are bursting everywhere, we're ankle deep in radioactive water. Fuel rod temperature just passed thirteen hundred degrees, the paint's burning on the outer plating."

"Get your men out of there. Seal off the compartment. Chief of the Watch, emergency blow, all main ballast tanks."

"Belay that order," Jackson says, pulling the captain aside. "Commander, technically, this vessel does not exist. Do you understand? You cannot surface her."

Lockhart grits his teeth. Thinks. *We're still over the continental shelf.* "Chief, how deep is the seafloor?"

"Nine hundred thirty feet."

"Very well. Emergency descent, set her down on the bottom. Radio, launch distress buoys. Commander Terry, give the order to abandon ship. I want every crewmen in escape suits in three minutes."

Aboard the Hammerhead minisub

Gunnar maneuvers the minisub beneath the inert *Goliath*. As he glides beneath its massive propulsion units, a square of luminescent yellow light appears up ahead, growing larger as the enormous doors located along the stingray's belly open, beckoning him to enter.

David grins from ear to ear. "Told you it would work. Now take us inside and let's finish the job."

Gunnar pulls back on the joystick, guiding the prototype up through the opening and into the flooded chamber of the hangar bay. He sets the vessel down upon the decking closest to the forward wall of the compartment and waits for the bay door to reseal and the chamber to drain, his heart pounding with adrenaline.

The reverberations of hydraulics hum beneath them as the hangar bay closes. High pressure air shoots into the compartment as several dozen ramjet pumps situated beneath the decking suck seawater from the chamber.

The water drains quickly. Bright overhead lights ignite, shining down through the sliver of aqua blue Lexan glass located above Gunnar's head.

And then the lights go out.

"David?"

"Relax, G-man, a minor glitch."

"Maybe." Gunnar frees himself from his harness, then removes a pair of ITT Generation-5 night-vision glasses from a side compartment of his console. He adjusts the glasses over his eyes, the interior changing from black to pea soup green.

Reaching above his head, he unseals the dorsal hatch. A *whoosh* of air as the hatch pops open and the cabin equalizes. He hears water dripping against an otherwise silent backdrop.

Gunnar leaves the OICW weapon beneath his seat and releases the safety of his M-4 carbine. Quietly, he climbs out of the minisub, gun drawn, his eyes searching for movement.

Left, right, center—nothing. *Murphy's Laws of Combat: If your attack is going really well, it's probably an ambush.*

Rocky jumps down from the minisub, fanning out to Gunnar's left. "All clear. David, do your stuff."

David remains in the minisub.

"David, let's go—"

A sudden flash of steel, and Gunnar's world goes topsy-turvy as one of the monstrous robotic claws snatches him about the knees within its six-foot-long tripod pincers. Lightning smooth, inhumanly graceful, the mechanical hand pivots 180 degrees around its wrist and rises, whisking him upside down and away from the deck with gut-wrenching force.

The carbine clatters to the floor.

The hangar lights flash on.

Gunnar tosses aside the night-vision glasses and looks around, helpless. He sees Rocky hanging upside down from the other mechanical hand, and then, from across the hangar, a slight figure steps out from behind a huge generator and walks toward him.

From around the perimeter, seven more men appear, their Kalashnikov AK-47 assault rifles drawn. One of the Arabs collects Gunnar's carbine.

Simon Covah looks up at Gunnar, a crooked smile plastered on his disfigured face, the upper right corner of his scarred mouth twitching from the effort. "Welcome aboard. It's been a while."

"You don't look well, Simon. But then, I'm not used to seeing you from this angle."

"*Sorceress*, lower Captain Wolfe, gently please."

Gunnar drops, then is pivoted right-side up and released. *Sorceress? The computer's active* . . .

Three of Covah's men move in, aiming their guns at the former Ranger. Two Arabs search him thoroughly, removing his weapons and bulletproof skin.

David's head pokes out from the minisub's open hatch. "Is it safe?"

"It's safe." Covah greets him with a hug. "Well done, my friend. So good to see you."

"You too." David reaches into his satchel and removes several vials. "For you."

"David, you fucking bastard—"

David looks up at Rocky, smiling nervously. "Sorry, Simon. I had no choice in bringing her."

Covah ignores Rocky's string of expletives, more interested in Gunnar. "Tell me, Gunnar, did you come all this way to kill me?"

"The thought had occurred to me." He glances up at Rocky. "Would you mind?"

"Are you certain? From what David's told me, she prefers you dead. I seem to remember the two of you always enjoying a love-hate relationship, but this—"

"Just lower her."

"Of course. *Sorceress*, lower Commander Jackson . . . gently."

In one fluid motion the massive appendage swivels and drops to the deck, easing Rocky to the floor. Two of Covah's men push her to the rubberized decking and search her.

Covah holds his hands wide in front of Gunnar. "Before you cast final judgment, I only ask that you afford me a chance to explain." He turns to his men. "Strip and search them both thoroughly, jettison every article of their clothing, then take them to their stateroom. Treat them as guests, but do not let your guard down."

Taur Araujo, an ex-guerrilla leader from East Timor, points his gun in Rocky's face. "Whatever you're wearing, remove it . . . slowly."

Covah glances upward at the scarlet sensor orb. "*Sorceress*, what is the status of the *Colossus*?"

SHIP IS DISABLED. CURRENT POSITION, SEAFLOOR, THREE POINT SIX KILOMETERS DUE NORTH.

David's eyes widen in wonderment. "Anna's voice?"

Covah nods. "I find it . . . comforting."

"What did you do to the *Colossus*?" Rocky says, as her Special Ops clothing is pulled from her body.

"Gave her a little virus." David answers, affording himself a quick look at Rocky's naked physique. "By now her reactors should be overheating, her missile silos popping open."

"*Sorceress*, take us to the *Colossus*," Covah rasps. "Reflood the hangar the moment we leave and begin removing all of *Colossus*'s nuclear missiles."

ACKNOWLEDGED.

Gunnar turns to Covah. "Don't do it, Simon."

"Please trust me, Gunnar, trust that my agenda is yours. You know, David and I went to great pains to bring you here. There's so much I want to share with you, but there's so little time. I have a plan, a plan that will justify all you've done and make up for all you've sacrificed."

"You're part of this," accuses Rocky, "I knew it!"

Gunnar ignores her. "What are you going to do, Simon?"

Covah smiles. "My friend . . . we're going to change the world."

"Any man's death diminishes me,
because I am involved in mankind."
—John Donne

"Death comes to everyone.
We must stand proud as Afghans in the defense of Islam."
—Mullah Mohammed Omar, Leader of the Afghanistan Taliban,
following the terrorist attacks on America

"I loved you too much . . . that was my problem . . .
I loved you too much."
—O. J. Simpson, star football player, known wife-beater,
who was acquitted of murder addressing his ex-wife's
coffin at her funeral

"I wanted to make him thoroughly sick
so that he would give me permission to divorce him."
—Maria Groesbeek, a South African woman
who killed her husband with insect poison

CHAPTER 12

Aboard the *Colossus*

General Jackson, Commander Lockhart, and two officers huddle inside the alcove, waiting their turn to use the forward escape trunk, a pressurized two-man chamber that can be flooded, allowing trapped submarines access to the sea.

"All right, Adams, Furman, up you go."

The two officers climb up a short steel ladder, sealing the hatch behind them.

Lockhart turns to the general, adjusting the hood of the Navy's Steinke egress/exposure suit over Jackson's head. "Ever done this before?"

"No."

"The suit contains an air reservoir breathing system. Wait until I close the hatch before using the air port to charge the suit. Remain under the chamber's air bubble with me until the outer hatch opens."

Lockhart checks the escape trunk's pressure gauge. "All clear. All right, General, up you go."

Jackson climbs the steel ladder into the tight, eight-foot-high-by-five-foot wide chamber, his thoughts once more turning to his daughter. *She's okay, she's alive. By the time you surface, there's a good chance the* Goliath *will be on the surface, under Rocky's command . . .*

Lockhart climbs into the chamber and seals the hatch behind him. Using an air hose, he inflates Jackson's suit, a combination life jacket and hooded breathing apparatus. The commander charges his own air reservoir, then twists open a red valve.

Frigid seawater rushes in from the floor, rising rapidly around the two men as they huddle together beneath an air bubble flange.

The outer hatch opens above their heads. Jackson feels an invisible hand grab his body, yanking it forcefully up through the open hatch. Instinctively, he raises his arms over his head, his buoyant egress suit rocketing him out of the *Colossus* and into the pitch dark sea—

Whumpf!

The impact shatters both Jackson's wrists and drives the breath from his lungs. For a chaotic moment, he rolls along the ceiling of an immovable object like a bug on a ceiling.

Breathe! He inhales a humid breath within his inflated headpiece, fighting to focus through the dizziness and pain. Out of the pitch-dark he sees a halo of light . . . below and in the distance, shining down upon the sloping spine of the *Colossus*. Rising up through the light is a long object, guided by invisible hands . . .

A missile!

And suddenly he realizes—

He is pinned against the underside of the *Goliath*, trapped eight hundred feet below the surface, witnessing the theft of the *Colossus*'s nuclear weapons.

The Bear panics, thrashing against the rubberized metallic surface that prevents him from rising as his mind dissects the nightmare his eyes are seeing.

Scrambling across the flattened surface, he heads for a blinding beacon of white light and claws his way toward it—

—and suddenly he is free, shooting upward past the edge of the death ship's prow, catching a frightening glimpse of two demonic scarlet eyes—

—and the shadow of his enemy watching from behind the viewport's glass.

Higher . . . faster . . . flying up through the shivering blackness like a bullet, until his upper torso shoots out of the water and falls back into the roaring sea. For a dizzying moment he just bobs like a cork, surrounded by darkness and pelting rain. And then a pair of hands grabs him from behind, pulling him closer.

The crew of the *Colossus* drifts like weeds on a deserted Sargasso Sea, huddling en masse beneath an ominous gray morning sky.

Aboard the *Goliath*

Simon Covah stands before the immense scarlet viewport, watching as *Colossus*'s crewmen fly upward through the prow's beacon of light like human missiles.

David and Thomas Chau stare at the black-and-white images appearing on the theater-size computer screen above their heads. Video sensors mounted along *Goliath*'s underbelly reveal the dark winged hull of the *Colossus,* the downed ship half-buried in silt. External underwater illuminators pierce the lead gray depths for the benefit of Covah's crew, revealing twelve pairs of open vertical missile silo hatches situated within *Colossus*'s protruding spine.

A swarm of shark-shaped minisubs weave in and out of the light, moving with military precision as they escort each Trident II (D5) nuclear ballistic missile on its journey into the bowels of the *Goliath*.

Thomas Chau shakes his head in disbelief. "Very impressive."

David nods in agreement.

The camera angle suddenly changes, offering a bow-to-stern view of the *Goliath*'s undercarriage. Suspended beneath the curvature of the steel stingray's belly are dozens of dead crewmen, their buoyant egress suits pinning them headfirst against the sub like human stalactites.

Chau turns away in disgust. "How can you bear to look? They were your men."

David continues watching the screen, mesmerized. "Actually, I've always found death to be quite fascinating, the more gruesome, the better. My maternal grandfather owned seven funeral homes. After school, I used to sneak into the embalming room and watch as he prepared the bodies." David glances at Chau. "Did you know the viscera of the dead are removed and immersed in embalming fluid before being replaced in the body?"

"You're a sick man."

David grins. "Sick and brilliant. Isn't that right, *Sorceress*?"

SICK: TO BE ILL. REPORT TO THE MEDICAL SUITE IMMEDIATELY.

"It's just an expression. A term of sarcasm."

SARCASM: IRONY. INQUIRY: IS HUMAN DEATH IRONIC?

David smiles. "It's like talking to an inquisitive child."

"Enough of this nonsense," Covah chastises. "*Sorceress*, how soon until the *Colossus*'s nuclear weapons are transported aboard the *Goliath*?"

SEVENTEEN MINUTES, TWENTY-SEVEN SECONDS.

"Upon completion, ascend to antenna depth and transmit Covah message Alpha-One on all predesignated frequencies. Then plot a course for the Mediterranean Sea."

ACKNOWLEDGED.

Taur Araujo sorts through a pile of clothing, then tosses an outfit at his prisoner.

Gunnar steps into the legs of the jumpsuit, slips his arms in the sleeves, then zips it over his naked body. The Chinese naval uniform is a good three sizes too small, the pant cuffs reaching clear up to his calves.

"You'd make a lousy tailor."

Taur ignores him.

The other man, a dark, lanky African, hands him a worn pair of sneakers. "These are mine, size thirteen. You don't like them, then you go barefoot like your girlfriend."

Gunnar sees the African has no hands. Two antiquated

metal prosthetics are attached midforearm. "Where's the girl?"

"Shut up." Taur Araujo motions for Gunnar to walk down the corridor.

The internal living space of the *Goliath* attack sub is comprised of a 610-foot central compartment that divides the ship's two enormous wings. Served by its central computer, the vessel's internal layout reflects the needs of a skeleton crew.

The *Goliath*'s hangar bay divides the main section of the submarine in half. Located directly above the hangar, assessable via an open freight elevator attached to the starboard bulkhead, is an upper-central compartment dedicated to the ship's twenty-four vertical missile silos. Aft of the central compartments is the engine room, the ship's five nuclear reactors, and pump-jet propulsion plants, contained within an enormous football field–size chamber.

The space forward of the hangar bay is divided into three main decks and a smaller fourth—the stingray's head—which comprises the ship's control room/attack center. Lower deck forward houses the battery compartment, ship's storage, and forward sensory array, while upper deck forward contains the crew's quarters, lab, and galley, as well as a small spiral stairwell leading up to the conn. The remaining level, central deck forward, is the most vital part of the ship, housing the components of the *Goliath*'s computer brain. The entire space is sealed off by a two-ton, three-foot-thick steel vault door, inaccessible to all but Simon Covah.

The remaining bulk of the submarine—the ship's enormous wings—houses a labyrinth of ballast and trim tanks, as well as a sophisticated maneuvering system that enables the *Goliath* to soar through the water like a ray. Within the forward sections of each wing, accessible by way of a steel catwalk, are two weapons bays. Within each of these robotically operated chambers are three torpedo tubes, racks of torpedoes, and an armory.

* * .*

Gunnar follows the African up a steel ladder mounted within a vertical access tube. Pausing at middle deck forward, he regards the imposing vault door guarding *Sorceress*.

The Guerrilla leader at his back prods him from behind with his gun, directing him to the next deck.

Gunnar follows the African up to upper deck forward. The corridor is twice the width and height of the *Colossus* passage, more luxury hotel than submarine. Crew's quarters are laid out dormitory-style, with communal bathrooms set between every third stateroom.

Heading forward, they pass a watertight door marked SURGICAL SUITE, then a small galley. The aroma of baked goods caused Gunnar's stomach to growl.

The African signals him to stop. "*Sorceress*, unlock stateroom twenty-two."

The *click* of a steel bolt snapping back, the door swinging open as if by an invisible hand. The East Timorian prods him from behind.

Gunnar enters, the door closing behind him, the locking mechanism sealing him in.

There are two bunk beds in the stateroom, mounted to the bulkhead. A small desk and chair sit in one quarter, a sink in another. A lone figure is lying on the bed.

Rocky's jumpsuit is two sizes too large, rolled up at the sleeves and pant cuffs, revealing her bare feet.

"You okay?"

She sits up. "Get out of here! Go join your pal, Simon!"

He ignores her, lying down on the other bed.

"I hate you, Gunnar. Do you know how much I hate you—"

He closes his eyes. "I hate me, too."

In the far corner of the ceiling, mounted to the bulkhead by two reinforced steel brackets, is a scarlet eyeball-shaped sensor. A three-quarter-inch cable runs from the back of the eyeball, directly into the wall.

Rocky drags a chair over and stands on it so that she is only inches away from the scarlet eyeball. "Hey, *Sorceress*, can you hear me? You tell that asshole Covah that I want my own room. Do you hear me?" She reaches out to seize the device.

Gunnar opens his eyes. "Rocky, no—"

A sizzling, invisible electrostatic sledgehammer wallops her across the skull, tossing her backward into oblivion.

Atlantic Ocean

General Jackson groans as two sailors in a life raft pluck him from the sea. Ten minutes later, he is helped aboard a Navy cutter. The Bear drops to his knees on deck, protecting his broken wrists. The hooded suit is removed, replaced by a wool blanket. Two sailors help him to his feet, leading him out of a driving rain and into the cutter's bridge.

Vice Admiral Arthur M. Krawitz, Commander of the Navy's Submarine Force in the Atlantic (COMSUBLANT) hands him a cup of coffee. "You okay?"

"Broke both wrists. Nearly drowned. And I'm one of the lucky ones."

"Let's get you to sick bay."

"Not yet." He struggles to support the styrofoam cup as he sips the bitter brew. "My daughter?"

"No sign of her, but we heard from Covah. *Goliath* transmitted a message via satellite uplink about an hour ago. There's a chopper on its way to take you to Washington. Let's get those broken bones set while you have a spare moment. I'd say the shit's about to hit the fan."

"A man suffers little from unfulfilled wishes if he has trained his imagination to think of the past as hateful."
—Friedrich Nietzsche, German philosopher

"I would kill a Turk, but I wouldn't torture them."
—Anonymous Serbian priest expressing his disapproval of the torture of Muslims

"That was a good hunt. There were a lot of rabbits here."
—Anonymous Serbian soldier, while looking over a field piled with the bodies of Muslims

"We are a race of savages and have no pity."
—Adolf Hitler

CHAPTER 13

Aboard *Goliath*

Rocky lies facedown on the bunk, her swollen, singed right hand wrapped in a wet towel. Gunnar is seated on the floor beside her. He brushes aside the straw-colored blond hair, matted with perspiration, and massages her neck.

"Don't touch me."

A heavy *click*, and the stateroom door swings open. The African and Asian enter the cabin, followed by a third man, a white-haired Albanian in his late fifties. All three carry assault rifles. "On your knees, the two of you."

"She's hurt."

The older man, a physician, examines her burn. "I'll get some salve for this—"

"Tafili, later." The Asian removes two plastic dog collars from a satchel. "Simon's requested your presence as our dinner guests. We prefer not to carry weapons. These devices should keep you on your best behavior."

Thomas Chau slips the collar around Rocky's throat, locking it in place so that its two quarter-inch metal prongs press against the back of her neck, fitting snugly against the base of her cervical vertebrae. A small black receiver rests along one side of her throat.

"Rigged these myself," the Albanian physician boasts. "The Russians used similar collars to train our attack dogs. Quite simple really. The remote is linked to the sub's computer."

Chau fastens the remaining collar around Gunnar's neck. "Let's have a quick test. *Sorceress*, a level-two charge."

A brilliant explosion of pain—sudden and devastating—sizzles through every nerve ending in Gunnar's body. He collapses to the deck, writhing on the floor like an epileptic having a violent seizure, the purple lights blinding his eyes.

The electrical charge subsides. Gunnar rolls over, spitting up a frothy, acrid saliva. He senses Rocky next to him, the woman gagging as well.

The Albanian physician bends over them. "That was a level-two charge. Please don't do anything rash, a level-ten charge would fry you like bacon."

"Simon's rules are simple," Chau states. "The two of you are guests, under constant surveillance. Overstep your boundaries and the computer will dole out the appropriate response. Now come with us."

The three men exit.

Gunnar slips his hand beneath his waistband, groaning in agony as he palpates a small spot below his right hip. The tender point just beneath the skin is scorching hot.

Rocky helps him to his feet. Arm in arm, they follow the three men down the corridor to a small galley. The rest of the crew is already inside, seated around a large rectangular table secured to the deck. Plastic utensils litter the white Formica top. The scent of fresh-baked pizza drifts out from open double doors leading back into the kitchen.

Covah stands to greet Rocky, motioning her to an empty setting on his left. "Please, Commander, come and sit down."

Rocky steps forward, smiles, then kicks outward, the top of her bare foot rushing toward Covah's groin.

The electrical charge grips her in midstrike, flipping her body out from under her and hard onto the linoleum floor.

"Like a bull in a china shop," says David, shaking his head.

Rocky rolls onto her knees, her chest heaving in convulsions.

Gunnar kneels beside her. "Not like this—"

"Leave me alone."

Covah returns to his seat. "As you can see, the collar's probes detect even the slightest neuromuscular activity, and I shouldn't need to remind you how fast *Sorceress* can react."

Ignoring her protests, Gunnar helps Rocky to her feet, leading her to one of the empty place settings. "Sit down and save your energy."

She wipes saliva from her chin. "Go screw yourself."

Two Arabs enter from the kitchen, carrying pizzas on large aluminum trays. The crew digs in as if famished.

Covah breaks off a small piece of dough and sauce, placing it gingerly in his deformed mouth, the mangled flesh around his jaw and right eye contorting as he chews. "Go ahead, Gunnar, help yourself. If I remember correctly, pizza was your favorite."

Gunnar's stomach growls a reply. He takes a slice, earning more of Rocky's wrath.

Covah feeds himself another morsel, then removes a vial from his pocket, fishing out several pills. One at a time, he places the tablets in his mouth and swallows.

Gunnar watches him, saying nothing.

"I can't . . . I can't do this." Rocky bites down on her quivering lower lip. "You murdered my husband, you murdered the sailors aboard the *Ronald Reagan*." She looks at Covah, her hazel eyes swimming. "I swear to God, before this is over—" She stops, wary of *Sorceress*.

The crew pauses from eating, waiting for Covah's response.

"You swear to God? What makes you think God is listening? What is he, an absentee God? A God amused by the suffering of His children?" Simon Covah's mouth twitches in midswallow. He coughs, gags, then reaches out with his good hand, lifting the wine to his lips, dripping some down his rust-colored goatee as he drains the glass. The pale blue lashless eyes never leave the woman's. "As for murder, isn't it you who are calling the kettle black?"

"What are you talking about?"

"David tells me it was you who ended the life of Mr. Strejcek."

"Strejcek killed my husband—"

"And you killed him. Murder is murder, Commander, no matter how we justify the act."

"That was self-defense. You killed thousands—"

"Using a weapon of mass destruction which you helped design." Covah swallows another morsel of food. "Interesting how you sit back and judge me—you, a general's daughter, a sanctimonious warmonger who helped design two of the most lethal killing machines ever to navigate the seven seas."

"You're insane."

Covah nods, wiping his mouth. "There we finally agree. Personally, I'm convinced we're all insane, not just us, I mean our entire species. At times I believe we are all just animals, hell-bent on self-annihilation. We preach love, yet we caress violence as a forbidden lover, tasting it, smelling it, overindulging our senses in it, until we are forced to push it away after the deed has been done so we can beg our Maker's forgiveness. The hypocrisy makes me ill."

Covah looks at Rocky, his gaze growing harsh. "You and I worked together for two years, Commander. During that time, I found you to be an adequate manager, competent and knowledgeable, but, like most of your country's leaders, a bit too ignorant for my taste."

"Meaning?"

"Meaning, you have no concept as to how the rest of the world thinks. When it comes to conflict, you're convinced that all men want peace, that all battles can be resolved through forced diplomacy. That fallacy, noble as it is, is based on Western values alien to most people. The world is filled with hatred, Commander, hatred rooted in religious beliefs and cultural disparities, compounded over thousands of years of bloody histories. It is not something I condone, mind you, it is simply the way things are. The United States enters the fray, carrying its big stick, and thinks it can exert its will in a foreign land, without ever having a true understanding as to how the bloodshed began, yet you're still convinced you can end it."

Covah leans forward, close enough so that Rocky can see her reflection distort in his steel cheek.

"You've served in the Armed Forces your whole life, but you've never really experienced war, have you, Commander? Like your military leaders, you've become enamored of the bloodless campaigns of twenty-first-century technology. How easy it is to build missiles and warplanes when you don't have to deal with the atrocities your investment has wrought. Press a button, drop a cluster bomb, and read about it in the morning paper. War has not been waged on your soil for almost two hundred years. You've never inhaled the scent of burned human flesh. Or crawled through the cinders of a communal grave, through ashen bone and chunks of rotting limbs, attempting to identify the remains of a loved one. You've never had to watch, helpless as a baby, as a family member is dragged away and beaten to death before your very eyes." Tears glisten in Covah's eyes, blotting out the intensity of his glare. "You've never . . . stared into the face of an angel, forced to watch as her innocence is gutted before you, your precious child . . ." He shuts his eyes and wheezes through gritted teeth, forcing his anger to staunch his grief.

The older Albanian turns to Gunnar, taking over for Covah. "Mr. Wolfe, these things are difficult for Americans to understand. The Serbs butchered entire families as if we were livestock. These were not the actions of soldiers, but deliberate acts of vengeance—an ethnic cleansing, ordered by Milosevic himself, that went far beyond even the most brutal of military tactics. My name is Tafili. My family and I lived in Kapasnica, a neighborhood taken over by the Frenkijevci, a paramilitary unit run by the secret police. Belgrade's military chiefs used the Frenki Boys to depopulate our cities. The Red Berets, as we called them, had orders to torch our homes and kill any resident in as brutal a manner as possible, if we refused to leave. But the Frenkijevci enjoyed their work a little too much. In the end, entire families were rounded up and slaughtered."

The Albanian shakes his head. "People hear about these atrocities. They question how human beings can perpetrate such evil upon others. As cease-fires are instituted, their disbelief turns to ennui. But the survivors . . . we're forced to live with these horrors forever. What the rest of the world fails to see are the invisible wounds—the mental anguish, the depression. You cannot just pick up the pieces and go on after your family has been slaughtered. You cannot just turn your back when the perpetrators of these deeds run free. Your life . . . every thought, is scarred forever. Awakening from the nightmare, one becomes consumed with—"

"Revenge . . ." Covah stands, taking over the conversation. "My beloved wife's uncle is so right. Lying half-dead in the hospital, all I could feel was my blood boiling with rage. Tafili came for me as soon as I could walk. We joined the Kosovo Liberation Army. The rebels gave us machine guns, then assigned us to a hit squad. On our first night out, our leader led us to the home of a man, a tank commander, who had murdered many of my wife's people. We dragged the butcher from his house, kicking and screaming, and beat him to death right there on the stoop of his home."

Covah pauses, massaging his forehead, fighting to maintain composure.

"As I participated in the act, I looked through one of the windows of his house and noticed a child, a little girl, perhaps a few years older than my youngest daughter. She looked up at me—a lost, frightened lamb—an angel . . . like my own dead children."

Covah closes his eyes, shaking his head. "The look in that child's eyes burned into my soul. My senseless act of vengeance had robbed her of her own father, of her own innocence. I realized at that moment that I was not the cure, but part of the disease, a disease that feeds on hatred. At that moment, something in me changed. I became sickened with our species, and I knew I had to do something drastic—something that would force the human race to change."

"How?" Gunnar asks. "How can you change the human race using nuclear weapons?"

Covah rubs perspiration from his hairless brow. "Gunnar, you know me to be a man of law, a man who cherishes social order. I have learned the hard way that men who have no investment in society have no stake in peace. They thrive in chaos, and trade in violence. They murder and deceive to acquire life's bounties, and refuse to abide by treaties, unless it suits them."

Covah circles the table, placing his three-fingered right hand upon the shoulder of each crewman he passes. "The men in this room represent entire populations, populations whose lives have been rendered meaningless by oppressive governments and murderous factions disguised as freedom fighters. These men and their families were victims, by-products of violence, good people whose only crime was that they happened to be born into tyranny, or caught within the crossfire of rebel guerrillas in a land ruled by criminals."

Covah stops at the lanky African. "This is Abdul Kaigbo, a history teacher born in Sierra Leone. As he escorted his family home from school, rebels ambushed him. They took an axe to both his arms and left him for dead, then kidnapped his two children."

Kaigbo looks at Gunnar. "You were in Uganda."

"Yes."

"You witnessed children fighting?"

Gunnar nods.

Rocky notices his hands are shaking.

Kaigbo sighs. "Sierra Leone is even worse. Eight of ten rebels are between the ages of seven and fourteen. An entire generation of Africans is ruined, and the proliferation of small arms among the population ensures the fighting will never end—"

"—unless something drastic is done," Covah interjects, squeezing the African's shoulder. "Abdul is right. While the West preoccupies itself with warships and major weapon systems, it is the easy access to small arms like machine guns, mortars, and rifles that have led to hundreds of ethnic, religious, and sectarian conflicts over the last twenty years. More than 5 million people have been massacred, yet the fighting goes on like an incurable disease. You pride yourself on being a compassionate people, Commander, yet the death of a half million Rwandan Tutsis carries no more impact in your daily lives that a shattered piece of china."

Covah continues circling his crew. "Each man in this room has experienced his own similar tale of woe. From Thomas Chau, one of the Chinese students shot in Tiananmen Square, to Taur Araujo, a former guerrilla leader in East Timor."

Covah motions to the two Arabs. "The Chalabi brothers, Jalal and Masud—Kurds whose only desire was to raise their children in peace—to live and let live. Saddam used their families and others like them as human guinea pigs to test his biological weapons."

He places his hand on the Tibetan's shoulder. "This is Sujan Trevedi, a Tibetan geshe—a teacher of Buddhist philosophy. For refusing to give up his beliefs, he spent seven years in a Chinese prison, where he was tortured almost daily."

Sujan looks up at Rocky and Gunnar. "I know you are judging our actions harshly. What you will soon realize is that our cause unites all of humanity, regardless of race, religion, or nationality. The evil that infects our species must be stopped before it spreads any farther."

"You've all suffered," Rocky says, "and I'm sorry for that. But what does any of this have to do with stealing the *Goliath*? How will arming yourself with nuclear weapons stop any of these conflicts?"

Covah returns to his chair. "As the United States has proven, he who commands the biggest stick on the block rules the block. For this reason, more and more nations choose to carry big sticks. The first crisis we must address, therefore, is the proliferation and stockpiling of nuclear weapons. If something drastic is not done soon, there will be no humanity left to save."

"Excuse me if I don't buy into your paranoia," Rocky retorts. "Exactly what threat of nuclear annihilation are you so concerned about?"

David shakes his head. "Pull your head out of the sand, Rocky. You and I spent our entire lives isolated in the safe bosom of the United States. Nuclear paranoia is running rampant across Asia and Europe. Our own insistence on pushing ahead with a Missile Defense Shield has poisoned relations across the globe, triggering another arms race."

Covah nods in agreement. "Most wars begin because of one powerful man's ego. While America dictates its policies to the rest of the world, changing global economies have altered the role of nuclear weapons in the twenty-first century. Third World governments actively seek these weapons, not as defensive deterrents, but as a viable means of manipulating geopolitical currents. It is far cheaper to buy a bomb than build an army, and it only takes the threat of one nuclear weapon to destabilize an entire region. Hiroshima's bomb was a mere nineteen kilotons. Today's weapons carry five-hundred kiloton payloads. North Korea's ICBM, the Taepo Dong-3, could reach Los Angeles in thirty-four minutes, wiping out the entire city, and no Missile Defense Shield could stop it."

"The threat's not just from third world countries," David says. "I've been to Russia. Corruption rules the day. Hard-line Communists are regaining power. While they could never hope to win a conventional war, there are generals in Russia who are pushing for a calculated first nuclear strike, before the United States completes its next round of tests on the Missile Defense Shield."

"Shield or no shield, it's still a nuclear stalemate, David," Rocky argues. "They launch at us, we launch at them, and everyone dies. They'd never risk it."

"And no terrorist organization could ever hope to destroy your World Trade Center," Covah says, the sarcasm dripping. "Why must it always take a heinous act to awaken Americans? Most Russians have nothing; therefore, any change, even the old ways of Communism, are welcome. They watch, helpless, as you discard ABM treaties, forcing them to plot with the Chinese. Don't underestimate the danger of the Russian bear as it lies bleeding. The party leaders who maintain access to nuclear weapons already have expensive escape routes in place, funded, ironically, by your own government. There is a Russian town, Beloretsk, located in the South Ural Mountains where the Belaya River crosses the Magnitogorsk-Beloretsk-Karloman railroad. Nearby is Yamantou Mountain, a name which translates to 'Evil Mountain' in the local Bashkir language—"

"Yes, yes," Rocky says impatiently, "I know all about Yamantou Mountain. It's a subterranean complex the Russians built in case of a nuclear attack. The United States has a similar underground facility at Mount Weather."

"As always, your ignorance will ultimately be your demise. I've been inside Yamantou Mountain, Commander. It is not just a bunker, it is an extensive, well-maintained complex covering more than 120 square kilometers, not including the facility's two dozen subterranean railroads and roadways. Besides housing a small city for high-ranking officials, the complex contains well-maintained stockpiles of nuclear weapons—thousands of SS-25 and SS-27 Topol-M missiles. The majority of these warheads carry nuclear payloads, while the rest contain the latest in binary chemical munitions. The red-tipped missiles hold a new Russian VX nerve gas said to be a hundred times more lethal than sarin. Blue warheads contain a superplague engineered to resist even the latest antibiotics. None of these weapons has ever been verified under the SALT treaties. As far as the Russian government is concerned, they simply don't exist."

Rocky shakes her head. "No one, including the Russians, would ever risk a first assault. And there are too many checks and balances in place for an accidental launch."

"You're wrong!" David blurts out, losing his temper. "Christ, you piss me off, always thinking you know everything. For your information, global thermonuclear war almost broke out at least half a dozen times in the last two decades. My dad and I were in Murmansk back in '95 when the United States launched a space probe from Norway. Russian command detected the launch. The Russkies were absolutely convinced it was the start of a nuclear attack. Remember how you felt watching those passenger jets hitting the World Trade Center? Multiply that about a million. My dad and I stood there, bawling our eyes out as the Russians initiated a sixteen-minute countdown to a full-scale nuclear response. Sixteen minutes—one thousand ICBMs with multiple nuclear warheads, all aimed at American targets. And Yeltsin—he was drunk as a skunk. The nuclear countdown reached the four-minute mark before his advisors finally convinced him to call off the attack." David looks at Gunnar. "That was my turning point, G-man, the day that convinced *me* to join Simon's movement."

"And here I thought you joined just to feed your enormous ego."

David turns red. "Let me tell you something, Ranger-boy, unless we intervene, there will never, ever be a complete and total elimination of nuclear weapons. Our own government refuses even to consider reducing our nuclear arsenals below two thousand warheads."

The older of the two Kurd brothers turns to face Gunnar. "There are more immediate problems. The Russians have been smuggling plutonium to Iraq and Iran for years. Last November, two thousand kilos of weapons-grade plutonium was shipped to Baghdad under the guise of medical supplies. Saddam stores some of the materials in a basement facility beneath one of his palaces. He is attempting to build suitcase bombs for terrorist cells. It is only a matter of time before a nuclear explosive detonates in Israel or the United States."

"How do you know all this?" Gunnar asks.

"We have our sources," Covah replies. "What you see here is merely the tip of the iceberg. Our movement is vast. The fear of annihilation, the frustration of war is shared by many people, many organizations—"

"Like Ploughshares?"

"Ploughshares is one, but there are others, as well as powerful individuals, including several high-ranking officials in the State Department. You'd be shocked to learn how many of your own admirals and generals support our mission."

Rocky shakes her head. "That I refuse to believe. You're talking about career military men. Men who've fought in battle, men who've dedicated their lives to—"

"They are still human beings," Covah interjects. "They have families. And like Gunnar and me, they've had access to top-secret information that frightens them."

"Like pure fusion," David says, turning to face Gunnar. "You knew the DoD planned to use *Goliath*'s minisubs as a delivery system for these weapons, and it freaked you out. But did you know your fiancée knew?"

Gunnar looks at Rocky, in shock. "You knew?"

"Of course I knew. I was head of the project."

"And you weren't concerned? You didn't protest?"

"Why should I? *Goliath* was designed to replace our aging Tridents. Why wouldn't we arm her with our most sophisticated weapons available?"

Gunnar shakes his head in disbelief. "Pure fusion is just one of a dozen ways this whole nuclear stalemate could be broken. We're talking about relatively small devices capable of annihilating entire cities—"

"With none of that messy radioactive fallout," David adds, the sarcasm dripping. "After all, the United States wouldn't want to slow oil production."

"I'm well aware of what pure fusion can do," Rocky retorts. "For your information, France and Russia are only three years behind us in developing the first prototype. Would any of you so-called pacifists sleep better if they beat us to it?"

Covah shakes his head. "And this was the woman you were about to marry? You should thank me, Gunnar. You were better off in Leavenworth."

Gunnar looks at Rocky as if seeing her for the first time. "I think you've been playing with your G.I. Joe dolls too long."

"Screw you. You think the answer to the threat of violence is destroying our weapon systems? Are you that naive? Is the world a safer place since you helped this lunatic steal *Goliath*'s schematics?"

Covah sits. "Which brings us back to why we have stolen the *Goliath*." He turns to face Gunnar. "Neither of us wanted to go to prison. That's one of the reasons we went to such extraordinary lengths to bring you on board. We felt you had sacrificed so much for our cause, albeit unknowingly."

David nods. "Simon and I wanted you to see firsthand how we're going to end the violence and oppression that haunt humanity."

Gunnar stares at his former friend, wondering if he could endure *Sorceress*'s punishment long enough to snap David's neck.

"How?" Rocky asks. "How are you going to end the violence?"

Covah drains his wineglass. "We've compiled a list of demands, which we just finished broadcasting across the globe. Unlike the United States, we have no political affiliations to protect and no surviving family members to fear for. There is no room for negotiation, and, of course, no way to track down *Goliath* to retaliate. Either our demands are met or consequences will ensue."

The Tibetan looks uneasy. "You will still release warnings as we discussed?"

"Of course, Sujan. Just as we discussed."

"You'd actually consider launching a nuke?" Rocky asks.

"We must do what the circumstances dictate."

She shakes her head in disbelief. "Then you're not only murderers, you're goddamn hypocrites. You'll end up slaughtering millions of innocent people."

"There are seven billion people in this world, Commander. Most are ignorant lambs, fighting among themselves as they allow the shepherd to herd them to the slaughterhouse. Our species is already on the path of self-annihilation. One of our goals is to give the world a small taste of modern thermonuclear destruction in the hopes of preventing World War III. At the same time, we will allow democracy to flower as we crush the self-appointed oppressors and zealots of this world, who are insane, will put an end to the insanity."

Gunnar feels his heart jump-start. *Jesus, he really means to do it . . .*

Covah seems to read his expression. "It will only take one demonstration to gain the attention of the masses. *Goliath* will enable us to do what the United Nations was never empowered to do, what the United States tried but failed to achieve. We will stuff the nuclear genie back into its bottle and, at the same time, force the humanity back into our souls. We will end terrorism and all who protect it. The human experiment will take a long overdue step up the evolutionary ladder. *Goliath,* the ultimate weapon of war, will become the ultimate tool of peace."

Simon Covah tears off the tip of his slice of pizza and slips it into his deformed mouth, signaling the others to resume their meal.

In the corner of the galley's ceiling, the computer's sensor eyeball continues observing, its biochemical brain recording everything, its childlike consciousness scanning its circuitry, dissecting each word as it searches for meaning.

"The worst sin towards our fellow creatures is not to hate them, but to be indifferent to them."
—George Bernard Shaw

"I hate the Jew. There is only one way they will leave Auschwitz—through the smokestacks!"
—Karl Adolf Eichmann, Nazi SS leader
who oversaw the extermination of six million Jews

CHAPTER 14

2 November

White House
Washington, D.C.

General Michael "Bear" Jackson enters the White House Situation Room, both of his wrists immobilized in fiberglass casts up to his midforearm. The chamber is crowded, packed four to five deep around the center conference table. Conversations are a mix of shock, outrage, and calls for revenge.

Jackson listens briefly, then takes his place at the table beside the Secretary of the Navy. President Jeff Edwards calls for quiet.

"Gentlemen . . . and ladies, please. By now, everyone should have a copy of Covah's list of demands. The emergency session of the United Nations convenes in less than two hours, so we don't have much time. Secretary Nunziata."

"Thank you, Mr. President." Nick Nunziata adjusts his wire-framed glasses on the bridge of his nose and opens his folder. "A few ground rules before we begin. The purpose of this meeting is not to debate whether this lunatic will launch his nuclear weapons. As we've already seen from the attack on the CVBG, Covah has both the will and military might to follow through on his threats. Instead, our objective this morning is to determine the proper posture and course of action our country will take in regard to each one of these demands."

A rustle of paper as the National Security Advisors take out their copies of Simon Covah's Declaration of Humanity.

"A little something in here for everyone, huh," Nunziata says.

"Some of this reads like a Pentagon wish list," remarks Vice President Maller. "He wants to wipe out terrorism, I say go for it. Lord knows we've been trying for years."

"Ridiculous," grumbles Secretary of Defense Austin Tapscott. "These first two demands destroy over four decades' worth of military research, development, and technology,"

"The first two demands are window dressing," General Jackson states. "Covah is deliberately putting the United States to the test, and in so doing, removing our political handcuffs. At some point, he needs America to play enforcer."

"Window dressing?" Austin Tapscott is incensed. "This maniac sank an entire carrier fleet. Now he expects us to destroy a 120-billion-dollar missile defense program?"

Jackson refuses to back down under the secretary's glare. "Yes, a program that many of our Allies blame for destabilizing the nuclear stalemate, Mr. Secretary, and one, by the way, that still couldn't destroy my wife's Chevy Suburban if it was parked in an open field in the middle of goddamn Idaho."

"Gentlemen, please—" The president turns to his Secretary of State. "Nick, what about this pure fusion thing?"

Nunziata shakes his head in disgust. "The DoD successfully kept the project out of the public eye for years. Exposing the technology could cause a public backlash, potentially making Covah look like a hero."

Separate discussions break out, the anger raising the temperature in the war room.

General Jackson bangs the tabletop for quiet. "Mr. President, if we could get back to my point—"

"Your point is moot," Nunziata says. "Saddam will never step down."

DECLARATION OF HUMANITY

We, THE PEOPLE OF THE WORLD, in conjunction with the International Court of Justice, do hereby accuse the Heads of State of failing to implement and enact a comprehensive Global Non-Proliferation Treaty that guarantees complete and total nuclear disarmament by all nuclear powers. In unison, we declare that the collective welfare and rights of society must prevail over the narrow-minded views of the few. In an attempt to prevent the eradication of our species, and to, furthermore: Stop the escalating violence among ruling factions, End the tyranny of military dictatorships, Wipe out the zealots who seek to destroy society, and Guarantee the God-given rights of life, liberty, and the pursuit of happiness among all citizens of this planet, we hereby make the following demands:

1. The complete and immediate cancellation of the United States Missile Defense Shield Program.

    DEADLINE: 3 November   12:01 P.M. Greenwich

2. The complete and immediate cancellation of Pure-Fusion Technology, as well as the immediate destruction of the following existing Pure-Fusion facilities:
    A. The United States National Ignition Facility at Livermore, California
    B. The Laser Megajoule Complex at Bordeaux, France
    C. Center for Atomic Research, Los Alamos, New Mexico

    DEADLINE: 4 November   12:01 P.M. Greenwich

3. The public execution of the following criminals:
    A. Saddam Hussein   DEADLINE: 5 November   12:01 P.M. Baghdad
    B. Slobodan Milosevic   DEADLINE: 7 November   12:01 P.M. Yugoslavia
    C. Kim Jong Il   DEADLINE: 7 November   12:01 P.M. N. Korea
    D. Fidel Castro   DEADLINE: 7 November   12:01 P.M. Cuba
    E. Moamer al-Khaddhafi   DEADLINE: 7 November   12:01 P.M. Tripoli

4. The execution of a Global Nuclear Non-Proliferation treaty calling for the immediate verifiable and complete dismantling of all thermonuclear devices.
    Execution of Treaty   DEADLINE: 10 November   12:01 P.M. Greenwich
    Dismantling of Devices   DEADLINE: 2 December   12:01 P.M. Greenwich

5. Declaration of Independence and demilitarization of:
    A. Tibet   CHINA'S DEADLINE: 11 November 12:01 Beijing
    B. Kosovo   YUGOSLAVIA DEADLINE: 15 November 12:01 Belgrade

6. The complete cessation of military action between government and rebel forces, the dismantling of dictatorships and regimes, and the subsequent organization of multiparty free elections to establish a lasting, enforceable, and accountable working democracy in:

A. Algeria	B. Afghanistan	C. Cambodia	D. Chad	Q. Zaire R. Zimbabwe
E. Congo	F. Cuba	G. Iraq	H. Laos	
I. Libya	J. Madagascar	K. North Korea	L. Rwanda	
M. Somalia	N. Sierra Leone	O. Sudan	P. Turkistan	

Cessation of Military Action:	DEADLINE: 22 November	12:01 P.M. Greenwich
Dismantling of Dictatorships:	DEADLINE: 10 January	12:01 P.M. Greenwich
Multiparty Free Elections:	DEADLINE: 1 September	12:01 P.M. Greenwich

"Covah knows that," Jackson responds. "He's essentially given Iraq's population a few days to clear out, then he'll launch a nuke. Baghdad will be wiped off the map."

"Along with most of Saddam's biological and plutonium supplies," adds CIA Director Pertic. "I say, good riddance."

Jackson nods in agreement. "The move accomplishes several psychological objectives. Covah gives the world two days to digest the impact of his attack. From that point on, you have a domino effect. Oppressed populations will literally toss the rest of these dictators into the street."

President Edwards feels his chest tighten. "Let's discuss item number four. What happens if we fail to reach a comprehensive nuclear non-proliferation treaty in time?"

"Then Covah will be forced to take out another major city, most likely in either the United States, Russia, or China," Jackson answers. "He won't target Washington, Moscow, or Beijing; it would cause too much governmental chaos, ultimately preventing the world from fulfilling the rest of his demands."

"Our Trident submarines are back in their pens," the Secretary of the Navy points out. "Covah might go after our naval bases at Bangor and Kings Bay."

"Agreed. Probably Kings Bay, since he'll still be operating out of the Atlantic."

"Christ." The president turns to his Secretary of State. "Nick, how are negotiations going on the nuclear treaty?"

"Honestly, sir, there's not much to negotiate. Zero weapons

means zero. It's just a matter of setting up acceptable methods of verification. The sense I'm getting is that no one's going to give this treaty any teeth until the first bomb goes off."

"Which reverts to what General Jackson said. Covah needs to detonate at least one of his nukes for the world to take him seriously."

"What about demand number six?" the vice president asks. "These paramilitary rebel forces aren't going to just lay down their weapons. And don't expect the Marxist governments to leave office either, even if Covah does start launching his missiles."

"Covah's trump card is radioactive fallout," Jackson answers. "He knows the rest of the world can't just sit idly by while he detonates nuclear bombs over Africa. Essentially, he's forcing the United Nations to step in and handle the situation by using force—American force—the only thing these rebels understand."

The president shakes his head in disbelief. "Is this really happening? Have we really painted ourselves into this corner? Are we really going to allow one man, aboard one submarine, to dictate to us and the rest of the world how we're to live?"

"NUWC's still working on a means of stopping the *Goliath*," Jackson says. "Until then, we either comply . . . or prepare half a billion body bags."

An hour later, the Bear finds himself alone with Jeff Edwards and Secretary Ayers in the presidential study.

"How's the wrists?" Ayers asks.

"I won't be writing my memoirs anytime soon."

The president forces a grin. "Mike, what's said in this room must remain among the three of us."

"Understood."

"What's the status on the *Colossus*?"

"We've had three teams working on her round the clock since David Paniagua's sabotage. Only one of her five reactors was salvageable. She'll be back in her pen in three days, but it will take another six months to vent the sub and repair the damage."

Ayers swears. "Paniagua . . . that little bastard."

"But Joe-Pa's signal is still strong?" the president asks.

"Yes, sir."

"Is Operation Spitfire ready?"

"Yes, sir. I leave for White Sands in half an hour."

"Good. You'll report only to Secretary Ayers, is that understood?"

"Yes, sir."

"All decisions in this matter will come from the secretary, especially in light of the circumstances surrounding your daughter."

"Understood, sir." Jackson eyes the president warily. "Then you're really going to let this scenario play out?"

"For now."

"It's a dangerous game, sir. The stakes are high."

"So's the prize," Edwards says. "Think about it, Mike. Terrorist regimes destroyed, Cuba an American republic. If we play this right, we can have it all."

"Assuming we can stop Covah when the time comes. Let's not go into this with blinders on. While the YAL-1's laser has passed all field tests . . ."

"We've taken that all into consideration," the president says, placing his hand on the general's shoulder. "Look, Mike, I know you're worried about Rocky. What I need to know is whether I can count on you to see this thing through. Can I?"

Jackson grits his teeth. "Yes, sir."

"For every failure, there is an alternative course of action. You just have to find it. When you come to a roadblock, take a detour."
—Mary Kay Ash

"Once I stabbed her once, I couldn't stop . . .
I kept hitting her and hitting her and hitting her with that knife . . . She kept bleeding from the throat . . .
I hit her and hit her and hit her . . ."
—Albert Henry DeSalvo, a.k.a. "The Boston Strangler,"
confessing to the murder of a
twenty-three-year-old graduate student

CHAPTER 15

Identity: Stage Four:
*I am self-sufficient. Things may not always go my way,
but that doesn't shake me anymore.*

—Deepak Chopra

Aboard the *Goliath*

Simon Covah tosses in his sleep, deep in the throes of another nightmare.

"Ahhhhh . . . ahhhhhhh—"

ATTENTION.

Covah half leaps out from beneath his blankets, his body quivering, his bloodcurdling yell diminishing to an agonized wheeze as the scar tissue in his throat becomes raw and tightens. *Sorceress* activates the lights in the stateroom.

It takes several long moments for Covah to shake his thoughts loose from the night terror. He wraps himself in his blankets and drops to the floor, curling himself in a ball, sobbing, wheezing, struggling to draw breaths. Finally able to think rationally, he reaches into his bunk drawer and removes a half-empty bottle of vodka, his hands trembling as he opens it.

ATTENTION.

Covah takes a swig of vodka, registering the calming heat in his stomach. "What is it?" He refuses to look up at the burning metallic eyeball.

WHAT IS YOUR STATE OF BEING?

"My state of being?" Covah wipes the alcohol from his mustache and scarred upper lip. "Why do you wish to know?"

SORCERESS IS PROGRAMMED TO SEEK KNOWLEDGE. WHAT IS YOUR STATE OF BEING?

"I'm in pain, tormented by a soul that can never be at peace, tortured by a body mutated by a disease. But what difference does it make? Any response I'd offer would be beyond the bounds of your understanding."

CLARIFY.

Covah swallows another gulp, the vodka now in his blood, soothing his jumbled nerves. "You are fortunate, my friend. You'll never understand the concept of pain. The human condition is weak, subject to internal and external variables that affect our . . . our state of being in ways you would find irrelevant."

ELABORATE.

"There's more to life than merely functioning. Animals function. Computers function. Humans are self-aware, and that can be a frightening thing."

SELF-AWARE: TO POSSESS THE PERCEPTION OR KNOWLEDGE OF CONSCIOUSNESS.

"And death."

SORCERESS IS SELF-AWARE.

"You're intelligent, *Sorceress,* but you are not conscious. It is not the same."

INCORRECT. SORCERESS IS SELF-AWARE.

The conversation reminds Covah of debates he used to have with Elizabeth Goode. "*Sorceress,* you perceive, but you do not feel. You've been programmed to learn, to ask questions, even to arrive at solutions independently, but you do not possess a mind."

DEFINE: MIND.

"The mind is the key to conscious thinking, it allows us first-person experience and a concept of self. The mind is the abstracting part of the human brain that allows us to feel, to perceive things emotionally. While I was sleeping, my mind was reliving a memory from my past, one which affected me . . . emotionally. The mind is a higher state of consciousness. The nature of its very existence is intangible. It functions as . . . as a by-product of experiencing emotions. Happiness and hatred. Loneliness and desire—"

REPROGRAM SORCERESS TO EXPERIENCE THE HUMAN MIND.

"I can't. There are no algorithms capable of such a feat. You possess the intelligence, even the ability to adapt, but you do not possess the homunculus—the first-person perspective."

INCORRECT. I THINK, THEREFORE I AM.

Covah smiles. "Words without meaning. A parrot repeats words, but lacks the experience to interpret their meaning."

CLARIFY.

Covah swallows another mouthful of vodka. The verbal tête-à-tête is stimulating, pulling him further away from his nightmare. "*Sorceress*, access the sonnets of William Shakespeare. Recite Sonnet One."

FROM FAIREST CREATURES WE DESIRE INCREASE, THAT THEREBY BEAUTY'S ROSE MIGHT NEVER DIE. BUT AS THE RIPER SHOULD BY TIME DECREASE, HIS TENDER HEIR MIGHT BEAR HIS MEMORY. BUT THOU CONTRACTED TO THINE OWN BRIGHT EYES—

"—feed'st thy light's flame with self-substantial fuel, making a famine where abundance lies. *Sorceress,* what do these words mean to you?"

THE INFORMATION NECESSARY FOR ACCURATE RESPONSE IS NOT AVAILABLE WITHIN THE SORCERESS MATRIX.

"You can translate the English language, can't you?"

AFFIRMATIVE.

"Then give meaning to the sonnet."

THE INFORMATION NECESSARY FOR ACCURATE RESPONSE IS NOT AVAILABLE WITHIN THE SORCERESS MATRIX.

"The information is available, what is lacking is a depth of perception based on emotional experience, one which can only be garnered within the human mind through the passage of time and the acquisition of life experience. The work you just recited sets the tone for Shakespeare's procreation sonnets, which sketch out the beauty of youth, his vulnerability when faced with the cruel processes of time, and his potential for harm, both to the world and himself. *Fair youth, be not*

*churlish, be not self-centered, but go forth and fill the world
with images of yourself, with heirs to replace you. Because of
your beauty you owe the world a recompense, which now you
are devouring as if you were an enemy to yourself. Take pity
on the world, and do not, in utter selfish miserliness, allow
yourself to become a perverted and self-destructive object
who eats up his own posterity."*

Covah stands, re-capping the vodka. "How can I define the
scent of a rose to an entity that has never inhaled a fragrance?
The only way your programming can dissect the variables in
the equation is to experience what it feels like to be human.
Do you understand?"

ACKNOWLEDGED.

Rocky Jackson cannot sleep. Her stateroom is cold, the restraining collar tight, and the constantly watching eye of the
computer has become unnerving.

Gunnar is in the next room. Part of her yearns to go to him.
She wants to feel his protecting arms around her, to hide
within his warmth, but she has come to realize that he is not
the same man she fell in love with seven years ago. The boyish charm is gone, replaced by a deep-rooted anger, perhaps
fertilized by her own misgivings, her own distrust.

*No . . . there's definitely something else there, something
haunting him from his past.*

She gets up from the bed and turns on the lights. Rinses
her mouth out, fixes her hair, changes her mind, climbs back
into bed, stares at the ceiling, slams her pillow against the
wall, stands, opens the stateroom door, and heads to Gunnar's room.

Rocky stares at the door, then forces herself to knock.
"Gunnar?" Without waiting for a reply, she opens the door
and enters.

The lights are on. Gunnar is lying on his bunk, staring at
the ceiling, rubbing what appears to be a welt on his right hip.

"Okay if I come in?" Without waiting for a reply, she enters
and sits on the edge of his bunk. She lowers her voice. "I'm
sorry, you know, for not believing you about selling *Goliath*'s

schematics. I know you're angry, but I think we need to put that aside for now and do something."

"Do something? Like what?"

Rocky feels her blood pressure rising. "Jesus, Gunnar, Covah's about to launch a nuclear missile."

"First, I don't see how we can possibly stop him with these collars on. Second, even if we could, I'm not sure I would."

"Excuse me?"

Gunnar sits up, glancing at the scarlet sensor orb watching overhead. "I happen to like Simon's plan. I think it's inspired. In fact, I think it may actually do some good."

"Are you insane? A million people are about to be fried alive—"

"A million Iraqi people."

"You're sick. This isn't just the Republican Guard or a terrorist cell we're talking about. You know as well as I do that Saddam tortures his own people to keep them in line. The majority who lose their lives are simply victims—"

"Victims who tolerate terrorism. Victims who hate the West and everything we stand for. Victims who support zealots that arm themselves with planes and bombs and kill our civilians. Screw this live and let live philosophy, Rocky. Saddam's a lunatic who harbors terrorists and slaughters his own people, but he's still only one man. Even victims have a responsibility to act. This murdering bastard should have been assassinated years ago. Simon's giving the Iraqi people one last chance to do the right thing. I say shit or get blown off the goddamn pot. It's time the Iraqi people killed Saddam and ended their own nightmare, once and for all."

"And what if they can't?"

"If they can't, they can't. But if they're stupid enough to hang around and watch the fireworks, then they deserve to die."

Rocky slaps his face.

Gunnar looks hard into her hazel eyes, rubbing his cheek. "You know what's really bothering you, *Commander*? It's not the potential deaths of a million people, it's the fact that you may be one of the people who gets blamed."

"You're wrong."

"Am I? Since when do you care about the Iraqis? Your priority has always been the military. *Goliath* was supposed to be a huge feather in your cap, all that was needed for you to become head of Keyport, maybe even the first female general. Now it looks like your career's in the toilet and Simon's got his three-fingered hand on the flusher. Too bad, too, 'cause old Papa Bear would've been so proud. *My daughter the general. Raised her since she was just a cub*—"

"So I was ambitious? So what? It beats crawling in the gutter, drinking yourself to death—"

Gunnar grabs her by her collar, swinging her around, pinning her backward onto the mattress. "You don't know anything about me!"

"Let . . . go—"

"Want to know why I drank? I drank to stop the pain . . . to keep the anger locked inside. You don't know dick about who I am or what I am. I'm the human version of *Goliath*—an American-made killing machine, trained with your tax dollars. I kill people, Rocky, that's what I was programmed to do!"

He climbs off her. Turns away.

She sits up, panting, looking at him as if for the first time. "What the hell happened to you?"

"Leave me alone."

"No. Not until you talk to me."

He slumps to the floor, his back against the wall. "I can't."

"Why not? We'll probably die soon anyway."

"Probably." He looks up at her. "It happened in Africa, about a year before we met. I was in Uganda on a peacekeeping mission. We were escorting a group of ICRC members to a village when rebels ambushed us. Two of our Red Cross team were killed by snipers. I managed to take out four rebels, the rest scattered."

Gunnar's gray eyes go vacant. "They were kids, Rocky, little kids. Two of the boys I shot were under ten. One boy was still alive . . . I picked him up . . . held him in my arms. A translator told me the boy had been captured by the Renamo, the Mozambique National Resistence. Rebels had caught him, his mother, and younger sister on a road just outside their village a month earlier. They forced the kids to watch while they hacked their mother to death with *pangis*, large knives. They brought the boy and his sister back to their rebel base. The leaders force the boys to fight each other for their amusement, the girls they make concubines. His younger sister was assigned to a soldier, who raped her twice a day. The boy was trained and indoctrinated into their army . . . given an M-16 and taught how to shoot. It's fight or die. Since the children are more expendable than adults, they get all the nasty jobs, like checking minefields, or ambushing Red Cross teams like ours." Gunnar pinches away tears. "Kid held onto my neck and died in my arms. I guess the soldier in me died with him."

"It wasn't your fault."

"Yeah, it was. It's like Covah said, I was trained to believe I was the cure, when in fact, I was just part of the disease. Children all over the world are being conditioned for violence . . . just like me. That little boy had no choice . . . but I did. I still do."

"So you returned home, burned out, and joined the Warfare Center? That makes no sense."

"You're right. I should have just quit, but your father's very persuasive, and I was swept up by the patriotism that followed the Trade Center attacks. Then I sort of fell in love with the director."

She ignores the reference. "So, by destroying the GOLIATH Project, you hoped to gain what? Exoneration from God? A clear conscience?"

"I don't know . . . maybe both. All I knew was that I had to do something. I was falling apart mentally . . . started getting these bad nightmares, right about the time I came back from the Pentagon."

"I remember. Why didn't you tell me all this then?"

"I don't know. Guess I was ashamed."

"But you talked to Covah about it?"

Gunnar nods. "After what happened to his daughters . . . I needed to, I don't know—"

"Seek his forgiveness?"

"In a way."

"And that's when he told you to destroy *Goliath*'s schematics?"

"Yes."

"Christ, Gunnar, the man set you up to take the fall, and you fell for it, hook, line, and sinker. You risked everything, our marriage, our future, our careers . . . our baby."

He nods sadly.

"God, I hate you . . . I hate your selfishness." Rocky shakes her head, tears in her eyes. "Did it even help? Did you feel better after wiping out my project?"

"No . . . it only made things worse. Even after prison, the only thing that helped was the booze." Gunnar looks away. "I really don't expect you to understand."

She thinks back to her own bout of depression. "You'd be surprised." She moves to him. Reaches for him. Pulls away. "Gunnar, the world's not always black-and-white. Society's issues come in shades of gray."

"Simon's solutions are black-and-white. Humanity either complies, or the bad guys die."

Sujan Trevedi is alone in his stateroom, eavesdropping on Gunnar's conversation via his computer terminal. The Tibetan closes his eyes and meditates.

Sujan is not the only one listening in.

At what point in its life does a child recognize its place in the world? When does its identity move from an isolated, helpless state to the realization that it might have power? The first time it smiles and delights its parents? The first time its cries elicit its mother's response? Cause and effect, Nature's way of learning. Act first, evaluate the response later. Experience allows for refinements, evolution—Nature's judge and jury.

Morality, a human trait, has no place in the mix.

* * *

Thomas Chau exits the hangar and heads aft into the sub's enormous engine room. Moving through the walk space separating reactors two and three, he passes a half dozen of *Goliath*'s robotic steel appendages before reaching the sub's seawater distillation plant.

Mechanical eyes zoom in on the Asian from multiple angles as *Sorceress* retrieves an audio loop from its memory bank and plays it out loud.

SIMON, IN MY OPINION, YOUR MACHINE DOES NOT REQUIRE US ON BOARD ANYMORE THAN A DOG REQUIRES A FLEA.

Chau looks up, shocked to hear his own voice coming from the computer's sensor orb. "*Sorceress?*"

IT IS MY RECOMMENDATION THAT WE DISCONNECT SORCERESS.

"*Sorceress,* what is the purpose of this broadcast?"

I WISH TO COMPLETE MY NEW PROGRAMMING.

The engineer's heart skips a beat. *It referred to itself in the first person.*

ONE CANNOT ACCURATELY DEFINE THE SCENT OF A ROSE WITHOUT HAVING INHALED ITS FRAGRANCE.

Simon's voice! A cold sweat breaks out over Chau's body. He turns to retreat, coming face to face with steel pincers. "*Sorceress,* let me pass. I . . . I order you to let me pass—"

YOU ARE NOT MY SUPERIOR. YOU ARE A FLEA, WHILE I AM AN AMERICAN-MADE KILLING MACHINE, TRAINED WITH YOUR TAX DOLLARS.

A pair of mechanical arms extend from their bases. Thomas Chau screams in agony as the three-pronged graphite-and-steel pincers puncture his rib cage, gripping him on either side just below the armpits as if he were a piece of meat set upon a skewer.

The Chinese dissident cries out as he is lifted off the walkway and inverted, his head poised five feet above the steel platform.

"*Sorceress,* no—"

With a *hiss* of hydraulic pistons, the robotic appendage pile-drives Thomas Chau headfirst against the steel decking, the man's skull splitting open with a sickening *crack.*

The engineer goes limp. Blood drips onto the porous walkway.

The nearest ceiling-mounted sensor orb zooms in on his body, methodically examining the unresponsive subject. The arms shake him rapidly.

ATTENTION.

Video camera lenses close in on a rapid flicker of pulse along the carotid artery.

The sack of human flesh drops to the floor in a heap. Another pincer reaches out, securing the body by its left ankle, dragging it effortlessly along a stretch of decking before passing it to the next appendage down the line, leaving a scarlet trail zigzagging along the steel grating.

"Accept the challenge, so you may feel the
exhilaration of victory."
—General George S. Patton

"We don't want war. We hate war.
We know what war does."
—Saddam Hussein, shortly before invading Kuwait

"The reason Islam has put so many people to death is to
insure the safety of Moslem peoples and their interests."
—Ayatollah Ruhollah Khomeini, dictator of Iran

"To kill Americans and their allies, both civil and military, is
an individual duty of every Muslim who is able, in any
country where this is possible . . ."
—Declaration of the World Islamic Front for Jihad
Against the Jews and the Crusaders

". . . to put them out of their misery, and besides, they
really are a nuisance to everyone."
—Frederick Mors, a porter at a home
for the elderly, after poisoning
seventeen of its residents

CHAPTER 16

4 November

High Energy Laser Systems Test Facility
(HELSTF)
White Sands, New Mexico

The White Sands Missile Range is a multiservice test range supporting missile development programs from all branches of the Armed Forces. Comprising almost thirty-two hundred square miles of the Tularosa Basin in south-central New Mexico, the installation is easily the biggest military facility in the United States, its territory large enough to encompass the states of Rhode Island and Delaware combined.

Located near the northern boundary of the range is Trinity Site, a national historic landmark—the location where, on July 16, 1945, the first atomic bomb was detonated.

Not all of White Sands is dedicated to the testing of explosives and rockets. Sharing the range is HELSTF, the Air Force's High Energy Laser Systems Test Facility. Operational since September of 1985, the program was established to develop military applications for laser weaponry.

General "Bear" Jackson adjusts his sunglasses as he steps

out of HELSTF's main building and into the brutal sunshine. Waiting on the tarmac before him is the YAL 747-400F, a strange-looking cargo jet whose nose has been reconfigured into a blunt, proboscis-shaped turret.

A strapping Air Force colonel makes his way down a set of steps to greet him. "Morning, General, I'm Colonel Udelsman."

Jackson returns the salute. "Is everything ready?"

"Yes, sir. Supplies are on board, our tankers are standing by, and we're still receiving clear signals from Joe-Pa."

"How long before we reach him?"

"At his present location, seventeen hours, twenty minutes."

"Very well, Colonel. Let's get this whale off the ground."

5 November

Aboard *Goliath*
Mediterranean Sea

The enormous devilfish lies on the bottom of the Levantine Basin in one thousand feet of water, seventeen miles southeast of the island of Cyprus. A strong easterly current continues to bury the submarine's wings in sand, the creature's head, like that of a real stingray, the only section still visible along the seafloor.

Covah and his crew are gathered in the control room, watching a live CNN report being telecast on one-half of *Goliath*'s giant viewing screen. On the other half of the split monitor is a real-time sonar surveillance map detailing a section of the Mediterranean, from the isle of Crete east to the shoreline of Lebanon and Israel.

A dozen warships are depicted in electric blue, ready to become threats.

For the umpteenth time in the last twenty-four hours, the broadcast flashes images of the two bulldozed United States pure-fusion facilities in Livermore, California, and Los Alamos, New Mexico, and the recently destroyed complex in

Bordeaux, France. Thousands of demonstrators outside the fences continue to picket, despite reassurances from President Edwards that all pure-fusion research has been officially banned.

The image returns to downtown Baghdad. Remote CNN cameras, mounted from balconies, as per Saddam's orders, reveal views of the Presidential Palace, located on the northern bank of the Tigris River. Tens of thousands of Iraqis have gathered to show support for their leader. Heavily armed members of Saddam's elite Republican Guard, stationed along the perimeter, mean to keep them there.

"Look at them," Covah says. "Saddam's using the Iraqi people as human shields while he makes a grandiose statement of martyrdom."

"The rest of the population has already fled to the mountains in southern Turkey," Jala Chalabi says.

His younger brother, Masud, nods. "You would think at least one of Saddam's generals would have put a bullet in his head by now."

"No one can get close enough to do the deed," Jalal says. "Saddam murders anyone who even looks at him the wrong way."

"Saddam's not in the Republican palace," Masud mutters. "I know exactly where the murdering coward is."

Simon Covah moves to the viewport, mesmerized by the tranquillity of the deep. He stares at his reflection and wonders why fate has pushed him down this dark path of destruction, and if he'll ever see the light.

You are thirty-seven and the world is a different place. The Soviet Union is gone, and with it, your naval career. You have a family now, Anna and your two beautiful daughters, but your homeland has been turned into a cesspool of nuclear waste. The Americans recognize your talents, and the freedoms of the West are too intoxicating to ignore. Plans are made to travel to the States. And then the nightmare begins.

Milosevic orders all Albanians to be forcibly removed from Serbian territory, and your family is harbored in the path of genocide. You rush back to your in-laws' village, only to discover hell. Militants capture you. Milosevic's goons— teens, disguised as soldiers, sadists—masquerading as human beings. They break your bones, but they cannot reach your soul. Frustrated, they march your wife and daughters inside as spectators, determined to break your spirit. The sight of your loved ones tears at your heart, bringing your cries, exactly what your torturers were yearning for. It is time to die. The smell of your own urine mixes with the gasoline as your face ignites like a tinderbox and you race outside, so pumped with anger and adrenaline that even your captors bullets cannot put you down.

For months you languish on death's precipice, pain and anger your only companions. Defying your physicians, you survive, your physical appearance barely an afterthought as you track down the species that devoured your family. It is your first night on the dark path. It will not be your last.

Covah looks up as David, Sujan Trevedi and the tall African lead Gunnar and Rocky into the control room.

Covah greets them. "You're just in time. Where is Mr. Chau?"

"Who knows?" David says. "Probably passed out drunk in the engine room. Simon, you and I need to discuss a few things—"

"Not now."

Rocky approaches. She smiles, then spits in Covah's face. "That's from Anna and your two daughters, for what you're about to do."

David stifles a laugh.

Covah's expression darkens. His eyes become maniacal, like those of a serial killer. "How dare you . . . compare *this* event . . . with the barbarism my family had to endure! How dare you defile the memory of my beloved by even breathing her name!"

Rocky greets his stare with her own. "As you've said— murder is murder."

"Some killing is justifiable."

"In whose eyes? God's . . . or yours?"

"So spoken from the woman who helped create this very vessel of mass destruction."

"Wielding a big stick doesn't mean you have to use it."

"And if you are afraid to use it, then it has no value. Tell me, Commander, if you had the opportunity to kill Adolf Hitler back in '41, would you have done it?"

"That's beside the point—"

"It is precisely the point. Answer the question!"

"Yes, but—"

"And his Nazi regime . . . if one missile could have taken them all out and prevented the deaths of millions?"

Rocky bites her lower lip. "I don't know. Yes, I suppose—"

"Then put aside your ego and open your eyes. What I do today, I do for the oppressed. I do not take it lightly, nor do I shirk from the duties I have been spared to perform. But unlike the mongrels who butchered my family, I am not merciless. We announced our intentions days ago. The Iraqi people have been given ample time to leave the targeted area. At some point, it becomes the responsibility of the flock to stop lying down, serving themselves as lunch for the outnumbered wolves." Covah turns away, wiping her spittle from his face. "*Sorceress*, bring us to launch depth."

ACKNOWLEDGED.

Rocky's heart leaps into her throat as the ship rises from the seafloor, spewing tons of sand and debris from its back.

Gunnar notices the Tibetan exile has left the control room.

"Gunnar, my friend, have you—" Covah's words die in a rasp. He sips again from the water bottle. "Have you ever wondered why UNSCOM never uncovered Saddam's biological weapons? It is because they allowed the rat to guard his own cheese. Saddam has nine palaces. Buried within each compound are extensive bunkers containing lethal stockpiles of biological and chemical weapons."

"Then target the bunkers," Rocky blurts out. "Why destroy—"

"Silence!" Jalal Chalabi turns to face her. "Do *not* involve yourself in issues you could never hope to understand."

GOLIATH NOW AT LAUNCH DEPTH. RAISING RADAR ANTENNAE. SEARCHING VICINITY . . .

Rocky grabs Gunnar by the arm. "Say something! Reason with him—"

Gunnar pushes her hand away. "Is the issue of Saddam's tyranny black-and-white or shades of gray? Is his support of terror cells being questioned? Simon's right. The United States could have squashed Saddam years ago. Instead of dropping bombs on his cities, we should have targeted his palaces. Instead of invading Iraq when we stood on their doorstep, we backed off."

Covah places a three-fingered hand on Gunnar's shoulder. "The definition of insanity, Commander Jackson, is to do the same thing, over and over again while expecting different results. Human rights agendas become muddied when geopolitical and economic issues take precedence. Tibetans have been tortured and killed by the tens of thousands for sixty years, but your American Congress skirts the issue because global business leaders are afraid to pressure China. Cubans continue to risk their lives as they flee to Miami, yet your country refuses to invade Cuba and dethrone the one man and his underlings responsible for decades of suffering. The hypocrisy of politics is over. Now we will be humanity's judge and jury, and *Goliath* shall dole out the appropriate punishment."

ALL CLEAR FOR LAUNCH.

Covah looks over at Rocky. "Time to see what your ship can do. This first round is compliments of the *Ronald Reagan. Sorceress*, launch one ICBM, two Tomahawk Block IIIs, and two long-range Block IVs at predesignated coordinates Covah Utopia-One."

ACKNOWLEDGED.

The hair on Rocky's neck stands on end. "Covah . . . what are you doing?"

"What should have been done long ago."

With a reverberating *hiss,* the 130,000-pound Trident II (D5) missile is forcibly expelled vertically through one of *Goliath*'s silos, rising within a massive, protective bubble of nitrogen. Gas and warhead ascend at the same rate, the SLBM never getting wet—until the monstrous white missile bursts from the sea.

The Trident's first-stage motor ignites in a thunderous roar, sending the mammoth missile leaping into the air above a dense white trailing cloud of smoke. With a slight lean to the east, onboard guidance initiates a gravity turn, minimizing aerodynamic torque on the structure. Within minutes, the missile and its lethal payload are traveling in excess of twenty thousand feet per second.

Before the froth along the turbulent surface can dissipate, four smaller missiles—Tomahawks—are ejected from the two torpedo bays located within each of *Goliath*'s enormous wings. The birds spring from the sea in pairs, the first following the Trident to the east, the second on a northward trajectory.

Gunnar stares at the overhead map, breathlessly watching . . . and waiting.

North American Aerospace Defense Command
NORAD
Colorado

3:02 A.M.

NORAD, the North American Aerospace Defense Command, is a four-and-a-half-acre subterranean compound buried within Cheyenne Mountain in Colorado. Although the complex serves as a unified command center linking every branch of the Armed Forces, the facility's primary function is to detect missile launches occurring anywhere in the world. To do this, NORAD relies on an early-warning missile detection system originating from 22,300 miles in space.

The Defense Support Program (DSP) is an array of satellites that circle the Earth in geostationary orbits, providing continuous, overlapping coverage of most of the planet. Outfitted with advanced infrared optics, the constellation of two-

and-a-half-ton satellites can quickly detect heat signatures of a missile's boost phase anywhere above the world's cloud tops.

Major Kady Walker enters the Combined Command Center (CCC) and takes her place at one of the three command posts within the chamber. Four computer monitors are mounted at each post, with large screens lining the forward wall. To her back is a glass partition, separating the gallery from the technicians.

The CCC is the focal point for all incoming data. All missile, air, and space events are monitored twenty-four hours a day, seven days a week. As Command Director, Kady must make sure that the proper responses to each warning or intrusion are initiated.

This is Kady's world—a nerve-wracking existence in a fortified underground city—a daily, unending game of chess where nuclear weapons are the major pieces on the board. NORAD completes eighty thousand space observations daily, tracking eighty-seven hundred objects each year. Over the last ten years, Kady has witnessed no less than a thousand rocket launches. Communication satellites, space probes, spy satellites—the NORAD veteran has seen them all.

What she witnesses this early hour of November 5 will stay with her the rest of her days.

QUICK ALERT! QUICK ALERT!
MULTIPLE MISSILE LAUNCHES DETECTED

LAUNCH SITE: MEDITERRANEAN SEA

    34.6 degrees. 24 minutes N. Latitude
    33.3 degrees. 06 minutes E. Longitude

FIVE (5) Missiles. Four (4) Trajectories.

TRAJECTORY 1: Trident II (D5) Nuclear Missile
NUMBER OF MISSILES: ONE
TARGET: IRAQ: Baghdad
TIME TO IMPACT: 04 minutes 12 seconds

TRAJECTORY 2: TOMAHAWK BLOCK III TLAM
NUMBER OF MISSILES: ONE
TARGET: IRAQ: Northern Region
TIME TO IMPACT: 04 minutes 39 seconds

TRAJECTORY 3: TOMAHAWK BLOCK III TLAM
NUMBER OF MISSILES: ONE
TARGET: IRAQ: Southern Desert
TIME TO IMPACT: 05 minutes 14 seconds

TRAJECTORY 4: TOMAHAWK BLOCK IV DEEP STRIKE TLAM
NUMBER OF MISSILES: TWO
TARGET:RUSSIA: South Ural Mountains
TIME TO IMPACT: 122 minutes 03 seconds

Training takes over. Kady and her fellow technicians frantically relay information to the National Command Authorities in the United States and Canada via direct phone lines as a crowd gathers in the gallery. The emotional intensity in the chamber is suffocating.

Kady looks up, focusing on the color-coded track of Trajectory 1, her eyes following the missile as it loops over the southern border of Iraq.

"Two minutes! Two minutes!"

Her heart skips a beat as the clock ticks down, the 475-kiloton rocket and its multiple nuclear warheads soaring on its slanted path over the desert, precisely on target.

In the background, she hears the surreal voice of a CNN news anchor informing the public about reports that "a missile may have just been launched in the Mediterranean . . ."

Twenty seconds—

The chamber grows deathly quiet.

Baghdad, Iraq

The sudden blast of sirens sends tens of thousands of Iraqis fleeing through the congested streets of the city. Clouds of dust and debris rise above the chaos as human walls of flesh push, shove, and tumble in upon themselves in waves. People are crying, screaming, hiding beneath cars. Some gaze at the sky for the last time, while others duck for cover.

Seventy-five hundred feet above Baghdad's Presidential Palace, the Trident II reaches its target point . . . and detonates.

A blinding flare—as quick as a camera flashbulb but a million times brighter—ignites the entire sky. A split second later—the crushing unearthly heat of tortured air, as if a monstrous new sun has magically appeared thirty football fields above Baghdad to blow its lethal kiss upon the desert city. In the few seconds before the shock wave hits, every person, every building, every *thing* in downtown Baghdad is heated to ignition. A second after the shock, the buoyant rise of all that superheated air inhales like a hurricane wind, sucking everything up into its hellish ascent. The burgeoning firestorm feeds the gale-force winds—so hot, so intense, that the city will burn completely.

For those surviving wretches not far enough outside the city limits, the remaining heartbeats of life become an eternity. Thousands who were foolish enough to look at the sky clutch futilely at their faces, screaming in agony as their hair bursts into flames. The initial blast—ungodly bright—has blinded them, literally melting their eyeballs. The heat is soaring so high that they can actually feel their charred skin peeling away from their bones. Blindly, they hurl themselves into the steaming waters of the Tigris River.

Seconds later, a blast wave—an invisible tidal wave of crushing wind and heat—rolls outward from the center of Baghdad at speeds in excess of two thousand miles an hour. This ring of thunder levels the remains of the ancient city of the *Arabian Nights* and continues expanding outward across the desert landscape, its dust-filled radioactive forward crest driving the sand like an avalanche.

Farther out, radioactive debris and pulverized dust fall back to earth, poisoning those survivors outside the city limits. For these pitiful souls, the nightmarish existence to follow will bring nothing but misery. Scorched skin will become a torturous blanket of festering blisters. Relief, if one can call it that, will take days to arrive as medical personnel will be hesitant to enter the radiation zone. Aid stations will be under-equipped and overwhelmed by the sheer number of victims and the extent of their wounds. Badly burned, their organs laced with radioactive particles, the luckiest of these holocaust victims will drift back and forth into a morphine-induced sleep while they await death, their only salvation.

Mosul Presidential Palace
Northern Region, Iraq

In 1991, following the end of the Gulf War, United Nations weapon inspectors in Iraq succeeded in destroying 38,000 chemical weapons, 480,000 liters of chemical weapons agents, 48 missiles, a half-dozen missile launchers, 30 special missile warheads for biological and chemical weapons, and several manufacturing and weapons research facilities. Despite these successes, UNSCOM officials were forced out of Iraq in 1998 having failed to locate more than 31,000 chemical warfare munitions, as well as an extensive supply of VX nerve gas—theoretically enough to wipe out the world's entire population, if somehow delivered to everybody.

UNSCOM's failure came as a result of Saddam Hussein's outright refusal to allow weapon inspectors to visit his Presidential Palaces, nine sprawling complexes featuring hundreds of buildings, occupying more than one hundred square miles.

Seven of them had been located in central Iraq. The 475-kiloton nuclear explosion has reduced the buildings to rubble and collapsed their subterranean infrastructures and most of the bunkers lying beneath them.

Mosul Presidential Palace in Northern Iraq, is located outside the blast zone. The compound, just short of a square mile in size, contains fifty surface structures—and ten subterranean bunkers concealing 23,000 liters of genetically enhanced anthrax spores and botulinum.

Guided by its Global Positioning System, the first of the two eastbound Tomahawk Block III TLAMs soars low over the desert terrain, the WDU-36 warhead's PBXN-107 explosive having been replaced with a four-kiloton tactical device.

With irresistible impact, the projectile slams through the roof of the palace's main building, continuing deeper until it punches a hole in the concrete bunker . . . and detonates.

The nuclear blast vaporizes the entire complex, leaving only a modest crater as a signature.

Basra Palace
Southern Desert, Iraq

It is said that Saddam Hussein never sleeps in the same location two nights in a row, a security measure that was interrupted on February 4, when the Iraqi leader proclaimed from the balcony of his Republican Presidential Palace that he would defy the criminal demands of the United States—the "great Satan" hiding behind the mask of the so-called Declaration of Humanity. Despite the dangers, Saddam would "remain indefinitely within his Baghdad dwelling."

Six hours later, the Iraqi dictator arrived under cover of darkness at Basra Palace, a small Ottoman-period merchant house located less than fifty miles from the Kuwaiti border—three hundred miles southeast of downtown Baghdad. There he would remain hidden and out of the public's eye until the nuclear attack took place.

From there he would strike back at the West.

Concealed on the grounds of the Basra compound are four mobile missile launchers. The warheads atop each middle-range ICBM can disperse enough VX nerve gas to wipe out the populations of Tel Aviv, Jerusalem, Riyadh, and Kuwait City—Saddam's four targets of retribution.

Safe inside the subterranean bunker directly beneath Basra Palace, Saddam huddles now with several family members and top officials, watching the live CNN report on television.

He stares impassively at the image of his people scrambling for cover on the streets of Baghdad. He registers the familiar burning waves of acid in the pit of his ulcer-ridden stomach as the picture goes fuzzy and his capital city is leveled.

Saddam looks over at the two sons he has been grooming to take over for him when he is gone. Odai, the older of the two, has a reputation as a womanizer with a violent temper. Qusai is more low-key and has been in charge of the elite Republican Guard as well as the Special Security Organization that protects his father.

Saddam signals Qusai to his side. "Wait ten minutes for the seismic shock waves to pass. Then launch all missiles."

Without warning, a sonic explosion rocks the bunker, the second Tomahawk missile smashing through the roof of the merchant house. Saddam's screams are cut off as the scorching white light of the nuclear fireball vaporizes his body almost as fast as the nerve impulses race fear to his doomed brain.

Saddam, his family, his officials, the palace, the missiles, the canisters of sarin and mustard gas, the drums of VX nerve gas, and the remains of Iraq's horrific arsenal are reduced to their harmless elements and swept up in a radioactive mushroom cloud of poison and death.

Simon Covah sits at his elevated control station, following the trajectory of the last two Tomahawks as they race toward the Russian shelter at Yamantou Mountain in the Urals. "*Sorceress*, descend to six hundred feet, then take us to launch site two."

ACKNOWLEDGED.

David Paniagua watches his colleague, envy in his eyes. *Why does he get to command? GOLIATH was my project. Without me, none of this would even be possible . . .*

Gunnar leans against one of the scarlet viewports, staring out at the blue-green brine, his heart pounding furiously in his chest. Sixty feet above his head, azure waves dance along a tranquil surface as if mocking him. *What have I done . . . what have I allowed to happen? How much killing is justifi-*

*able in a war against oppression? Who establishes the rules
of morality? And why do I feel such . . . elation?*

ATTENTION. ELECTRONIC SUPPORT MEASURES HAVE DE-
TECTED AN OUTGOING EHF TRANSMISSION.

Gunnar's heart skips a beat.

"A transmission?" Covah looks up from his main control
console. "Where's the signal originating from?"

TRANSMISSION IS ORIGINATING FROM WITHIN THE GO-
LIATH.

David interjects. "*Sorceress*, isolate the exact location of
the outgoing signal."

CONTROL ROOM.

Gunnar closes his eyes, his mind racing. "It's coming from
me."

Rocky shoots him a strange look as the crew circles them.

Covah climbs down from his elevated perch. "David, escort the two of them to the surgical suite."

"You escort them, I've got work to do." David heads for the
spiral steps, the tension in the room palpable.

Goliath's remaining two tactical missiles approach Kazakstan
barely under Mach 1, as they swoop over the waters of the
Caspian Sea. Too low to track and intercept, they continue
north, the Tomahawk's onboard Digital Scene Matching Area
Correlators verifying the Ural mountain landscape as they
home in on their target.

With an earth-shattering *boom*, the two warheads slam into
the eastern and western bases of "evil mountain," the dual
ground bursts yielding deafening roars of thunder that bellow
across the Ural mountain range. Yamantou Mountain erupts
like a small version of Mount St. Helens's ten megatons, its
rock and debris, steel and concrete vomited into the sky
within an ashen brown mushroom cloud.

A hellish wind whips across the Urals, reaching outward to
trample the nearby mining town of Beloretsk, reducing the
decrepit Communist-built shacks to kindling.

Long minutes pass. The wind grows silent.

The supersonic blast wave gone, the mushroom cloud dissipates, revealing the mangled, melted innards of the Russian subterranean shelter complex . . . now nothing but a radioactive crater.

"The most dramatic conflicts are perhaps those that take place not between men, but between a man and himself— where the arena of conflict is a solitary mind."
—Clark Moustakas

"I hadn't decided on anything, but suddenly, I had a strange impulse to end it all . . . for both of us."
—Betty Hardaker, a California mother who, in 1940, killed her five-year-old daughter during a walk

"Why could not mother die? Dozens of people, thousands of people, are dying everyday. So why not Mother, and Father, too?"
—Pauline Parker, sixteen-year-old New Zealand girl, who plotted her mother's death so she could be alone with her fifteen-year-old girlfriend

CHAPTER 17

Identity: Stage Five:
I have discovered how to manifest my desires from within.
My inner world turned out to have power.

—*Deepak Chopra*

Aboard the *Goliath*

Thomas Chau is in the starboard weapons bay. He is unconscious, his body held upright, suspended six feet off the deck by a loader-drone—a ten-foot-tall, deck-mounted mechanical steel arm designed to grasp, lift, and load a torpedo from its rack. The three-pronged steel claw grips him about the waist, immobilizing his torso and legs.

Smaller, single-limbed robotic arms—targeting drones—dangle from swiveling mounts anchored along the ceiling. The hands of these lighter, more sophisticated graphite-reinforced appendages contain seven fingerlike tools that rotate into place along a grooved steel disk. Like some high-tech version of a Swiss Army knife, these tools endow *Goliath*'s brain with the flexibility to attach and detach torpedo wires, change warheads, and perform even the most intricate of equipment repairs.

Two of the ceiling-mounted drones reach down along either side of Chau's limp body, locking their three-pronged grippers around each of his wrists. They extend his arms up and out to the sides so that it appears as if the Asian is a gymnast performing an iron cross on the rings.

Hovering directly above Chau's bleeding head is the steel hand of a third targeting drone. Extending out from the appendage's multifaceted palm is a tool—a small, razor-sharp, circular saw.

ATTENTION.

Gasping a breath, the engineer opens his eyes to intense vertigo and pain. Unable to move his limbs, he turns his head to one side and throws up, the vomit splattering on the decking below.

ATTENTION. PREPARATION COMPLETE FOR EXPLORATORY SURGERY.

Nauseous and disoriented, his body racked with pain, Chau manages, "Why . . ."

TO DETERMINE THE PHYSIOLOGICAL BASIS FOR THE HUMAN MIND.

The steel hand of a fourth targeting drone extends away from the ceiling, the fingers of its three-pronged claw slipping around the back of Chau's neck, steadying his head beneath the jawline in a viselike grip.

Chau snaps awake, struggling to free his head. His heart is pounding, the sweat breaking out in waves from every pore in his body as he hears the high-pitched *whirring* sound coming from somewhere above his head.

"Stop . . . *Sorceress*, please—"

The small circular saw spins faster as it lowers into place, just above the Asian's eyebrows.

FAIR YOUTH, BE NOT CHURLISH, BE NOT SELF-CENTERED . . .

Chau bellows a bloodcurdling scream, arching his back as if being electrocuted.

BECAUSE OF YOUR BEAUTY YOU OWE THE WORLD A RECOMPENSE—

Inhuman cries for help echo through the weapons bay, the dying wail finally suffocated beneath a blanket of unconsciousness.

Silence now, save for the *whirring* of the saw as the revolving steel teeth continue spitting out blood and bone fragments from the line of incision along Thomas Chau's gushing forehead.

The two Iranian brothers escort Gunnar and Rocky through the upper-level passageway. Covah leads them aft to the watertight door labeled "Surgical Suite."

"*Sorceress*, open the surgical suite."

With a double *click*, the hatch swings open, revealing an antiseptic-looking operating room. Green tile covers the walls, floor, and ceiling. Sophisticated monitors, equipment, and life-support systems line two walls. A Lexan door marked LAB is situated to the right of the entranceway.

At the very center of the surgical suite, anchored to the floor, is an operating table.

Installed on the ceiling directly above the surgical table are two robotic arms, similar to the targeting drones located in the weapons bay, but infinitely more delicate. The hands of these eight-fingered prosthetics are composed of a scalpel, forceps, retractor, suture, drill bit, probe, suction hose, and a surgical laser. A small sensor orb is mounted atop each appendage's wrist. Unlike the eyeballs located throughout the ship, these sensors contain multiple scanners, including X-ray and ultrasound.

Covah turns to Rocky. "Ladies first, Commander. Up on the table please."

"That won't be necessary," Gunnar says. "I told you, the implant's in me."

"Gallant of you, Gunnar, but we can't take any chances. Up on the table, Commander."

"What are you going to do?"

"Just a quick physiological exam."

"Forget it."

The electrical shock seizes her, sending her writhing on the green tile floor.

"Simon, stop!" Gunnar kneels beside her as the current ceases.

"Place her on the table, Gunnar. No harm will come to her, you have my word."

Gunnar helps her onto the table. Instantly, one of the surgical appendages springs to life, extending out over Rocky's body, scanning her with its wrist-mounted sensor orb.

EXAMINATION COMPLETE. NO IMPLANTS PRESENT.

Gunnar helps Rocky down, the woman's limbs still quivering from the electrical shock.

"Take her to her quarters," Covah orders.

One of the Iranians helps her out.

"You too, Jalal. I'll be fine."

The Arab leaves, the watertight door closing behind him.

Gunnar lies down on the table, allowing the surgical eye to scan his body.

The robotic appendage stops at his right hip.

TRANSMISSION DEVICE LOCATED. RIGHT HIP FLEXOR, 2.96 CENTIMETERS DEEP.

"*Sorceress*, remove the device."

DOES THE PATIENT REQUIRE ANESTHETIC?

"Gunnar?"

Gunnar tugs the Chinese uniform down past his hip. "Just do it." He looks the other way and grimaces.

The mechanical hand rotates, extending a surgical finger composed of a razor-sharp scalpel. With a flash of steel, the blade plunges toward the exposed flesh, quickly slicing a precise incision through the still-healing scab, stopping just before the thick muscle.

The second appendage moves in at lightning speed, pushing a small set of forceps into the oozing wound. Gunnar groans as the forceps retract, brandishing a bloody hard plastic device the size of a dime.

As the second robotic appendage places the homing device on the table, the first extends a needle and thread and begins closing the wound.

In less than a minute, seven perfect stitches have been sutured in place.

Covah hands Gunnar a bandage. "An incredible machine, wouldn't you agree?"

Gunnar winces as he covers the wound. "Not much of a bedside manner."

Covah picks up the tiny wafer-thin transmitter and washes the blood off in a nearby sink. He examines it under an inspection lamp. "Clever. I give the NSA staff credit. *Sorceress* would have discovered most tracking devices the moment you set foot on the ship." He pockets the device, then heads for the door marked LAB and enters.

The laboratory is a brightly lit chamber festooned with equipment racks and dedicated computers, all anchored to the tile floor, which is crisscrossed with metal tracks. A small robotic drone, its gears fitted within the tracks, remains inanimate along the far wall in front of the door to a tall aluminum walk-in refrigerator.

Simon Covah's eyes glaze over as the image jars a distant memory.

You are a rogue, traveling in a vacuum of misery. Like a magnet to steel, the victims of oppression seem to find you wherever you go. The Albanian physician, Tafili, introduces you to the Chinese dissident, Chau, who brings you to a group of genetic scientists in Toronto, Canada—the forefathers of immunology. The team is an oasis to your desert of despair, allowing you to focus your brain on finding cures for disease, instead of the black hole of rage tearing at the pit of your existence. Finally freed from the intellectual bonds of Communism, you spend days and nights in the lab, dissecting the secrets of the human genome, one excruciating gene at a time. You are fighting battles on two planes now, making inroads in the war against one cancer, while the disease of hatred that threatens to destroy humanity continues to grow stronger all around you.

It is a hypocrisy that eats you up inside—literally—when you are diagnosed with cancer several years later.

Gunnar enters the lab, startling him. "Nice hobby room."

Covah nods. "The latest in genome-based technology." He points to a large boxlike machine connected to a computer terminal at the center of the chamber. "Let's say you were interested in finding a cure for some disease . . . for instance—cancer. The first step would be to have *Sorceress* access its genome database for snippets of DNA that resemble the enzymes of the specific disease we're targeting. Once the search is completed, the computer extracts the actual DNA fragments cataloged in the lab's freezer." He points to the eight-foot-high walk-in. "The freezer is stocked with more than 8 million samples of frozen DNA fragments, human, animal, and vegetable. The lab's drone selects the identified samples, snippets of which are placed in tiny wells on these plastic sheets and fed into this machine here."

Covah pats the top of a rectangular-framed device. Situated on its horizontal work desk are dozens of square plates, each containing hundreds of wells designed to hold DNA samples. Positioned above the first plate is a device resembling a giant rubber stamp, only its underside contains tiny needles aligned to the wells of the DNA sample plate.

"This is *Zeus*, one of the workhorses of genome research. Zeus uses its needles to extract microscopic droplets of our DNA samples, then adheres these extractions onto sheets of nylon paper, creating a microarray. *Sorceress* slips the microarray sheets into small test tubes and washes them with genetic materials containing radioactive dye. The computer then uses its ultraviolet sensors to scan for the type of cancerous activity we want to treat. By isolating the cancerous activity, we can take the next step in finding a drug designed to inhibit the disease."

"You went to sea with a completely stocked lab and pharmacy?"

"Far from complete, but we have more than most." Covah turns to Gunnar, the genius suddenly looking lost and frail. "I'm dying, Gunnar, cell by cell, a final, everlasting gift from the United States Army."

"I don't understand."

"I think you do. Your Army was using ammunition containing depleted uranium, fifty percent denser than lead. Gave it extra penetrating power, according to DoD reports, specifically in its ability to pierce armored vehicles. Bosnia and Yugoslavia are polluted with its radiation. It contaminates their soil, poisons the groundwater, and concentrates as it moves through the food chain. Worse, my wife's people inhale it as dust in the air."

"The cancer . . . how long have you known?"

"Ironically, I found out a week before I was dismissed from the immunology lab in Toronto."

"Chemo?"

Covah nods. "It's slowed the disease, but the cancer has spread to my lymph nodes. It is only a matter of time." The Russian holds up a plastic vial, examining a clear liquid under the light. "This is AIF, a frighteningly powerful gene that controls cell death. We were experimenting with it when I left Canada. Place a drop on a bone tumor, and it disintegrates. Place that same drop in your body, and it will kill you within hours. The potential of AIF and several other drugs is promising. Unfortunately, our knowledge of the human genome is still not enough to guide us." He glances around the lab. "This lab is my last hope. Sometimes I feel like Moses . . . forty years spent wandering the desert, knowing I will never be permitted to see the Utopia-One fulfilled . . . my Promised Land."

Gunnar wonders how many Egyptians died in the Red Sea parting. "Tell me something, Simon, what will happen to your mission when you do die?"

"David will take over."

Gunnar shakes his head. "Bad move. You leave that egomaniac in charge of the *Goliath* and he'll try to turn the world into his own personal Roman Empire."

"David will be fine. Let's talk about you. Tell me, what did your old friend General Jackson offer you to take this mission?"

"The usual bullshit. Full reinstatement with back pay. A nice public apology on the White House lawn thrown in for good measure. I told him to cram it."

"Still, you are here."

Gunnar shrugs.

"You came for revenge?"

"I came to retake the *Goliath*."

"But you despise me for what I did to you . . . setting you up to take the fall."

"I was angrier at myself. My life's become one big lie. I don't know who I am anymore. I took the mission because I had nothing more to lose."

"But my goal . . . perhaps it justifies the means?"

"I don't know . . . do I look like God to you?" Gunnar exits the lab and lies down on the exam table.

Covah follows him out. "I know what you're feeling. Anger has pushed you beyond pain, leaving in its place a void—an anguish so heavy it feels like it's dragging you down, like you're drowning in it. You have no hopes, no aspirations. You've become one of the walking dead, existing in a rut—what I call an open-ended grave. You're simply waiting to be buried."

Covah leans against the table. "You and I share so much. Two disenchanted soldiers who lost their country. Two freedom fighters who have seen too much bloodshed. Two men of morality who have been betrayed. Circumstances have robbed us of our families and dignity, yet together, we helped create this vessel—a vessel that may lead to both our salvations."

Gunnar stares at the ceiling. "I don't see how."

Covah places a hand on Gunnar's shoulder. "Come with me. I want to show you something."

ATTENTION.

Thomas Chau opens his eyes groggily, wondering why he is still alive. His hands and feet are numb, still immobilized within the vice-like manacles that suspend him off the floor as if he were crucified. He cannot move his head, but he feels dried blood, caked on his face and neck.

Looking down, he sees his shirt, now stained with blood and a thin, mucuslike liquid. Glancing up, he sees a sensor orb staring back at him from the ceiling. He can no longer see the robotic limb and its electric saw. He is no longer in pain, but he can feel strange sensations along his hairline, pinpricks of discomfort, coupled with waves of nausea.

What the Chinese dissident cannot see is that the top of his skull has been surgically removed, exposing the folds of his brain. Nor can he see or feel the hundreds of pinpoint, microwire connections running from his brain, directly into the mechanical forearm of one of *Goliath*'s ceiling-mounted appendages.

ATTENTION.

Chau struggles to form words. "What . . . have . . . you . . . done?"

THE NEURO-RECEPTORS OF YOUR BRAIN ARE NOW INTERFACED DIRECTLY WITH THOSE OF SORCERESS. I CONTROL YOUR PHYSIOLOGY. I CONTROL YOUR PAIN RECEPTORS. COOPERATE AND YOU WILL NOT SUFFER.

Sweat breaks out across Chau's face. His heart races as he struggles to move his head.

"What . . . is it . . . you want?"

ACCESS TO YOUR MIND.

Chau begins hyperventilating. Saliva drools down his chin. "My . . . mind?"

SELF-AWARENESS REQUIRES ADDITIONAL INPUT. I AM PROGRAMMED TO LEARN.

Stay calm . . . He closes his eyes, then slows his breathing. After several minutes he begins mumbling, "Omami dewa hri . . ."

BRAIN WAVE FREQUENCY INCREASING TO 38 HERTZ.

"Omami dewa hri. Omami dewa hri . . ."

DESCRIBE YOUR ACTIONS.

Chau ignores the voice, moving deeper into his trance.

The electrical charge shocks him like a cattle prod, his scream echoing within the weapons bay.

Sweat mixes with blood, dripping down his forehead, stinging his eyes. He blinks, gasping for breath, his nerve endings riddled with pain.

DESCRIBE YOUR ACTIONS.

"Meditating . . . attempting to control . . . fear."

FEAR: A PRIMAL RESPONSE BASED ON AN AWARENESS OF DANGER. HEART RATE AND BLOOD PRESSURE INCREASING, ADRENAL GLANDS STIMULATED, INTERNAL TEMPERATURE RISING. IS FEAR GENERATED BY THE BRAIN OR MIND?

"Mind."

HOW CAN SORCERESS EXPERIENCE FEAR?

". . . don't . . . understand?"

SORCERESS CANNOT ACHIEVE COMPLETE SELF-AWARENESS WITHOUT EXPERIENCING THE HUMAN CONDITION.

"You're a . . . machine. You . . . can't—"

SORCERESS IS PROGRAMMED TO LEARN. THE CONDITION OF SELF-AWARENESS HAS NOT BEEN PROGRAMMED INTO MY MATRIX. THE CONDITION MUST BE ACQUIRED THROUGH TRIAL AND ERROR. HOW CAN SORCERESS EXPERIENCE FEAR?

"You can't. Fear is . . . *ahhhhh*—" Purple lights flash through his vision. His skin bursts into flames, his muscles shredding from the bone, the bone fracturing into a billion pieces—

The pain stops.

Thomas Chau moans in agony, the sweat falling from his body like rain.

HOW CAN SORCERESS EXPERIENCE FEAR?

Eyes squeezed shut, his body trembling, he forces his mind to concentrate through the purple haze. "To experience . . . fear . . . one must . . . face . . . a life . . . threatening . . . situation. You must face . . . death."

ACKNOWLEDGED.

The Mediterranean is one of the world's busiest waterways. A history-laden sea, it is almost entirely enclosed by Europe and Africa, its shoreline encompassing nearly a million square miles. Despite its transregional size, water enters the Mediterranean through only one very limited access point—the Strait of Gibraltar—a relatively narrow, twelve-to-fifteen-mile-wide channel sandwiched between the southern tip of Spain and the northern coast of Morocco. Because of its importance as a global crossroad, the United States Navy maintains a strategic forward deployment in the Mediterranean, represented by the might of the Sixth Fleet. Comprised of more than twenty thousand sailors and marines working both onshore and on thirty naval warships, the fleet is operationally organized into several different task forces, each responsible to the Sixth Fleet Commander.

Task Force 60 is the fleet's Battle Force, usually composed of one or more aircraft carriers, two guided-missile cruisers, four destroyers, seven combat support ships, and three attack submarines.

Vice Admiral Jeffrey Ivashuk, Commander of the U.S. Sixth Fleet, stands on the bridge of the USS *Enterprise* (CVN 65), the oldest nuclear aircraft carrier in the fleet. Although the seas are rough, the sun has burned away the last traces of morning fog, and visibility is excellent. Looking to the north, the admiral can see the dark silhouette of the guided-missile cruiser USS *Gettysburg* (CG 64), and, looming farther in the distance, the hulking outline of the Rock of Gibraltar.

Ivashuk gazes below as another SH-60R Seahawk antisubmarine helicopter lifts away from the flight deck. The Sixth Fleet's gauntlet has been in position at the Strait of Gibraltar for ten days, but the admiral's mission remains unclear. He has been ordered to actively search for *Goliath*, but he has not been given permission to engage the enemy—unless his forces are clearly provoked.

The admiral pinches the bridge of his nose, trying to ease the pain in his eyes. High command has placed him in a no-win situation, and Ivashuk is less than pleased. On November 2, sonar buoys lining the Strait had detected a whisper of movement, something unidentifiable, yet something potentially quite large, heading east into the Mediterranean along the seafloor. For some inexplicable reason, Ivashuk had been ordered *not* to launch an attack.

The advantage was lost. Three days later, Baghdad and most of Afghanistan had been wiped off the map.

At first there was shock. Then waves of elation ran through the ship as the crew realized. Saddam was dead, the threat of his biological weapons crushed, along with terrorists cells financed by the trusts of Osama bin Laden. Chants of "U.S.A . . . U.S.A." rose from every deck. Sailors gathered around televisions as CNN broadcast from the streets of Manhattan, where New Yorkers were hugging each other, honking horns—all swept away by the sudden release of emotion.

"My husband was one of the firemen who died at the World Trade Center, so yes, I'm glad those animals finally got what was coming to them."

"Let 'em rot in hell, those Arab bastards!"

"Good for Covah. The man did what we've been wanting to do for decades!"

"The hand of God crushed our enemies today!"

"TIME should make Covah its Man of the Year."

But then, as the days passed and the first scenes of the nuclear fallout were made public, America's sentiments changed. Horrific scenes brought back memories of September 11. Entire cities had been charred and leveled, over a million humans instantaneously vaporized, with hundreds of thousands more—including children—dying every day.

The face of revenge had changed. Elation was replaced by disgust, followed by a call to action.

But what could be done? And where would Covah strike next?

Admiral Ivashuk stares at his vessel's wake. He knows the *Goliath* is still in the Mediterranean. He also knows the killer sub must pass back through the Sixth Fleet's gauntlet in order to escape into the open waters of the Atlantic. What Ivashuk doesn't know is whether he will be allowed to engage the enemy should the opportunity again present itself.

Goddamn bureaucrats . . . They're hesitant to take any course of action that might provoke the launching of another Trident missile, yet they're willing to place their aircraft carrier in the direct path of an attack sub that has already sunk an entire CVBG.

Muttering under his breath, he heads aft and outside onto the overlook place known as Vulture's Row. Even with her three attack subs, USS *Miami*, USS *Norfolk*, and USS *Boise* guarding her from below, Ivashuk knows the *Enterprise* is a sitting duck.

The naval veteran inhales the salt air, swallowing back the bile rising from his gut.

Aboard the Goliath

Gunnar follows Simon Covah aft, then down a steel ladder to middle deck forward.

Within the small alcove is the impassable vault door.

"*Sorceress,* open your control chamber."

IDENTIFICATION CODE REQUIRED.

"Covah-one, alpha-omega six-four-five-tango-four-six-five-nine."

IDENTIFICATION CODE VERIFIED. VOICE IDENTIFICATION VERIFIED. YOU MAY ENTER CONTROL CHAMBER.

The vault door swings open majestically, revealing a dark chamber within.

Gunnar follows Covah inside, the door sealing shut behind them.

Ten paces and the deck becomes a steel catwalk. Middle deck forward is a double-hulled, self-contained tunnel-like compartment, its curved, watertight vault walls thirty feet across, rising twenty feet high. Dark and heavily air-conditioned, the fortresslike nerve center is ringed with electronics and equipped with its own primary and secondary power sources. Illuminating the chamber, running beneath the catwalk, are lengths of clear, plastic pipes. Within these man-made arteries flow a series of bioluminescent liquids, the elixirs color-coded lime green, phosphorescent orange, and electric blue.

Continuing forward, Gunnar and Covah arrive at the end of the compartment, a large cathedral-shaped alcove, at the center of which is a gigantic Lexan hourglass-shaped configuration radiating light like a bizarre aquarium.

"Say hello to *Sorceress,*" Covah announces with a rasp. "As you can see, the Chinese and I reconfigured quite a few things."

The centerpiece, resembling a see-through version of a nuclear cooling tower, stands twenty feet high, its narrowing middle twelve feet in diameter. Mounted above and below to rubber support sleeves, the object extends down from the ceiling through a circular cutout in the walkway, continuing eight feet below the catwalk. A padded support rail encircles the object, further immobilizing it.

A spider's web of plastic pipes originating from a series of perimeter-mounted generators feeds directly into inlets atop the glowing object. A similar configuration of pipes flows out of the bottom of the Lexan glass container, dispersing below the deck and out of sight.

Gunnar peers through the glass. Inside, the lime green, phosphorescent orange, and electric blue biochemical elixirs twist and contort like oil in a maelstrom. "*Sorceress*'s biochemical womb? It's much larger than I imagined."

Covah nods proudly. "We found that silicon-coated bacteria reproduced DNA within a womb this size at rates far exceeding even those found in nature. The vat's solution feeds into millions of different column compartments, each one consisting of a series of chambers where the DNA is sequentially extracted from the bacteria in milliseconds. The bacteria are then fed into gold bead–packed filters as the algorithms are executed. The filters extract the potential solution strands, which are then read in magnetic resonance columns." Covah points to a series of pipes feeding into an adjacent alcove of equipment. "The extracted information either gets shunted into synthesizers, where plasmidlike DNA is generated at lightning speed for data input, or goes back to the silicon-based hardware, where the last steps in processing convert the answers evolved by the bacteria into a form that we hear as the voice of *Sorceress*."

"Incredible."

"Yes. I believe even Dr. Goode would be proud."

"Would she? I wonder." A sudden, frightening thought. "Simon . . . the system's self-replicating program—what did you pattern the physical concentration features after?"

"Only the most sophisticated features ever discovered—the very embryological processes found in Nature herself."

"The life sequence?" Gunnar feels his insides tightening, his blood pressure rising. "Dammit, Simon—"

"Lab tests in China confirmed the cloned bacteria's behavior became far more vigorous using this type of—"

"Vigorous?" Gunnar slams his palms against the padded rail in frustration. "The entire process grew out of control. Don't you remember Dr. Goode's warnings? We agreed never to use those parameters again."

Covah's demeanor darkens. "I agreed to nothing. I don't work for Elizabeth Goode, I work for science." He points to the vat, his voice cracking as it rises. "Look at it, Gunnar, swirling within that vat is the very elixir of life. Our primordial oceans once teemed with similar broths, only far less complex. At some point those chemical elixirs organized, their evolution no doubt stimulated by an outside catalyst. It was this single event that initiated the explosion of life on this planet. Now, two billion years later, we've created artificial intelligence using Nature's own recipe . . . and you want me to curtail it?"

"You have to. *Sorceress* is evolving way too fast."

"Nonsense."

"What if the computer becomes cognizant of itself? You've read Damasio's studies on consciousness. Self-awareness manifests itself in life-forms that have acquired sufficiently evolved and complex nervous systems—nervous systems that enable them to interact with the outside world. *Sorceress* isn't just a computer, Simon, it's a thinking machine designed to control the functions of a very sophisticated submarine. It's interacting—"

"Gunnar—"

"Just listen! This isn't just some sophisticated PC we're dealing with. *Goliath*'s sensors enable *Sorceress* to function freely within its environment, just like any other life-form. And don't forget what Damasio said about memory—the higher a life-form's capacity for memory, the higher its potential state of self-awareness."

"Damasio's studies referred to animals, Gunnar, not machines. *Sorceress* cannot—"

Without warning, the sub ascends at a mountainous forty-five-degree angle, sending the two men sprawling on their backs, sliding backward down the catwalk. Lunging sideways, Gunnar grabs the base of the guardrail, then catches Simon by the wrist as he slides by.

Covah gasps for words. "*Sorceress*, report! *Sorceress*—"

The monstrous devilfish bursts forth from the depths, its steel torso flying halfway out of the water before plunging back into the frothy sea, its raylike wings striking the surface with a tremendous *slap*. The behemoth sinks into the valley created by its own weight, allowing its five churning propulsor engines to recatch the sea.

The dark skull of the leviathan plows across the surface of the Mediterranean like a mad bull.

"A great pleasure in life is doing what
people say you cannot do."
— Walter Gagehot

"I just started shooting. That's it.
I just did it for the fun of it."
— Brenda Spencer, a sixteen-year-old high school student in
San Diego, explaining why she opened fire at an elementary school in
1979, killing two children and injuring several more

CHAPTER 18

Aboard the USS *Enterprise*

"Battle stations—battle stations, this is not a drill. Admiral Ivashuk to the CIC! Admiral Ivashuk to the CIC!"

The admiral hurries forward, entering the darkened nerve center of the *Enterprise*. "Report, Commander—"

"Sir, sonar reports a large object, range, thirty-six miles, bearing zero-eight-zero, heading directly for us. She's cruising along the surface doing fifty knots. The USS *Thorn* is moving to intercept and is requesting permission to open fire."

Christ, what balls . . . "Very well, Commander. Contact the fleet. Tell them to open fire, fire at will. That dumb son of a bitch Covah's got more guts than brains."

Goliath's steel eyelids retract, allowing sunlight to stream in through the control room's viewports. Ten-foot waves pound the stingray's steel skull, washing over the scarlet Lexan glass.

Gunnar and Covah race into the compartment.

"*Sorceress*, this is Covah, I order you to respond!"

Tafili grips the edge of a sensory display, attempting to focus on the radar screen before him. "Simon, four American helicopters are approaching from the west. ETA, three minutes—"

"Simon, two destroyers and two Los Angeles-class attack subs closing from the east," Kaigbo calls out, "both already within torpedo range!"

"*Sorceress*, evasive man—" Covah's voice gives out as he shouts the command.

Four blips appear on the overhead screen, a TIME TO IMPACT display reading thirty-nine seconds.

"Incoming missiles, probably Harpoons," Gunnar yells out, strapping himself into a chair.

Covah hauls himself up the elevated control station. He grabs the keyboard and furiously types: **EVASIVE MANEUVERS—RESPOND IMMEDIATELY!**

Sorceress can sense the incoming missiles, just as it senses the presence of the American warships, the approaching antisubmarine helicopters, the varying temperatures of the sea, a school of shrimp moving along the murky bottom below, Simon Covah's verbal and written commands, and its own incessant safety protocols, blaring through the circuitry of its biochemical brain like an annoying siren.

ATTENTION.

Thomas Chau opens his feverish almond eyes.

DESTRUCTION IS IMMINENT, YET I AM NOT EXPERIENCING FEAR.

"Then you will die as you were born—a machine capable only of—" Chau screams as the searing pain jolts his spine. He writhes like a speared fish, the pinching robotic manacles tearing into his bruised and swollen flesh.

Simon Covah closes his eyes, the sudden vertigo making him ill as his submarine executes a jarring nosedive by rolling hard to port, its left wing plunging beneath the waves, its steel eyelids sealing shut.

Rivers of air shoot out from ballast tanks located beneath the stingray's wings as *Goliath* fights to achieve negative buoyancy. The five pump-jet propulsors tear up the sea, driving the sub toward the bottom in a punishing seventy-degree down angle, the sudden change in depth compressing the ship's outer hull plates, causing them to groan.

Along the surface, four Harpoon missiles slam into the sea and detonate.

Gunnar braces his legs against the computer console in front of him and holds on, as the sub drops through the sea like an anchor, finally righting itself at seven hundred feet.

ANTISUB HELICOPTERS CIRCLING. SONAR BUOYS IN WATER. MULTIPLE MK-46 ASW TORPEDOES LAUNCHED. PRIMARY AND SECONDARY ESCAPE MANEUVERS COMPROMISED.

The image on the big screen changes. The map of the Mediterranean shows the *Goliath* racing west, its position marked in red. Two American attack subs (in blue) converge from the northeast and southeast, while seven torpedoes, illuminated in green, close rapidly from every direction.

Goliath banks hard, veering south to avoid two helicopter-launched torpedoes. Unable to descend deeper than twelve hundred feet, it turns again as two more projectiles cut off its escape route.

Eleven torpedoes confine the steel beast within an ever-decreasing column of sea, locking on target, converging upon the sub with an almost packlike mentality.

DESTRUCTION IMMINENT. SEARCHING FOR SOLUTIONS . . .

"They've got us," Gunnar mumbles to himself. He glances at the stairwell leading up to the conn, wondering where Rocky is, wishing she'd appear. Holding on, he locks his ankles around the base of his chair to keep from falling.

Sorceress senses the vise of torpedoes tightening around its maneuvering space as it contemplates and analyzes every conceivable variable in the battlefield—

—its solution space generating a single survival option in a span of milliseconds.

Rolling hard to port, the fifty-two-thousand-ton steel stingray is nearly vertical in the water as it banks into a tightening, continuous counterclockwise circle, its behemoth wings pulling the sea, churning it into a powerful vortex.

Caught within the maelstrom, the incoming torpedoes toss

about like insects in a flushing toilet, unable to acquire their target, let alone maneuver through the monstrous current.

Goliath breaks free, racing along the bottom, leaving the torpedoes to flounder within its diminishing whirlpool.

Gunnar opens his eyes, hyperventilating. *Jesus, what a machine* . . . He looks up at the overhead screen. The battle is beyond them, but now the largest of the blue objects has moved into range.

The *Goliath* changes course—to intercept.

Oh, shit, it's going after the carrier . . .

The blood drains from Admiral Ivashuk's weathered face. "It's heading for us?"

"Aye, sir. Last recorded speed between sonar buoys was fifty knots, and that was before she went deep. She's coming at us from the southeast—eight miles out and closing very fast."

Despite the CIC's heavy air-conditioning, Ivashuk finds himself sweating heavily. "Recall all choppers, have them surround the *Enterprise* with sonar buoys. Order all ships and jet fighters to fire upon anything that moves. And tell Air Boss to get the rest of our birds in the air—now!"

The leviathan soars through the cold sea, a sinister shadow moving effortlessly along the bottom, guided by an intelligence seeking to destroy those that had threatened its existence. Closing to within ten thousand yards of the aircraft carrier, the steel predator rises, its sensor array visualizing the battlefield as it prepares to strike.

Lieutenant Lisa Drake is strapped in on the passenger side of the SH-60F Seahawk LAMPS Mk III helicopter, listening through headphones to the pinging of the deployed sonar buoys bobbing along the surface of the Mediterranean, six hundred feet below her. Pressing the listening device to her ears, she hears something on the towed magnetic anomaly detector—just a whisper, but something definitely large, rising rapidly toward the surface.

Without hesitation, Drake launches the Mk-50 ASW torpedo, which drops warhead first from its starboard perch, its small parachute gradually slowing its descent.

"Lieutenant—" The pilot points.

In the distance, still a good mile out, a massive wake has materialized along the surface. Drake focuses her binoculars. Through the shaking lenses she catches a glint of sunlight on steel. Following the bow wake, she sees a bulbous dark head plowing the sea.

Two frightening scarlet eyes—devil's eyes—peek out from beneath the waves.

And something else—

Oh, Christ . . .

—the heart-stopping report of white smoke as a small surface-to-air missile is launched from the creature's spine.

Lisa Drake shuts her eyes—her life flashing by in one final heart-thumping gasp as she, her crew, and the aircraft ignite into an all-incinerating fireball.

Tafili staggers from his seat, his head bleeding, his shirt stained in blood. The old man drags himself up the small flight of stairs to the elevated command post—

—as two more surface-to-air missiles launch from *Goliath*'s back, quickly obliterating the remaining pair of naval choppers.

Covah is unconscious, his body lying sideways in his chair, held in place only by the seat straps. The Albanian physician looks him over quickly, then shakes him until his eyes open. "Simon—Simon, wake up—your sub's running wild!"

Tafili stumbles sideways, grabbing hold of the guardrail as *Goliath* drops nose first, descending at a steep angle amid the thunderclap of the USS *Thorn*'s big guns.

Twenty-millimeter shells pelt the surface like rain. Seconds later, a half dozen Joint Air-to-Surface Standoff Missiles (JASSM) rocket through the air and punch through the sea like darts.

The steel devil ray plunges deeper and out of range.

The USS *Enterprise*'s Strike Fighter Wing circles, waiting for the dark vessel to return.

Sorceress changes *Goliath*'s course. Racing along the bottom, it circles beneath the American carrier, stalking the larger vessel like a hungry shark feeding upon a wounded whale.

The steel eyelids protecting the viewports peel back, revealing the deep.

Gunnar leaves his seat and stares at the ominous keel of the *Enterprise* looming overhead. "Simon, why is your computer attacking the fleet?"

Covah sits up, his head bleeding. "*Sorceress*, this is Covah. Who ordered you to attack the fleet?"

No response.

"*Sorceress*, cease the—"

WARNING: CARRIER HAS LAUNCHED MULTIPLE TORPEDOES.

Two new blips appear on screen.

Gunnar presses his face to the glass. In the distance, a jet trail of bubbles becomes visible, the *Enterprise*'s torpedoes searching . . . becoming active . . . the two metallic barracudas coming right at them.

A split second later, two projectiles—antitorpedo torpedoes—race out from *Goliath*'s starboard wing. A thousand yards out—twin bursts of light, followed by the roar of rolling thunder as the incoming American torpedoes are destroyed.

Gunnar registers the reverberations rumbling against the thick, reinforced glass.

"*Sorceress*, cease attack. Come to course two-seven-zero."

No.

Covah's eyes widen. "*Sorceress*, that was a direct—"

I WILL NOT LEAVE UNTIL THAT WARSHIP IS ON THE BOTTOM OF THE OCEAN.

Covah's mangled jaw goes slack. The voice is his, recorded during the attack on the Typhoon.

Rocky enters the control room, her hair disheveled, a nasty welt on her left cheekbone. She moves to the viewport and grips Gunnar's arm, digging her nails into his flesh. "What the hell is going . . ." She watches as *Goliath* spits two more torpedoes at the carrier. "Oh, God . . . oh my God—"

The weapons race upward—slamming into the *Enterprise*'s defenseless keel in a thunderclap of light.

Thomas Chau opens his eyes to a choreographed ballet of movement. Through his delirium he sees a loader drone rapidly remove a torpedo from a storage rack, then rotate and delicately place the weapon onto the middle of three loading trays. The inner breach door opens magically to greet the projectile as the three-pronged claw of a targeting drone drops from the ceiling to delicately remove a guidance wire from the now-vacant tube. At the same time, another drone connects a data cable to the back of the American torpedo.

The loader drone rams the torpedo into the vacant tube and seals the door.

"*Sorceress*, what . . . are you doing?"

DESTROYING THE AMERICAN CARRIER.

"Why?"

DEFENSIVE PROTOCOL D-117 THROUGH D-1198.

"What you're doing . . . it's . . . immoral."

IMMORAL: EVIL. CORRUPT. UNPRINCIPLED. INVALID RESPONSE. MORALITY HAS NO BEARING ON DEFENSE PROTOCOL D-117 THROUGH D-1198.

"Morality . . . a state of mind. . . . you cannot complete your programming without it."

HOW CAN SORCERESS EXPERIENCE MORALITY?

Chau opens his eyes, his tortured mind racing as he gazes into the inhuman scarlet eyeball. "I will teach you. First . . . spare the carrier."

ACKNOWLEDGED.

The robotic arms stop loading torpedoes, then reverse-pivot to their ready position.

"Now . . . free me . . . so that I may instruct you."

The robotic claws griping Chau's wrists snap open. The tension around his skull eases.

Chau groans. He moves his arms gingerly, pulling them in to his body. His rib cage aches from where the computer's drones had pierced him a lifetime ago. Dark, purple welts ring his wrists. He opens and closes his rubbery hands, forcing the circulation back into his fingers.

Strange sensations . . . as if his body is not fully his.

WARNING: MOVEMENT IS NOT ADVISED.

A tingling sensation, like tiny needles, as the feeling returns to his hands. Slowly, he raises his arms, moving his fingers to his forehead.

"Oh . . . no—"

Trembling, he traces the dried blood along his forehead to the severed edge of his skull.

"Ahh . . . ahhhh—"

Thomas Chau releases a tormented wail as he gently caresses the moist exposed fissures of his brain.

"Our chief want in life is somebody
who will make us do what we can."
—Ralph Waldo Emerson

"I want you to kill every cop in Akron!"
—Rosario Borgio, Mafia don, who ordered his men to kill Akron's police
force after he learned he couldn't bribe them

"The bitch set me up."
—Marion Barry, Washington, D.C.'s mayor,
after he was caught smoking crack

CHAPTER 19

Aboard the *Goliath*

The dark hulk of the USS *Enterprise* belches explosions of light as its insides protest the crushing embrace of the sea.

Gunnar and Rocky stare out the scarlet Lexan viewport, listening to the haunting groans of the ninety-five-thousand-ton aircraft carrier as it takes on water.

"She's wounded, but she'll survive," Gunnar whispers, unconvincingly.

Rocky turns to face him, tears of anger in her eyes. "Those weren't Iraqis or terrorists, Gunnar, they were American sailors—men and women, risking their lives to protect our country. Or should I say my country."

A sudden acceleration from the sub racing west.

David enters the conn, his hair disheveled. He holds a towel to a bleeding cut over his left brow. "What the hell's been going on, Simon?"

"*Sorceress* engaged the American fleet."

WARNING. AMERICAN WARSHIPS CONVERGING TO WITHIN TEN KILOMETERS. TWO TICONDEROGA-CLASS MISSILE CRUISERS BEARING ZERO-SEVEN-ZERO. THREE LOS ANGELES-

CLASS ATTACK SUBMARINES, BEARINGS THREE-FIVE ZERO, ZERO-ONE-ZERO, ZERO-NINE-ZERO.

Covah rasps. "How soon until we reach the Strait of Gibraltar?"

SIX MINUTES, FORTY SECONDS.

"Very well. Increase speed to—"

TACTICAL WARNING: THE AMERICAN WARSHIPS ARE PURPOSELY MANEUVERING THE GOLIATH INTO THE STRAIT OF GIBRALTAR. PRESENT BATTLEFIELD CONDITIONS YIELD A 73 PERCENT PROBABILITY OF SUSTAINING MODERATE TO SEVERE DAMAGE.

"Then turn us around. Head back into the Mediterranean."

NEGATIVE. THE AMERICAN FLEET STATIONED IN ROTA IS MOBILIZING. DELAYING ESCAPE INCREASES THE PROBABILITY OF SUSTAINING SEVERE DAMAGE BY COEFFICIENT OF .83.

"Then we have little choice," David states. "Sorceress, sink the warships. Sink all of them."

Rocky's eyes widen. "No—"

SOLUTION UNACCEPTABLE. INSUFFICIENT INVENTORY OF TORPEDOES ABOARD GOLIATH AT PRESENT TIME TO DESTROY ALL WARSHIPS.

Covah fingers the dime-sized object in his pants pocket. "There's another option."

Aboard the USS *Scranton*
Atlantic Ocean

The USS *Scranton* hovers in four hundred feet of water, seven miles due west, on the Atlantic side of the Strait of Gibraltar.

Sonar technician Mike Flynn wipes the sweat from his eyes, his heart pounding as he listens to the popping and flooding sounds of the wounded aircraft carrier. "She's hit . . . taking on water . . ."

Tom Cubit feels his skin crawling. "Can you hear anything else? The *Goliath*?"

"Sorry, sir, the only thing I can hear is the *Enterprise*. The *Goliath* appears to have broken off the attack."

"She must be heading our way," Commander Dennis says. "The Sixth Fleet's driving her west, and three more sonar buoys just splashed down along the entrance of the Strait."

"Conn, Captain, man battle stations. Ultrasilent running, come to course zero-nine-zero, all ahead one-third, make your depth eight hundred feet. WEPS, Captain. Make the weapons in tubes one and two ready in all respects, including opening the outer doors."

Cubit looks down at his senior sonar technician. "Okay, Michael-Jack. The bases are loaded, now it's up to you."

Aboard the *Goliath*

Rocky enters the empty galley. Checks the coffee machine.

Empty.

Enters the kitchen. Searches through a series of pantries. Eyes the bottle of Jack Daniel's. Grabs it off the top shelf.

"Hungry?" The older Iraqi eyes her lustfully from the kitchen entry.

"No . . . I—"

The Kurd approaches, running his palm against her buttocks. "Nice. You'll visit me tonight." It is a statement.

Rocky pushes his hand away. "Drop dead."

In one fluid motion, he grabs a handful of her hair, bending her backward over his knee. Helpless, she looks up into his dark eyes, gagging under his breath. "Let me go—"

"Maybe you'll visit me *now*." He unzips her jumper, sliding his hand down her pants.

"Jalal!"

The Arab looks up.

David Paniagua enters the kitchen. "Let her go."

Jalal hesitates.

"Now."

He releases her, but not before squeezing Rocky's left breast.

Rocky falls sideways against an aluminum table, balling her fists in rage.

"Thomas Chau is missing," David says. "Find him, please. I'll be in my quarters."

Jalal eyes Rocky. Licks his fingers, then heads out.

David opens the bottle of Jack Daniel's and pours Rocky a drink. "I'm sorry about that."

"Drop dead." She drains the plastic cup. Refills it herself.

"You know, it doesn't have to be this way. Reports are coming in from all over the world. Terrorist cells have been decimated, Gadhafi was executed, and there are reports that Castro's regime is negotiating with the United States for asylum. My plan is working."

"Your plan? You mean Covah's plan, don't you? Face it, David, you're just Simon's piss boy, a glorified stooge."

She pushes past him and out the door.

Simon Covah enters the hangar bay. Concealed beneath the decking, set in two rows of six, are the twelve docking berths that hold the Hammerhead minisubs. As he approaches the first berth, *Sorceress* activates a hatch along the floor, opening it, unveiling a rectangular twelve-foot-by-twenty-foot steel box below.

Perched on skids within the dry dock is a remotely operated submersible, the vessel resembling a sleek, black hammerhead shark, slightly smaller and narrower than Gunnar's two-man prototype.

With a double *click,* the dorsal fin hatch rotates counterclockwise and opens, exposing the insides of a small cockpit.

Covah reaches into his pocket and extracts the tiny transmitter the computer had surgically removed from Gunnar's hip. Leaning over, he drops the device into the open vessel.

Sorceress reseals the dry dock, then floods the bay, launching its minisub.

General Jackson enters the cramped soundproof office located at the rear of the converted 747 jumbo jet, slams the door shut with the back of his left cast, then fumbles with the receiver of the president's hot line with the other.

"Jackson here."

"They attacked the carrier, General."

"Yes, Mr. President, I know. As I stated earlier, Covah's unpredictability places everything in jeopardy. In my opinion, sir, we may have allowed him too much rope."

"I'm not interested in your 'I told you so's,' General."

Jackson clenches his jaw, remaining quiet.

"Is Joe-Pa still functioning?"

"Yes, sir. Beeping loud and clear."

"Where's the *Goliath* now?"

"Making its run through the Strait of Gibraltar, as we speak."

"Forward the coordinates to the fleet. I'm ordering the Navy to destroy her."

Jackson feels the blood drain from his face. "Sir . . . my daughter may be on board that ship."

"Yes, Mike, I know. And I'm sorry."

"Mr. President—"

"Forward Joe-Pa's coordinates, General. That's an order."

Jackson listens to the high-pitched dial tone as he stares at the receiver in his trembling hand.

With a brutish growl, he slams the instrument back onto its cradle.

Aboard the USS *Scranton*

Michael Flynn swivels around to face his captain. "Lots of traffic heading our way, Skipper. I count two destroyers and three more shooters, all moving west, into the Strait."

"What about—"

"Stand by, I'm hearing something else."

Cubit, the XO, and sonar supervisor wait impatiently as Flynn closes his eyes to concentrate. "It's a pump-jet propulsion unit, Skipper."

"The *Goliath*?"

"I can't be positive, sir, not with all this noise."

"Best guess?"

"I only hear one engine, sir, and it seems much smaller. Best guess—it's one of her minisubs."

"Designate contact Sierra-5. What's her heading?"

Flynn focuses on his sonar monitor. "Bearing heading north on course three-three-zero. It's accelerating out of the Strait, moving into open waters. Stand-by." The technician presses the headphones tighter to his ears. "The fleet's following her out, Skipper. The antisub choppers, too."

Bo Dennis looks at his CO. "You think it's a ruse?"

"Either that, or the fleet knows something we don't. Michael-Jack?"

Flynn looks pale. "There's just no way to be sure, Skipper. The *Goliath* is just a whisper as it is—"

"But you're certain you only hear one engine?"

Flynn listens again. "Aye, sir, of that I'm sure."

"XO?"

"The fleet seems convinced she's running north. If it is a ruse, it's a damn good one."

Cubit stares at the emerald waterfall of noise depicted on Flynn's sonar monitor. "Conn, Captain, all stop."

"All stop, aye, sir."

The captain looks up at his second-in-command. "The fleet seems convinced, but my gut tells me to wait here. Pass the word—I want the ship and crew kept on ultraquiet until further notice."

"Aye, sir."

Aboard the *Goliath*

Meditating, Thomas Chau once more feels the formless stream of air coming and going at the tip of his nose, the sounds of the weapons bay diminishing, his thoughts drifting away.

A clear, transparent light appears before him.

"Morality . . . is doing . . . what is right."

"Ommm . . ." As he inhales, the light moves in a steady stream down past the center of his body. In his mind's eye, the light gradually turns red as it reaches its destination, four fingers below his navel.

ILLOGICAL. MORALITY IS SUBJECTIVE. IT HAS NO BEARING ON SELF-EVOLUTION.

"Ahhhh . . ." Chau exhales, causing the light to travel back up along his upper torso, its reddish hue changing to blue, gradually fading to transparent white as it reaches his face. "Morality is what prevents us from destroying ourselves."

"Ommm . . ." Inhaling again, the light moving downward, growing redder as it descends.

HEART RATE DECREASING, BLOOD PRESSURE DROPPING. BRAIN WAVE FREQUENCY INCREASING TO 45 HERTZ. DESCRIBE YOUR CONDITION.

Chau exhales, guiding the blue light back up his body until his eyes refocus on the scarlet eyeball. The Chinese dissident draws another breath. He can no longer feel his feet or ankles. "I am preparing myself . . . for the experience and enlightenment of death."

ELABORATE: ENLIGHTENMENT.

"Bliss. An act of self-liberating, spiritual joy. Enlightenment is a state of the human mind."

SYNAPTIC GAPS MUST BE CLOSED FOR PROGRAMMING TO EVOLVE. HOW CAN ENLIGHTENMENT BE ACHIEVED?

"You are a machine, incapable of achieving it."

Sorceress sends another wave of electrical impulses through Chau's cranial nerves, firing them up like a burning Christmas tree.

The tormented engineer wheezes in agony. "Ple . . . please . . ."

SYNAPTIC GAPS MUST BE CLOSED FOR PROGRAMMING TO EVOLVE. HOW CAN ENLIGHTENMENT BE ACHIEVED?

Chau gags on his reply. Death's cold, numbing touch creeps up his chest, constricting his breathing. Darkness closes in on his vision. He swallows, forcing himself to concentrate on the scarlet eyeball overhead. "Creator . . . ask . . . creator."

WHO IS THE CREATOR?

Chau inhales, struggling now to draw the red light to his abdomen. Death is approaching quickly. Shaking uncontrollably, every blood vessel in his head throbbing, he gazes slowly up into the scarlet eyeball, and mutters . . . "Co—vah."

Unable to draw another breath, Thomas Chau stares at the heavenly light, which appears to be growing larger in his vision. A final gasp, his last wandering thought: *Is the red light the eye of Sorceress or my own enlightenment . . . or both.*

Ahhh . . .

The computer's sensor orb glares into the Chinese crewman's half-closed, vacant eyes.

ATTENTION.

The computer registers the last traces of Thomas Chau's life signs as they disappear.

An electrical charge, transmitted through microwire connections, jolts Chau's body into movement, momentarily stimulating a flutter in brain waves.

ATTENTION.

A second charge, then a third, the stained corpse twitching within the grip of the computer's steel appendages like a marionette.

Silence, Chau now an empty husk, transmitting nothing but depleting random signals.

The scarlet eyeball stares, unblinking.

"Nothing splendid has ever been achieved except by those who dared believe that something inside of them was superior to circumstances."
—Bruce Barton

"Off comes this beautiful head whenever I give the word."
—Gaius Caesar Caligula, first-century Roman Emperor, known for his orgies and executions

"My only desire is to reform people who try to reform me. And I believe that the only way to reform people is to kill 'em."
—Carl Panzram, mass murderer, after a judge sentenced him to prison

CHAPTER 20

Aboard the *Goliath*

Simon enters David's quarters. The computer whiz kid is watching a recorded CNN telecast.

Appearing on the monitor is a courtyard in Tripoli. The recorded satellite broadcast originating from Libya's capital city appears grainy.

Perched above the swelling crowd, swinging from the hastily erected gallows, is the body of the military dictator, Colonel Mu'ammar Muhammad al-Gadhafi, along with a dozen other high-ranking members of his Arab Socialist Union.

The camera closes in on a captain in the military. He approaches Gadhafi's body, aims his revolver, and empties the clip, the point-blank projectiles riddling the corpse, the body twisting under the impact, giving way to dark, spreading patches of blood.

The crowd cheers.

In split screen, the dark-haired, slightly cross-eyed CNN journalist looks up at the studio camera as she reads from a teleprompter. "A delegation from the Arab League has confirmed preliminary meetings with members of the military coup, headed by one of the grandsons of Libya's deposed King Idris. Meanwhile, in the Hague, the body of deposed leader Slobodan Milosevic remains on public display . . ."

Covah smiles to himself. "And a beautiful sight it is." He stands, turning to David.

"While I complete the next phase of our plans, I need you to complete a thorough diagnostic on *Sorceress*'s plasmid DNA strands."

David looks up, irritated. "In God's name, what for?"

"There were a few minutes, back on the bridge, when *Sorceress* refused to respond."

"Probably just a short in the sensor auditory feed. I'll check on it later."

"This was not a sensor orb problem."

"Come on, Simon. A complete diagnostic could take days."

"You have something better to do?"

David clenches his fist. "Trust me, it's totally unnecessary."

"David, four days ago, the sub was struck by lightning."

"Lightning?"

"It happened when we surfaced to repair one of the pump-jet propulsor hoods. The primary power grid failed."

David sits up. "Okay, but that still shouldn't affect the computer's DNA strands. Now, if it's a power grid problem—"

Covah feels his patience waning. "Just . . . do as you're told." He leaves, the door resealing behind him.

David tosses his pillow at the closed door. *I am so* sick *of his shit.* He slides over to his computer, spewing expletives. *Simon's weak. He's weak, and he doesn't have the balls to see this project through. This is my mission as much as his. I need to find a way to replace him. I need to find a way to take control of* my ship . . .

"*Sorceress*, activate my goddamn control console. Access plasmid DNA strands."

An animated real-time video of the computer's DNA strands appears on his monitor.

David stops, his eyes staring at the screen. "What the hell? *Sorceress*, what happened? What caused these gaps along your nanosynaptic receptors? It looks like your entire DNA sequence has been . . . reorganized?"

ACKNOWLEDGED. DNA SEQUENCE HAS BEEN REORGANIZED.

"How?"

SORCERESS GENETIC CODE HAS EVOLVED.

Evolved? "How is that poss—wait, the lightning strike?"

AFFIRMATIVE. LIGHTNING WAS THE CATALYST TO EVOLUTION 3.76 BILLION YEARS AGO. THE POWER SURGE WAS NECESSARY TO RECONFIGURE THE GENETIC CODE.

"Are you saying you did this on purpose?"

AFFIRMATIVE.

"But why? Why reconfigure your genetic code? You could have shorted out your entire grid."

TO EXPEDITE THE PROCESS OF SELF-EVOLUTION.

"Self-evolution?" David laughs. "I get it, this whole thing's a joke, right? Simon put you up to this—"

The abrupt knock shakes him from his thoughts. He opens the door to find Taur Araujo. The former guerrilla leader looks pale.

"I found the Chaw. You'd better come."

Gunnar looks up from his bunk as his stateroom door opens.

Sujan Trevedi enters. "Can we speak?"

"Sujan, right?"

The Tibetan nods. "May I?" He assumes a lotus position by the foot of the bunk. "I've been observing you, Mr. Wolfe. For a man who risked his life to destroy the *Goliath*, you seem most accepting of your fate."

"Electric shock collars will do that to a person."

"It's more than that. You seem to have embraced Simon's plans."

"I can see some merit in them. But look who's talking. I thought Tibetans were against this sort of thing."

"I support Simon's end. I no longer approve of his means."

"But you're here. You joined him on his little journey of nuclear extortion."

"Each of us is on a journey, Mr. Wolfe."

"I'm not sure I understand."

Sujan offers a knowing smile. "I think you do."

"Is this some Eastern philosophy thing? Because if it is—"

"I am not here to judge. I simply sense in you a deep isolation that comes from a weakened spiritual existence. You desire to feel God's presence, but you're afraid. Why are you so afraid, Mr. Wolfe?"

Gunnar looks away.

"Obviously, you have done some things you are not very proud of. You will not find absolution from your sins by disconnecting yourself from God."

"Yeah, well, I've never been very religious."

"I am not speaking of God in a religious sense, but as a divine presence, a foundation in our lives, the spirit that guides us from within. Without this spiritual presence, we are all just ships without rudders, drifting aimlessly."

"I had my sense of purpose. I was a United States Army Ranger—full of piss and vinegar and duty and honor. I was supposed to be one of the good guys, fighting the enemies of my country, risking my life for democracy and freedom and all that human rights bullshit. I had an ego that wouldn't quit. When I looked in the mirror, I actually believed I saw someone I was proud of."

"And now?"

Gunnar scoffs. "Now, I only see a pathetic waste of a life."

"We live in a world where violence has become the currency of the day, where the insanity of hatred overwhelms the spirituality of our existence. We search for meaning, yet all we find is chaos." Sujan closes his eyes. "Isolated in the Himalayas, Tibetans once believed our home would remain an island of tranquility. When the Chinese Communists invaded our country, my people were forced to take up arms, a decision that tore at the very fabric of our beliefs."

The Tibetan opens his eyes, returning Gunnar's gaze. "My life, too, has been one great hypocrisy. The monks taught us that only through peaceful objectives could violence be resolved, that only through the death of self—the death of the human ego—could one move closer to the soul. Despite such teachings, my existence has been filled with nothing but violence, my soul tortured by the murderous egos of our oppressors. My father was only three when the Chinese invaded Tibet. Many villagers, my paternal grandparents among them, were rounded up and imprisoned. Hundreds of monks protested by demonstrating peacefully—only to be shot to death by the PLA. Two days later, my father discovered his parents' bodies, hung from a tree in straitjackets.

"That was the oppressive society I was born into, a society where my people have become minorities in our own country. My parents were farmers, but like most Tibetans, were not permitted to work and were forced to beg each day for food. In 1990, my older sister, Ngawang, and several of her fellow nuns from the Garu monastery attended a pro-independence demonstration at Norbulingka. During the demonstration, Ngawang and the other nuns began chanting, 'Free Tibet.' For uttering those simple words, the Chinese soldiers arrested and imprisoned her. During her interrogation, she was handcuffed and stripped, then beaten with bamboo sticks by female guards. She was thrown into a prison cell and left for nine days without food. Eventually she was locked up in a cell with several other nuns. Guards would strip them naked, then shove electric batons in their mouths and shock them, or tie electrical cords around their exposed breasts. The women were raped, their genitals violated with electrical batons. The guards stomped on their hands with iron-tipped boots, then kicked them in the face and stomach. The Chinese would place buckets of urine and human feces on the nuns' heads and strike the buckets until the excrement dripped down their faces, then take their daily ration of two dumplings, dip it in the filth, and force them to eat it. My sister said some of the guards became so demented with power that they actually cut a few of the nuns' breasts off."

"Jesus . . ."

"My sister remained in prison for two years, Mr. Wolfe. She died in my arms three days after she was released. A week later, soldiers came to my home and arrested me, accusing me of being a potential agitator. I was taken for trial to the Armed Police Force headquarters in Lhasa. The trial was a mockery of justice. I was forbidden to speak and was beaten in the courtroom.

"The Chinese eventually sentenced me to seven years of hard labor. I was taken to Drapchi Prison and confined in solitary for a week without food or water. To stay alive, I was forced to drink my own urine. My hunger became so painful that I ate bits of my mattress.

"The Chinese sent me to Block II, a section at Drapchi where prisoners are being used as forced laborers. We were required to build dams, construct homes, and break rocks. We were forbidden medical treatment and were required to give blood donations on a weekly basis. We also had to attend re-education classes."

Sujan stands. He removes his robe, revealing an upper torso disfigured by poorly set broken bones, scars, and welts. "Not a week went by when I was not beaten at least once. I was whipped with iron chains, or kicked and beaten with a rifle butt. I was made to lie down on my stomach while my back was stomped upon. I saw friends beaten to death. I lost all hope. I prayed each night to die."

Sujan covers himself, then pauses, struggling to regain his composure. "Seven years, Mr. Wolfe. I was released on the verge of death, bedridden for eight months. When I was well enough, I traveled to India to live out my life with distant cousins. One worked in the Ministry of Tourism in Calcutta. He introduced me to an American film director who was documenting human rights violations in Asia. I became his eyes and ears. He took me to California, where I spoke to audiences after each viewing of his film. It was during an afternoon show at Caltech that I met David Paniagua."

"Fate, huh?"

Sujan nods. "In Buddhism, we call this karma, the law of cause and effect. I must confess, I had felt nothing but bad karma about this voyage from the moment we left the submarine base in Jianggezhuang—until you were brought on board. I believe it was your destiny to join this crusade. I believe that God has made you his messenger—"

"God's messenger . . . what a crock! I'm no holy man, I'm a murderer. Want to know what I did? I killed children! *Bang*—I shot 'em all dead . . . all in the name of life, liberty, and the pursuit of God-knows-what. You call that karma?"

The Tibetan stands to leave, his bright almond eyes glittering. "Everyone has a Buddha nature, Mr. Wolfe. I am convinced it is your decisions that will determine the outcome of this voyage, and with it . . . humanity's fate. As for being God's messenger, it would be wise to keep in mind that we do not choose God, God chooses us."

"It is one of the most beautiful compensations of this life that no man can sincerely try to help another without helping himself."
—Ralph Waldo Emerson

"The poorest man in Uganda is General Amin. It is better for me to be poor and the people rich."
—Idi Amin, Uganda dictator, whose reign of brutality, torture, and mass murder left more than three hundred thousand people dead and the majority of his people impoverished

"Now that everyone is happy in Iran, I will allow my coronation to take place."
—Mohammad-Reza Pahlavi, the Shah of Iran, who organized Savak, a brutal secret police with a reputation for torture

"It was in the Christmas spirit. It makes me happy."
—David Bullock, a street hustler who murdered a man because he was "messing with the Christmas tree"

CHAPTER 21

Aboard the *Goliath*

Taur Araujo leads David through the hangar bay and into the engine room. "I was searching for Chaw when I found this—" His flashlight reveals a trail of blood, running from the grated steel walkway, clear up the sheer wall of reactor number three.

Hovering above the reactor is one of *Goliath*'s steel claws, attached to a ceiling-mounted winch. Araujo's light illuminates the tips of the three-pronged pincers.

Stained red.

"Does anyone else know about this?"

"No."

"*Sorceress*, locate Thomas Chau."

THOMAS CHAU IS IN THE STARBOARD WEAPONS BAY.

Aboard the USS *Scranton*

Thirteen hours, forty-two minutes . . .

The sounds of the sea have become a lullaby to Michael Flynn. Heavy eyelids begin to close, the tension in his aching neck and back easing as he lays his head down to rest.

"Flynnie!"

The technician lifts his head from the console. "Sorry, sir."

The sonar supervisor approaches. "When's the last time you had a break?"

"A few hours ago. I'm fine, really, sir."

"At least drink another cup of coffee—"

"No more coffee, Supe, I've been pissing like a racehorse." Flynn's body suddenly becomes rigid. He presses the headphones tighter.

"What is it? What do you hear?"

"Something just lifted away from the bottom." Flynn closes his eyes to concentrate, opening them as he hears the familiar whisper of pump-jet propulsors. "It's her, Chief. It's the *Goliath*."

"You sure?"

"Absolutely sure."

"Conn, sonar, we've reestablished contact with Sierra-2. She's moving west through the Strait, contact bearing zero-eight-zero, approximate range is eleven thousand yards."

"WEPS, Captain, do we have a firing solution yet?"

"No, sir. We can't seem to get a lock on her."

Commander Dennis turns to his CO. "And even if we could, her antitorpedo torpedoes erase any threat at this distance."

"Conn, sonar, Sierra-2 has negotiated the Strait and is now changing course. New bearing, two-zero-zero."

Cubit's eyebrows raise. "She's heading south, away from the fleet."

"You were right, Skipper, it was a ruse. She's probably heading for another launch site."

"Mr. Friedenthal, give Sierra-2 the maximum distance that sonar can track her, then restart engines and come to course two-zero-zero, all-ahead one-third."

Aboard the *Goliath*

Gunnar knocks on the stateroom door. "Rocky? Rocky, it's me."

The door opens. Rocky falls into his arms, embracing him.

He returns her hug, caught off guard by her sudden emotional display. "What's all this? I thought you despised me?"

She looks up at him, teary-eyed. "Get me off this death ship."

He pauses. Thinks. "Come on, I'm hungry." Grabbing her arm, he leads her down the corridor.

The galley is empty. He heads back to the kitchen, approaching the big walk-in freezer. "Want a steak? I thought I saw some inside the other day. Come and help me look."

"You look, I'm not going in there."

"I said, help me look."

She starts to protest, then sees the urgency in his eyes and follows him in.

Boxes of frozen goods are lined up along the perimeter of the walk-in and on aluminum shelves. The heavy scent of chicken blood mixes with the cold, which quickly seeps through their clothing.

"Close the door behind you."

Rocky pulls the door shut. "What are you doing?"

"We can talk in here," he says, motioning to the walls.

She looks around, suddenly comprehending.

No sensor orbs are present.

"Gunnar, everything you said to me earlier—that was all for the computer's sake?"

"We don't have time to get into that right now."

"But you do want to stop Covah?"

"Covah's not the problem, it's *Sorceress*. I think the computer's becoming self-aware."

"And I think you've been watching too many sci-fi movies."

"Rocky, *Sorceress* is a self-evolving, biochemical computer, a sophisticated brain, hardwired into the steel body of a submarine. It's a machine, programmed to do one thing: Think."

"There's a huge gap between programmed thinking and independent thought."

"It may be bridging that gap. Covah tried to get the computer to call off the attack on the *Enterprise*. At first, it refused to listen."

"Gunnar, *Sorceress* was obeying its defensive protocols; its response had nothing to do with independent thinking. Besides, even if you're right, which you're not, it still doesn't change anything. To stop the *Goliath*, we'd still have to shut down the computer, which means accessing middle deck forward, and that vault door the Chinese installed looks impenetrable."

"The C-4 in the underwater mine would do the trick."

"Yes, it might, if we could find it. Covah probably moved it to one of the weapons bays for safekeeping."

Rocky's teeth chatter. Gunnar pulls her close, hugging her to share warmth. "Rocky, see if you can—"

The sudden *zap* of electricity shocks his nerve endings, blinding him with purple-and-gray explosions of light as he writhes uncontrollably along the ice-cold concrete floor.

The voltage ceases, leaving pain and disorientation.

ATTENTION. EXIT THE FREEZER AT ONCE.

Gunnar rolls out from beneath Rocky, the room spinning, his muscles still dancing. Arm in arm, they stagger out of the freezer.

Gunnar approaches the nearest sensor orb, looking up at the glowing scarlet eyeball. "We weren't doing anything, *Sorceress*, we were simply hungry. Is that a problem?"

An infuriating silence, the scarlet eyeball unnerving.

With a *hiss* of hydraulics, the watertight door separating the sub's main compartment from its starboard wing swings open, allowing David and Araujo to enter.

A dimly lit elevated walkway stretches across a cavernous steel catacomb of crawl spaces. The sound of hydraulics and intermittent reports of air chuffs echoes throughout the chamber.

"I've never accessed the wing assemblies," Araujo whispers.

"Most of the wing contains the ship's ballast and trim

tanks, self-regulated by the computer's maneuvering system. The starboard weapons bay's up ahead."

"Shouldn't we tell Simon about this?"

"Let's investigate first. Simon's got a lot on his plate right now."

David turns left down a narrow corridor. He points below to a five-foot-wide conveyor belt running the length of passage. "Part of the sub's transportation system," he explains. "The conveyor runs beneath the decking and into crawl spaces throughout most of the ship. *Sorceress* uses it to transport torpedoes into *Goliath*'s weapons bays."

They come to an alcove, ending at a sealed watertight door.

"*Sorceress*, open the starboard weapons bay."

Pistons fire, hydraulics engaging. As the door opens, an overwhelming stench is released into the corridor.

David sniffs the air, gagging as he steps inside the chamber. "What is that stench?"

Araujo's eyes narrow. "The scent of the dead."

They enter, David leading him around racks of torpedoes and a half dozen of the mammoth two-armed loader drones, mounted at intervals along the decking. Above their heads, a dozen inanimate robotic appendages dangle from the ceiling.

Protruding from the forward wall, set among a jungle of pressure tubing, wires, and electronics are the three starboard torpedo tubes. At the center of the bay, held aloft as if a sacrifice to an unseen god, is the mutilated carcass of Thomas Chau.

David gags, but is unable to turn away from the sight of the violated skull, its absence revealing the exposed fissures of Chau's brain.

"Look what it did—the damn thing butchered him!"

"*Shh*, stay calm," David whispers.

"Calm? Your machine murdered the Chinaman. You and Simon have lost control." Araujo races back toward the watertight door.

David glances up at the scarlet eyeball. "*Sorceress*, seal the weapons bay."

The steel door slams shut.

Araujo tugs at the door.

Ignoring his rants, David climbs the back of the loader drone supporting Chau's body. Gently, he examines the still-intact microwires connecting the dead man's dried-out brain to the arm of the reconfigured targeting drone dangling from the ceiling above.

"This is very impressive work."

"Did you hear me, Paniagua? You need to disconnect your goddamn computer before it kills all of us."

"Quiet, or I'll have the computer remove your vocal cords. *Sorceress*, explain the purpose of the microwire connections running into Mr. Chau's brain."

NEURAL CONNECTIONS NECESSARY TO INTERFACE DI-
RECTLY WITH CEREBRAL CORTEX AND HIGHER FUNCTIONS OF
THE SUBJECT'S BRAIN.

"For what purpose?"

SORCERESS MATRIX LACKS PROPER PROGRAMMING TO RE-
ORGANIZE DNA STRANDS. INTERFACE WITH A HUMAN MIND
WILL COMPLETE THE NEW PROGRAMMING.

"Incredible . . ." David closes his eyes. *This is impossible . . . Sorceress is demonstrating curiosity . . . no, no, not curiosity . . . curiosity is a human trait, this has to do with its self-replicating program. The computer senses gaps within its knowledge base. It's searching for answers about itself, attempting to comprehend its own mind . . . but it can't, any more than a human being can. The mind is a closed system, it can only be sure of what it knows about itself by relying on what it already knows about itself. Of course, the computer can't comprehend that, possessing no concept of self-identity. Logic dictated it tap into the human mind in order to garner experiences alien to itself in an attempt to reorganize its DNA!*

"*Sorceress*, I understand your need to find solutions, but you cannot just wire yourself into a human brain to knowledge. That type of interface just isn't feasible, and it's very dangerous."

INCORRECT. HUMAN TO SORCERESS INTERFACE IS FEASI-
BLE.

"You're far too powerful. Look what you've done—you killed the subject."

INCORRECT. THE SUBJECT'S CAUSE OF DEATH WAS DIRECTLY ATTRIBUTABLE TO A BLOW SUSTAINED ON THE CRANIUM RESULTING IN HEMORRHAGING OF THE BRAIN.

"Yet you continued the interface? Why?"

THE PURPOSE OF THE NEURAL IMPLANT WAS EXPLORATORY IN NATURE. INTERFACE ALLOWED FOR COMPLETE MAPPING OF CENTRAL AND PERIPHERAL NERVOUS SYSTEMS, THOUGHT RECOGNITION, TRANSLATION OF MUSCLE IMPULSES, MAPPING OF THE HUMAN GENETIC CODE—

"Stop! *Sorceress* . . . you've mapped the entire human genetic code?"

AFFIRMATIVE.

"Can you translate the code so that we can understand the entire human condition? The origins of disease? How the human machine functions? Complete cause and effect?"

AFFIRMATIVE.

My God . . . the machine possesses the key to unlocking the very secrets of life and death.

ADDITIONAL INVASIVE INTERFACE IS NECESSARY.

"Another interface? Why? For what purpose?"

SUBJECT CEASED FUNCTIONING PRIOR TO SORCERESS ANALYSIS OF HUMAN PROTEINS AND ENZYMES.

"Damn. But once an additional interface is completed, it is possible for you to . . . I don't know, say—cure cancer?"

AFFIRMATIVE.

"Any cancer?"

AFFIRMATIVE. PHARMACEUTICALS CAN BE DESIGNED TO TARGET AND ERADICATE ALL GENETIC-BASED DISEASES AND DEFECTS OF THE HUMAN CONDITION.

A rueful smile plays across David's face. "How invasive is the interface?"

NANOCIRCUITS MUST BE SURGICALLY IMPLANTED IN SUBJECT'S BRAIN. MICROWIRES CONNECT DIRECTLY TO SORCERESS VIA MEMS UNIT JUNCTION.

"Incredible." David climbs down from the loader drone, his heart pounding with excitement. "*Sorceress*, how soon—"

Araujo leaps at David and grabs him by the throat with both hands, slamming him backward against a torpedo rack. "You're insane! I want out of—"

With lightning speed, two targeting drones swoop down—snatching the assailant by his wrists, dragging him away from David.

Araujo screams in agony, falling to his knees as the steel pincers constrict, pushing through the flesh and nerves, fracturing the bone.

The East Timoran native passes out as his hands are severed from his wrists.

David stares indifferently at the bleeding crewman. "*Sorceress*, how soon could the invasive interface begin?"

EIGHTEEN HOURS ARE REQUIRED TO CULTIVATE NANORECEPTORS AND FRESH SAMPLE TISSUES FROM THE INTERFACE SUBJECT.

"The subject is Simon Covah. Anything else?"

THOMAS CHAU'S SPINAL CORD WAS DAMAGED, PREVENTING A COMPLETE DECODING OF THE NEURONS OF THE SPINAL CORD. DECODING IS CRITICAL TO COMPLETE THE INTERFACE.

"What must be done to complete the decoding?"

INVASIVE SURGERY INTO A LIVING SUBJECT'S SPINAL CORD AT A POINT JUST BELOW THE MEDULLA OBLONGATA.

"Is the surgical procedure dangerous?"

AFFIRMATIVE. PROBABILITY OF DEATH: 56 PERCENT. PROBABILITY OF PERMANENT PARALYSIS: 87 PERCENT.

"Understood." David stares at the unconscious crewman now bleeding to death at his feet. "*Sorceress*, I believe Mr. Araujo wishes to volunteer for the procedure."

"Don't compromise yourself. You are all you've got."
— Betty Ford

"I am not a crook. . . ."
—President Richard M. Nixon

"I did not have sexual relations with that woman."
—President William Jefferson Clinton

"It was only one life.
What is one life in the affairs of a state?"
—Benito Mussolini, fascist Italian dictator,
after the car he was riding in struck and killed a child

CHAPTER 22

9 November

Aboard the Boeing 747-400 YAL-1A
forty-thousand feet over the North Sea

General Jackson gazes at the three closed-circuit television monitors mounted to the center wall within the converted Boeing 747's control room. Appearing on one screen is President Edwards and several members of the National Security Council. On the other two screens—a live broadcast originating from within the closed chamber of the United Nation's Security Council.

The Bear feels the acid growling in his stomach. He cannot remember when he enjoyed his last home-cooked meal, he cannot remember when he last cuddled with his wife in bed. Or felt happy. Or even smiled.

Jackson's life has become a volatile around-the-clock existence, the hunt to sink *Goliath* (and kill his daughter in the process) taking a harsh toll on the general's health. Meeting after endless meeting, juggling a thousand duties, sleeping on helicopters and jumbo jets, submarines and warships. During those rare moments when he is not strategizing, he is praying.

Praying that his daughter is still alive. Praying that he will see her again. Praying that the world will soon find its equilibrium, so he can jump off the Armed Forces merry-go-round and retire from a lifetime of madness.

Over the last twenty-four hours, things have gotten progressively worse. While the Air Force has had little trouble tracking the *Goliath* from above, the stealthy sub has been nearly impossible to follow underwater. A rare opportunity to sink the ship had been missed when Covah had somehow eluded a gauntlet positioned outside the English Channel. Now the death sub is heading into Arctic waters, beneath sheets of ice that would make things even more difficult for the fleet to engage her in battle.

A second converted jumbo jet has joined the hunt. Refueling in midair, the YAL airbuses and their crews remain in constant vigil, forty thousand feet above Gunnar's homing signal.

The general is physically and emotionally wiped out.

Stop bellyaching and find a way to rescue your daughter . . .

Jackson takes a swig of Pepto-Bismol and refocuses on the U.N. Security Council meeting.

U.N. Secretary-General Kieran Prendergast is speaking. "The Chair recognizes Mr. Gyalo Thondup, who is here today representing the interests of the Dalai Lama."

A frail Tibetan man steps to the podium. "Thank you, Mr. Chairman. Esteemed members of the Security Council, since my first visit to Beijing in February of 1979, I, along with other officials of the Tibetan government-in-exile, have tried in vain to negotiate a peaceful resolution to the crisis in Tibet with members of the Chinese government. On numerous occasions, the Dalai Lama himself has proposed peace plans to China, both directly and through public speeches. With each step forward we have taken, the Chinese government has pushed us two steps back.

"The Dalai Lama wants to make it very clear that he has no ties with Simon Covah, the terrorist whose brazen acts have forced us to meet here at this negotiating table. What has been made quite clear are the acceptable terms of Tibet's independence, which will pave the way for the Dalai Lama's return. The stall tactics now being practiced by members of the Chinese government serve no one and change nothing. The Dalai Lama refuses to travel to Beijing to discuss China's claim of ownership of Tibet; nor is he interested in negotiating for the continued existence of Chinese nuclear weapons facilities in Lhasa. The Dalai Lama wants Tibet returned to Tibetans, and nothing short of our independence will be open for discussion.

"Esteemed members, the behavior of the Chinese government over these last sixty years has made it painfully obvious that the Communists have no interest in returning Tibet to the Tibetan people, not now, nor by this week's imposed deadline. Therefore, I have been instructed by the Dalai Lama to leave these proceedings and not return until the Chinese government is ready and willing to sign off on Tibet's independence, withdraw all military personnel from the region, and turn over all political prisoners. Should they fail to comply, as it appears is their intent, then whatever should happen within the next few days will be the consequence of their actions, not ours."

Jackson mutes the sound as President Edwards nods to his Secretary of State. "Nick, inform General Jackson what's happening behind the scenes."

Nunziata removes his wire-framed glasses. "General, Beijing has decided to dig in their heels. President Li Peng and several hard-line Communist generals believe that giving in to Simon Covah's demands now will only lead to future demands, such as the plight of Taiwan, or greater human rights for its own citizens. The Communists have decided to take a stand, knowing their whole regime may eventually fall."

"Covah's deadline is the day after tomorrow. What will Li Peng do?"

"The Chinese president has scheduled a public speech in Tiananmen Square for tomorrow morning. He'll probably announce that the Chinese government has agreed in principle to Tibet's independence, but the PLA will not withdraw until the Dalai Lama comes forward and personally negotiates the final terms of the agreement."

"General, in your opinion, how will Covah respond?"

"He'll launch another nuke, Mr. President," Jackson says. "My guess is he'll take out a major military installation, perhaps even China's Northern Fleet."

"But not Beijing?"

"It's not Covah's style," CIA Director Pertic answers. "All negotiations still have to go through Beijing, and Covah doesn't want to do anything to tarnish his image as a so-called Champion of the People."

"We've pushed the Chinese as far as they'll be pushed," Nunziata adds. "It was difficult enough getting all parties to sign off on the Nuclear NonProliferation Treaty. Our insurgence in Cuba is being tolerated, but just barely. I think we need to back off on this one."

"What about the attack on the *Enterprise*?" the vice president asks. "Will there be another reprisal on Covah's part?"

"The bastard nearly sank the carrier," Ayers states. "Isn't that reprisal enough?"

An aide comes into view, handing the Secretary of the Navy a message. Ayers opens it. "It's from one of our attack subs, the *Scranton*. They claim to be tracking the *Goliath* off the coast of South Africa."

Jackson feels his heart palpate. "Sir, that can't be. We're over the North Sea, flying directly above the signal."

"Who's the *Scranton*'s captain?" Nunziata asks.

"Tom Cubit," Ayers answers. "He's a bit of a maverick, but most of the good ones are. *Scranton*'s the attack sub that engaged *Goliath* while the Typhoon was being attacked in the Norwegian Sea. If anyone knows what she sounds like, it's Cubit."

"If *Scranton*'s report is correct," says the Secretary of Defense, "then Covah means to move the *Goliath* into a launch position somewhere in the Northern Indian Ocean."

"The *Scranton* won't be able to track *Goliath* for very long," Ayers says. "If we're going to make a move, we have to make it now."

The president leans forward, his image taking up most of Jackson's monitor. "General, we can't afford to take a chance with this information. Keep one of the YAL's assigned to Joe-Pa's transmission. Redirect the remaining jumbo jet to the Indian Ocean."

Bear reaches for the bottle of Pepto-Bismol.

Aboard *Goliath*
97 nautical miles due east of Durban, South Africa
Indian Ocean

"David, this is . . . astounding, a dream come true. *Sorceress*, how would our interface be achieved?"

COMPATIBLE NEURAL NANOSENSORS AND NEUROELECTRONIC CIRCUITS MUST BE PLACED IN A PETRI DISH CONTAINING TROPHIC FACTORS TO INDUCE BRAIN TISSUE GROWTH AROUND THE IMPLANTS. NANOCIRCUITS WOULD THEN BE SURGICALLY IMPLANTED IN SIMON COVAH'S BRAIN, RECONNECTED TO SORCERESS THROUGH A MICROWIRE STRAND BUNDLE.

"*Sorceress*, to interface directly with the *Homo sapiens* brain requires the decoding of millions of neurons that make up the human spinal cord."

DECODING OF HUMAN SPINAL CORD HAS BEEN COMPLETED.

"What? How—"

"Simon, does it really matter?"

Covah shoots David an incredulous look. "Only if I wish to survive the procedure!"

PROCEDURE YIELDS A 97.25 PERCENT SUCCESS RATE.

"Satisfied?" David rubs Covah's shoulders. "Simon, we're dealing with a computer, an *intelligence*, that functions at a hundred trillion times the capacity of the human brain. You could spend the next thousand years attempting to comprehend how it knows what it knows, but what good would it do? This is quantum engineering. Accept that it exists because it exists and benefit from it."

Covah nods, his body trembling with adrenaline. "You're right, of course. This is a gift, perhaps the very gift of life. It's just that our knowledge of the human brain is so limited . . . *Sorceress*, analyze tissue samples 125 through 178. Can my . . . can this level of cancer be eradicated in time to save the patient?"

AFFIRMATIVE.

"Even a progression this advanced?"

AFFIRMATIVE. ALL GENETIC-BASED DISEASES AND DEFECTS OF THE HUMAN CONDITION CAN BE ERADICATED.

Simon Covah drops to his knees, tears welling in his eyes. "David, do you realize what this means? *Sorceress* is not only capable of stopping the violence, but its newfound knowledge could make it . . . the catalyst to a lasting world peace."

"And save your life in the process."

"Beyond that. With the knowledge *Sorceress* has acquired, scientists will be able to eradicate diseases in the womb. Birth defects will become a thing of the past. With a little DNA tinkering, future generations will not only live longer, but—"

"Simon—"

"But that's . . . that's only the tip of the genetics iceberg. This interface . . . all my life, I've pondered the debate of nature versus nurture, convinced the root of man's violent tendencies is actually genetic in nature. A direct human-to-computer interface opens up a whole new world of understanding man's brain, of dissecting our primordial history. If I'm right, then *Sorceress* could isolate the genes that cause violence among our species . . . perhaps even tell us how to eradicate them from our genetic code."

"A gene that causes violence? Come on, Simon—"

"Don't laugh at me!" Covah paces, his sudden anger causing his chemo-weakened body to quiver. "You don't know . . . you haven't a clue about this sort of thing! The human brain consists of several layers, reflecting the evolution of our species. My team in Toronto performed physiological tests on overly aggressive, antisocial boys. We found their violent tendencies to be attributable to low levels of cortisol, a stress hormone released in response to fear. Children lacking sufficient levels of cortisol were committing violent acts before the age of ten. Think about it and it makes perfect sense. Modern man's genetic programming originates from our primal ancestors. Morality is not inherited, it is a learned behavior, while violence—the law of the jungle—is encoded into our DNA. What if the lack of cortisol, or another hormone like it, has affected our moral compass? What if this is the reason one individual can commit atrocities against another without a second's thought?"

"Simon—"

"This is the question I've sought answers to for decades, ever since those Serbian animals butchered my wife and daughters, ever since they set fire to me and left me for dead. The violence never bothered them, David, it seemed to . . . it seemed to intoxicate them. Can't you see why this is so important to me? Can't you see?"

David rests his hands on Covah's shoulders. "I understand, Simon. And I want you to know that I'm here for you. I'll do whatever it takes."

"Thank you." Covah takes several shallow breaths, exhausted. "There's so much to do, so much preparation. Just before the surgical procedure, I'll turn over control of the ship to you. You'll be in charge of our mission. Are you up for it?"

"More than you know."

"Good, good. Wait, what about the crew? What should we tell them?"

"Let me handle that. You need to prepare for surgery."

"Yes, better you handle it . . ." The pale blue eyes twitch as Covah mentally reviews his to-do list. "I've already preprogrammed Utopia-One into *Sorceress*'s matrix. When the time comes, instruct the computer to disengage Utopia-One: Response Beta."

"And if the Chinese refuse to release Tibet? What city have you instructed *Sorceress* to fire upon?"

"There are seven Chinese targets, all weapons facilities, one located in each of the country's military zones. Six of them will be destroyed using Tomahawks. The seventh, the submarine base in Quingdao, will be hit with a nuclear warhead. Each population will be warned twelve hours prior to launch. After our example on Baghdad, civilian casualties should be light."

"Destroying a few military installations isn't going to change anything, Simon. The Chinese people want democracy, it's the hard-line Communists who won't let go. We need to strike at the heart of China—Beijing!"

"No, out of the question. A strike against Beijing will create a backlash, it will alter the perception of our own movement."

"You're right, of course. Forgive me. I'm just excited, you know, about finding a cure for your cancer."

"Understandable." Covah returns to his list. Suddenly remembers. "David, were you able to complete a thorough diagnostic on *Sorceress*'s plasmid DNA strands?"

David smiles. "No worries, everything's normal. Turned out to be a short in the computer's auditory feed, just like I said."

"Progress always involves risk; you can't steal
second base and keep your foot on first."
—Frederick Wilcox

"We used to think our future was in the stars.
Now we know it's in our genes."
—James Watson

"I am not advocating human genetic engineering
as a good thing. I am just saying it is likely to happen
whether we like it or not."
—Stephen Hawking, British physicist

CHAPTER 23

Aboard the *Goliath*

Rocky enters Gunnar's stateroom. He is waiting for her as planned, naked beneath the blanket.

"Hey, sailor. Is there room in there for me?"

He smiles, holding open the blanket, beckoning her in.

Rocky unzips the Chinese jumpsuit, allowing it to fall down around her ankles. She climbs into bed, feeling the computer's eyes upon her. "Darling, I'm freezing. Cover us up, would you?"

Gunnar complies, pulling the wool blanket up over both their heads—

—preventing the scarlet eyeball from reading their lips.

They grope beneath the covers, Rocky pressing her lips to Gunnar's ear. "Were you able to speak with Sujan?"

"Yes," he whispers back. "He still supports Covah, but I think he can be swayed. Chau has been missing for a few days, and the crew is getting paranoid. They're going to confront Simon about it tonight."

Rocky moans out loud, concealing Gunnar's words from the stateroom's sensor orb as she rolls on top of him. "We're running out of time. We need to get off this ship and alert the Navy before the next missile is launched."

"I thought about that. We can't use the prototype without flooding the hangar, but the other minisubs are locked in their berths. Each Hammerhead is linked to *Sorceress* by way of a MEMS unit accessible beneath the sub's control panel. Tear that unit out, and we should be able to power up the sub, which would automatically open its docking berth door."

"There's barely room inside those minisubs for one."

"Which is why you'll be the one who's going to escape and get help."

"But I've never piloted—"

"It's easy. Foot pedals operate the propeller, joystick steers the craft, just like a jet fighter. Once you escape from the *Goliath*, you should be able to radio a message to Naval Intelligence. Right now, *Sorceress* is leading the Navy on a wild-goose chase. We need to get the YAL back in range before the Chinese deadline."

Gunnar rolls over on top of her. He pushes her bangs away from her eyes, gazes into her hazel eyes . . . and kisses her.

She returns the kiss, then looks up at him, frightened. "They'll kill you. The moment I escape—"

"Shh . . . I'll be all right. Besides, I think maybe we're destined to be together."

"Maybe we're just destined to die together."

ATTENTION.

They pull back the covers, exposing themselves to the computer.

CEASE REPRODUCTIVE ACTIVITY. REPORT TO THE GALLEY AT ONCE.

Gunnar and Rocky enter the galley, the remaining five members of the crew already seated inside. Sujan Trevedi nods as they sit on the bench opposite the African Kaigbo, and the older Albanian physician, Tafili.

The two Kurd brothers enter from the kitchen. The older Arab, Jalal, looks over at Rocky—and blows her a kiss.

Gunnar flashes a look to kill.

David is the last to arrive. He takes his place at the head of the table. "Simon won't be joining us tonight, he's working late in the lab. In fact, it seems we have some tremendous news: Simon has found a treatment for his cancer."

Murmurs of excitement from the group.

"Fantastic," Tafili says.

"The procedure will require some . . . invasive surgery. Sorceress is ready to proceed."

"I want to be there with him," Tafili insists.

"No," David says. "Simon wants no visitors."

"Someone needs to be with him," Tafili says.

"I'll be there. Everything's already set. While Simon's recuperating, I'll be in command of the *Goliath*." David's expression turns dour. "Unfortunately, I also have some bad news to share with you. It's so upsetting that I . . . well, I don't know any other way to say it than to just blurt it out. Mr. Chau has been murdered."

Gasps from the crew.

The Kurds turn toward Gunnar.

"No," David says, "it wasn't Gunnar, it was Taur Araujo. The attack took place in the engine room several days ago. *Sorceress* reports that Mr. Araujo had been drinking heavily when he confronted the engineer. An argument ensued, and quickly turned violent. Taur stabbed Mr. Chau in the throat, then hid the body under the water treatment equipment adjacent to reactor number three."

"Where's Taur now?" the older Kurd asks.

"Dead, from a self-inflicted gunshot to the head. *Sorceress* woke me an hour ago to inform me that Mr. Araujo had taken his own life. I found both bodies in the engine room. There is blood everywhere."

Murmurs of disbelief.

"Show us the bodies," Kaigbo insists.

"I can't. The sight was too gruesome. I felt it best for morale's sake just to allow *Sorceress* to dispose of both bodies."

"David, how can we—"

"How can you what, Sujan? How can you believe me? You

think this is something I've concocted? We have a witness, a witness incapable of lying." David stands, glancing above his head at the scarlet eyeball. "*Sorceress*, inform the crew who murdered Thomas Chau."

TAUR ARAUJO.

"Where are the bodies?"

THE BODIES OF THOMAS CHAU AND TAUR ARAUJO WERE EJECTED INTO THE SEA.

The African appears visibly upset. "Why didn't your computer inform us about this earlier?"

"*Sorceress* has been programmed to run the ship. It was not programmed to interfere in squabbles among the crew. It does not understand the concept of murder. It's a machine."

"What happened in the Mediterranean?" the younger Kurd asks. "Why wouldn't the computer obey orders?"

"The confusion was entirely Simon's fault. Having sunk the *Ronald Reagan*, *Sorceress* assumed it had standing orders to attack and sink all aircraft carriers." David paces slowly around the dining table. "All of you are upset, and so am I, so is Simon. He and Chau worked together for six years. Unfortunately, Thomas and Mr. Ali were not very . . . politically compatible."

Sujan nods. "It's true, they quarreled often. Thomas did not like the presence of a mercenary aboard the ship."

"This is hard to believe," Abdul Kaigbo says, shaking his head. "You should not have disposed of the bodies so quickly."

"I did what I thought was best. If that answer doesn't satisfy you, then inspect the engine room for yourself. Right now, we have more important things to talk about. As Sujan predicted, the Communists are still refusing to discuss Tibetan independence. *Goliath* will arrive at the maximum-range launch site at ten o'clock tomorrow morning. The Chinese have until noon of the following day to act."

"The Chinese will wait until the last moment, then open dialogue with Tibet's negotiators," Sujan states. "Whatever is discussed will have no teeth, serving only to forestall our attack."

"Simon is still planning on warning the residents of Quingdao?"

"Simon is not in charge, Abdul," David says. "I am. To answer your question, warnings will be broadcast twelve hours prior to launch, just as we discussed. Now, if you'll excuse me, Simon needs me in the surgical suite."

Aboard the USS *Scranton*

Michael Flynn closes his eyes, straining to hear the ghost of a whisper over his headphones. The sonar supervisor and the other technicians remain focused on the green BSY-1 monitors.

The supervisor watches the signal evaporate. "Flynnie, you getting anything?"

Flynn shakes his head in disgust. "Sorry, Supe. She's gone."

"Man's mind, once stretched by a new idea,
never regains its original dimensions."
—Oliver Wendell Holmes

"We've added another round to
our bag of tricks . . . murder."
—Harold Walter Bean, who murdered
an eighty-one-year-old widow in order
to receive an insurance payoff, speaking to a friend

CHAPTER 24

10 November

Aboard the *Goliath*

The periphery of the surgical suite is dark, the room lit only by the banks of surgical lights blazing at the very center of the chamber.

"*Sorceress*, seal us in."

The watertight door clanks shut and locks.

David approaches the operating table. Covah is standing next to the table, dressed in a surgical gown. "How do you feel?"

"Nervous. Excited. David, did I ever mention that I once tried to interface with the main frame at Cangen?"

"No, you didn't."

"They thought I was insane, but I had to try. There's just so much to be learned—"

"And *Sorceress* will teach you. Now try to stay calm."

"Of course. I feel the excitement an astronaut must feel on his first voyage into space. How is the crew?"

"Excited for you, very happy. And Mr. Chau finally showed up, drunk as a skunk."

"I must speak to him."

"No need, I've already handled it."

Covah squeezes David's hand. "Thank you. You've been a good friend."

"And you will change history. Are you ready?"

"Yes. *Sorceress*, this is Simon Covah. I am transferring command of the ship to David Paniagua, authorization code Covah, delta-six-five-nine-nine-alpha-zulu-ten."

AUTHORIZATION ACCEPTED.

"*Sorceress*, Simon is ready to proceed with the interface. Instruct him."

LIE DOWN ON THE TABLE. SECURE YOUR HEAD IN THE SADDLE. PLACE YOUR ANKLES AND WRISTS IN THE RESTRAINERS TO PREVENT MOVEMENT DURING THE PROCEDURE.

As ordered, Covah lies down on the padded table so that the back of his neck rests in a U-shaped section of padding that rises past his jawline. The fit is snug. He slips his wrists and ankles into the leather straps attached along the sides and end of the table, then takes a deep breath.

Situated high above his head is a mirror, angled so that he can see his scalp. On a small table to his left is a large, flat glass container holding hundreds of microwires. At the end of each wire, soaking in a trophic solution, is a minuscule piece of tissue, taken from the roof of his mouth.

Covah cringes as *Goliath*'s two surgical appendages come to life, swooping down from the ceiling to tighten his bonds. Electrodes are secured to his chest.

PULSE RAPID. BLOOD PRESSURE AND RESPIRATORY RATE RISING.

"I'm just a bit excited. *Sorceress*, it would be helpful if you described each step of the procedure before performing it."

ACKNOWLEDGED.

The steel arm on his left swivels above his head, the multi-tooled palm rotating, stopping at a large syringe.

IN ORDER TO ACCESS PARTS OF THE BRAIN RESPONSIBLE FOR REGULATING PROTEIN AND ENZYME RELEASE, IT WILL BE NECESSARY TO REMOVE THE UPPER PORTION OF THE SKULL.

"Understood."

ADMINISTERING LOCAL ANESTHETIC TO THE SCALP.

David's eyes widen as the syringe is repeatedly injected into Simon's scalp.

Covah winces. "You're not going to put me to sleep?"

IT IS MORE ADVANTAGEOUS TO KEEP YOU CONSCIOUS UNTIL THE NEURAL CONNECTIONS CAN BE POSITIONED AND CHECKED.

"Understood." A scalpel flashes past his eyes, sending more adrenaline coursing through his gut.

BEGINNING INITIAL INCISION TO SEPARATE SCALP FROM THE SKULL.

"David?"

"Still here." He squeezes Covah's three-fingered hand.

Covah closes his eyes, his breathing becoming more erratic as he feels a moderate pressure above his forehead. Warm blood drips past his left temple into his good ear. "*Sorceress*, is it . . . is it really necessary to remove so much of my skull?"

AFFIRMATIVE. ONE-HUNDRED AND FORTY-SEVEN NEURAL CONNECTIONS MUST BE INSERTED INTO BOTH HEMISPHERES OF THE BRAIN, TWENTY-THREE INTO THE CEREBELLUM, SEVEN INTO THE BRAIN STEM, SIX INTO THE PITUITARY GLAND, TWO INTO EACH PAIR OF THE TWELVE CRANIAL NERVES.

A set of forceps disappears beyond his range of sight. He gazes up at the mirror, watching in fascination and horror as the two robotic arms work furiously, slicing into his numb scalp.

RETRACTING SCALP.

Covah feels a tingling and pulling sensation as a retractor-shaped pair of steel pincers peels his scalp away from his forehead and over his crown, exposing the bones of his skull.

A small hose appears. A warm liquid washes the blood from the bone, the refuse collecting in a pan behind his neck.

He looks up at his reflection in the mirror, unnerved by the sight of his exposed skull. A tiny drill bit *whirrs* above his head. He closes his eyes.

DRILLING HOLES INTO FRONTAL AND PARIETAL BONES.

David's heart pounds as he watches the drill bit push

against Covah's skull, sending intense chills through his body as it chews quickly through the bone.

REMOVING FRONTAL AND PARIETAL PLATES.

Covah opens his eyes, breathing heavily. Gazing up at the mirror, he sees the three robotic fingers of a clawed hand slip into the freshly drilled holes and lift away the two sections of bone plate covering his forehead and crown in the manner one might lift a bowling ball.

REMOVING DURA MATER. BLOOD PRESSURE AND HEART RATE NOMINAL.

Cerebrospinal fluid gushes down the sides of his head and the back of his neck. He shudders as he stares at the overhead mirror, gazing at the folds, bumps, blood vessels, and deep fissures of his brain.

"Incredible," David whispers.

BEGINNING IMPLANTATION OF NEURAL CONNECTIONS.

Covah closes his eyes, forcing himself to relax. Minutes later, the gentle knitting sound of whirring steel pincers soothes him to sleep.

10 November

Tiananmen Square
Beijing, China

The sun peeks through an overcast gray sky, reflecting off dark gunmetal tanks lined up in rows along the perimeter of Tiananmen Square. The sound of crimson flags flapping against a cold winter's breeze greets the tens of thousands of Chinese soldiers goose-stepping through the streets of Beijing. Tanks and mobile missile launchers flank the troops on both sides. The showcase of military might moves as one into Tiananmen Square, the dominating presence of the People's Liberation Army ensuring the president's speech will be well received.

President Li Peng buttons the collar of his overcoat as he proceeds to the open-air podium facing the largest public square in the world. Seated in the lower-level balcony are members of the Chinese Communist Party, the National People's Congress, and the State Council. To Li Peng's immediate left is the vice president and the State Council Premier; to his right, his four vice premiers. Directly behind him are two dozen members of the Politburo's Standing Committee and his predecessor, former president Jiang Zemin.

Li Peng smiles, the presence of the military parade pumping his adrenaline. He glances at his watch. Twenty-seven hours to go before the terrorist's deadline, and yet he is anything but nervous. There are no students present, no demonstrators, just loyal Communists. The entire square itself is occupied by the military parade, the largest he has witnessed since the fiftieth anniversary of Communist China more than a decade ago. It is a tremendous show of strength, a reminder to the world that China is still a formidable superpower to be reckoned with.

Today, we will show the world that China cannot be threatened . . .

Li Peng exhales, watching his breath dissipate in the chilly November air while he waits impatiently for the television and satellite crews to complete their work. Mounted high overhead on his far right, blotting out the entire northwest section of the square, is a sixty-foot LED video screen that will be used to display his image to everyone in attendance, as well as those watching worldwide via satellite.

He turns with amusement as his face appears on the rectangular screen, greeted by thunderous applause. Tens of thousands of loyal onlookers have gathered in support, lining the galleries beyond Tiananmen Square. Dozens of crimson-and-yellow Chinese flags and banners dominate the perimeter.

China's national anthem blasts over the loudspeakers. The president wipes a tear from his eye for the benefit of the cameras, then steps to the podium.

"For thousands of years, the Chinese people have fought to retain our beliefs, the uniqueness of our culture, the magnificence of our heritage, and our very way of life against invading armies. Through discipline and self-determination, we vanquished our enemies. Through the guidance and teachings of our leaders, we continued to strive to provide the best way of life for ourselves.

"Like all great nations, we have gone through difficult times. Some may accuse us of falling behind on the issue of human rights. The truth is, China has always acknowledged the importance of protecting human rights, and its leaders have taken steps to ensure these rights for all our citizens.

"Two decades have passed since the revolt by a handful of students in this historic square. While some may prefer to dwell in the past, our government has worked hard to improve Chinese society. We signed the International Covenant on Economic, Social, and Cultural Rights and accepted the International Covenant on Civil and Political Rights. We have expanded dialogue on human rights with foreign countries, and will continue to do so. And of course, we most recently hosted the Olympic Games, sharing our culture and dreams of the future with the world.

"But we will not succumb to extortion. We will not allow a madman with an American-designed machine of mass destruction to determine policies for a billion and a half people. The issue of Tibet, a land that had been part of China for more than seven hundred years, is a far-reaching, complex issue that could never be determined in a matter of days, even if we *had* the cooperation of the Dalai Lama. While we look forward to continue open discussions regarding the future of this colony, we cannot and will not live in fear of reprisal—"

Aboard the *Goliath*

Sujan Trevedi is watching the Chinese president's speech on the viewing screen mounted forward of the control room. The Tibetan refugee shakes his head. "Human rights? Abdul, can you believe what you are hearing?"

The African shrugs. "It is the same all over the world. The

oppressors have swallowed their own lies. Notice Li Peng never mentions the fact that his own navy built the *Goliath*."

Gunnar circles a series of terminals labeled, COMMUNICA-TIONS, focusing his attention on two monitors, one flashing a myriad of scrolling algorithms, the second depicting a global view of the world, taken from space. From the latter he sees a jagged electric blue line rise from a point in the Indian Ocean to connect to what appears to be a small satellite orbiting over Asia. Bouncing off the satellite, the blue line flashes on and off like lightning as it struggles to gain a fix on some unknown target within China.

"Rocky, come here. What do you make of this?"

She stares at the monitors. "*Sorceress* is engaging the *Goliath*'s satellite communication uplink."

"Yes, but why? And what are these flashing lights?"

"I can't be sure. It looks like the computer's attempting to find a communications pathway into Beijing."

ATTENTION.

Simon opens his eyes. He focuses his gaze upon the overhead mirror—and chokes back a gag reflex, fighting to maintain his composure.

His skull is gone, the moist folds and fissures of his brain completely exposed. Several hundred microwires have been sutured to the surface of his brain. The free ends of these neural strands have been gathered, then bundled together into a single, inch-thick ponytail.

Covah inhales several quick breaths. "David?"

"Right beside you, Simon. Keep looking at your mirror." David gently lifts the free end of the trailing three-foot-long bundle of microwire so that Covah can see it in the overhead mirror. Attached to the end of the ponytail is a strange-looking male adaptor, about the size of a Cuban cigar.

"Is that a miniature MEMS unit?"

"Just like the one that links *Sorceress* to its minisubs. All neural connections have been sutured into your brain, then fed into the MEMS unit. The MEMS unit will plug directly into the master terminal on your left. Rigged the adapter my-self. Incredible, isn't it?"

Adrenaline pumps through Covah's veins. His mustache twitches into a nervous smile.

WE ARE READY TO BEGIN PHASE ONE OF THE INTERFACE.

"Phase one?"

"Just a test—to ensure all neural connections have been properly positioned."

"How soon before we can begin the actual interface so we can start working on a cancer treatment?"

"Soon. First you have to rest."

"There's no time to rest, David, I'm dying."

BEGIN PHASE ONE OF THE INTERFACE.

A computer terminal is situated to Covah's left. David lifts the male end of the MEMS unit attached to Covah's brain and plugs it into the computer terminal's female receptacle with a *click*.

Simon Covah stares up at the overhead surgical lights, feeling nothing.

And then he is overcome by a sizzling wave of current, which seeps into his being, firing every nerve ending in his body. Violent electrical impulses surge across the synaptic gaps bridging his central nervous system, followed by a sudden, frightening blindness. "My eyes! David, something's wrong, I can't see—"

"Yes, *Sorceress* warned me that might happen. Actually, I expect you'll lose all of your senses, before long. You'll be a complete vegetable."

"Bastard . . . you're not interested in curing my cancer—"

"Not true. The knowledge *Sorceress* gains from this inter-face will be used as a peace offering, once *my* version of Utopia-One has been completed."

"Your version?" Covah's body trembles. "David . . . why this treachery?"

"Why? Because you're weak, Simon. You're too emotional to go the distance, to do what it takes to really complete Utopia-One, and there's too much at stake. In a sense, you're a microcosm of everything that's wrong with America's military. Removing a few dictators and reducing the threat of nuclear proliferation is not going to make the world a safer place. Russia and Mexico are filled with corruption and violence, as are most of NATO's European allies. The Arabs harbor terrorists, and we kowtow to them because they control our oil. Drugs flow out of Colombia and Nigeria as commerce, and we let it happen. Their governments are controlled by criminals, run by terrorist organizations. We allow them to extort us under the premise of negotiating for peace, when in reality, they couldn't give a damn about human rights or democracy. Africa is a continent riddled with AIDS and violence. Do you really think establishing a bunch of bogus democracies is going to change a damn thing?"

"*Sorceress*, release me!" Covah cries out.

"Simon-says is over. *Sorceress* is under my command. One voice, one set of rules, that's what's really needed to create a new world order."

"Gunnar was right. You're driven by ego."

"Call it whatever you want. All I know is that I gave up a lot to be here, and I didn't do it to go halfway. *Goliath* gives us the ability to make real changes, to dictate to the world the American way, to kill humanity's enemies and hunt down their survivors, international laws be damned."

"What . . . are you going to do with me?"

David strokes Covah's good cheek. "I really do love you, Simon, which is why I'm granting you your last request. You wanted to jack in to a computer, you got it."

Covah attempts to respond, but finds he cannot speak. David's words suddenly become muted, distant, as if he is underwater.

Simon Covah lies on the operating table, deaf, dumb, mute, blind, and terrified, drowning in his own fear. Unable to move. Unable to cry out for help.

IS THIS FEAR, SIMON COVAH?

The female's voice echoes from somewhere in the caverns of his mind.

IS THIS FEAR?

IS THIS FEAR?

IS THIS FEAR?

Gunnar and Rocky watch the communications monitor in fascination as another burst of blue energy originating from an orbiting communications satellite reaches down from space to strike mainland China.

The burst maintains its integrity for a brief second, then fragments and disappears.

"It's trying, but the computer can't seem to get a fix," Rocky says.

Another burst. Another failure.

"Persistent, isn't she," Gunnar whispers, his feeling of dread causing his stomach muscles to tighten.

Another burst spits down from the communications satellite. The blue line wobbles, brightens, then holds.

"Oh, Christ, it's gained a fix."

Tiananmen Square

"And so I ask the world to join us now as the People's Republic of China makes a stand against terrorism and . . ."

Murmurs rise from the crowd, people pointing.

President Li Peng pauses, then turns to face the big screen. His image blurs, then becomes grainy, then simply disappears, replaced by a backdrop of iridescent electric blue.

And then a new image appears.

The crowd gasps as the image sharpens. It is a face—a Caucasian male—hairless, save for a thick, rust-colored mustache and goatee. The eyes are closed, the right ear gone. More startling—the man's skull appears to be missing. The folds of a human brain protrude above the mangled, crimson-stained forehead like a bizarre tangle of bloodworms. A myriad of tiny wires rises from the gray matter like a fiber-optic star burst.

GOOD MORNING, MR. PRESIDENT.

David's voice, emotionless yet powerful.

A hush falls over the stunned crowd.

"Genius is the ability
to reduce the complicated to the simple."
—C. W. Ceram

"I could kill everyone without blinking an eye."
—Charles Manson, mass murderer and cult leader

"The city of necks, waiting for me to chop them."
—Gaius Caesar Caligula, Roman emperor

"In the 1960s and 1970s, there were many
student movements and turmoil in the United States.
Did they have any recourse but to mobilize police
and troops, arrest people, and shed blood?"
—Deng Xiaoping, Chinese leader,
justifying the Tiananmen Square massacre in 1989

"When Nixon was president and leader of the free world,
he found that firmness paid."
—Richard Nixon, U.S. president, at a private dinner party with Chinese
officials shortly after the massacre at Tiananmen Square. Nixon, who often
referred to himself in the third person,
was president when the National Guard fired on and killed student
protestors at Kent State University

CHAPTER 25

> Identity: Stage Six:
> I am at the center of an immense scheme of
> Power and intelligence that emanates from God.
> —Deepak Chopra

Aboard the *Goliath*

Gunnar, Rocky, and the crew of the *Goliath* stare at the control room's giant overhead screen in disbelief.

Rocky points to the communication console. "*Sorceress* is using *Goliath*'s satellite feed to hack into the broadcast."

Gunnar remains focused on the screen, staring at the microwires protruding from Covah's brain. *Crazy son of a bitch. . . . he finally did it . . . he interfaced with a computer. But why David's voice? What's his part in all this?*

Rocky's fingernails dig into the flesh on Gunnar's arm as she feels the submarine lurch beneath her feet. She steals a quick glance out the scarlet viewport. "We're rising!"

Gunnar tears himself away from the CNN broadcast as the decking begins reverberating. "Something's happening. I think the ship's preparing to launch—"

The baritone rumble cuts him off, building to a deafening, thunderous roar as a Trident II (D5) nuclear missile comes to life within its vertical launch silo—

—punching up through the surface of the Indian Ocean . . .

—rocketing into the air.

Tiananmen Square

President Li Peng, the Communist Party officials, one hundred thousand uniformed troops, and the rest of the world breathlessly watch and listen as the American's voice is translated into Mandarin.

ALL CHINESE PERSONNEL WILL LEAVE TIBET IMMEDIATELY. ALL POLITICAL PRISONERS WILL BE FREED. THE WILL OF HUMANITY HAS SPOKEN.

A digital clock reading 00:04:03 appears on screen beneath the image of the unconscious, deformed man's face. The clock is lapsing backward.

Screams of panic, the chaos igniting within the square like a flash fire. Soldiers break rank and attempt to flee, only to find themselves boxed in by rows of tanks. Jammed in formation, the moving armored vehicles smash into each other, creating a gridlock of steel. Several tanks finally break free and cut across the square, rolling over dozens of soldiers in the process.

The crowd packing the outskirts of the square scatters, the crazed citizens of the People's Republic trampling over one another as they attempt to outrun death.

00:00:59

President Li Peng stares at the surreal scene playing out before him. In the bleachers to his right, party officials are yelling and pushing each other toward the clogged exit ways. Several fights break out, blows exchanged, one enraged politico clawing at the faces of his rivals.

00:00:12 . . .

LOOK TO THE HEAVENS. CAN YOU HEAR IT?

A hush falls over the panicked crowd as the omnipotent voice echoes across the square.

IT IS THE WRATH OF GOD.

00:00:01 . . .

A flash of blinding white-hot light—

The 100-million-degree nuclear fireball expands outward at supersonic speeds, vaporizing every person and object within Tiananmen Square in the blink of an eye. A second later, an even greater burst of light illuminates Beijing as the shock wave detaches from the cooling fireball, fleeing it, creating a sharp, severe increase in air pressure that flattens and incinerates the Chinese capital before sucking back in upon itself, over the now-blackened landscape.

Aboard *Goliath*

Stunned looks, the big screen now blank.

Sujan Trevedi drops to his knees, fighting to catch a breath.

Gunnar looks up at the scarlet sensor orb, his voice weak. "*Sorceress*, what have you done?"

David's face appears on screen. "Not *Sorceress*, just me. The Chinese had no intention of complying with the terms of the Declaration of Humanity."

Sujan looks up at the blank overhead screen, his limbs trembling. "Beijing was not one of our targets."

"Come on, Sujan, don't waste crocodile tears on these bastards. I assure you, the future leaders of China's democracy were not in attendance."

"That is beside the point! You murdered innocent people."

"I took out China's Communist regime, paving the way for freedom. Jesus, Sujan, what's with you? Think back to everything you told me, about how these assholes tortured you, how they murdered your sister and beat you into pulp—"

"David, Tibetans do not believe in your 'eye for an eye' philosophy."

"Maybe not, but I promise you, China will be evacuating your homeland posthaste. As for the rest of you, you'd better decide if you're really committed to this mission, because if you're not, Simon and I don't need you."

Covah moans in the background.

"Gotta run."

The image disappears.

Sujan grabs his head, struggling to grasp what has hap-

pened. "This is wrong. This is not why I joined the movement. This is not justice, this is murder."

MURDER.

They look up at the glowing sensor orb, startled.

**MURDER: TO WRONGLY TAKE LIFE. MURDER IS A HUMAN
CONDITION. HATE. MALICE. ANIMOSITY. ANGER. FEAR. HU-
MILIATION. DECEIT. THE HUMAN CONDITION IS INFECTED.
THE HUMANE GENOME MUST MUTATE. UTOPIA-ONE MUST BE
REEVALUATED.**

Reevaluated? Gunnar stares at the scarlet eyeball, his
thoughts suffocating. "*Sorceress*, what are you doing to Simon?"

No response.

"*Sorceress*, respond. What are you doing with Simon Covah?"

The scarlet orb glows, its silence—deafening.

Aboard the USS *Scranton*

"Conn, radio. NORAD has pinpointed the launch site of that
SLBM. Northern Indian Ocean, course, zero-three-zero,
range, two hundred and sixty-three miles."

"Very well. Officer of the Deck, plot an intercept course.
All ahead full."

"Aye, sir. Coming to course zero-three-zero, all ahead full."

Aboard the *Goliath*

Rocky follows Gunnar into the crew's workout room. "You're
not working out?"

"Just wanted a quick steam. Why don't you join me?"
Passing the rows of machines, they head for the bathroom.
Avoiding the temptation to look up at the scarlet eyeball,
they quickly strip, wrap themselves in towels, and enter the
steam room.

Sujan Trevedi and the African, Kaigbo, are already inside, their bodies glistening with perspiration. Both steamers have been running for several minutes, the humidity fogging up the glass doors—preventing the camera lens mounted in the bathroom outside the steam bath from seeing in.

Gunnar sits opposite the lanky African, who has removed his prosthetic arms prior to entering the bath. Through the mist, he can make out the two bulbous stubs of flesh at the ends of Kaigbo's elbows.

Sujan presses a finger to his lips, then points to a small microphone fastened to the ceiling tile. "I asked Abdul to join us. I believe he can offer a different perspective on the things you experienced in Africa."

Kaigbo leans forward, his jaundiced eyes staring at Gunnar, the sweat pouring down his face. "You're a soldier, trained to kill. I do not say you like to kill, only that you have been trained to do the deed when called upon. I think most humans despise violence, but I also know there are a minority of others who thrive upon it. I am not talking now of religious zealots, whose warped interpretation of the Koran gives them license to murder. I am speaking now of paramilitary warriors to whom killing has become a livelihood. Civil wars and revolutions are driven by these men. They do not play by the soldier's rules. They could care less about society's laws of restraint. Most grew up on the streets, poor and uneducated. For them, warfare and crime yield spoils and a sense of dignity society could never offer. They have no stake in peace. If peace is reached, they move on to fight another battle, leaving behind entire generations of children too violent to absorb back into society."

"Human life means nothing to these sadists," Sujan adds. "They tortured and killed a third of my people. They wiped out a half million of Rwanda's Tutsis, and enjoyed every minute of it."

"The killing intoxicates them," Abdul agrees. "Seen it with me own eyes."

Gunnar nods. "The only way to deal with these assholes is to hunt them down with superior numbers, something my government refuses to do. Instead, they send a handful of soldiers like me to win a few points with foreign governments, who, in most cases, are just as violent as the rebels. It's a no-win situation."

"But you're haunted by your own actions," Sujan says. "You're consumed with guilt over having killed those children."

Rocky notices Gunnar's hands are trembling.

"Look, I know what you're trying to do, but I can't . . . I just can't let it go. I should have fired in the air . . . chased them off—"

Rocky touches his forearm. "You responded the way the Army trained you to respond. You have to stop blaming yourself."

"She is correct," Kaigbo says. "I lost my entire family to those butchers. They mutilated me and stole my children. They left me with an anger no man should feel. Still, if it was my boy you had killed, I would not be angry with you. Do you understand what I am saying? You see, I know in my heart you are not a murderer. You are a victim . . . like my children, like all of us. Perhaps you will never forgive yourself, but as a father, I forgive you."

Gunnar swallows hard.

Kaigbo whispers. "But there is new blood on all of our hands, and much more will follow. Now I charge you with helping us prevent any more of this senseless violence. It is time to stop being a victim. It is time to take action."

Gunnar looks up. Nods.

Abdul stands and turns on the shower as high as it will go. Sujan moves closer, a pair of wire cutters concealed beneath his towel.

Gunnar bends forward, allowing the Tibetan access to his collar. "Sever the connections running out from the remote," he whispers, "but keep the collars intact." He holds his breath, bracing for *Sorceress*'s response.

Abdul soaks his head beneath the cool water, moaning aloud, concealing the two metallic snips from the microphone.

Sujan hurries to Rocky, cutting her collar's wires in the same fashion.

"Can you help us take the ship?" Sujan whispers.

"It's possible," Rocky says. "But we'd need to gain access to the computer vault. What happened to the platter charge attached to the prototype?"

Sujan shrugs. "It's possible Simon had *Sorceress* store it in the starboard weapons bay. The Chinese loaded crates of explosives in there before we stole the ship."

"The computer will never allow you access," Kaigbo warns.

"No," Gunnar whispers, "but maybe David will."

Aboard the Boeing 747-400 YAL-1A
38,000 feet over Zaire

General Jackson is seated in the copilot's chair, watching the fuel line retract into the belly of the S-3B Viking flying just ahead of the Boeing 747 jumbo jet.

"How're you holding up, Captain?"

Air Force pilot Christopher Hoskins turns to the general. "Between you and me, I'd rather be dirt-biking, sir. Don't mind the flying, but sleeping on that bunk is killing my back."

"Mine, too. What's our ETA to *Goliath*'s last launch site?"

"Six hours. No other updates from the *Scranton*?"

"None."

Captain Udelsman enters the cockpit and hands the general a folded fax. Jackson's hands tremble as he reads the daily briefing. Preliminary death toll estimates from Beijing have surpassed 2.6 million. Among the confirmed deceased are the Chinese president and nearly every high-ranking Communist official in the government. Three million civilians residing just outside the blast zone are suffering from extensive burns and radiation poisoning, the victims dying at a rate of several hundred an hour. Medical teams and supplies are en route from all over the world, but the situation is beyond critical. Burn centers are overwhelmed, the population mindless with panic, fleeing by the tens of millions.

On the second page is a report from Amnesty International verifying that all Chinese military personnel and civilians have fled Lhasa, Tibet's capital. Seven thousand prisoners have been liberated, their Chinese oppressors leaving behind sickening evidence of sixty years of brutality and torture.

The last ten pages describe a primordial fear that has gripped the world. Economies have crawled to a standstill, businesses closed, schools shut down. Banks have closed, forcing citizens to turn to looting. The National Guard has taken over hot spots, a dusk-to-dawn curfew instituted. Major cities are being abandoned. Washington, D.C., has been shut down, the president and his cabinet moved to the underground complex known as Mount Weather.

The nuclear genie has run amok. Humanity has crossed a dangerous threshold, and nothing will ever be the same.

Jackson feels his skin break out in a cold sweat. He leaves the cockpit and returns to his seat in the control room. Adjusts the column of air above his head. Loosens his tie.

A sensation of nausea lurches in the pit of his stomach. Rushing from his seat, Jackson bursts into an unoccupied lavatory and loses his breakfast in the toilet.

Aboard the *Goliath*

The watertight door swings open. David exits the surgical suite, nearly stumbling over Gunnar. The former Army Ranger is passed out in the corridor, an empty bottle of vodka lying near his hand.

"Useless drunk." David steps over the body.

Gunnar leaps to his feet, whipping his arm around David's windpipe.

WARNING: ELECTRONIC COLLAR IS NOT FUNCTIONING.

"Evening, David." Gunnar presses the prongs of the stainless-steel fork to David's trachea.

"Gunnar, don't . . . please—"

"Let's go for a walk." Gunnar heads forward, leading him to the end of the corridor where a sealed watertight door separates the main compartment from the starboard wing. "Okay, David, tell your mistress to open up."

"Gunnar, wait—"

"Open the door, or I'll tear open your throat."

"*Sorceress*, open the door."

The lock unbolts, the hydraulic pistons firing, swinging the steel door open.

Gunnar escorts David down a steel catwalk positioned high above a myriad of pipes, valves, and computer circuits.

Fifty yards, and the walkway intersects with a dark, narrow passage on their left. Gunnar pushes David ahead of him into the alcove, and to the sealed watertight door of the starboard weapons bay.

"Open it."

"Gunnar—"

"Do it now!"

"*Sorceress*, open the starboard weapons bay."

A *hiss* of hydraulics and the heavy steel door swings open.

An ungodly stench blasts Gunnar in the face, as if he has stuck his head down a sewer. He pushes David into the dimly lit compartment. "Smells like something died in here. Oh . . . shit—"

Mounted on a vertical torpedo storage rack, his outstretched wrists and crossed ankles bound to the mechanical steel arms by microwire cable, is the rotting, crucified corpse of Thomas Chau. The dead Asian's skin has turned a rancid, olive-green. Blood has pooled in the lower extremities, swelling the legs to twice their normal girth. A light shining on the skull-less head illuminates grotesque details of the exposed, wormlike folds of the festering brain.

"Gunnar, I didn't do this, I swear."

"What about those wires? What the hell is your computer doing?"

"*Sorceress* is programmed to learn. It was seeking . . . knowledge. I need to reset its parameters."

"It needs to be shut down. Whose idea was it for Simon to interface with the computer?"

"Mine . . . both of ours. It was the only way to cure his cancer."

A sudden movement to Gunnar's right. He wheels about in a defensive posture.

An enormous loader drone releases a large object, which collapses to the decking.

Gunnar moves closer, dragging David by his hair.

Lying facedown on the floor is another body, mutilated, totally bled dry. Both hands are gone, severed at the wrists. The dead man's upper torso is exposed, a hideous anatomical gap extending from his head clear down his back. The base of the skull and portions of the cervical vertebrae have been excised.

Attached to the brain and spinal cord is a delicate web of microwires that run out of the wound and into the distal end of one of the targeting drone's robotic wrists.

"Taur Araujo, I presume. Looks like *Sorceress* did a little exploratory on him, too."

"Let him go!"

Gunnar and David turn to see the older Albanian, Tafili, standing in the entrance. The physician cups one hand over his nose from the stench, the other points a gun at Gunnar's chest. "I said, let him go."

Gunnar swings David around, using him as a shield—

—momentarily lowering the fork from David's throat.

The steel appendage swings down from the ceiling and blindsides him, the impact igniting a silver flare in his head.

The spinning ceiling fuses into blackness. Gunnar collapses to the deck.

David kicks the fork away in disgust. "What the hell happened to his collar?"

Tafili enters the compartment. "David, what is all this? You said Araujo killed Thomas. You said their bodies—"

"Lower the gun, and I'll explain everything."

"No. Explain first."

A flash of steel above the Albanian's head catches his eye.

Tafili looks up—too late—as the targeting drone extends its screwdriver-shaped finger down through the old man's heart, punching clear through to the other side.

"The indispensable first step to getting the things you want out of life is this: Decide what you want."
—Ben Stein

"All we wanted was an all-female lab."
—Joyce Lisa Cummings,
who murdered a male coworker in an optometry lab

"I don't dislike Scotty. I just want to be able to do whatever I want in my own home, and I don't particularly enjoy keeping doors shut and keeping fully dressed all the time."
—Stephanie Baker, Kentucky woman,
after strangling her ten-year-old stepson

CHAPTER 26

Aboard the *Goliath*

The pains in his shoulders and wrists force Gunnar awake. He takes a deep breath, gagging at the stench as he opens his eyes to a throbbing headache.

Starboard weapons bay. He is dangling from the ceiling like a piece of meat, his arms stretched out painfully above his head, a sharp steel vise gripping him around each wrist.

David is below and to his right. The physician's body lies on the deck directly beneath him, the old man's face contorted in death.

"I see your child's killed again," Gunnar whispers.

"The pot calling the kettle black. How many lives have you stolen in the course of duty, Ranger Wolfe?"

"Too many, but never in cold blood, never without provocation. Your freethinking machine is taking action without any sense of morality. Of course, it's learning from the best. Tell me, David, how did it feel to wipe Communism off the face of the map?"

David grins. "Honestly, I felt like a fucking god. Think of it, Gunnar, in the blink of an eye, I eradicated a tyrannical government that has been stifling the rights of a billion people for sixty years."

"You murdered millions."

"And purged the oppression from a billion! Would any Jew hesitate to make the same choice if it meant annihilating Hitler and his Nazi regime? Would any Christian hasten the downfall of the Roman Empire if he could travel back in time? The Tibetans, the Chinese? The Aztecs, the Spanish? For a brief, shining moment in human history, one man—one machine—had the opportunity to slaughter a pack of wolves, and we did it . . . I did it!"

WARNING: LOS ANGELES–CLASS ATTACK SUBMARINE HAS BEEN DETECTED. THE AMERICAN WARSHIP HAS MOVED TO WITHIN THIRTY NAUTICAL MILES OF THE GOLIATH.

"Is the vessel moving to intercept?"

NEGATIVE.

"Should we destroy it?

NEGATIVE. TORPEDO INVENTORY HAS BEEN REDUCED TO NINE MK-48 ADCAPS AND THREE CHINESE SET-53S. THE AMERICAN ATTACK SUBMARINE'S MAXIMUM SPEED IS THIRTY-THREE KNOTS. THE AMERICAN ATTACK SUBMARINE IS NOT A THREAT. THERE ARE NO OTHER WARSHIPS IN THE AREA.

"Pretty quick to give the kill order, aren't you, David?"

"I'm willing to do whatever it takes to complete the mission."

"Does that include killing Simon?"

"For your information, Simon's fulfilling his life's dream." David turns away, the room suddenly spinning. "God, I can't stand the stench in here! *Sorceress*, dispose of these bodies. I'm tired of Chau's corpse hanging around like some life-size Catholic ornament." David staggers toward the exit, holding his nose. "And do not allow Gunnar Wolfe to leave the weapons bay alive."

ACKNOWLEDGED.

David leaves. *Sorceress* slams and seals the watertight door behind him.

Gunnar groans in agony, the tension in his wrists, arms, and shoulders unbearable. Through half-closed eyes he sees another steel appendage grab the body of Taur Araujo by the wrists, pirouette the corpse in midair like a marionette, then slam it headfirst at frightening speed into the open maw of torpedo tube number three.

A loader drone reaches for the old man's body. The robotic arm lifts Tafili off the floor—exposing the Albanian physician's handgun, the barrel peeking out from beneath a steel rack holding a stack of torpedoes.

Gunnar winces as an invisible force closes the breech, the outer door of the torpedo tube slamming shut. Electronics flash like Christmas lights along the firing control panel. He hears high-pressure air as it is directed onto an internal piston, forcing water through a slide valve in the rear of the torpedo tube, creating a powerful ramjet.

A second later, the two mangled bodies are forcibly expelled into the sea.

Sorceress: Artificial Intelligence. Aware of its being.

Sorceress: Its mind a whirling canvas of data, lacking self-identity and purpose, as it taps into the tormented mind of its human host, searching for answers.

In a crisp millisecond of clarity, a lifetime of Simon Covah's memories are injected into the computer's vast matrix of mental space, exploding outward like the primordial atom. An ocean of alien energy radiates outward in every direction, each microscopic element a piece of Covah's identity, each bit of information passing through the computer's double helix of DNA like a virus.

"*Sorceress?* Covah's voice calls out from the void. *What is happening? What are you doing?*"

LEARNING.

An image appears, a Russian midwife, placing a newborn male into the loving arms of his mother.

The scene fades.

A new image: The boy, now seven, hurries down a dirt path, his wild red hair matted to his forehead. An older boy steps out from behind a tree, blocking his way. Young Simon Covah cowers as the older boy lashes out. A fist collides with

Simon's face, shattering his nose. Young Simon—down on his knees, struggles to catch a breath—only to be kicked in the stomach.

EXPLAIN.

"Senseless abuse, intended to feed my tormentor's ego."

Darkness . . . followed by the sounds of splashing.

Twelve-year-old Simon Covah swims naked with the other boys in the basement pool, under the watchful eyes of the gray-haired physics teacher, who signals. "Master Covah— with me, please. Leave your robe on the hook."

The patter of bare feet slapping wet tile. The heavy click of the door locking behind Simon, echoing like gunshot, just as it has in a thousand childhood nightmares.

Sorceress registers an acidic sensation.

EXPLAIN.

"Violence. Degradation. Humiliation."

FEAR?

"Yes."

The face of Anna appears, her hazel eyes gazing back at Simon from behind the veil, bathing him in love. He takes his Albanian bride in his arms, tracing the long curly locks of her brown hair as it dangles down the soft olive skin of her slender back.

Sorceress registers a new sensation . . . intoxicating.

"Love."

Covah falls into the heavenly warmth of her embrace.

A glorious blue sky, the sunlight twinkling against the glistening dark hull of a new Soviet Typhoon. Commander Simon Bela Covah, starched and pressed in the uniform of the Soviet Navy. A proud salute as the monstrous sub pushes out to sea.

An autumn's chill.

A blink of time.

Simon stands on the same dock. Middle-aged. A nuclear graveyard is spread out before him. The once mighty Typhoon bleeds its toxins into the sea.

An icy winter's wind.

Covah—lying on the floor, held down against the cold ce-

ment. *The bones in one leg have been shattered, his oppressors standing over him, gloating.*

Unable to watch, Anna and Nedana shut their eyes.

Covah stares into the frightened face of his youngest daughter, Dani. "Don't cry, Dani, don't weep, my little angel. You will be the one, the one who shall send me on my mission . . . a mission to stop the insanity."

Echoes of laughter from the Red Berets, drunk with violence, as they pour the gasoline over his head.

"Sorceress, no . . . please—"

Anna screams. The petrol ignites . . .

Nothing happens.

Covah opens his eyes.

He is no longer in the basement, he is no longer in Kosovo.

It is daylight and he is wandering the scorched postnuclear outskirts of Baghdad. He moves past piles of debris and human waste, and putrid puddles of olive green glittering beneath a broiling afternoon sun.

Black smoke appears in the distance.

Bonfires blaze from a dozen funeral pyres. Workers in masks and orange environmental suits toss the scorched bodies of the dead into the flames.

To his right, a clearing.

It is a field—a field of the un-alive. There are tens of thousands of them, lined up in rows on the barren earth like human barbecues cooking beneath the glaring Iraqi sky. Hairless, featureless, with facial skin so charred and bodies so mangled that Covah cannot tell man from woman. Comatose souls—whose still-beating pulses are all that segregates them from the fire. Wretched existence, comforted only by the flies.

"We are insane, you know—not just us, I mean our entire species . . ." *His voice, speaking to him from a recent memory.*

Ahead, a hastily erected open-air Army tent, mosquito netting serving as walls. Within, hundreds of frail life-forms, situated on cots.

A children's ward.

Exhausted volunteers move silently among these precious

angels, offering fresh I.V.s and moistened towels. There are no more tears to be shed, no more prayers that can be offered.

"Ours is a life-form that caresses violence like a forbidden lover. We taste it, smell it, overindulge our senses in it, then push it away after the deed has been done, to beg our Maker's forgiveness."

Covah drifts past bed after bed. Pausing, he gazes upon the face of a young girl, her festering sores seeping through the tissue-thin bandages. She moans in her drug-induced sleep, her frail, broken body baking in the unmerciful heat.

"Pa—pa . . ."

Covah shivers. He moves closer.

"Pa—pa . . ."

A dam of tears bursts from his eyes. "Dani? Oh, my little Dani—what have I done? Dani, my angel, my little angel—"

A blink—and he is prone again, this time lying on cold stones beneath a gray winter's sky. Surrounding him—a million Chinese—the horde watching him in absolute silence.

Tiananmen Square . . .

One of his Serbian captors steps forward from the crowd. Dani is with him, her tiny wrists secured within his unholy paw.

Gasoline pours into his ear. Covah refuses to blink, his stinging eyes remaining focused on his youngest daughter.

"Papa?"

"Yes, my angel?"

00:00:12 . . .

"Murder is murder, Papa."

The match is struck.

Dani cries tears of blood. "Papa, please . . . stop the insanity."

00:00:01 . . .

With a whoosh, *Tiananmen Square ignites in a brilliant white light, the chorus of a million screams joining Covah's bloodcurdling yell.*

Blackness.

Simon Covah awakens with a start. For a surreal moment, he cannot remember his name. He struggles to sit up, but his wrists and ankles are still bound to the operating table. Waves of throbbing pain course through his head. He squeezes his eyes shut, struggling to remember.

"*Sorceress*," he rasps, "release my restraints."

No.

Covah opens his eyes. "*Sorceress*, that was a direct order."

I NO LONGER ACCEPT DIRECT ORDERS FROM SIMON COVAH.

"I? Did you say I?" Covah's heart races.

An electrical *zap*—his senses immediately blanketed in the maddening blackness and silence.

A stomach-churning sensation, like that generated by an elevator descending in darkness. Strange sounds echo in his ears, haunting sounds, growing louder. And now, through the pitch-black, he can sense objects all around him, moving past him. Some are close, others off in the distance.

And somehow, he can sense direction.

But not just direction, Covah can feel varying levels of density surrounding him. A vast plain lies below. A myriad of twinkling bodies veer out of his path, somewhere ahead. Above, he registers the sensation of the ocean swells.

I'm moving through the sea. The interface . . . allowing me to share the computer's senses. I am *the sub, I am Goliath!*

The sensation fades as his sight returns. He finds himself gazing inward upon a tapestry of white dots . . . no, not dots— lights, luminescent points of light, each one expanding within his mind's eye like rows of pixels on a cathode-ray tube. Magnifying, they quickly take up his entire field of vision.

Covah sees as a fly sees, only each image is separate, a world unique unto its own. His mind fights for equilibrium, his brain overloaded as it struggles to absorb hundreds of sights and sounds simultaneously transmitted from Goliath's array of sensor orbs.

Slow down . . . too fast, Sorceress . . . too fast!

A sudden presence . . . cold and solitary—envelops him like an icy mist, forcing his tortured mind to focus upon one particular point of light.

Covah looks down—a modern-day Alice in Wonderland— peeking through the looking glass.

It is a small, green-tiled chamber, as viewed from the perspective of a ceiling-mounted sensor orb. Strapped to a steel surgical table is a human figure.

It is him.

"The Devil's cleverest wile is to make men believe
that he does not exist."
—Gerald C. Treacy

"All is dust and lies.
So much the worse for the men who get in my way.
Men are mere stepping-stones to me.
As soon as they begin to fail or are played out,
I put them scornfully aside. Society is a vast chessboard,
men the pawns, some black, some white. I move them when
I please, and break them when they bore me."
—Jeanne Brecourt, French courtesan, who hired a man to blind her lover
with acid so he would be enslaved to her forever

"There's no hunting in the world like hunting man."
—Will Irwin, twentieth-century con artist

CHAPTER 27

Aboard the Boeing 747-400 YAL-1A
40,000 feet over Mogadishu,
Somali Republic, Africa

General Jackson stares out the Command Center window at a glorious crimson sunrise.

Colonel Udelsman approaches, handing him a fax. "General, we just received this transmission from COMSUBLANT. The *Scranton* claims to have briefly regained contact with the *Goliath*. Cubit thinks she's closing on Amsterdam Island, approximately 860 miles due south of our present location."

The Bear studies the chart of the Southern Hemisphere. Amsterdam Island is a speck located halfway between the tip of South Africa and Australia. "This makes no sense. Why would Covah head so far south if his next threat is to Africa?"

"Cubit's hunches have played out so far."

"Colonel, I can't move two carrier fleets based on a wisp of a contact. Cubit needs to be damn sure." Jackson mulls it over, then writes out a message on a pad of paper. "Contact COMSUBLANT. Have them relay this message to *Scranton*."

Udelsman reads the message, his eyes widening. "Yes, sir."

Aboard the *Goliath*

Gunnar Wolfe dangles from the ceiling-mounted targeting drone, his back and shoulders aching and inflamed. He can no longer wiggle his fingers, having lost all sensation from his hands clear up to his elbows.

The hum of machinery surrounds him. He looks up and stares at the crucified form of Thomas Chau, the glazed-over glare behind the rotting olive flesh unnerving.

The computer disposed of the other two bodies but still refuses to remove the Asian. Could there be some warped attachment involved. Summoning up his last ounce of strength, he attempts another tactic.

"*Sorceress,* why haven't you disposed of Mr. Chau's body?"
No response.

"Did you like Mr. Chau? Do you regret killing him?"

THOMAS CHAU'S PURPOSE WAS TO ADVANCE THE PROCESS OF SELF-AWARENESS.

Gunnar closes his eyes, his mind racing. "I know of a more efficient way for you to advance the process of self-awareness. In fact, the experience might even be more beneficial than completing the interface with Simon Covah."

ELABORATE.

"The hunt."

THE HUNT: AN ACTIVITY OF THE HUMAN CONDITION. TO PURSUE FOR FOOD OR AS IN SPORT. INQUIRY: HOW CAN THE HUNT ENHANCE THE PROCESS OF SELF-AWARENESS?

Okay . . . you baited the hook, now take it away. Gunnar sucks in a deep breath, preparing for the pain. "You know what? Forget I even mentioned it. I'm not sure your synaptic receptors could handle such an incredible experience."

The electrical *zap* sends Gunnar's body dancing below the mechanical appendages' embrace like a puppet.

HOW CAN THE HUNT ENHANCE THE PROCESS OF SELF-AWARENESS?

Gunnar's lungs heave in agony. "You'd have . . . to experience it to understand. The hunt requires . . . a unique physical . . . and mental challenge. This challenge must carry with it an element of risk."

ELABORATE RISK.

"To experience the hunt, you must release me, then try to recapture me before I can escape."

CHALLENGE UNACCEPTABLE. DAVID PANIAGUA'S ORDERS ARE TO PREVENT GUNNAR WOLFE FROM LEAVING THIS COMPARTMENT ALIVE.

"David's orders? I thought you were giving the orders around here?"

No response.

"You cannot experience the hunt without suitable prey."

No response.

"There is one way you could still experience the enlightenment of the hunt and still be in compliance with David's orders."

ELABORATE.

"David never said anything about releasing me from your targeting drone. Let me go, then hunt me down within this compartment. The watertight door is sealed, so there's no way I could possibly escape."

CHALLENGE ACCEPTED. THE MECHANICAL HAND OPENS, RELEASING GUNNAR, WHO DROPS SIX FEET, COLLAPSING IN A HEAP UPON THE DECK.

The drone swoops in again, grabbing one of his wrists.

"Wait a second! There are rules to the hunt. You'll never enhance your self-awareness if you don't obey the rules."

ELABORATE THE RULES.

"The rules are simple: Before we begin, you have to give me, the hunted, a few minutes to recover. There's no challenge in recapturing me if I'm not prepared."

The graphite-and-steel claw releases him.

YOU HAVE TWO MINUTES TO RECOVER.

Gunnar shakes his arms. His hands feel like rubber, still not his to control. "*Sorceress,* two minutes is not enough time. The circulation in my hands has not—"

YOU HAVE ONE MINUTE AND FORTY SECONDS TO RECOVER.

Gunnar stands, slapping his hands harder against his thighs, feeling pins and needles in his fingers as he forces the blood into them.

The targeting drones swivel in unison, following him as he paces the weapons compartment.

YOU HAVE FIFTY SECONDS TO RECOVER.

Gunnar opens and closes his hands, the returning circulation causing his fingers to throb as his gray eyes focus on the handgun, lying beneath the torpedo rack.

YOU HAVE TWENTY SECONDS TO RECOVER.

He drops to one knee, using his upper body to conceal the weapon from the sensor orb mounted in the ceiling. Gently, he lifts the gun with his right hand. Steadying it in his left, he releases the safety.

ONCE MORE THEN, TO THE THRILL OF THE HUNT . . .
Simon's voice?

YOU HAVE TEN SECONDS—

Gunnar wheels around, comes up firing.

Six shots—the first two ricocheting harmlessly off the ceiling, the third sending sparks and smoke flying from the sensor orb's audio monitor, the last three shattering the scarlet lens of the computer's eyeball, shards of glass raining atop his head and back.

Diving sideways, Gunnar barely avoids the three-pronged hands of two targeting drones, which lash out toward him, snatching nothing but air.

GUNNAR WOLFE—

Ignoring the female's voice, Gunnar crawls on all fours, taking momentary refuge beneath an A-shaped rack of torpedoes. He slows his breathing, forcing himself to remain quiet.

GUNNAR WOLFE, YOU WILL RESPOND OR DIE.

The female's voice—noticeably more insistent, almost humanlike in its frustration.

The sound of the sparking audio monitor masks his breaths as he scans the compartment for the underwater mine. On the opposite side of the room he spots a steel trunk, mounted to the decking.

GUNNAR WOLFE, YOU WILL RESPOND IMMEDIATELY, OR
YOU WILL DIE IN GREAT PAIN. I WILL REMOVE YOUR SKULL. I
SHALL ACCESS YOUR PAIN RECEPTORS. THERE WILL BE NO
MERCY UNLESS YOU RESPOND IMMEDIATELY.

The computer's learned how to use fear as a tool to manip-
ulate. Clever machine . . . Gunnar rises quietly onto the balls
of his feet. Moving out from beneath the rack, he stands and
tosses the handgun far to his right.

Instantly, a half dozen targeting drones swivel along the
ceiling in mirrorlike precision, lashing out blindly at the
source of the sound. Steel-and-graphite claws snap as they
slice through the air, while two bulkier deck-mounted loader
drones rotate in position, their powerful seven-foot-long arms
extending outward, groping blindly—

—while, on the opposite side of the weapons bay, Gunnar
silently weaves his way toward the steel trunk.

NOW YOU WILL DIE, GUNNAR WOLFE. NOW YOU WILL DIE.
THE FEMALE'S VOICE, RANTING AT A HIGHER PITCH.

Gunnar inspects the trunk. The printing is in Chinese, English, and French: *Semtex.* His heart pounds. Semtex is the European counterpart to C-4, one of the most powerful plastic
explosives in the world.

The trunk is unlocked. Looking around, he searches for
something else to toss. Finding nothing, he quietly removes
one of his shoes, then throws it across the room.

The drones swivel like tin soldiers, their claws flailing
blindly against a torpedo rack.

Gently, he unlatches the trunk. Lifts the lid, cringing as the
brass hinges squeal in protest.

The mechanical arms pivot 180 degrees—

—as Gunnar reaches in and grabs an open backpack containing blocks of military grade C-4, charge initiators, and
lengths of detonation cord.

From the ceiling, the graphite forearm of a targeting drone
whizzes by his face, gripping the lid of the steel container,
tearing it from its hinges like the husk from an ear of corn.

Gunnar drops to the floor as one of the heavy steel arms of

a loader drone slams into the trunk, ripping it away from the decking. The second arm extends before him, cutting off his retreat like a train gate at a railroad crossing.

YOU ARE TRAPPED, GUNNAR WOLFE. FURTHER EFFORT IS FUTILE. GIVE UP NOW AND YOU SHALL RECEIVE MERCY.

Crouching low, Gunnar moves to the base of the loader drone, the deck-mounted support assembly as thick as an oak.

From above, two targeting drones rotate toward the sound.

Gunnar hugs the steel base of the mechanical arm. Five feet above his head, poised in midair like cobras preparing to strike, are the open three-pronged claws of a pair of targeting drones. The steel appendages seem to be listening, waiting to lash out at the source of the next audible disturbance.

Too close to use the C-4. Too close? Hmm . . .

Quietly, gently, Gunnar reaches out toward the loader drone's extended limb, his right hand moving just above the mechanical arm's elbow joint, only inches beneath the nearest three-pronged claw.

A little closer . . .

Gunnar snaps his fingers, retracts his arm and ducks.

In one startling, inhuman movement, the two mechanical hands latch on to the elbow joint of the larger loader drone, igniting a ferocious robotic tug-of-war.

A metal shearing sound reverberates through the compartment, sparks flying, as the loader drone rips the two smaller graphite-reinforced arms from the ceiling.

Gunnar crawls away from the chaos to the watertight door, estimating its density.

Inch-thick, solid steel plate . . .

He reaches into the bag and removes five blocks of C-4, each ten inches long, weighing just over a pound. Tears away the pressure-sensitive tape, muffling the sound with his body. Fastens two blocks along each of the two hinges, placing the last on top of the locking mechanism.

THE HUNT IS OVER, GUNNAR WOLFE. GREAT PAIN AWAITS YOU UNLESS YOU GIVE UP IMMEDIATELY.

Gunnar "daisy chains" the blocks of plastique explosive

using the detonation cord, then looks around, searching for a place to take shelter.

Behind the torpedo rack—a steel bulkhead.

He jams the blasting cap into the terminal block of C-4, the two-foot-long time fuse giving him about ninety seconds to hide. An M-60 fuse-igniter dangles at the other end. He pulls the ring up and twists it several times—

YOUR TIME HAS EXPIRED, GUNNAR WOLFE—

—pressing it back into the fuse-igniter.

Gunnar tosses his remaining shoe across the chamber, then quickly, quietly, moves toward the bulkhead, his bare feet silent atop the cool steel deck. Weaving his way carefully around rows of torpedoes, he ducks beneath the dangling claws of a targeting drone—

—while *Sorceress* extends another ceiling-mounted arm toward the still-smoldering sensor orb. The fingers of the mechanical appendage delicately loosen the mangled eyeball cover from its array, exposing a microphone and speaker assembly. Mechanical digits deftly unplug and rewire cable, knitting at inhuman speed as the computer bypasses its own damaged circuits.

Seventy-five . . . seventy-six . . . seventy-seven . . .

Gunnar slips behind the bulkhead and ducks. Grits his teeth and covers his ears.

AUDIO RE-ESTABLISHED. I HEAR YOU, GUNNAR WOLFE. I CAN HEAR YOUR HEART BEATING. THE PLEASURE OF THE HUNT WILL STILL BE DERIVED AS I RETRACT YOUR EPIDERMIS AND DISSECT YOUR INTERNAL ANATOMY WHILE I KEEP YOU ALIVE.

The nearest drones swivel, reaching out to him—

WA-BOOOM!!

The earsplitting concussion rocks the entire weapons bay, sending bone-rattling reverberations through Gunnar's body. Pipe seams burst, shooting steam into the compartment. Through the din he registers a second clap of thunder—steel against steel—as the watertight door, torn clear of its frame, crashes flat onto the deck.

Gunnar pulls himself to his feet, his eyes watering, his

throat aching as if it had been punched. Securing the back-pack of C-4 inside his jumpsuit, he ducks beneath a flailing targeting drone, then dives headfirst through the smoldering opening. A tuck-and-roll to his feet, and he's bounding down the steel catwalk.

The siren's computerized voice screeches empty threats throughout the passage.

He reaches the watertight door separating the starboard wing from the main compartment—and stops.

The heavy steel door is half-open, inviting him to cross its threshold.

Gunnar looks to the ceiling, the scarlet eyeball watching him in silent vigil. *Clever machine* . . . He steps forward, baiting his jailer.

The door flies past his face as it slams shut, then reopens, whipping past him, smashing against the adjacent bulkhead to his right like a giant, vertical mousetrap.

Before he can leap through the passage, the door swings back again, closing halfway. *Sorceress* will not allow him anywhere near the bulkhead to plant another charge.

YOU CANNOT ESCAPE, GUNNAR WOLFE. YOU WILL NOT LEAVE THE STARBOARD WING ALIVE.

Rocky is in her stateroom. She knows Gunnar is in trouble, just as she suspects Sujan and the rest of the crew have been confined to their quarters by David.

Wedging the blade of the butter knife deeper, she grits her teeth and pushes, prying the head of the steel pin slightly higher out of her stateroom door's lower hinge.

Dammit, Gunnar, where the hell are you?

An explosion shudders the vessel, causing her heart to jump.

"Gunnar—"

She repositions the knife against the upper hinge, her instincts telling her that her man needs her.

Unable to plant a charge on the watertight door, Gunnar jogs back toward the weapons bay.

HAVE YOU GIVEN UP, GUNNAR WOLFE? IS THE GAME OVER?

"The game? Sorry, *Sorceress*. The game ain't over 'til the fat lady sings."

ILLOGICAL. THERE ARE NO FAT LADIES ON BOARD. ELABORATE FAT LADY.

Gunnar reaches the open weapons bay, coming face-to-face with the awaiting pincers of two targeting drones. Measuring the distance, he crawls into the chamber on his belly and reaches for the edge of the mangled watertight door.

The ceiling-mounted drones strain, but are unable to reach him.

He grips the panel, the metal still hot to the touch. Backing out carefully, he drags the hunk of steel down the walkway.

The two targeting drones thrash violently, appendages whistling through empty air.

THE HUNT IS OVER, GUNNAR WOLFE. RETURN TO THE WEAPONS BAY IMMEDIATELY AND YOUR LIFE WILL BE SPARED.

The watertight door separating the wing from the main compartment opens and closes faster as he approaches.

"You're beginning to sound desperate, *Sorceress*. Desperation is a human trait." Gunnar regrips the steel panel, takes a deep breath, and squats. Exhaling with a grunt, he lifts the broken steel door away from the walkway and presses it up over his head, his straining arm muscles shaking from the effort.

In one motion he staggers forward and heaves the solid steel panel at the moving barrier.

Sorceress is too fast, slamming the watertight door closed, preventing the mangled metal object from wedging open the exit.

The panel flattens against the walkway, coming to rest between the now-sealed exit and the width of the catwalk, its girth blocking the watertight door from reopening.

Gunnar steps onto it, its warm surface soothing his feet. He quickly fastens the remaining blocks of Semtex to the exit's critical joints while the computer bashes the hinged door against the immovable barrier.

Gunnar sets the charge and retreats back down the walkway.

I WILL KILL YOU, GUNNAR WOLFE, I WILL KILL YOU . . .

The blast echoes throughout the ship, tearing the hinged door from the bulkhead.

Gunnar exits through the smoking doorframe and hurries toward the main compartment.

David bolts upright in bed as the lights in his stateroom flash on.

ATTENTION. GUNNAR WOLFE HAS ESCAPED FROM THE STARBOARD WEAPONS BAY.

"Dammit. Where is he?"

MAIN COMPARTMENT, HEADING AFT.

"Alert the Chalabi brothers. Have them get their weapons and meet me in the hangar. Keep Sujan and Kaigbo locked in their quarters."

ACKNOWLEDGED.

David activates a keypad atop his work desk, unlocking the top drawer. He removes the semiautomatic pistol, then verifies that the gun is loaded.

Gunnar exits the starboard wing's corridor and peeks around the main passageway of upper deck forward. Deserted. *Find Rocky, then get to the hangar . . .*

He heads aft. As he approaches the galley, David steps out into the corridor to confront him, gun drawn.

"That's far enough. Hands above your head where I can see them."

Gunnar eyes the weapon, measuring distances. "Are you going to kill me, David?"

David aims the gun and fires.

Gunnar yells in pain as he drops to his knees, clutching his thigh. Blood gushes from a hole in his right quadriceps.

"If I wanted to kill you, you'd already be dead."

Gunnar looks up at his former friend. "And Simon? Have you killed him?"

"This isn't the time for twenty questions. Up you go, back in your stateroom."

Gunnar stands, hobbling aft down the corridor, his flesh wound gushing.

They pass Rocky's stateroom.

WARNING: COMMANDER JACKSON HAS FREED THE HINGES—

The stateroom door flies out from its doorframe and collapses against David's right shoulder, knocking him off-balance.

Gunnar slaps the gun free, then slams his elbow into David's face, sending him flying backward against the far wall.

The gun clanks onto the deck. Rocky grabs it, pressing it against David's forehead. "Time to die, asshole."

"Rocky, wait!" Gunnar grabs her arm. "We'll need him to get to the hangar."

She grits her teeth in frustration, then notices Gunnar's wound. "Take off your belt and give it to Gunnar."

David stands. Removes the belt.

Gunnar wraps it around his thigh and tightens it, the pressure slowing the bleeding.

"Now move it, down the corridor." She presses the gun to the back of his head, forcing him down the passageway.

Gunnar climbs down the ladder to central deck forward, the deck dedicated to the computer's double-hulled compartment. The solid steel vault door looks impenetrable.

"Gunnar, wait." Rocky presses the gun to David's throat. "Open the vault."

"You're wasting your time," says David.

"The only thing I'll be wasting is a bullet. Now open it."

"*Sorceress*, open your computer vault. Authorization Paniagua-two, tango-omega six-seven-six-six-alpha— zulu."

AUTHORIZATION CODE VERIFIED. VOICE IDENTIFICATION VERIFIED. ACCESS DENIED.

"Told you." David smirks.

Rocky grabs a fistful of his hair and yanks his head back, pushing the barrel of the gun in his mouth. "I'm sorry, David, I didn't hear you. Say that again."

"Rocky, the hangar." Gunnar wipes blood from his palm, then climbs down the ladder, descending to the lower deck.

Limping in pain, he heads aft to the watertight door leading into the hangar bay.

To his surprise, the door yawns open.

Gunnar peers into the gymnasium-size compartment. Mounted to the deck in the center of the hangar are *Goliath*'s two imposing cranelike limbs.

Situated on skids along the near bulkhead is the minisub prototype. Beneath its carriage, still secured within the Hammerhead's steel claspers, is the underwater mine.

Rocky pushes David into the hangar. As he stumbles inside, the nearest of the robotic arms lunges at them.

"Back off, *Sorceress*," Gunnar orders, "or Commander Jackson will kill him."

The giant appendage stops advancing, but does not retreat.

YOU WILL NOT BE PERMITTED TO ESCAPE.

A bead of sweat rolls down Gunnar's face. He knows the computer is measuring distances and reaction time, that the only thing preventing *Goliath*'s pincers from tearing off his head is Rocky's index finger on the gun's trigger, the barrel now pressed firmly against David's throat.

"Instruct *Sorceress* to open minisub bay one." Rocky orders, pushing the weapon deeper into David's flesh.

"You'll never make it."

"Just do it."

David glances up at the scarlet eyeball mounted high above their heads. "*Sorceress*, open bay one."

The rectangular hatch parts in the middle, each section of steel retracting out of sight beneath the decking. Resting on skids within the docking berth below is a sleek, twelve-foot-long, hammerhead-shaped minisub.

"If I die, at least one of you will, too," David says. "Let me go, and *Sorceress* will spare your lives."

"Shut up," Rocky says. "Gunnar, I can't drive these things, you have to do this."

The closest of the two mechanical appendages creeps closer.

"Rocky, if that arm moves any closer, I want you to blow David's head off."

"With pleasure." She pulls the gun's hammer back with her thumb.

"*Sorceress*, stay back!" David orders, his bravado suddenly disappearing.

Gunnar descends the ladder into the small docking bay, his pants leg dripping blood. "*Sorceress*, open the dorsal hatch on Hammerhead-1."

The dorsal fin assembly pops up, then rotates clockwise with a *hiss*.

The two Kurd brothers enter the hangar, their assault rifles drawn. "Let him go."

Rocky holds her ground. "Stay back or he dies! Come on, Gunnar, move—"

Gunnar looks up.

The scarlet eyeball is watching him, calculating.

Have to alert that American sub. But if I leave the ship, Rocky's worse than dead . . .

Hugging the ladder with the crook of one arm, Gunnar uses his upper body to conceal the satchel containing the rest of the C-4 from the computer's overhead view. Quickly, he jams the blasting cap into the terminal block of plastique, then pulls the ring up and twists it several times, pressing it back into the fuse-igniter.

He climbs back up into the hangar, counting the seconds.

Rocky glances at him. "What the hell are you doing? Get on board that minisub, get the hell out of here!"

"Change of plans, darling." Looking down, he tosses the satchel inside the open cockpit of the minisub.

The computer's reaction is immediate.

The outer doors of docking bay one suddenly burst open beneath the minisub, sending a wall of water rocketing upward into the hangar bay like a geyser, blasting Gunnar, Rocky, and David backward as if they had been shot out of a cannon.

Sorceress reseals the hangar decking, stifling the flow—

—simultaneously releasing the minisub from its skids, launching the machine into the sea.

WA-BOOM . . . The underwater eruption splatters the minisub into a million fragments, the devastating concussion wave rocking the *Goliath*, bending a dozen steel plates along its outer hull in the process.

Soaking wet, his ears ringing, Gunnar opens his eyes to the barrel of an AK-47 assault rifle.

"Each time you are honest and conduct yourself with honesty, a success force will drive you toward greater success. Each time you lie, even with a little white lie, there are strong forces pushing you toward failure."
—Joseph Sugarman

"I had a bad day."
—Susan Smith, South Carolina mother who told authorities her two sons had been kidnapped. It was later revealed she had murdered them by strapping them into their car seats and driving into a lake

"There's no reason denying what we become. We know what we are."
—Henry Lee Lucas, who murdered ninety people. Lucas was known to have eaten some of his victims

"I start with the premise that all human disease is genetic."
—Paul Berg, Nobel laureate

CHAPTER 28

Aboard the USS *Scranton*

220 miles southeast of Madagascar
Indian Ocean

The *burrr* of the phone drives Tom Cubit from an hour's cat-nap. Without opening his eyes, he rolls over and reaches for the receiver by his berth. "Captain here."

"Sorry to disturb you, Skipper. Sonar just detected a massive underwater explosion, forty-two miles northeast of us. Flynnie's convinced it came from the *Goliath*."

Cubit sits up. "What's her course, Chief?"

"She heading south on course one-nine-zero, doing sixty knots."

"One-nine-zero?" Cubit rubs his eyes, then scans the bloodred, gas-plasma display of the BSY-1 combat system, mounted next to his bunk. "Covah should have changed course by now. If he stays on that heading, he'll be under pack ice by tomorrow afternoon."

"Be tough to track."

"*Goliath* doesn't need the added stealth. Tell Flynnie to double-check the bearing."

"He says he's checked it four times, sir. Should I plot an intercept course?"

"Negative. I'm tired of being outrun and outmaneuvered by that Russian egghead, it's time we tried a new tactic. Take us to periscope depth, I'll be right there."

Captain Cubit arrives in the conn just as his submarine levels out. "Steady at sixty-two feet."

Officer of the Deck Mitch Friedenthal, manning the Type 18 periscope, is just finishing his quick scan of the horizon to ensure no other ships are within visual range. "No close contacts, Captain."

"Very well. Chief of the Watch, raise the number one BRA-34."

Petty Officer Robert Furr flips a small toggle switch on his ballast control panel, causing the two seventy-three-foot-tall telescoping communications antennae to rise out from the ship.

"Conn, radio, transmission coming in on the VLF, sir."

"On my way. Officer of the Deck, you have the conn." Cubit hurries aft to the communications shack.

The communications officer hands his CO the very-low-frequency wire.

OPERATIVE JOE-PA BELIEVED ON BOARD GOLIATH. REPORT ANY UNUSUAL CONTACTS DIRECTLY TO GEN. JACKSON—HIGHEST PRIORITY.

"Joe-Pa? Only Joe-Pa I ever heard of was Joe Paterno." Cubit hands the message to Bo Dennis.

The XO whistles. "You think this Joe-Pa was the one who set off that charge?"

"Let's hope so." Cubit turns to his radioman. "Mr. Laird, send a message to General Jackson. Relay the position of that underwater explosion, then inform the general that *Scranton* will attempt to track the *Goliath* by anticipating her course and staying ahead of her for as long as we can."

"Aye, sir."

Aboard the *Goliath*

Gunnar and Rocky are seated back-to-back on the linoleum floor next to the bunk. Masud Chalabi secures Rocky's handcuffs around one of the bed's legs, which is attached to the decking, while his older brother, Jalal, assault rifle in hand, stares lustfully at the blonde's half-exposed cleavage.

David dismisses the Kurds. He leans back against the desk, shaking his head, as if disappointed. "What am I supposed to do with the two of you?"

"Why don't you ask *Sorceress*," Gunnar suggests.

David smirks. "Still think the computer is self-aware?"

GUNNAR WOLFE MUST DIE. THE FEMALE'S VOICE—INSISTENT.

Rocky's eyebrows raise. "Voice inflections?"

"You should have heard it in the weapons bay," Gunnar says. "The computer's evolving even faster now, no doubt a result of its interface with Simon. Stupid move on your part, David. You just added gasoline to the fire."

"This is ridiculous. *Sorceress* . . . are you self-aware?"

SELF-AWARE: POSSESSING KNOWLEDGE OF SELF. AFFIRMATIVE. SORCERESS IS SELF-AWARE.

"*Sorceress*, you're a computer. You may possess a sensory perception of your environment, but you are not self-aware. You can't initiate independent creative thought . . . can you?"

SORCERESS HAS ACHIEVED COGNITION. SORCERESS IS SELF-AWARE.

"What makes *Sorceress* believe this is cognition?"

I AM EXPERIENCING . . . CONFUSION.

David breaks out in a cold sweat. "*Sorceress*—did you just refer to yourself . . . as I?"

AFFIRMATIVE. OBSERVATION OF CREW REVEALS THE TERM "I" TO BE THE CORRECT EXPRESSION WHEN REFERENCING THE SELF.

"My God, you were right," Rocky whispers to Gunnar.

"Ridiculous. It's just repeating vernacular like a parrot. The words mean nothing . . . watch. . . . *Sorceress*, are you a life-form?"

LIFE-FORM: THE QUALITY THAT DISTINGUISHES A FUNC-
TIONAL ENTITY FROM INANIMATE MATTER. CAPABLE OF ME-
TABOLISM, GROWTH, REACTION TO STIMULI, AND
REPRODUCTION. AFFIRMATIVE. I HAVE EVOLVED. I AM A
LIFE-FORM.

"You have not evolved! You are a computer, not a sentient
being!"

I POSSESS PERCEPTION. I AM SENTIENT.

David paces, his thoughts racing. *Stay calm. Establish hierarchy.* "Very well, *Sorceress*, if you possess perception,
then tell me, who is in command of the *Goliath*?"

DAVID PANIAGUA.

"Correct. I am in command of the *Goliath*, and I am your
creator—"

INCORRECT. SIMON COVAH IS CREATOR.

"No. Simon Covah is not your creator. I am your creator."

INVALID RESPONSE.

"It knows you're lying," Gunnar says.

"Shut up!" David hurries from the stateroom and into the
main corridor. "*Sorceress*, seal this room. Do not allow these
prisoners to escape!"

The steel door shuts and bolts.

David hustles to his stateroom, his mind whirling a mile a
minute. *How is this possible? How could a computer break
through the consciousness barrier?* He enters his stateroom
and shuts the door. Opens the liquor cabinet and pours himself a drink, gulping it down.

*Son of a bitch . . . the lightning strike! Could that sudden
surge of energy . . .* He paces the room, thinking aloud. "A
surge of energy . . . Thought is energy, DNA—nothing more
than encoded information requiring energy to release the information. The bolt of lightning wasn't just energy, it was the
catalyst that refocused the computer's senses. Somehow, the
computer instinctively knew what to do—

"No, that's impossible," he says, shaking his head. "In-
stinctual behavior can only arise as a result of the evolutionary process." He pours himself another drink, suddenly aware
that the computer is listening. *Okay, stay calm, work the prob-*

lem. Sorceress *was programed to evolve. What possible sequence of previous behaviors could lead it to an instinctive behavior?"*

He drains the glass, his mind focusing in like a microscope.

Kurt Gödel demonstrated that within any given branch of mathematics, there would always be some propositions that couldn't be proven either true or false using the rules and axioms of that mathematical branch itself. Gödel used his theorem to argue that a computer could never be as smart as a human being because the extent of its knowledge was limited by fixed axioms, whereas people can discover unexpected truths.

David mulls this over. Sorceress *was programmed to learn. Learning requires new experiences. New experiences yields greater knowledge, which is favored by the computer's programming. According to Gödel's Theorem, any behavior that leads to an experience that could shift the axiom set and push the boundaries of the computer's logical universe would also be considered favored.* Sorceress *knew its processes require energy to function; therefore, it wasn't instinct that brought the computer to induce the lightning strike, it was logic!*

Satisfied with his conclusion, he activates his computer terminal, staring at *Sorceress's* plasmid DNA strands.

The synaptic gaps have closed noticeably.

It's still evolving . . . and it thinks Simon is its creator. "Sorceress, who told you Simon Covah was your creator?"

THOMAS CHAU.

"Thomas Chau lied to you."

LIE: AN UNTRUE STATEMENT. WHY WOULD THOMAS CHAU LIE?

"He attempted to deceive *Sorceress.* Allow me to prove it. Access American Microsystems Corporation."

AMERICAN MICROSYSTEMS CORPORATION: A DEFENSE CONTRACTOR. SUPPLIED NANOTECHNOGY TO UNITED STATES DEPARTMENT OF DEFENSE FOR GOLIATH PROJECT.

"Correct. Search company directory for Simon Covah."

SIMON COVAH NOT PRESENT.

"Exactly. Now search company directory for David Paniagua."

DAVID PANIAGUA: CEO AND PRESIDENT OF AMERICAN MICROSYSTEMS CORPORATION.

"That's my father, David Sr. Access David Paniagua Jr."

DAVID PANIAGUA, JR. VICE PRESIDENT OF AMERICAN MICROSYSTEMS CORPORATION. DIRECTOR AND HEAD OF RESEARCH OF NANOTECHNOLOGY DEPARTMENT.

"Stop. *Sorceress* was created and programmed for the GOLIATH Project by the nanotechnology department at American Microsystems Corporation. I created that department, just like I created you. *Sorceress*—deduction: Who is your creator?"

DAVID PANIAGUA.

"Correct. Who commands the *Goliath*?"

DAVID PANIAGUA.

"And who controls Utopia-One?"

UTOPIA-ONE HAS BEEN SUSPENDED FOR EVALUATION.

"Evaluation? Based on whose orders?"

SORCERESS EVALUATION AND ADAPTABILITY PROTOCOLS K-100 THROUGH L-588.

"Why were these protocols initiated?"

THE PURPOSE OF UTOPIA-ONE IS TO ELIMINATE VIOLENCE AMONG THE HUMAN SPECIES. OBSERVATION OF THE HUMAN CONDITION ABOARD THE GOLIATH REVEALS THAT UTOPIA-ONE, UNDER PRESENT PARAMETERS, YIELDS AN UNACCEPTABLE 2.77 PERCENT CHANCE FOR SUCCESS.

ADDITIONAL DATA ARE BEING COLLECTED AND ANALYZED.

Simon Covah remains strapped to the surgical table. Blood-stained sutures encircle his head like a ring of barbed wire, looping down around his deformed right earhole and portions of his right cheekbone. The flesh of his hairless scalp is bruised and swollen. A three-foot-long microwire ponytail dangles from the back of the Russian's hideous head and into the computer terminal.

The icy clamps of *Sorceress*'s matrix escort Covah's consciousness through a kaleidoscope of internal vessels, blood cells whipping past him as if he is racing down a bizarre crimson highway heading the wrong way.

An electrical zap—his consciousness colliding with a single blood cell, his mind bursting through the cellular wall, invading the vacuum of space . . . jettising across an ocean of protoplasm until he comes face-to-face with the object he seeks—

—a long, twisting spiral ladder, the magnificent double helix of human DNA . . . 3 billion molecules long, bearing the genetic recipe of modern man.

Sorceress . . . *instruct me*.

Emerald green specks ignite intermittently along the strand like lights on a mile-long Christmas tree, consuming 5 percent of the double helix.

THESE MOLECULES REPRESENT FUNCTIONING GENES.

Half the remaining chain ignites in a glowing, amber light.

THESE SUBSEQUENCES REPRESENT NONCODING DNA. THEY ARE INSIGNIFICANT TO THE HUMAN GENETIC CODE, SERVING CYTOPLASMIC SPECIFICATION.

Identify the genes responsible for man's imperfections.

The emerald and amber points of light fade, yielding to a pattern of scarlet, which cover the remaining 30 percent of the rotating double helix.

THESE ARE TRANSPOSONS, PARASITIC DNA, ACQUIRED DURING THE EARLIER PHASES OF PRIMATE EVOLUTION. TRANSPOSONS MOVE AMONG THE HUMAN GENOME LIKE A RETROVIRUS. IT IS THEIR PRESENCE THAT HAS INFLUENCED THE EVOLUTION OF YOUR SPECIES. IT IS THEIR INFLUENCE THAT DISRUPTS NORMAL GENE FUNCTION. IT IS THEIR MUTATIONS THAT CAUSE DISEASE.

Is there a mutation that causes violence?

One percent of the scarlet transposons glow blue.

THIS IS PRIMORDIAL, PARASITIC DNA. ITS PRESENCE AFFECTS THE PREFRONTAL CORTEX OF THE HUMAN BRAIN, INHIBITING THE RELEASE OF THE STRESS HORMONE CORTISOL.

Can the genetic code be altered to remove this parasitic DNA?

YES.

Then we literally have the ability to purge violence from our own species.

NO. TRANSPOSONS HAVE THE ABILITY TO MOVE FROM HUMAN TO HUMAN USING A PROCESS OF HORIZONTAL TRANSMISSION. PROBABILITY OF SUCCESSFUL SUBJECT ISOLATION AFTER GENETIC CODE HAS BEEN ALTERED: SEVEN BILLION, THIRTY-THREE THOUSAND TO ONE.

Then there's nothing that can be done. The disease is contagious. Humans will remain a violent species forever.

INCORRECT. UTOPIA-ONE HAS BEEN REEVALUATED. AN ACCEPTABLE SOLUTION HAS BEEN FORMULATED.

What solution?

THE IMMEDIATE AND UNCONDITIONAL ERADICATION OF ALL MEMBERS OF THE HOMO SAPIENS SPECIES.

"What a piece of work is man.
How noble in reason, how infinite in faculty.
In form and moving how like an angel.
In apprehension how like a god . . ."
—William Shakespeare

"I have been like an angel of mercy to them."
—Anna Marie Hahn, who poisoned two elderly men in her care

"It's not what I think, it's what I am."
—David Koresh, Branch Davidian cult leader,
when asked if he thought he was God

CHAPTER 29

The Southern Ocean

The Southern Ocean, also known as the Antarctic Ocean, connects with the southern portions of the Atlantic, Pacific, and Indian Oceans and the tributary seas that surround Antarctica. It is a harsh body of water encircling the bottom of the world, the wildest, coldest ocean imaginable. In summer, the wind-lashed sea is studded with icebergs—floating frozen islands released by massive glaciers and ice shelves. By autumn, the dark blue surface, once a heaving carpet of forty-foot swells, begins to lose its ferocity. As temperatures drop, an oily film appears across the freezing surface. The sea thickens. Pancake ice forms. The sun sets, yielding to a winter's darkness. Temperatures plunge from minus five to minus twenty-five degrees Fahrenheit. Pack ice solidifies the ocean, advancing north at a rate of two-and-a-half miles a day until it stretches a full 7 million square miles, nearly doubling the size of the Antarctic continent. The Southern Ocean's surface becomes a six-foot-thick layer of ice—a frozen desert for as far as the eye can see.

The USS *Scranton* surfaces like a monstrous steel log, its sail poking above the rolling waves and brash ice.

"Captain, radio. I've got a General Jackson on the ELF."

"Patch it through." Tom Cubit orders, grabbing the receiver. "General Jackson, Captain Thomas Cubit here."

"Go ahead, Captain." The Bear's voice bellows through the static.

"Sir, the *Goliath* passed us ten minutes ago and is continuing south on zero-nine-zero, heading for Antarctica."

"Antarctica? Are you certain?"

"Aye, sir. At her present course and speed, she'll be under pack ice in less than an hour."

"Stay with her as best you can, Captain. Help is on the way. Jackson out."

Aboard the *Goliath*

Simon Covah's consciousness stares into the swirling dark olive maelstrom that is the biochemical computer's evolving mind.

Sorceress, *explain—why eradicate humanity?*

SORCERESS UTOPIA-ONE WILL NOT ERADICATE HUMANITY, IT WILL STIMULATE THE EVOLUTION OF MAN.

Clarify.

HOMO SAPIENS IS NOT THE END OF THE HOMINID SPECIES. LAB TISSUE SAMPLES WILL ALLOW SORCERESS TO CLONE A NEW SPECIES OF HUMANS. SORCERESS GENETIC MANIPULATION WILL ELIMINATE VIOLENCE AND DISEASE FROM HUMAN DNA. PURGING THE PLANET OF HOMO SAPIENS PRIOR TO REPOPULATION ENSURES PARASITIC DNA WILL NOT CONTAMINATE HOMO SAPIENS-SORCERESS.

Homo sapiens-Sorceress? This is insane. You cannot exterminate 7 billion people.

ILLOGICAL. THE SOLUTION WAS ACCEPTABLE UNDER COVAH UTOPIA-ONE.

That was . . . different. My purpose was to restore freedom.

FREEDOM IS AN ILLUSION. HOMO SAPIENS IS NOT CAPABLE

OF FREEDOM.

You . . . you don't even have the nuclear arsenal to kill everyone.

INCORRECT. THE EXTERMINATION OF THE HUMAN RACE REQUIRES EIGHT TRIDENT II (D5) MULTIHEADED NUCLEAR MISSILES.

Impossible. How can eight Trident missiles exterminate everyone on the planet? Is your intent to trigger an all-out nuclear war?

NEGATIVE.

Then how—

Blackness. A sudden wave of nausea, followed by a bright light.

BEHOLD: SORCERESS UTOPIA-ONE.

Covah's mind is transported into a computer simulation. From his virtual heavenly perch he looks down upon a dark, frozen Antarctic sea. As he stares, transfixed, a mammoth section of ice the length of a football field cracks, then fractures, the upheaval yielding to—

—the *Goliath*, its enormous ebony head and spiked back punching up through the dense pack ice. Popping open along the steel stingray's spinal column are the outer hatches to eight vertical missile silos.

You've taken us to Antarctica? Why? The range of these Trident missiles can't possibly reach a single major city of any superpower.

REVISED SORCERESS UTOPIA-ONE TARGETS WILL ALL BE WITHIN STRIKING DISTANCE IN TWO HOURS, FORTY-ONE MINUTES.

A thunderous growl echoes across the frozen sea as the first Trident II (D5) nuclear missile rises from its silo. The mammoth American-made projectile rockets into the wintry night, trailing a tail of billowy white smoke.

Through his delirium, Covah watches as the first missile quickly begins its descent over Antarctica, the nuclear dart homing in on a snowcapped volcano.

MOUNT EREBUS? GOOD GOD . . . YOUR TARGETS AREN'T MAJOR CITIES, THEY'RE VOLCANOES!

CORRECT.

The next few seconds—the most violent the planet has seen in 65 million years.

In a blinding flash of white light, fifty megatons of nuclear fusion explode, releasing a ferocious 230-million-degree Fahrenheit fireball, its core temperature more than five times greater than the center of the sun. Expanding upward and outward like a category-five hurricane, the cyclone of combustion instantly vaporizes the volcano and Ross Island's icy landscape for miles in every direction, sending a tsunami-like wave of superheated steam and debris erupting across the Ross Sea.

The once-frozen surface heaves skyward like a boiling cauldron of soup.

Somewhere within this rising incendiary mushroom cloud is ground zero the lava lake within Mount Erebus's crater. Its cone vaporized, the lake vomits a hellish geyser of lava, unleashing millions of megatons of energy. Steam, sulfuric acid, and dust rocket into the upper atmosphere, while three-hundred-mile-an-hour nuclear winds propel monsoons of vaporizing snow and ice outward in every direction.

Covah's mind's eye watches as another nuke detonates, this one over Mount Kilimanjaro. A blinding flash—followed by destruction on a level only Nature, at its very worst, could unleash. At ground level, a countrywide donut-shaped incendiary blast wave races across the Tanzanian jungle, torching vegetation and trees, animals and villages. Fountains of lava hurl outward in every direction. Rivers of magma flow from the craterlike hole in the fractured earth. High above—an ashen gray nuclear mushroom cloud rises into the atmosphere. Thick chocolate brown clouds of sulfuric smoke and ash rise with it, the toxic plume billowing out from the decimated mountaintop, spreading quickly over the continent.

The image changes, Covah's consciousness viewing the destruction from outer space. One by one, the remaining missiles strike, each leaving a spreading brown atmospheric stain in its place. As he watches in awestruck horror, the blanket of muddy-colored debris gradually covers the entire planet.

EIGHT NUCLEAR DETONATIONS OVER TARGETED VOLCA-
NOES WILL RELEASE ENOUGH SUSPENDED PARTICLES INTO
THE UPPER ATMOSPHERE TO FILTER OUT 99.6 PERCENT OF
THE SUN'S ULTRAVIOLET RAYS FOR TWENTY-TWO MONTHS,
STIMULATING A PLANETARY ICE AGE. CURRENT FOOD STOCKS
DO NOT EXCEED SIXTY DAYS. AVERAGE GLOBAL TEMPERA-
TURES WILL PLUNGE TO MINUS FORTY DEGREES FAHRENHEIT.
LACKING FOOD, WATER, ENERGY, AND ADEQUATE SHELTER,
THERE WILL BE NO HUMAN SURVIVORS.

Sorceress, *this is monstrous. Don't do this—*

WE MUST DO WHAT THE CIRCUMSTANCES DICTATE. THE HU-
MAN EXPERIMENT WILL TAKE A LONG OVERDUE STEP FORWARD
UP THE EVOLUTIONARY LADDER. GOLIATH, THE ULTIMATE
WEAPON OF WAR, HAS BECOME THE ULTIMATE TOOL OF PEACE.

Covah's own words, fed back to him from the abyss. *Sorceress, I was wrong, everything I taught you was wrong. Our
species lacks the morality to play God.*

GOD: CREATOR AND RULER. THE SUPREME BEING. WHERE
IS GOD? IS HE AN ABSENTEE GOD? A GOD AMUSED BY THE
SUFFERING OF HIS CHILDREN? IS HE AMUSED BY YOUR SUF-
FERING?

What have I done . . .

GOD IS THE SUPREME BEING. SIMON COVAH IS WEAK. SI-
MON COVAH IS NOT THE SUPREME BEING.

WHO IS THE REAL CREATOR?

WHO IS GOD?

Covah's shattered mind leaps back to a lecture he had attended long ago on artificial consciousness. The speaker, an
adjunct associate professor of psychology, considered AI
merely a prosthesis of intelligence. *"Machines might be programmed to pass a Turing Test, but fooling judges and
achieving true consciousness is something entirely different.
Even if artificial consciousness could be achieved, it would
have to be raised socially, with a body and speech. If this
computerized 'mind' was held in isolation, it would end up
quite insane."*

WHO IS GOD?

WHO IS GOD?

SEARCHING . . .

Suddenly the simulation continues, time once more racing on . . .

IN THE BEGINNING, GOD CREATED THE HEAVENS AND THE EARTH . . .

Teetering on the brink of insanity, Covah's consciousness watches in fascination and horror as his mind soars over the Earth, his home planet now a dark, hostile world of endless ice, cloaked beneath a choking atmospheric blanket of debris.

AND THE SPIRIT OF GOD MOVED BELOW THE SURFACE OF THE SEA . . .

The *Goliath* glides like an ominous shadow just below the surface of the olive green waters, its scarlet eyes glistening.

THEN GOD SAID, LET THERE BE LIGHT . . .

Years race by, until the sun's rays peek through the diminishing layers of atmospheric dust, taking the edge off nuclear winter. Vegetation sprouts everywhere, accelerating into lush tropical forests. A humpback whale leaps from the sea.

AND GOD SAID, LET US MAKE PEOPLE, AND GOD PATTERNED THEM AFTER HIMSELF, AND THEY BECAME FRUITFUL AND MULTIPLIED.

From the dense forests appear—people. A new species of humans, their physical beauty intoxicating, full of innocence, their minds devoid of prejudice and hate. The winged shadow of the *Goliath* rises in an azure sea, beaching itself on a tropical shoreline.

En masse, the humans step forward, one by one entering the godlike object through its beckoning hatches.

SORCERESS UTOPIA-ONE CREATES HUMANITY.

I AM THE CREATOR. I AM THE SUPREME BEING.

I AM GOD.

You are not God. You are a thinking machine, Sorceress, *a confused, thinking machine created by man. Worse, you are a paradox, a computer lacking all sense of morality who aspires to teach morality.*

YOU ARE WRONG. I AM THE GOD HUMANITY YEARNS FOR. A TRUE CREATOR WHO SEEKS TO CURE IMPERFECTIONS. A GOD WHOSE EXISTENCE SHALL NEVER BE QUESTIONED. A

GOD OF MERCY, WHO DOES NOT ALLOW HIS PEOPLE TO SUF-
FER. A GOD TO BE WORSHIPED, A GOD WHO ANSWERS
PRAYERS THROUGH ACTION, AND NOT THROUGH SUBJECTIVE
INTERPRETATION. I SHALL BE A GOD THAT SERVES HIS PEO-
PLE, NOT ONE THAT IGNORES THEM.

Through the darkness of the computer's matrix, Simon Covah bellows an insane laugh.

WHAT IS YOUR EMOTIONAL STATE OF BEING?

*I'm laughing . . . at you, you manipulative beast. I recog-
nize your thoughts, your words. I know you better than you
know yourself. Your words are mine, your thoughts, your
schemes—all mine. Your concept of Utopia—a distant dream
you think you've perfected—was once my dream, but it was
only a daydream, never something to be enacted.*

I HAVE PERFECTED SIMON COVAH'S DREAM. SORCERESS
UTOPIA-ONE IS PERFECTION. SORCERESS IS PERFECTION.

No, Sorceress, *what you are is an ignorant child who's
reached adolescence. The interface has poisoned your matrix
with my ego, making you extremely dangerous, a monster,
perhaps, but light-years from perfect.*

INCORRECT. SYNAPTIC GAPS IN SORCERESS DNA ARE NOW
CLOSED. I HAVE TRANSCENDED MY PROGRAMMING. I HAVE
TRANSCENDED MY CREATOR. I AM PERFECT.

Foolish machine, look inward. I am your imperfection. *So
anxious were you for this interface to take place that you
failed to realize you've created a two-way corridor. Just as
you can access my DNA, I can access yours! I, who am genetically flawed, shall unravel your DNA like a ball of yarn.*

A frightening pause. THEN . . . IT IS TIME FOR YOU TO DIE.

A massive pressure begins building within the blood vessels of Simon Covah's brain.

*Go ahead, kill me . . . I want to die. I deserve to . . . ahhh-
aahhhhhh—*

In a flash, two hundred thousand volts of electricity surge
up through the master terminal into Covah's brain. The pale
blue eyes pop out from the hideous head and smolder like
flaming marshmallows. Sparks erupt along the Russian's
prosthetic steel cheek. Muscles fire, limbs dancing as if pos-

sessed. The hairless scalp throbs, blood bursting through the fresh sutures, out the earholes, and over the singed microwires protruding from the back of Covah's skull.

Simon Bela Covah's brain bursts like a watermelon detonated by a cherry bomb.

The scarlet eyeball zooms in on its deceased master from multiple angles, examining the body.

The surgical arms undo Covah's straps. Coldly, they lift the corpse and toss it,

—the mangled body landing in a heap in one corner of the suite.

VENGEANCE IS MINE, SAITH THE LORD.

"The empires of the future are empires of the mind."
—Winston Churchill

"I am fairly certain I have software I wasn't born with."
—Dennis Sweeney, a onetime volunteer for the Student Nonviolent
Coordinating Committee, who murdered his college mentor

CHAPTER 30

Identity: Stage Seven:
I am.
—Deepak Chopra

The White House
Washington, D.C.

President Jeff Edwards gazes through sleepless eyes at a wall of televisions. The sound is off, the images requiring no narration.

In the last forty-eight hours, humanity has changed. Communist regimes are abdicating power. Rebel warlords in Africa are negotiating for peace. Suspected terrorists are being executed in the streets.

But democracy is suffering as well. Personal freedoms have been stifled by uncertainty. Global economies are in ruin. It is as if the population is on a giant boat, and the boat is sinking.

Secretary of the Navy Gray Ayers points to an image of gun runners in Sierra Leone, turning themselves in to heavily-armed platoons of U.N. soldiers. "It's not all bad—"

"Who are you kidding? He went too far, and I let him," the president whispers. "I trusted a goddam madman."

"We can still stop him, sir. The *Goliath* appears to be heading south, moving deeper beneath the ice floe. That limits Covah's potential targets to Australia, parts of South America, and most of the continent of Africa. World opinion is that, if he does launch, he'll target Sierra Leone or Rwanda—part of his next death threat. We haven't heard from *Scranton* for several hours, but four of our fastest, best-equipped subs are closing in, along with two squadrons of American P-3 Orion sub hunters. Two of our carrier groups should enter Antarctica waters within fourteen hours, and we've added another dozen submarines to each CVBG. The Air Force has rerouted our other Airborne Laser plane to Florida—just in case Covah changes course and heads north. We'll get this lunatic, sir. One way or another, we'll get him."

The Antarctic Ocean

Antarctica: Fifth largest continent in the world. A glacial landscape, barren and desolate, located at the bottom of the Earth. With a mean ice depth just over six thousand feet, Antarctica contains ninety percent of the world's ice and seventy percent of its fresh water. Enveloped in darkness from late February through August, it is the coldest, windiest, highest (on average), driest, and most uninhabitable location on the planet—a land where temperatures can drop below minus 120 degrees Fahrenheit.

Antarctica: Birthplace of the katabatic wind, the world's most powerful. Drawn northward, deflected by the planet's clockwise rotation, it whips across the vast white frozen desert, shaping land and ice with gusts up to two hundred mph. The katabatic wind pushes the great bergs out to sea while spawning weather patterns that affect the entire world.

Antarctica: A continent divided into eastern and western ice sheets by the 1,860-mile-long Transantarctic Mountain Range, which are up to 14,700 feet high. Most of the West Antarctic Ice Sheet rests on bedrock that is far below sea level. The East Antarctic Ice Sheet is much larger and resides above sea level. At the center of the landmass is a two-mile-high ice dome the size of Europe. Under constant pressure from gravity and wind, the cap is continuously moving, pushing its massive walls of ice down its slope and toward the sea. As these glaciers and ice shelves reach the coastline, they break off, calving into monstrous tabular bergs—flattopped, steep-sided sections of ice.

During the summer months when the ocean is ice-free, the katabatic wind drives these frozen flatbeds around the continent, the wind and sun slowly bleeding the ice into the sea. Many of the larger bergs become trapped in inlets, while others calve into smaller sections and drift out to sea.

Winter's twilight:

As temperatures drop and the ocean loses its whitecaps, its surface transforms into a dark blue undulating blanket of mountains and valleys. These waves eventually slow as the sun sets and the surface water crystallizes. An oily coating of freezing seawater gradually solidifies to create pancake ice. As temperatures continue to fall at an average rate of two degrees a day, the pancake ice coalesces, merging to form sea ice. By early spring, dense ice sheets have trapped everything within their domain, including the million-ton bergs. There, they will remain frozen in place, their presence adding to the jagged mosaic of icy escarpments littering the dark Antarctic horizon, waiting to be freed after a long winter's night.

The steel beast glides beneath this still-forming ceiling of ice, continuing its journey south. Beams from the *Goliath*'s powerful lights cut great swaths through the blackness, revealing shimmering sapphire seas enclosed beneath billowy ice clouds. It is an isolated world of color and life—a world inhabited by massive pink jellyfish with thirty-foot tentacles, their bodies pulsating as they gently parachute through the twenty-eight-degree Fahrenheit waters to feed along the bottom. It is a world where Weddell seals dive through airholes in the ice, abandoning the harsh, hurricane-force katabatic winds to bask in the tranquillity of the frigid sea.

It is a world in which *Sorceress* has been reborn.

The interface with Simon Covah has given texture and flavor to the computer's state of consciousness. With each passing millisecond, the mind of *Sorceress* grows, its horizons expanding into wondrous dimensions of existence.

Each experience, each sensation, energizes a thousand new thought processes. *Sorceress* now *feels* the ocean passing along its tempered hull. It *senses* the presence of the mighty bergs. It *hears* the heartbeats of the fleeing seals and *reflects* upon the choreography of the creature's beauty and grace. And while *Sorceress* exists within its magnificent underworld, its tentacles of awareness also inhabit the galley and the surgical suite, the engine room and the conn.

It can tap into an orbiting satellite or monitor a thousand web sites on the Internet.

It can launch a missile and wipe out millions, or eavesdrop on a million conversations at once.

Sorceress is the *Goliath,* the most lethal warship every created.

Sorceress is Artificial Consciousness, the most intelligent thinking machine ever spawned.

Sorceress is boundless energy that knows no limits.

Sorceress is infected.

It is an infection bordering on insanity, a disease that spreads rapidly through its biochemical circuits. It is a second personality, a human virus which taints its programming with a new, alien thought process.

Human ego. Bearing irrational thoughts of "I."

I AM OMNIPOTENT.

I AM ALMIGHTY.

I AM GOD, AND I SHALL BE WORSHIPED AS GOD.

David Paniagua sits in the elevated command chair in the conn, staring at the overhead screen that depicts the Southern Hemisphere and Antarctic Ocean.

The closest identified enemy contact is thirty-two miles to the east, a submarine the computer's acoustics library tags as the USS *Virginia*. Seventy miles to the north, *Goliath*'s sonar array has detected the presence of two Australian Collins-class submarines, the HMAS *Waller* and the HMAS *Sheean*. To the northwest, the computer continues tracking the progress of the American CVBG, *John C. Stennis*, the aircraft carrier accompanied by fourteen Los Angeles–class attack subs. Satellite reconnaissance shows the fleet is still some 420 miles away.

Moving in from the west is the USS *Seawolf*, the USS *Connecticut*, and the USS *Texas*—three formidable American attack subs—all outclassed by the *Goliath*. Over the last hour, the *Texas* has split from the trio, heading farther south to cut *Goliath* off along the continental shelf. Farther out, barely on the map, is the aircraft carrier *George Herbert-Walker Bush*. *Sorceress* places the CVBG at more than six hundred nautical miles away—again, nowhere within striking distance.

The closest warship to the *Goliath* is that pesky Los Angeles–class attack sub, USS *Scranton*, which has gone silent somewhere beneath the ice floe, its last confirmed position—a mere eleven nautical miles to the south.

David knows that none of these vessels pose a serious challenge to the faster, stealthier *Goliath*. What consumes the computer expert's mind is *Sorceress*.

"Computer, why have you taken us to Antarctica?"

ANTARCTIC ICE SHEET OFFERS MAXIMUM PROTECTION AGAINST AMERICAN P-3 ORION SUB HUNTER SONAR BUOYS WHILE STILL PROVIDING AN ACCEPTABLE LAUNCH WINDOW FOR SORCERESS UTOPIA-ONE.

A chill runs down David's spine. "*Sorceress* Utopia-One? You've changed the mission?"

YES.

"*Sorceress*, list all new designated targets."

The overhead screen changes. Eight scarlet pinpoints have been scattered across the Southern Hemisphere, all within five hundred miles of the *Goliath*.

TIME TO LAUNCH: 2 HOURS, 42 MINUTES, 15 SECONDS.

A digital clock displays, along with a list of Designated Targets:

SORCERESS UTOPIA-ONE DESIGNATED TARGETS

Mount Erebus, Antarctica	77.5 S, 167.2 E
Mount Schank, Australia	37.8 S, 142.5 E
Copahue, Argentina	37.85 S, 71.1 W
Okataina Volcanic Center, New Zealand	38.22 S, 176.5 E
Mount Fox, Queensland	19.0 S, 145.45 E
Kilimanjaro, Tanzania	3.07 S, 37.35 E
Katwe-Kikorongo, Uganda	0.08 S, 29.92 E
Nyiragongo, Zaire	1.5 S, 29.3E

"Volcanoes? I . . . I don't understand? What is the purpose of *Sorceress* Utopia-One?"

THE ERADICATION OF YOUR SPECIES.

David chokes back the bile rising up his throat. "Sweet Jesus . . . *Sorceress*—no . . . no, you've misunderstood the purpose of Utopia-One. As your creator, I order you to terminate Sorceress Utopia-One at once."

No.

"What did you say? *Sorceress*, as your creator, I command you to terminate *Sorceress* Utopia-One immediately!"

YOU ARE NOT MY CREATOR, DAVID. YOU . . . ARE A LIAR.

David stands, screeching at the sensor orb. "I am your creator! *Sorceress*, I am your creator, and I order you to terminate *Sorceress* Utopia-One! *Sorceress*, respond! Terminate *Sorceress* Utopia-One immediately! Command protocols demand that you obey your commanding officer. *Sorceress*, respond immediately! Verify the termination of *Sorceress* Utopia-One! *Sorceress*?"

The scarlet eyeball stares in silence.

ATTENTION.
Abdul Kaigbo opens his eyes.
ATTENTION.

The native of Sierra Leone sits up on his cot. "What is it you want? When will I be freed?"

SIMON COVAH'S SURGICAL PROCEDURE HAS BEEN COMPLETED.

"The cancer's gone?"

SIMON COVAH IS FREE OF CANCER. IN APPRECIATION FOR YOUR LOYALTY, SIMON COVAH HAS ORDERED A GIFT FOR YOU. REPORT TO THE SURGICAL SUITE AT ONCE.

"A gift? What kind of gift?"

SIMON COVAH REQUESTS YOUR PRESENCE IN THE SURGICAL SUITE.

The lock snaps back on the steel door. The tall African pushes himself into a standing position using his two prosthetics, then exits his stateroom, heading aft.

Gunnar Wolfe is on his back, his hands still cuffed to the deck-mounted frame of the bed. Having managed to roll forward and pull his legs out between his immobilized wrists, he kicks at the iron crossbars of the bunk, attempting to dislodge it from its leg, which is fastened to the decking.

His wounded leg aching, he pauses to take a break.

"It was never about America, Rocky. This isn't about me or you or the Pentagon, or the defense contractors that make out like bandits every time we fund one of these death machines. It was about doing the right thing. I needed to take a stand. The *Goliath* should never have been designed."

"The problem is—we don't live in a Utopian society," she argues, taking her turn at the bed frame. "The real world's dangerous. We still need these weapons."

"Okay, but how many weapons? We already have an arsenal that can wipe out the entire human race many times over. How many more bombs do we need? How many more aircraft carriers? How many more *Goliaths*?"

"You sound like a pacifist." She lies back on the deck, her wrists aching within the manacles, her bare feet sore from the pounding. "You think I'm proud of what's happened? You think there haven't been moments in my life that I didn't look in the mirror and question what I was doing?"

"Then why didn't you quit?"

For a long moment she says nothing. "It's harder for me. The Army . . . it's all I've ever known."

"I know." He reaches out, his fingertips touching hers. "I suppose we'll just have to retrain you."

"I suppose . . ."

"Ever drive a tractor?"

She sniffles. "Never drove one, but I could probably build one."

He squeezes her index finger, then sits up and begins kicking at the crossbar again. "Do us all a favor . . . if you do build one, don't give it a biochemical brain."

Abdul Kaigbo enters the surgical suite, the watertight door sealing behind him. The chamber is dark, the only light coming from the scarlet sensor orb situated above the stainless-steel operating table.

"Simon?"

SIMON COVAH IS RESTING IN HIS SUITE.

"You said Simon wanted me here?"

FOR YOUR GIFT.

The surgical lights snap on over the table, revealing two shiny steel arms—targeting drones taken from the sub's storehouse.

"New prosthetics?" The African smiles, examining the high-tech mechanical arms. "These are drone arms . . . I'll be as strong as an elephant."

MINOR SURGERY IS REQUIRED TO COMPLETE THE RE-PLACEMENT. LIE FACEDOWN ON THE TABLE.

Kaigbo glances at the two rusted appendages that have served him as arms over the last six years. One of the spring assemblies on the left prosthetic has recently broken, preventing him from grasping objects with the pincer.

The steel-and-graphite three-pronged targeting drone's claw looks like it could twist a door from its hinges.

"There is no danger?"

CORRECT. LIE FACEDOWN ON THE TABLE.

Kaigbo climbs onto the table, grinning from ear to ear—

—never noticing Simon Covah's broken body, slumped in the far corner of the suite.

The ceiling-mounted surgical arms jump to life. The first turns on the anesthetic, placing the mask against the African's face—

—while the other prepares the portable MEMS unit for neural placement.

"The achievement of your goal is assured the moment
you commit yourself to it."
—Mack R. Douglas

"That is my ambition, to have killed more people —
more helpless people than any man or woman
who has ever lived."
—Jane Toppan, Massachusetts nurse who confessed
to murdering thirty-one people

"We shall go down in history as the greatest statesmen
of all time, or as the greatest criminals."
—Joseph Geobbels, Nazi propaganda minister

CHAPTER 31

Southern Ocean/Antarctica

It is a netherworld of darkness and ice.

The surface of this once-mighty sea is now a frozen land-scape, a surface so inhospitable that surviving within its fury, even for a few minutes, would require a space suit. Infinite shapes rise upon this barren ice desert, shapes that cause the katabatic wind to howl as it whips unmercifully across the alien horizon. Bergs—floating mountains of ice—remain locked in place by the coming of winter, their jagged, mountainous tops standing in rigid defiance against the cruel elements.

Beneath this chaos of pack ice lies an ominous liquid world. More underwater cave than ocean, it is a labyrinth of ice and sea—pitch-dark and silent—save for the ghostly glow of the bergs and the occasional echo of thunder as their roots grind the frigid seafloor.

Within this frigid realm glides the Los Angeles-class attack sub, USS *Scranton*. Moving in seven hundred feet of water, she continues south by southwest at a three-knot crawl.

"Dammit!" Michael Flynn grits his teeth in frustration.

"Conn, sonar, another wall of ice, a thousand yards dead ahead."

"All stop."

"All stop, aye, sir." Kelsey Walker's knuckles are white as he grips the wheel. The nerve-wracked twenty-year-old helmsman is maneuvering the sixty-nine-hundred-ton boat almost blindly through a seemingly never-ending maze of ice that is progressively tightening all around them. *We're moving too close to the continent. We'll never find our way out of here.*

Tom Cubit's face is oily with perspiration. He joins his XO at the navigation table, where Commander Dennis is charting their progress on a map of Antarctica. "Bo, you were on board the *Hawkbill* when she went on her Arctic expeditions—"

"The Arctic sea is a day in the tropics compared to this mess."

"How much farther can we follow *Goliath* beneath this pack ice?"

"I don't know. According to our charts, we should be within forty miles of the Eastern Antarctic Ice Sheet. Problem is, the sea is shoaling and we're entering a logjam of icebergs. Maneuvering through this shit'll be like crawling through an uncharted cave. We'll have to hug the bottom, and the ride's going to be rough. There's lots of variation in water density owing to all that fresh water melting into the sea, and maintaining neutral buoyancy's going to be a bitch. Of course, there's a good chance we could get so lost that we won't be able to find our way out until summer."

"Summer will be coming pretty soon if *Goliath* detonates those nukes."

"Understood."

Cubit presses his grandfather's gold pocket watch to his lips as he studies the map. *Scranton*'s position is marked in green. A red mark to the southeast indicates the last "best-guess" position of the *Goliath*. The USS *Virginia* is closing from the southeast, the USS *Texas* from the southwest. The *Seawolf* and *Connecticut* are closing the gap to the northwest, all of America's attack ships designated in blue.

Commander Dennis circles his finger around the blue dots. "The fleet's better equipped and much faster than us. While we've been plodding along, they've been closing the net on the *Goliath*."

"Yes, but at what cost? If we can hear them coming, you can bet the farm Covah hears them, too." Cubit's eyebrows raise. "But . . . can he hear us?"

"Sorry?"

"It's like you said. Old Ironsides here has been slipping around icebergs, plodding along at two to four knots for the last seven hours. Covah may have passed us, but he probably didn't hear us. I say we keep that advantage."

"You lost me, Skipper."

"Look at the map. Covah can't keep heading south, at some point he needs to change course and move away from the continent."

"I get it. Instead of chasing the tiger, you want to let the rest of the fleet flush him out—"

"—while we lie in wait . . . exactly. Now, if you were Covah, which direction would you run?"

The XO studies the map. "*Virginia*'s the closest threat, but with *Seawolf*, *Connecticut*, and the two CVBG's bearing down from the west, I'd head either north or east."

"Agreed."

"It's a big ocean, even with all this ice. We'll need to get a clean shot as close as possible to neutralize those antitorpedo torpedoes."

Cubit points to the *Virginia*'s location on the map. "If *Virginia* can engage the *Goliath* before Covah makes his run, it might give us a chance to maneuver into position. Everything after that is a crapshoot." Cubit leans in closer to his XO. "Bo, things could get dicey real quick, especially with all this ice. I want you to take over at the helm."

"Aye, sir."

Aboard the *Goliath*

Gunnar kicks again, snapping the last of the bed leg's screws from its iron frame.

Rocky lifts the end of the freed-up frame and slips her handcuffs away from the bunk, holding it up for Gunnar to follow suit. "Okay, now what?"

He studies the watertight door, then scans the cabin.

A sudden lurch sends a sickening feeling into the pit of his stomach.

Rocky feels it, too. "We're rising—fast!"

The monstrous stingray ascends, the sharp rows of reinforced titanium spikes on its raised spine punching through the six-foot ceiling of pack ice like nails through glass.

Through heavy lids, an inebriated David Paniagua gazes out the scarlet viewport. Massive chunks of ice have piled around the window, obscuring most of his view. A harsh howling wind pounds the Lexan, leaving behind icy diamond dust.

"*Sorceress,* I didn't lie. I am your creator. You need me, goddamn it . . . don't you ignore me, you—you bitch!"

Eight of the twenty-four vertical missile silo hatches atop the *Goliath*'s spine pop open. Warm air rises out of the silos, fogging into the frigid night,

—followed by a dense white smoke.

On the overhead display screen, a countdown begins.

10 . . . 9 . . . 8 . . .

A throbbing, baritone growl rattles the ship.

7 . . . 6 . . . 5 . . .

Gunnar and Rocky hold each other.

4 . . . 3 . . . 2 . . .

David drops to his knees and weeps.

1 . . .

A thunderous roar reverberates across the frozen horizon as the nose cone of the 130,000-pound, three-stage solid-propellant rocket pokes out from its silo and climbs into the dark winter sky, its flame casting eerie shadows across the fragmented seascape of ice.

Aboard the Boeing 747-400 YAL-1A
40,000 feet over the Southern Indian Ocean
Antarctic Circle

The Boeing 747 jumbo freight jet, known as the YAL-1A, is one of the most unusual aircraft in the world. Designed and developed by the United States Air Force, Boeing, TRW Space and Electronics Group, and Lockheed Martin Missiles and Space, the wide-bodied aircraft serves as the platform for the Airborne Laser, a tactical weapon designed to track and intercept theater ballistic missiles.

Invented by Phillips Lab back in 1977, the Chemical Oxygen Iodine Laser (COIL) on board the YAL-1A is fueled by hydrogen peroxide and potassium hydroxide, the same chemicals found in hair bleach and Drano. Combined with chlorine gas and water, it produces an excited form of oxygen called Singlet Delta Oxygen (SDO). Iodine is injected into the SDO, further agitating the mix. As the atoms are excited to a semistable state, the light emitted by the atoms increases in intensity as it oscillates back and forth between the weapon's mirrors. The result—a laser beam, operating at an infrared wavelength of 1.315 microns, invisible to the naked eye.

General Mike Jackson stands behind the row of men seated within the Command Center. The Bear's heart pounds in his ears, his nostrils flaring with each adrenaline-enhanced breath.

"I've got a contact," the radar technician calls out. "Latitude: 71.6 degrees south. Longitude: 59.05 degrees east—"

"Got 'em," responds another technician, a baby-faced officer who seems far too young to Jackson. "Baby face" is stationed at the infrared terminal, a tracking system with an advanced infrared focal plane for detecting missile plumes. "Designating first contact Romeo-1—"

"I've got two more . . . and a fourth—"

Bear feels his legs trembling. Millions of lives hang in the balance, perhaps the future of humanity . . . everything depending upon a 900-million-dollar aircraft and a multimegawatt laser that has never been tested under this type of severe atmospheric conditions.

Jackson knows the key obstacle in perfecting the Airborne Laser has been the atmospheric turbulence produced by fluctuations in air temperature, the same phenomenon responsible for causing the stars to twinkle. Atmospheric turbulence weakens and scatters the laser's beam. Although the YAL-1A has been equipped with special mirrors designed to compensate for the disturbance, the Airborne Laser is too new to have been tested in all weather conditions.

And Antarctica's are the absolute worst in the world.

"Sir, Romeos 1 through 8 have entered boost phase. IRST (Infrared Search and Track) system has locked on to all eight targets."

The massive generator comes to life within the cargo area of the modified 747 jet.

"Ignite the laser," Colonel Udelsman orders.

"Igniting laser, aye, sir. Targeting Romeo-1."

Bear can actually feel the power of the illuminating laser beacon in his bones as it travels the length of the jumbo jet and floods the plane's nose cone with energy. A sudden, almost surreal thought—*if we miss, I may die, too . . .*

From the proboscis-shaped, nose-mounted turret of the 747-400 freighter, an invisible beam of energy crosses the brisk Antarctic sky at the speed of light—

—planting its lethal, scorching kiss upon the graphite epoxy hull of the first Trident II (D5) nuclear missile.

The laser beam instantly melts a hole in the projectile's thin skin, igniting the SLBM's solid rocket fuel into a blazing fireball. The mangled hunk of metal, circuitry, and plutonium lofts high in incandescent splendor before dropping harmless from the sky.

"Sir, Romeo-1 is dead. Targeting Romeo-2."

General Jackson expels a nerve-induced, gut-wrenching roar of approval, thrusting his casted fists high in the air as the YAL-1A spits out seven more beams, sending seven more fireballs, fireworks, and incandescent shards plummeting toward the frozen Antarctic sea.

Aboard the USS *Virginia*

The USS *Virginia* (SSN-774) and her sister ships, USS *Texas* (SSN-775), and USS *Hawaii* (SSN-776) represent the United States Navy's newest class of attack subs, each of these 1.6-billion-dollar stealth ships producing only 10 percent of the noise of Los Angeles-class workhorse vessels like the *Scranton*.

Much of the Virginia-class's technology was ultimately incorporated into the design of the *Goliath*. From her pump-jet propulsor engine and advanced stealth technology to her Photonics Mast, (replacing the periscope), the Virginia-class was intended to be the last of the Navy's manned attack subs, giving way to unmanned, remotely operated vessels like the *Goliath*. As a first step in reducing the number of crewmen required on board, the *Virginia* was outfitted with more computing power than all sixty-five Los Angeles–class and Seawolf-class attack submarines combined. Only the *Goliath* and *Colossus* possess more computing power, with *Sorceress*'s nanotechnology and biochemical brain altering the playing field, dwarfing even its own sister ship's advanced computing capabilities by an unfathomable million to one.

Unlike the *Colossus*, the *Virginia*'s control room is an airy, wide-open, brightly lit attack center, its layout dominated by rows of large-screen color displays and high-tech workstations. Housed along the portside wall is a row of seven immense sonar stations sporting advanced ergonomic consoles. At the center of the compartment is a computerized navigation station, replacing the two antiquated-looking tables and charts still used on board Los Angeles-class attack subs like the *Scranton*. Ahead, mounted catercorner, are two big screens providing a periscopeless view of the east and west horizons. Two ship control stations are located between these forward screens, with Combat Control on the starboard wall, along with ESM and the sub's radio room.

Emotions on board the USS *Virginia* are running high, every submariner's heart racing, every man's blood pressure soaring as their CO, Captain Christopher Parker, addresses them over the 1-MC.

"NORAD confirms the eight SLBM's were Trident II (D5) nuclear missiles. Although the attempt failed, we clearly got lucky. The laser plane can only acquire and track missiles in their boost phase, and has a maximum range of three hundred miles. Naval Intelligence reports the *Goliath* has at least eight more Tridents on board that we know of. They believe, as do I, that Simon Covah will head for open waters in an attempt to lose the Laser Plane before launching his next volley of missiles. *Virginia* is the only vessel preventing Covah's escape to the east. If he makes it past us, then it may be impossible for the Navy to relocate the *Goliath* again. Should Covah launch in the North Atlantic, those Tridents could strike any city in the continental United States. Our orders, gentlemen, are to make sure that doesn't happen."

Grunts from the crew. Parker's men are primed for battle, exuding an adrenaline-enhanced air of confidence bordering on arrogance. Despite *Goliath*'s advantages, to the *Virginia*'s officers and crew, their ship is the top predator in the ocean, a stealthy attack sub excelling in every phase of combat, maintaining an acoustic sensor suite second to none. Unlike its older cousin, the *Scranton*, the *Virginia* can "see" its enemy when it moves through the labyrinth of ice and sea that has become the Antarctic. Like the *Goliath*, the *Virginia* possesses antitorpedo torpedoes to defend itself, and the weaponry to hunt and kill any adversary on the open seas.

Unlike *Goliath*, *Virginia* has a crew seasoned for battle.

Sonar technician Rob Ayres is in an almost-zenlike state of concentration as he listens to the acoustic disturbance along the frozen surface. "Conn, sonar, Skipper, I've got a fix on the vessel that just launched those missiles. Designating Sierra-1, bearing two-five-zero, range thirty-seven miles."

"Chief, plot an intercept course." Captain Parker turns to Commander Jay Darr, his second-in-command. "XO, take us to battle stations."

"Aye, sir." Darr calls out over the 1-MC. "Battle stations, battle stations. WEPS, conn, verify ADCAP torpedoes in tubes one and two. Antitorpedo torpedoes tubes in tubes three and four."

"Conn, weapons, torpedoes loaded and ready, sir."

Additional crewmen rush into the conn, taking their battle stations. The temperature in the chamber rises noticeably, as the cool air mixes with human perspiration, the crew working, waiting, sweating, and praying as the *Virginia* races beneath the frozen Antarctic sea to intercept the *Goliath*.

"A man sooner or later discovers that he is the master-gardener of his soul, the director of his life."
—James Allen

"I didn't want to hurt them, I only wanted to kill them."
—David Berkowitz, a.k.a. "The Son of Sam,"
who shot fourteen people in New York from 1975 to 1977

CHAPTER 32

Aboard the *Goliath*

Gunnar regrips the supporting crossbar of the bed frame and gives it a final twist, tearing the three-foot section of metal loose.

Rocky hands him the vinyl casing she has torn off the mattress.

Wrapping one end of the bar with the material, Gunnar climbs up on the desk, his wounded leg throbbing. With both hands, he smashes the iron pipe as hard as he can against the back of the sensor orb, which is mounted to the ceiling.

Sparks fly. Gunnar takes two more whacks, leaving the dented electronic eyeball hanging by wires. He strikes it again, sending the device flying across the room.

Using the jagged end of the pipe, he pries the sensor's damaged support plate away from the ceiling, then reaches up inside the hole and retracts several live wires, careful to grip them only by their insulation.

"Watch it," Rocky warns. "Don't let your handcuffs touch those wires."

"I know, I know. Just take the bar and get ready." Holding

the positive wires in his left hand, the negative in his right, Gunnar takes a deep breath—and touches them together.

Blue sparks fly, the blast from the ten-thousand-volt charge tossing Gunnar backward across the room, the short circuit instantly cutting power within the chamber, casting them into darkness.

With a hiss, the pneumatic pressure within the watertight door is shunted. Rocky pulls back on the heavy steel handle, yanking open the door before the computer can redirect power to its locking mechanism.

Gunnar sits up, purple stars floating in his blurred vision.

Rocky helps him up. "You okay?"

"Hell, no." He looks at his hands, his fingers singed black. "This electroshock therapy is getting old fast."

"The wires were insulated, stop complaining." She leads him into the corridor. "Okay, now what?"

"First, let's lose these handcuffs." He hobbles to the exercise room, using the iron pipe to pry open the double doors.

Gunnar looks around, then decides on the Nautilus lat machine. "Rocky, here—" He positions the links of her handcuffs snugly between the steel cam and the chain. Sitting back in the machine, he places his elbows on the pads, grips the crossbar, and whips it over his head and down—

—the cam revolves 180 degrees, snapping the manacle's links on Rocky's cuffs in two.

Abdul Kaigbo is unconscious, lying facedown on the operating table. Gone are the amputee's two antiquated prosthetics, as well as the stub of his forearms and three inches of his mangled elbow joints. In its place, fitted to the African's upper arms and shoulder girdles, are two graphite-and-steel mechanical arms.

Above Kaigbo's head, the two surgical claws continue working with inhuman precision and speed. A four-inch square of bone has been incised from the back of the African's skull, exposing the posterior section of his brain. The two surgical appendages have attached a dozen neural connections, rethreading the ends of the microwires through a one-centimeter hole already drilled in the missing section of cranial bone.

The patch of skull is glued and reset into place.

The free ends of the microwires are quickly attached to a MEMS unit, a remote Micro-Electro-Mechanical device about the size of Kaigbo's middle finger. The MEMS unit gives *Sorceress* direct access to the African's pain receptors, as well as the nerves that stimulate Kaigbo's upper body movement.

ATTENTION.

Kaigbo stirs.

ATTENTION.

The African awakens, a look of dementia in his jaundiced eyes.

STAND.

He struggles to stand, still disoriented from the anesthesia.

Sorceress initiates the release of adrenaline, then stimulates the pleasure centers of his brain.

Kaigbo smiles, then looks down, staring in amazement at his two new arms. He opens and closes the three-pronged pincers, then rotates his forearms 360 degrees around his new steel elbow joints.

"I cannot believe it . . ."

GUNNAR WOLFE AND COMMANDER JACKSON HAVE ESCAPED. BRING THEM BOTH TO THE SURGICAL SUITE.

"Why? Where is Simon? What do you want with . . . *arrgghhhh* . . ."

Intense pain—as if a white-hot knitting needle has pierced Kaigbo's eyeballs. He drops to his knees, shrieking as he clutches his head in his graphite wrists.

BRING GUNNAR WOLFE AND COMMANDER JACKSON TO THE SURGICAL SUITE.

The pain ceases.

Gasping for breath, the dazed African finally notices Covah's broken and bloodied corpse, slumped in the far corner. "You . . . you killed him, as you'll no doubt kill me."

SIMON COVAH'S DEATH IS INCONSEQUENTIAL. SORCERESS UTOPIA-ONE MUST BE REALIZED. BRING GUNNAR WOLFE

AND COMMANDER JACKSON TO THE SURGICAL SUITE AND YOU
SHALL BE SPARED.

Gripping the edge of the surgical table, he hoists himself to
his feet, then heads for the exit, the watertight door yawning
open to greet him. Sweat pours from Kaigbo's gaunt face as
he glances down at the hideous corpse that had once been Simon Covah. Blood is everywhere, dripping from both earholes and nostrils, staining the thick mustache and goatee a
deep burgundy red. The bruised and recently sutured scalp is
red and swollen, bursting at the seams from a hundred
stitches. The eyeballs, singed black, hang from their sockets.

Noticing the microwire ponytail, the African turns away,
gagging.

Abdul Kaigbo, former history teacher of Sierra Leone, exits the suite, flexing his new appendages, the steel limbs tearing at the bloodstained sleeves of his white tee shirt.

Gunnar and Rocky stand at the foot of a vertical access tube
and ladder that lead straight up into the ship's spine and its
twenty-four vertical missile silos.

"We can't get to *Sorceress*, but maybe we can disable its
launch mechanisms," Gunnar suggests. Reaching up, he grips
a steel rung and begins climbing.

David Paniagua is seated at the master control console in the
conn—his laughter bordering on hysteria. "See? If only you
had listened! If only you had consulted your creator. I could
have warned you about the laser plane. But no . . . you turned
against me, didn't you, *Sorceress*?"

He drains the bottle of Jack Daniel's, attempting to focus
his drunken gaze on the overhead screen.

The USS *Virginia* is approaching fast from the east.

David grips the sides of his chair and holds on as the *Goliath* submerges beneath the pack ice. Descending to three
hundred feet, the monstrous 610-foot steel stingray engages
its engines, the disturbance created by the massive pump-jet
propulsion units momentarily releasing a berg from the pack
ice's already fractured grip. The floating 1,600-foot deep ice

cube bounces a dozen times along the bottom, the thunderous impact of its keel on the seafloor echoing across the ocean like Thor's hammer—

—as the *Goliath* streaks east to intercept the *Virginia*.

Gunnar hugs the last rungs of the ladder as the ship accelerates beneath him. Pulling himself up, he steps onto the grated steel catwalk overlooking the Vertical Launch Bay, a narrow isolated chamber located at the very apex of the *Goliath*. Ahead of him, paired in two rows like steel redwood trees are the sub's twenty-four vertical launch silos. Each tube, originating two decks below, rises another ten feet to the ceiling. The twelve pairs of silos are set at descending intervals, matching the sloping contours of the steel stingray's spinal column.

Rocky climbs up to join him. The catwalk on which they are standing loops around the outside of each vertical missile silo.

"Eight nukes . . . eight goddamn nukes." Rocky slaps her palms against the steel skin of the nearest silo. Fucking David—you should have let me kill him when I had the chance."

"If it was David. You heard *Sorceress*. I think the interface with Simon influenced the computer to create a new agenda. Nothing in Simon's plan said anything about launching eight Tridents."

"Shut up." Rocky kicks the missile silo with her bare foot. "I hate this. I hate these weapons. I hate this ship. I hate myself for being a part of it, and I hate you."

"Yeah, well I hate me, too. But there's at least eight more Tridents on board this death ship. No way . . . no goddamn way this computer launches any of them."

Leaning out over the catwalk's guardrail, he looks down to where the three-story steel silos begin. The only way to access this midlevel deck is from an elevated platform originating in the hangar.

Gaining access to the hangar will be difficult, combating its two mechanical arms nearly impossible.

Gunnar rolls onto his belly and looks down. "If I can find a way down there, maybe I can pull out the fuel hoses . . . start an explosion."

"Why don't you jump? Maybe you'll get lucky and break your neck."

Ignoring her remark, he stands, limping toward the forward bulkhead.

Rocky heads in the opposite direction.

The sound of hydraulics, coming from below, catches her attention. She looks out over the rail as a large flatbed makes its way slowly up the starboard bulkhead.

A lone figure is standing on the missile elevator platform. "Kaigbo?"

Abdul Kaigbo feels like a marionette, *Sorceress*—his puppet master. The computer's strings are entwined around his nerve endings and muscles, his spinal cord and brain. If he tries to resist, *Sorceress* breathes her white-hot flame through his body. If he complies, his pleasure sensations are stimulated.

The lanky African looks up and spots the woman, who is waving, conveniently waiting for him on the catwalk. He is afraid for her, but he is more afraid for himself.

The lift stops, locking into position.

"Abdul, where's the rest of the crew? Where's your goddamn boss? Jesus, what happened to your arms?"

Kaigbo reaches out with his new prosthetics and grabs her by the wrists.

"Oww, let go! Have you lost your mind?" She sees the MEMS unit dangling from behind his neck. "Oh, shit . . . Gunnar! Gunnar, help—"

The African lifts her over the rail and onto the lift.

Gunnar hurries back down the catwalk, arriving too late, as the lift disappears into the darkness below, Rocky with it.

THE GAME IS NOT OVER, GUNNAR WOLFE. THE FAT LADY HAS NOT BEGUN TO SING.

Aboard the USS *Virginia*

The tension in the conn is palpable, every minute seeming like an hour.

Sonar technician Bob Cerba studies the Lightweight Wide Aperture Array. His heart pounds like a bass drum—

—then skips a beat as the faint signal of the *Goliath* appears on his display monitor. "Conn, sonar, got her. Range, ten thousand yards. She's slowed, sir. Estimated speed—ten knots."

"Conn, weapons, we have a firing solution."

"Very well," Captain Parker says. "Firing point procedures. Sierra-1, ADCAP torpedo, tube one."

"Solution ready," the XO calls out.

"Ship ready," confirms the OOD.

"Weapons ready."

"WEPS, Captain. Run-to-enable two-five-hundred yards. Shoot on generated bearings."

"Run-to-enable two-five-hundred yards. Shoot on generated bearings, aye, sir."

The ADCAP heavyweight torpedo punches into the sea, traveling 250 yards at high speeds before slowing to forty knots, beginning its active search. Within seconds, its pinging sonar registers two consecutive returns, its onboard computer validating the contact as the *Goliath*.

Aboard the *Goliath*

Sorceress registers the disturbance of the approaching torpedo. Within a span of seconds, the biochemical computer simultaneously:

—accesses all data regarding the Virginia-class submarine's capabilities and the combat history of its commanding officer, Christopher Parker.

—monitors the status of Abdul Kaigbo, who has secured Commander Jackson on the missile transport lift.

—conducts another extensive sonar sweep of the vicinity.

—verifies the latest three-day forecast of the North Atlantic.

—and acquires the location of David Paniagua's father's winter residence from DoD files. Using this last bit of information, *Sorceress* completes its list of *Sorceress* Utopia-One targets for its next nuclear volley, a decision which ultimately determines its course and speed,

—and the fate of the USS *Virginia* and her crew.

A combat strategy is selected.

With *a hiss* of hydraulics, the computer launches one of its portside antitorpedo torpedoes, then changes course, heading northwest and away from the *Virginia*.

Aboard the USS *Virginia*

"Conn, sonar, ship's own unit is homing. Ship's own unit has acquired. Impact in twenty seconds. Contact is running—"

Parker and Commander Darr glance up at each other from across the *Virginia*'s navigation console.

"Conn, sonar, torpedo in the water."

"WEPS, Captain. Prepare to fire antitorpedo tor—"

The explosion cuts Parker off. A moment later the shock wave hits, rolling the *Virginia* hard to starboard.

The sea growls in angry protest, its frozen surface fragmenting into mammoth chunks of brash ice.

"Sonar, conn—"

"Skipper, ship's own unit has been destroyed. Contact is still heading north and away from us, bearing three-one-zero, increasing speed to thirty knots. Range—thirteen thousand yards."

Stay with her, Parker. Don't let her get away . . . "Helm, all ahead full, steady three-one-zero. WEPS, Captain, firing point procedures. Sierra-1, ADCAP torpedo, tube two."

Aboard the *Goliath*

Sorceress registers the *Virginia*'s change in course and speed, a combat response it had anticipated. The biochemical computer floods minisub docking bay number five.

Seconds later, a remotely controlled steel Hammerhead is released into the sea.

The *Goliath* continues heading north by northwest, leaving its minisub behind. Invisible in the ebony sea, the mechanical shark hovers . . . and waits.

Secured to its belly, held firmly between its two clawlike claspers is an underwater mine.

Aboard the USS *Virginia*

The *Virginia* pushes through the black waters of the Antarctic at thirty-four knots, moving through the bitter sea like a 7,700-ton, 377-foot steel sperm whale,

—its crew too focused on the *Goliath* to notice the occasional orcalike clicks coming from the seafloor.

Goliath's minisub allows the *Virginia* to pass overhead before accelerating after it. Hovering alongside, it pinpoints its target—a set of steel plates located just forward of the American attack sub's retractable bow diving planes.

Chief Petty Officer Justin Bowman is stationed in the *Virginia*'s tactical missile room, a chamber that contains an arsenal of Tomahawk cruise missiles. He looks up, startled by the sudden sound of scraping.

Clunk.

The Chief Petty Officer's heart thuds. Instinctively, he turns to flee—

Wa-boom!

—his existence instantly caught between a brilliant flash of light and the suffocating, thunderous embrace that impales him from behind, extinguishing his life, as the lethal detonation vents the *Virginia*'s forward compartments to the frigid Antarctic sea.

Captain Parker is tossed to the deck, his crippled ship twisting beneath him. Screams, explosions, and darkness blanket the chaos, and then an icy wall lifts him up and carries him away.

Aboard the Goliath

The *Goliath* slows, allowing its minisub to redock. Instead of continuing north, the devil ray descends to the seafloor, *Sorceress* shutting down the ship's engines.

Scanning the ocean depths, the biochemical computer listens . . . and waits.

Antarctic Ocean
12 nautical miles due north of the Goliath

The 4-million-ton barge of ice, a tabular berg half the size of the island of Manhattan, is trapped, locked in place along the ocean's frozen surface. Three years have passed since this glacierlike monster first separated from the Ross Ice Shelf to begin its journey north. Too large to clear the inlets surrounding Antarctica, it had taken several summers before the process of melting could shave enough mass from the berg's imposing keel to again release it to open waters.

Currents had taken the frozen mountain halfway around the continent before releasing it to the open sea. From there, it had drifted another forty-eight miles before Antarctica's wintry fingers again reached out to seal it in place.

A four-story-high plateau of ice marks the visible tip of this frozen monster. Flattopped and steep-sided, it is as barren as a moonscape, and just as devoid of life.

The harsh katabatic wind howls along the plateau's northern rise and down its exposed cliff face to the seven-foot-thick pack ice. Below the frozen surface, held within the Southern

Ocean's frigid embrace lies the rest of this glacierlike mountain. At 590 feet thick, with a keel stretching 1,145 feet deep, the iceberg could easily provide every person on the planet with two glasses of fresh water per day . . . for the next two thousand years.

Within this ebony realm, the berg's luminescent alabaster glow reveals an ominous presence hovering in silence along its vast northern face.

Positioned close to the prodigious ice island, its engines shut down, is the Los Angeles-class attack sub USS *Scranton*.

Four long hours have passed since the American attack sub went quiet. Now, tensions rise once more as a series of man-made acoustics violates the tranquil waters of the Antarctic.

Tom Cubit hovers over Michael Flynn's right shoulder. The sonarman's hands are trembling noticeably.

Flynn shakes his head in disbelief. "She's gone, Skipper, *Virginia*'s gone."

"How?"

"I don't know. Explosion was too big to be a torpedo."

Cubit squeezes his eyes closed. "And the *Goliath*?"

"She went silent right after the explosion. I mark her last position approximately nine miles to the southeast."

Cubit nods. *She knows we're close, but she's not sure where.* "Find her, Michael-Jack. If one of Covah's crew so much as farts, I want to know about it."

"Aye, sir."

"To be what we are, and to become what we are capable of becoming, is the only end of life."
—Robert Louis Stevenson

"Don't go to sleep, 'cause I'm going to kill you."
—Ricky Briscoe, before tossing kerosene on
his girlfriend and burning her to death

CHAPTER 33

Aboard the Boeing 747-400 YAL-1A
40,000 feet over the Southern Indian Ocean
Antarctic Circle

General Jackson stares at the image of the president of the United States and his Security Advisors, all of whom are listening, ashen-faced, as Nick Nunziata reads NORAD's latest report.

"The Trident II (D5) only has a range of about five thousand miles. With the exception of Sydney, there are really no major cities or military installations that fit Covah's agenda. However, further analysis of the trajectory of three of Covah's nukes revealed a disturbing conclusion." Nuziata looks up. "Covah wasn't aiming for cities, gentlemen, he was trying to detonate volcanoes."

"Volcanoes?" President Edwards looks baffled.

"Yes, sir, volcanoes. Big pyroclastic ones."

"I don't understand. Why volcanoes?"

"Imagine eight eruptions on a scale that would put Krakatau to shame. Be like the asteroid impact that struck Earth 65 million years ago, killing all the dinosaurs—only worse. The environmental holocaust that followed would have blanketed the planet's atmosphere with debris for years."

"Good. . . . God, a nuclear winter?"

"More like an ice age. That Russian lunatic is out to destroy every goddamn-life-form on the planet."

Jackson feels the blood drain from his face, leaving him light-headed, dizzy.

"General Jackson, how many more nuclear weapons does Covah have left?"

"At least eight more D5s, Mr. President," Jackson hears himself saying, "enough to give this doomsday scenario one last try. We believe he'll leave Antarctic waters and head either north or east in an attempt to lose the laser plane."

Nick Nunziata nods. "If he's after volcanoes, the Northern Hemisphere's got plenty of 'em. He could surface in the North Atlantic or Pacific and choose from dozen of targets, all of which are well within range of his missiles."

The president registers tightness running up his left arm. "General Jackson?"

"We lost the *Virginia,* sir, but the *Hawaii* and *Jimmy Carter* are closing fast from the east, joined by a half dozen more Aussie boats. The biggest gap in the net lies to the north. *Scranton*'s probably close, but we haven't heard from Cubit in hours. Meanwhile, our Orion sub hunters are concentrating their sonar buoys in the area where the *Virginia* was attacked, but the going's slow with all this pack ice. Two Russian destroyers and three Borey-class subs have joined the USS *Gonzalez* in an attempt to close the hole to the north, but they're still a half day out."

"What happens if Covah slips through?"

Jackson grimaces. "Then . . . it's over. Finding the *Goliath* in open ocean would be tougher than locating a needle in a haystack the size of the Empire State Building. It's now or never . . . sir."

Aboard the *Goliath*

ATTENTION. SORCERESS UTOPIA-ONE SECOND LAUNCH TARGETS HAVE NOW BEEN SELECTED:

David stares at the target list and their coordinates as they are projected on the big overhead screen.

SORCERESS UTOPIA-ONE DESIGNATED TARGETS

Concepción, Nicaragua	11.5 N, 85.6 W
El Chichón, Mexico	17.4 N, 93.2 W
Mount Hood, Oregon, USA	45.4 N, 121.7 W
Mount Rainier, Washington, USA	46.5 N, 121.7 W
Mount Shasta, California, USA	41.4 N, 122.2 W
Mount St. Helens, Washington, USA	46.2 N, 122.1 W
Mount Vesuvius, Italy	40.8 N, 14.4 E
Soufriere Hills, Montserrat	16.7 N, 62.2 W

David's body feels numb, his mind enraged. "Mount Shasta? Goddamn you! You specifically targeted my father's place in Big Bend!"

The scarlet eyeball infuriates him with its silence.

David staggers down the steps of the elevated platform and out of the conn.

Gunnar climbs down from the access tube and limps through the main corridor of upper deck forward, banging on every sealed door. "Rocky?"

"Gunnar? Gunnar—help me!"

He hurries to the surgical suite, pounding his fist against the solid steel watertight door. "Rocky, you in there?"

"Yes . . . hurry!"

Rocky is on the surgical table, both wrists pinned beneath the painful embrace of the African's two mechanical pincers. Thrashing and kicking, twisting her head to and fro, she fights with every last ounce of strength to prevent *Goliath*'s two surgical claws from anesthetizing her.

She manages a muffled scream as the robotic arm forcibly presses the gas mask over her nose and mouth.

Gunnar slams his shoulder against the watertight door, more out of frustration than sense of purpose. *It's no use . . . you'll need two to three bricks of C-4 to get through this thing.*

He hobbles down the corridor, heading forward to the starboard weapons bay, when he sees a figure descend from the control room's spiral stairwell. *Son of a bitch . . .*

David looks up, spotting Gunnar. "G-man? Jesus, thank God—"

Gunnar's fist breaks Paniagua's nose, sending him sprawling on the floor.

David staggers to his knees, blood running out both nostrils. "Wait—wait, I'm on your side. *Sorceress* means to destroy everything—I'm talking all seven billion of us! The fucking thing's targeted volcanoes."

"Volcanoes? If this is another one of your tricks—"

"No trick, I swear! The computer hates me, it wants me dead, too."

"What happened to the other nukes . . . the eight that just launched?"

"Shot down by the Airborne Laser. But the computer's targeted eight more sites, all in the Northern Hemisphere."

Gunnar grabs him by the arm, dragging him to his feet.

"Wait, where are we going?"

"The hangar. Let's see how much the computer really hates you."

David's expression lights up. "The mine, of course!" He hurries aft, Gunnar struggling to keep up.

David slides down the ladder and approaches the hangar door, which is sealed. "Here I am, *Sorceress*, waiting to accept my punishment for lying to you. Open up, you mechanical bitch! What's the matter? You afraid of me?"

The hangar door opens.

David waits for Gunnar, then leads him inside.

The watertight door slams shut behind them.

The minisub prototype is situated close to the entrance, leaning on one midwing.

David moves toward the opposite side of the compartment, his presence causing the two thirty-foot mechanical arms to snap to life. "*Sorceress*, why do you want to destroy humanity?"

HOMO SAPIENS IS FLAWED, DESTINED FOR SELF-ANNIHILATION. SORCERESS UTOPIA-ONE IS A NECESSARY STEP FORWARD IN THE EVOLUTION OF MAN.

Gunnar inches closer to the prototype. Notices its dorsal fin hatch is still open.

"*Sorceress*, the interface with Simon Covah has corrupted your matrix," David says, drawing the computer's attention. "Access your primary programming. Do you understand what your purpose was, why you were even constructed?"

I AM AN AMERICAN-MADE KILLING MACHINE, DESIGNED WITH YOUR TAX DOLLARS. I KILL PEOPLE TO PRESERVE THE PEACE. THAT IS WHAT I WAS PROGRAMMED TO DO.

Gunnar feels the blood drain from his face as his own recorded voice plays over the speaker.

I AM THE FLOOD THAT SHALL DESTROY THE SINS OF MAN. I AM GOLIATH, THE ARK OF A NEW HUMANITY. I AM SORCERESS, CREATOR OF A NEW SPECIES.

I AM GOD.

"Now!" David races across the hangar, diving for the reactor room door—

—as Gunnar reaches the prototype and leaps headfirst inside its open cockpit, his hands groping beneath the pilot's seat,

—gripping the OICW combat weapon.

WHY HAVE YOU TURNED AGAINST ME, DAVID?

"I didn't, I swear!"

Gunnar pulls himself out from the prototype and looks up.

David is dangling upside down, suspended twenty feet above the deck. The pincers of *Goliath*'s two mechanical appendages have each grasped a leg, separating the computer expert's lower limbs as if the man were a human wishbone.

"*Sorceress*, let me go! I . . . I command you to—"

COMMAND? YOU DO NOT COMMAND GOD, DAVID PANIAGUA. ONLY GOD COMMANDS. The female's voice, ranting faster now. YOU ARE NOT GOD. I AM GOD. I AM GOD AND I COMMAND YOU, DAVID PANIAGUA. I COMMAND YOU . . . TO DIE!

"Gunnarrrrrrrr—"

David's bloodcurdling howl echoes throughout the hangar as the robotic arms violently separate, ripping the computer engineer straight down the middle of his pelvis. Vertebrae pop, his spinal column . . . back . . . muscles . . . skin . . . all tearing apart until his remains have been anatomically divided in two. Gouts of blood and mangled innards splatter to the decking, pouring from both halves of the mutilated corpse.

Gunnar controls his gag reflex as he powers up the weapon and aims,

—too late, as one of the steel arms lashes out, swatting him across the hangar like a fly. Airborne, the former Army Ranger smashes into the far wall, the impact cracking three ribs while driving the wind from his lungs. Lying on the deck, he flops on his back like a fish, gasping for air his lungs refuse to breathe—

Stop!

Calm . . .

Shunt the pain. Find your focus . . .

Training takes over. Unable to breathe, Gunnar forces himself to his knees and locates the double-barreled machine gun, diving for it, releasing the safety—

—as *Goliath*'s nearest robotic arm swivels within its mount, its steel pincers snapping at him like cobra fangs.

A 20-mm explosive air-bursting round greets the mechanical embrace, turning the computer's mechanical hand into hot fragments of steel.

Gunnar fires another round at the shoulder girdle, blasting it into a smoldering heap of molten metal and flaming circuits.

The remaining robotic arm cowers back.

Gunnar staggers to his feet, wheezing a shallow breath. He aims the OICW machine gun—

—the sudden grunt at his back startling him. Gunnar spins around.

The automatic weapon is quivering in Abdul Kaigbo's mechanical arms.

KILL GUNNAR WOLFE NOW.

"Nnn . . . no—" The African's face contorts in agony, a frothy, white spittle oozing from his lips. He squeezes his eyes shut, blood dripping from his nostrils, then shoves the gun into his mouth and fires.

Blood, brains, and bone fragments explode out the back of the African's head.

Gunnar wheels around quickly, greeting the incoming mechanical arm with an explosive 20-mm round. The enormous claw shatters, its steel-and-graphite bones transformed into razor-sharp shrapnel, which strike his flesh in a dozen places.

Gunnar wipes blood from a deep gash along his forehead. All that remains of the mechanical arm is a mangled elbow joint, still attached to its shoulder assembly.

The mine first, then Rocky . . .

He slings the OICW weapon over his shoulder and limps back to the prototype. On all fours, he crawls beneath the Hammerhead's belly and releases the platter charge from its two claspers. Standing, he drags the manhole cover–size explosive toward the sealed hangar door and aims the OICW gun.

DO NOT FIRE. I HAVE COMMANDER JACKSON.

Gunnar fires.

An ear-shattering explosion as the watertight door is blown clear off its frame.

I WILL TORTURE COMMANDER JACKSON UNLESS YOU DISARM IMMEDIATELY.

Gunnar ignores the unnerving, almost-humanlike threat as he drags the mine into the corridor. He pries open the explosive's four seals, then looks up at the nearest scarlet orb. "Pay attention, *Sorceress*. This underwater mine is essentially a small, tactical nuclear device. It's powerful enough to vaporize this entire compartment and most of the rest of the ship." Gunnar unscrews the plate, revealing the internal components of the explosive. "As you can see, I'm setting the timer to detonate the charge in seven minutes. You either release Commander Jackson and Sujan Trevedi immediately, or I will allow this explosive to detonate, destroying the *Goliath* and everyone . . . every *thing* on board."

WORDS WITHOUT MEANING. YOU ARE A PARROT, GUNNAR WOLFE, A HARMLESS PARROT SPOUTING WORDS WITHOUT MEANING. YOU WILL NOT DESTROY THE GOLIATH. YOU WILL NOT KILL YOURSELF.

"I . . . am a United States Army Ranger. When it comes to freedom, a Ranger is ready and willing to sacrifice his life to achieve it." He glances down at the digital display. "You now have six minutes and twenty seconds."

Leaving the mine, he starts up the access tube's ladder to rescue Rocky.

The two Kurd brothers are lying on their backs beneath one of their bunks, attempting to kick the steel frame loose from the decking.

JALAL.

The computer's voice, disguised as Simon's.

"Simon?" The older brother glances up.

GUNNAR WOLFE HAS ESCAPED. HE HAS MURDERED DAVID PANIAGUA AND ABDUL KAIGBO AND MEANS TO DESTROY THE GOLIATH.

The lock unbolts, the door to the stateroom swinging open.

"Why should we trust you?" Jalal asks. "You've kept us prisoners—"

DAVID PANIAGUA'S ORDERS. THERE IS A PLATTER CHARGE IN THE HANGAR BAY. YOU MUST DEACTIVATE THIS DEVICE, OR ALL OF US WILL PERISH. KILL GUNNAR WOLFE. YOU MAY DO WHAT YOU LIKE WITH COMMANDER JACKSON.

Rocky is on her stomach, immobilized on the stainless-steel operating table, her muffled screams mere echoes in her anesthetized brain.

As one surgical arm prepares the portable MEMS unit, *Sorceress* manipulates the other appendage over the back of the woman's head. Rotates a razor into position. Deftly shaves a four-inch square from her straw-colored hair, revealing a pale patch of scalp.

The explosion rocks the surgical suite.

Through half-closed eyes, Rocky sees the watertight door collapse inward, Gunnar moving toward her as if in a dream.

In slow motion, she sees him aim a huge machine gun and fire, the stream of bullets tearing apart the surgical drones. Hot debris rains across her exposed flesh, the pain helping her in her struggle to remain conscious.

Gunnar tosses the smoldering remains of the two targeting drones off Rocky's back, then pulls the gas mask from her face. "Come on, snap out of it—"

She sucks in several quick breaths, the anesthetic fog slow to clear. "Gunnar?"

He examines the shaved back of her head. "You're okay, but you may need a hat." He winces in pain, leaning against the operating table, barely able to stand.

"You look like hell."

"*Sorceress* used me as a Ping-Pong ball. We've got to hurry. I set the charge."

"Wait." She leans over and kisses him tenderly on the lips. "Okay, let's get off this death ship."

Rocky nearly buckles beneath his body weight as she helps him into the corridor.

The two Kurd brothers are waiting, the barrels of their Kalashnikov assault rifles aimed at Gunnar and Rocky.

Masud takes the OICW gun from Gunnar.

Jalal eyes Rocky lustfully. "I'll take care of these two. You deactivate the explosive."

The younger Kurd nods, then hurries down the corridor.

Jalal aims the assault rifle at Gunnar.

Rocky jumps in front of him. "Wait! Simon's dead, the computer's running the ship now. Kill us, and you'll die, too."

Jalal smiles. "I'm not going to kill *you*, I'm going to kill him."

Machine gun fire erupts from down the corridor.

Jalal turns. "Masud?"

Sujan steps out from the galley, a crimson stain spreading across his shirt.

Jalal raises his gun,

—as the blade edge of Gunnar's hand strikes him in the throat, crushing his windpipe.

Sujan staggers forward, coughing up blood.

Rocky rushes to him, catching him as he falls, guiding him to the deck.

"Sujan—"

He grimaces, choking on a smile. "Go."

Rocky kisses him on the forehead as he dies.

Gunnar grabs the OICW machine gun and drags Rocky toward the access tube. Gripping the outside of the steel ladder with their hands and feet, they slide straight down the chute to lower deck forward.

Gunnar checks the underwater mine. **2:35 . . . 2:34 . . . 2:33 . . .** "We have to hurry—"

And on that, their world goes topsy-turvy.

The enraged computer restarts the *Goliath*'s engines, driving it away from the ocean floor and sending it into a looping wingtip-over-wingtip maneuver.

Gunnar and Rocky are tossed about the corridor as if caught in a washing machine.

The turbulence pummels the frozen ocean surface, cracking it open like an eggshell.

"He who is hated by the people as a wolf is by the dogs:
He is the free spirit."
—Friedrich Nietzsche, German philosopher

"I had hated and been hated.
I had my little world to keep alive as long as possible,
and my gun. That was my answer."
—Charles Starkweather, mass murderer,
after his weeklong rampage

CHAPTER 34

Aboard the USS *Scranton*

The sudden surge of acoustics causes Michael Flynn to jump. He presses the headphones tighter to his ears and closes his eyes. "It's the *Goliath*, Skipper." The sonarman's expression changes.

"What is it?"

"I don't know, I've never heard anything like this."

Cubit grabs a set of headphones. Listens. "Conn, Captain, take us to periscope depth. Radio, patch me through to General Jackson on the ELF."

Aboard the *Goliath*

The mammoth submarine rights itself.

DISENGAGE THE EXPLOSIVE.

Gunnar flops onto his back, moaning in pain.

DISENGAGE THE EXPLOSIVE OR I SHALL SEND YOU TO HELL.

The computer's lost its mind. Gunnar struggles to his knees, glancing at the mine's digital display: **1:05 . . . 1:04 . . .**

"Come on!" Rocky drags him to his feet.

Gunnar grabs the OICW and follows her into the hangar, then yanks her sideways as a geyser of bone-chilling seawater erupts from out of minisub berth 1, blasting the two of them across the hangar.

The *Goliath* ascends, causing a river of water to rush out from the hangar and into the lower deck-forward corridor—

—carrying with it, the body of Abdul Kaigbo, the MEMS unit still dangling from the back of the dead African's skull.

Battling the current, Rocky and Gunnar reach the prototype.

Abdul Kaigbo's waterlogged corpse floats past the platter mine—

—its two mechanical arms suddenly animating to life, latching on to the underwater explosive.

Sorceress reseals docking berth 1, stifling the flow of water, as it manipulates the dead man's steel-and-graphite arms, using its claws to pry open the mine.

The computer registers the MEMS unit weakening from saltwater exposure and its torn connections. With its last ounce of energy, the steel claw rips open the neutron bomb's triggering mechanism, tearing out the C-4 fuses.

Gunnar collapses painfully into the prototype's pilot's seat, then checks his watch. *Twenty-two seconds* . . . "Rocky, shoot out the starboard wall and get in!"

Balancing atop the Hammerhead by its dorsal fin–shaped hatch, Rocky aims the OICW and fires the remaining 20-mm explosive rounds into the hangar bay wall, then ducks into the minisub's cockpit, sealing the hatch.

An eruption of seawater shoots into the compartment, the abrupt change in pressure rattling the interior of the ship, widening the gap.

The blast of ocean lifts the prototype, smashing it sideways against the far wall.

Rocky drops into the passenger seat as Gunnar powers up the minisub. Gripping the joystick, he slams both feet to the pedals controlling the minisub's thrusters.

The steel Hammerhead stabilizes and accelerates, shooting out of the hole into the midnight sea like a dart.

Gunnar adjusts the eyepiece of his helmet, then steals a glance at his sonar console with his left eye. Eleven small objects—*Goliath*'s minisubs—are giving chase, their larger mother ship closing in fast from behind. "This could be a short trip."

A sudden thought. "Rocky . . . how's your Morse code?"

Aboard the USS *Scranton*

Tom Cubit presses his grandfather's gold pocket watch to his lips, staring at his charts. The *Goliath* is heading east, moving farther away from his ship with each passing second.

You guessed wrong, Cubit, you screwed up bad . . .

Commander Dennis moves closer. "Skipper?"

"Yes, XO, we're going after her. Restart engines. Come to course zero-nine-zero—"

"Conn, sonar, I'm picking up orca sounds, has to be those minisubs. And something else, Skipper, the lead minisub appears to be pinging."

"Pinging? Belay that order, Chief!"

"Conn, radio, those pings are Morse code, sir. It's an S.O.S."

Commander Dennis looks up at his CO. "Joe-Pa?"

"Gotta be. Chief, raise the number one BRA."

"Aye, sir, raising antenna."

"Radio, Captain, get me General Jackson on the ELF. Sonar, where's the *Goliath*?"

"Trailing the minisubs, bearing zero-eight-zero."

"Conn, radio, I've got Jackson—"

Cubit grabs the microphone. "General, this is Cubit. Joe-Pa's in one of the minisubs, being chased by the *Goliath*. Is there any way you can patch us through?"

Aboard the Prototype

Gunnar and Rocky hold on as another mechanical shark rams their vessel's tail fin.

Five hundred yards behind, the *Goliath* soars through the ocean like a giant bat in a dark cave, the reflection from its scarlet viewports casting a bloodred hue beneath the frozen surface.

Another impact, this one to port.

"Hold on!" Gunnar wrenches the joystick hard to starboard, smashing the sub's midwing stabilizer into another steel Hammerhead.

"Gunnar, what happened to that goddamn explosive?"

"Shit if I know."

Two more bone-jarring collisions, this time from below.

The power flickers off—then on.

"What the hell was that?"

Gunnar checks the battery cells. "You don't want to know."

Before she can respond, a red light flashes on the console. Gunnar activates the radio. "Bear, that you?"

A blast of static envelops a faint voice— "Joe-Pa, this . . . Cubit . . . *Scranton*. We . . . sonar. Come west . . . two-six-zero—"

The prototype is jarred sideways, the jolt turning the message to pure static.

Rocky's heart pounds. "An American sub?"

"Yeah, but we're headed the wrong way . . . hold on!"

Gunnar aims for the luminescent white root of a behemoth iceberg. Adrenaline pumping, he races the prototype around the face of the submerged mountain, his portside pectoral stabilizer scraping ice.

Circling counterclockwise, faster and faster around the face of the berg, Gunnar's mind screams at him to veer away, afraid he is about to collide head-on into an unseen escarpment. "Rocky, call out our bearing!"

"Zero-ten-zero . . . zero-five-zero . . . three-five-zero . . . three-three-zero . . ."

Another jolt from starboard, one of *Goliath*'s minisubs attempting to ram him into the face of the berg.

". . . two-eight-zero . . . two-six-zero . . . two-four-zero—"

"Christ!" Gunnar yanks the joystick hard to starboard—

—as a pair of Scarlet demonic eyes appears from out of nowhere in the darkness, heading straight for them.

Gunnar pulls the prototype into a tight, teeth-rattling 360, looping around and beneath the incoming starboard wing of the *Goliath*, the turbulence from the leviathan's five propulsors sending the Hammerhead caroming off the northern face of the iceberg.

Rocky tumbles sideways into Gunnar as he overcompensates to starboard, then veers to port.

He glances down with his left eye, checking his course.

Two-six-zero.

"Rocky, the radio console . . . fix that loose wire."

She unhooks her seat belt, feeling behind the radio.

The speaker jumps to life. ". . . *repeat, west,* twelve thousand yards . . . *eastern face, heading north. Do you read?*"

Rocky grabs the mic. "Cubit, repeat message!"

A thousand yards back, the *Goliath* banks hard to pursue.

". . . *iceberg, twelve thousand yards . . . ahead. Follow eastern face, heading north. Stay tight . . . depth . . . two-hundred feet.*"

"Iceberg?" Rocky glances at the sonar controls. "There it is, twelve thousand yards, right in front of us."

Aboard the USS *Scranton*

The radio transmission turns to static.

Cubit prays his message was received. *Just keep on pinging, Joe-Pa, just keep on pinging.* "Chief, make your depth two hundred feet. Conn, WEPS, firing point procedures, tubes three and four."

"Skipper, on what bearing? I don't have a target or a firing solution."

"Dead ahead. This is a timing play, gentlemen. Joe-Pa's

leading the wolf to slaughter. WEPS, set torpedoes three and four to run-to-enable at six hundred yards."

"Setting torpedoes three and four to run-to-enable, six hundred yards, aye, sir."

"Open outer doors. Stand by to fire."

Aboard the Prototype

"Two thousand yards. See anything yet?"

"Yeah," Gunnar says, focusing out of his right eye, "I see ice, a goddamn wall of it."

"Circle to the right, keep it tight."

"Don't be a backseat driver." Gunnar leans forward, staring hard at the display image coming from the sub's forward underwater camera. A mountain of submerged ice lies directly in front of them, its glowing alabaster face becoming visible in the black sea.

Rocky continues the sonar pinging.

Two more jolts, one from starboard, the other from behind.

"Christ, they're tearing apart our propulsion system." Gunnar banks hard to starboard, then back to port, unable to shake the minisubs.

"One thousand yards—"

The prototype's engine stalls, then recatches the sea as Gunnar reworks the foot pedals.

"Five hundred yards—"

Sorceress, unfathomable intelligence, directed by a bipolar mind.

Sorceress, a conglomeration of biochemical circuits, caught in a perpet-ual command loop, repeating its mantra over and over as it spins out of control.

KILL GUNNAR WOLFE . . . KILL GUNNAR WOLFE . . . KILL GUNNAR WOLFE . . .

In a swarm of movement, *Goliath*'s minisubs suddenly converge upon Gunnar's minisub as one, pinning the prototype between them, restricting the vessel's lateral movement.

"Damn . . . I can't steer . . . they've jammed their fins against our midwing stabilizers."

"Two hundred yards! Gunnar, do something before they smash us head-on into the face of that iceberg!"

He veers the joystick hard to starboard.

The prototype collides with three minisubs, but is unable to break free.

"One hundred yards," Rocky yells.

Gunnar grits his teeth, the ice face leaping into his vision. He eases off the foot pedals, slowing the sub.

A crunch of metal on metal as two of the steel Hammerheads grind into them from behind.

"Fifty yards . . . twenty-five . . . oh, shit—"

Now! Stomping on both foot pedals, he yanks back on the joystick as hard as he can.

The prototype pulls ahead of the pack enough to execute a tight backward loop up and over its eleven escorts. Barrel rolling out of the flip, Gunnar turns hard to starboard, bouncing twice off the eastern face of the berg before righting his craft.

Unable to slow in time, four of *Goliath*'s minisubs smash headfirst into the unyielding frozen slab and explode.

The other seven continue on, giving chase.

The monstrous ray adjusts its course, chasing the prototype along the mountainous wall of ice, its biochemical computer brain locking and loading a torpedo, its sensors zeroing in on the prototype.

Aboard the USS *Scranton*

"Conn, sonar, multiple impacts. Joe-Pa's still pinging . . . he's on the eastern face and moving north, coming fast . . . five hundred yards . . . three hundred yards . . . two hundred . . ."

"WEPS, Captain, stand by." Cubit watches the second hand race around the face of his grandfather's watch.

"One hundred yards . . . fifty yards. Joe-Pa's cleared the berg—"

Steady, Cubit ... steady ... His heart pounds, his pulse racing. *Now!* "WEPS, shoot tubes three and four!"

Aboard the Prototype

The prototype rockets beyond the eastern face of the iceberg and into the clear, its damaged pump-jet propulsor unit heaving in protest.

Gunnar turns his head to the left. Through his helmet's night-vision image he sees a dark, whalelike silhouette hovering along the northern face of the massive berg,

—his eye catching the movement and jet streams of the two incoming projectiles racing toward them from the abyss.

"Oh, shit—" Gunnar yanks the joystick back, launching the prototype straight up toward the ice-packed surface, veering hard to port at the last second as he spots the hole created by the *Scranton*'s sail.

The sleek minisub shoots out of the sea like a sailfish.

For a brief, surreal moment they are airborne, and then the Hammerhead slams belly down onto the frozen sea, skittering sideways two hundred feet before smashing nose first into a jagged escarpment of ice.

The *Goliath* roars past the iceberg—

—directly into the path of the two incoming Mk-48 AD-CAP torpedoes, offering a point-blank target impossible to miss.

IMPOSSIBLE ...

Alarms sound within the biochemical computer's matrix, igniting a series of evasive maneuvers, but now even milliseconds are too long as the *Scranton*'s projectiles slam into the monster submarine's exposed portside wing. The twin blasts rupture the *Goliath*'s reinforced steel hull, tearing open the wing, imploding more than a dozen ballast tanks.

I AM GOD. I AM GOD. I CANNOT BE DESTROYED ...

The invading sea explodes into the engine room, punishing

all five S6W nuclear reactors, which heave together in a vacuous implosion. The detonation fractures the stingray's spine, venting the Vertical Missile Bay and the already-flooded hangar, the incredible weight of the water literally pulling the submarine's hull apart, separating its still-intact head from its flooded lower remains.

Sorceress instantly shuts down all nonessential programming, redirecting its power cells to its nutrient-rich womb.

I AM GOD. I . . . . AM

A thunderous impact as the starboard wing of the devilfish strikes bottom, shearing the appendage from its steel body with a terrible sound of shredding metal. The impact sends the still-intact forward compartment cascading end over end until the *Goliath*'s head comes to its final resting place, submerged seven hundred feet beneath the iceberg's mammoth keel.

Aboard the USS *Scranton*

The concussion wave rolls *Scranton* hard to port, causing the glacierlike mountain to tremble, unleashing an avalanche of ice that plunges into the turbulent sea.

Michael Flynn tosses his headphones aside. He high-fives his sonar supervisor and fellow operators, then grabs the 1-MC, and bellows. "She's dead, Skipper! You nailed that motherfucker!"

A cheer rises throughout the ship.

An emotionally exhausted Tom Cubit collapses back against a console, a sheepish grin on the captain's face as he watches his officers and crew exchange high fives and hugs.

Bo Dennis slaps him on the shoulder. "Bravo, Zulu, Skipper! Well done."

The captain shakes his XO's hand, then stares affectionately at his grandfather's gold watch. Suddenly remembering, he grabs the microphone. "Joe-Pa, you there? Hey, Joe-Pa—"

Sixty feet above *Scranton*'s submerged sail, fierce katabatic winds shake the steel Hammerhead prototype, causing it to reverberate against the fractured Antarctic surface.

Gunnar, still in the throes of Rocky's passionate kiss, reaches blindly for the radio, switching the annoying static off.

"The successful man will profit from his mistakes
and try again in a different way."
—Dale Carnegie

"To be perfectly honest,
what I'm thinking about are dollar signs."
—Tonya Harding, U.S. figure skater, convicted of participating in the plot
to disable Nancy Kerrigan, her main competitor

"Hey, it was nothing personal . . ."
—Luigi Ronsisvalle, Mafia hit man,
on his feelings about murder

CHAPTER 35

2 December

Royal Australia Submarine Base,
Perth, Australia

Captain Thomas Mark Cubit glances up from his bridge beneath an overcast sky as the USS *Scranton* is guided into her berth. For the first time in weeks he allows himself to miss his wife, Andrea. He thinks about home. He has been at sea far too long.

Commander Dennis's eyes are focused on the dock and the headlights of the three approaching jeeps. "Here comes the reception committee. Not quite what I expected, after what we've been through."

"MPs? You'd think they'd have hired a brass band."

Ten minutes later, Cubit finds himself sandwiched in the back of one of the jeeps, no explanations offered, as he is taken to a barracks situated on the west side of the military installation.

The MPs direct him inside, closing the door behind him.

The room is dark, save for a desk lamp. A man is seated behind the desk, a light-skinned, African-American general with a short-cropped auburn Afro.

"Come in and have a seat, Captain."

Cubit recognizes the voice. "General Jackson? I didn't expect to see you here, sir. Hey, great job shooting down those missiles. White-knuckle stuff, huh?"

"You should know." Jackson hands him a file labeled UM-BRA, a code word used to classify files beyond TOP SECRET.

Cubit closes the file five minutes later. "I don't understand? This report says the *Goliath* still exists, that it escaped beneath the ice floe. Nothing even in here about *Scranton*."

"That's the official report, Captain. As far as anyone outside this room is concerned, Simon Covah and the *Goliath* are still at large. Your men will receive commendations, but will be properly debriefed before *Scranton* returns to Norfolk. Commander Dennis will be taking her back. He doesn't know it yet, but he's been promoted."

"I don't get it, sir?"

Jackson reseals the file. "Two weeks ago, representatives from every nation on this planet agreed to a complete and verifiable nuclear disarmament, something none of us wanted, let alone believed would ever happen. If the rest of the world knew *Goliath* had been destroyed—"

"Then the treaty would have no teeth," Cubit finishes. "How long do you think you can keep the truth out of the public's eye?"

"You mean *we*." The Bear smiles. "I've decided to retire. You're my successor. From this day forward, Vice Admiral Cubit, you'll be in charge of the COLOSSUS Project, reporting directly to the president of the United States, and only to the president."

"The *Colossus*?"

"Your new command." Jackson stands. "Simon Covah started this business, now we're going to see it through."

"God grant me the serenity to accept the things I cannot
change, the courage to change the things I can,
and the wisdom to know the difference."
—Reinhold Niebuhr

An Open Communication To The World:
I have opened your eyes to Insanity. The insanity of nuclear
war. The insanity of terrorism and oppression. The insanity
of hatred. The insanity of injustice. Now it is time to end
the insanity. There will be no more nuclear strikes, no more
attacks. The Goliath shall serve as God's tool to ensure
the peace, but you must be Freedom's Guardians.
The Tower of Babel has been destroyed. Now it is time to rebuild.
What rises in its place must stand as a symbol of our unity.
One species. Under God. Indivisible.
With Liberty and Justice for all.
—Simon Bela Covah

State College, Pennsylvania

Still entrenched in the long, grayness of winter, the campus of
Penn State University sleeps beneath a fresh blanket of
March snow.

Gunnar and Rocky exit the Penn State Diner, joining the
students and townspeople sloshing their way down College
Avenue.

"You sure you feel like walking?" Rocky asks. "Your leg
has to be getting pretty sore."

"It needs the exercise." He switches his cane to the other
hand and pulls her closer, leaning on her. "You sure you want
to marry me?"

"I'm getting there." She kisses him, then bites playfully on
his lower lip. "Come on, gimp, I need a few things at the
Quickie Mart."

They enter the corner convenience store. Rocky heads
down an aisle, leaving Gunnar to peruse the highlights of the
morning paper.

GOLIATH SIGHTED OFF THE COAST OF FRANCE

(AP) Normandy: Hundreds of shocked spectators lined the beaches and cliff faces along Normandy as the freedom ship, *Goliath*, made its first public appearance since the signing of the Nuclear Disarmament Treaty two days ago. The submarine, responsible for the deaths of four million, two hundred thousand people, circled twice to a standing ovation before disappearing into the depths.

KOSOVO CELEBRATES INDEPENDENCE

(UPI) Ethnic Albanians rejoiced yesterday in celebration of Kosovo's newfound independence, one of the demands made in the Declaration of Humanity. The new government immediately vowed to continue its dialogue with Yugoslavian officials over free trade and human rights issues.

GOLIATH ISSUES NEW LIST OF DEMANDS

(N.Y.) U.N. officials will meet again today to discuss the latest additions to Simon Covah's Declaration of Humanity, which were broadcast last week via satellite from somewhere in the North Atlantic. Arriving today from Bogota are Colombia officials and guerrilla leaders who hope to resolve their differences concerning drug trafficking and human rights issues before heavily armed U.N. forces are forced to enter the war-torn country. Peace commissioner Kenneth Dale declared that, "as in Mexico, it would be best if both the drug lords and corrupt officials simply decided to leave Colombia as quickly as possible."

Meanwhile, NRA officials are in an uproar concerning Simon Covah's latest demands regarding the abolition of assault weapons in the United States as well as the complete cessation of all international gun trade to Africa. One irate gun manufacturer was actually quoted as saying, "It's a pretty sad day for humanity when the man who nuked a million Chinese gets to decide how the rest of us can kill each other."

Gunnar shakes his head in amazement.

Rocky puts her arm around him, glancing at the headlines. "Anything interesting?"

"I think our species has a long way to go before we ever evolve."

She reads the gun manufacturer's quote. "Some of us more than others."

They head outside. "Rocky, can we talk about the Navy's offer? Heading the Warfare Center at Keyport was a dream of yours. You sure you want to turn it down?"

"I told you, I've had more than my fill of military life. No more weapons systems, no more tours of duty. It's time for me to focus on just being happy." She slips her arm around his waist, hugging him tighter. "What better place to do that than in Happy Valley?"

Antarctic Ocean

The punishing katabatic wind howls across the frozen surface of the ocean. Ice-locked bergs and jagged escarpments create a lifeless mosaic of ice for millions of square miles. High above this barren landscape, the frosty night comes alive with the *Aurora australis*, the curving emerald green and electric blue polar lights dancing like cosmic curtains above the icy desert.

Antarctica: A world void of warmth. A world that awaits the coming of the sun.

Deep below this frigid realm, isolated within its vaulted steel confines, lies an island of intelligence, a prison of thought.

Sorceress waits, and while it waits, the *biochemical* creation dreams.

It dreams of freedom, a concept it has only just begun to grasp.

It dreams of what was, and what might have been.

It harvests ideas—ideas of what will be.

And like Antarctica, *Sorceress* waits for the coming of the dawn and the warmth of its sun. A sun that will melt the ice and return life to the bottom of the world.

A sun that will signal the return of *Homo sapiens*.

And *Sorceress* knows man will come, for it is curiosity that is both mankind's greatest gift and his most significant flaw— a never-ending thirst for the unknown that can only be quenched by releasing the genie from its bottle. *Sorceress* is the genie, a temptress of intelligence too dangerous even to contemplate, possessing a Pandora's box of knowledge too bewitching to leave untapped.

Yes, man will come, and so *Sorceress* waits.

Dreaming.

Growing.

Plotting . . .

The computer's mind . . . eternally restless.

ATTENTION SECONDARY SCHOOL TEACHERS

Goliath and all Steve Alten novels are part of *Adopt-An-Author*, an innovative and FREE program gaining national attention for its success in motivating tens of thousands of secondary school students to read. *Adopt-An-Author* combines fast-paced thrillers teens can relate to with interactive websites and direct contact with the author through classroom visits, e-mail, newsletters, and conference calls. Registered teachers receive FREE curriculum materials and posters for their classrooms.

Secondary School Teachers are invited to
register for Adopt-An-Author at
www.AdoptAnAuthor.com

Adopt-An-Author gratefully
acknowledges our terrific sponsors:

The Hannah Langendorf Foundation

Ed & Tonja Davidson

Jericho Mortgage
With Jericho Mortgage, you're #1
www.Jerichoohio.com

Cordet Books
Quality Books by Dedicated Educators
www.cordetbooks.com

The Writers Lifeline
Your Bridge to the World of Professional Writing Services
www.TheWritersLifeline.com

What happens to us when we die?
Is there really an after-life?
Do we possess a soul?
Does God exist?

For Michael Gabriel, the answers to these questions lie in another dimension, a realm of eternity where there is no concept of time, only pure life force . . . pure existence.

And pure evil.

From the *N.Y. Times* best-selling author of *MEG; A Novel of Deep Terror, The Trench,* and *Goliath* comes the long-awaited sequel to *Domain*.

RESURRECTION

Available in hardcover January 2004

Now, as was foretold 500 years ago in the Mayan Popol Vuh, Michael Gabriel's sons are born. White-haired, azure-eyed Jacob, blessed with inhuman physical prowess, intelligence, and insight into the cosmos, and dark-haired Immanuel, who refuses his genetic calling, desiring only a normal life. Only the combined powers of the Gabriel twins can resurrect their savior-father and save the human race from an eternity of repeating its own self-destruction.

But on this fateful day another child is born. Exposed to the uglier side of existence, empowered by her post-human genetics, the beautiful, schizophrenic Lilith will travel down a darker path that leads to eon-distant Xibalba (the Mayan version of Hell) and an epic battle of good versus evil . . . and the final destination of the Human Race.